Cong. Church of Eastford
Eastford, Conn. 06242

ALULA-BELLE
BLOWS INTO TOWN

ALULa-BELLE
BLOWS INTO TOWN

Cover illustration by Marie Chapian
Book Design: Jon Ritt

Text and illustrations copyright © 1995
Marie Jordan Chapian

Published by Bethany House Publishers
A Ministry of Bethany Fellowship, Inc.
11300 Hampshire Avenue South
Minneapolis, Minnesota 55438

Printed in the United States of America

CONTENTS

the grouchy people
at Kneebend-on-Limber

WELCOME TO
KNEEBEND-ON-LiMBER
DON'T EAT ALL OUR
PEACHES AND DON'T
STAY too LONG *as long as you like*

When you come to Kneebend-on-Limber, please do stop and pick yourself a peach. Pick several if you like. Then sit down along the banks of the River Limber and nibble away to your heart's content.

In the town of Kneebend everything smells and tastes like peaches.

There's a popular saying you may already know. It goes like this:

You'll never have a worry
in the world as long as you're
sitting in the shade in Kneebend
eating a peach.

If you decide to stay a while, and I hope you do, you may notice a thick grove of trees off to the right of the riverbank. And just as you are feeling quite contented with a belly full of peach and a face covered with smile, you will get a big surprise.

Turn your head and look really hard into the shadows of the trees and see if you catch sight of a girl of about eight years old. She will be strolling along, kicking and crunching leaves under her feet while humming some little tune she made up.

Her name is Alula-Belle Button-Top Paintbrush Softshoe Pucheeni Magrew.

She will give you a "Hi-dee-hi-hi," which is her favorite greeting. And she will more than likely give you six or eleven peaches to take home with you.

If you want another surprise, take a peek into the shadows of the trees. You may see a turtle who is no ordinary turtle. He is not like other turtles who lump around in their shells taking forever to get anywhere. Nor is he a turtle who hides in his shell as if being forced to go to the dentist. *This* is a special turtle by the name of Jo-Jo Peach Jam, a Really Smart Turtle.

But that's not the end of the surprises. If you happen to look up, and I hope you do, you will see outlined against the sky, way up high in the tallest trees in the woods, the funniest, most crooked and colorful tree house you ever saw. Alula-Belle built and painted that house all by herself.

Kneebend-on-Limber is a happy and friendly place today, but it wasn't always that way. Oh no, far from it. To begin with, at one time there were no peaches here. Not one.

If that wasn't terrible enough, the people of Kneebend-on-Limber all had sour, horrible faces because they absolutely never smiled. Nobody ever told a joke or got tickled. They didn't sing or dance or act comical. They didn't draw pictures or play games. Nobody told any interesting stories; there were no good songs to sing or books to read. Those days were gloomy and boring, let me tell you. Life was dull, dull, *dull*.

But that was before Alula-Belle Button-Top Paintbrush Softshoe Pucheeni Magrew blew into town. Which is what she did. Alula-Belle Button-Top absolutely and positively *blew* into town.

ALULA-BELLE BUTTON-TOP BLOWS INTO TOWN

On a day quite like today—it was a Tuesday or a Saturday—an enormous wind rose up over the town of Kneebend-on-Limber. The wind blew so hard that people fell over sideways. They rolled on their bellies; they toppled on their noses. You couldn't stand up in such a wind—not even if you were wearing

your biggest boots.

The wind was so strong it blew poor Mrs. Lefse right out of her kitchen window. Away she bobbled down the street to the Patterplumps' driveway, where she remained lodged tight between their laurel bushes and new camper trailer.

Trees buckled in the fearsome wind, and birds hid in the leaves of the trees.

The River Limber tossed and flopped and splashed against its steep, grassy banks.

Fish hid at the bottom of the river and ducks and frogs swam to shore as fast as their little legs could swim. There they huddled among the rocks and reeds.

Dogs and cats ran to their owners, and squirrels and rabbits dove into any old hole they could find.

In Tony Cannoli's bake shop all the powdered sugar blew off the pastries. Clouds of sugar bounced through the air

In Tony Cannoli's bake shop all the powdered sugar blew off the pastries.

Jim Scrapnail and his Watcha-ma-callit

around the town, left and right.

Les Fussbucket's fruit stand teetered and toppled, and apples began to roll every which way. The apples bounced along the sidewalk and rolled all the way to the end of town.

Everything that was not nailed down went flying. Apples, papers, hats, coats, children' school books, you name it.

This put everyone in a foul temper. Not one person thought it was funny, not even Jim Scrapnail, the mechanic, who looked very funny indeed blown upside down in the whatcha-ma-callit in his garage

(nobody knows exactly what Jim fixes).

Being everyone was so annoyed and unhappy about the Big Wind, it was a surprise to one and all when they heard the most pleasant laughter coming from the very center of the storm.

"Is that you, Rufus Chuck, you miserable child?!" screamed Mrs. Chuck. "Stop that laughing this minute! We are having ourselves a bad day in a Big Wind, and that's no laughing matter!"

But little Rufus wasn't laughing. In fact, he was so scared he was barely breathing.

The wind blew and blew, and the more it blew, the sweeter and happier was the laughter coming from inside the storm.

The wind was like the sneeze of a giant because as fast as it had begun, it suddenly stopped. Just like that. Everything became very, very quiet.

Then came the biggest surprise of all! The wind deposited something amazing in the middle of the street. It was a shock to everyone. In fact, nobody had ever even dreamed of such a thing. There, in the middle of Main Street, were millions and millions of butterflies!

Sparkling, brightly colored butterflies were everywhere! They were fluttering around one little lump in the center of the street, and that lump was a strange-looking girl of about eight years old, with eyes as big as teacups, all shiny and bright.

The people came hurrying out of their shops and houses to look at the unusual sight. Clara Clearhead ran indoors for her camera.

"Look at all the butterflies!" They said to one another. "Did you ever? And what's *that*?"

Click! Click! went Clara's camera.

Russell Clearhead wasn't quite so fascinated. "Watch it, Clara!" he bellowed. "Could be a trick of some sort."

"Russell Clearhead, what on earth trick could butterflies play, for crying out loud?"

"There's a...a *creature* sitting in the middle of those millions of butterflies. It could be an alien from outer space. It could be dangerous. You never know!"

Click! Click! went Clara Clearhead's camera in spite of the warning.

The tiny girl sat cross-legged in the street. She had small, thin arms which she was waving outward in smooth circles for the butterflies to climb and flutter upon. She

7

seemed to be having a conversation with them. As the gentle laughter continued, the butterflies flew in the air around her head, landing on her shoulders, face and hands. It was the most incredible sight you ever saw. The town was spellbound.

Even grouchy old Mr. Fry-by-Night, who ran the We Never Close Diner, left his griddle and frying pan to watch the awesome sight.

The butterflies formed a long, brightly colored ribbon over the heads of the people.

(Les Fussbucket missed this part because he was so busy crawling around on the sidewalk picking up his spilled apples.) The butterflies' wings touched and glided together as they formed beautiful designs in the sky. They twirled and whirled and swirled until they looked like a long, silk robe—all red and yellow and blue and green and violet and orange.

The girl laughed and clapped her hands as she watched. The butterflies swooped down (and here's the part that shocked even Russell Clearhead and Mr. Fry-by-Night) and each one seemed to *kiss* the little girl's cheeks, like a mother kisses her boy or girl when children leave for school in the morning!

The tiny girl sat cross-legged in the street

The butterflies flew up into the sun with their bright wings fluttering, then they were gone. The girl waved happily after them. "I love you, too!" she called. And then she said something that sounded like "Mommy," but everyone was in such a state, it was hard to tell.

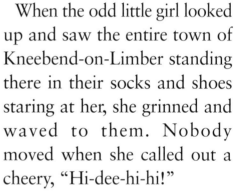

When the odd little girl looked up and saw the entire town of Kneebend-on-Limber standing there in their socks and shoes staring at her, she grinned and waved to them. Nobody moved when she called out a cheery, "Hi-dee-hi-hi!"

Finally, a boy named Ritchie Tick spoke up. "Who...who... are you?" he asked. Ritchie Tick was Rosie Tick's ten-year-old nephew who was not originally from Kneebend, but who had arrived for the weekend eight years ago. Ritchie Tick always said the meanest things. Instead of "Hello, and how are you," he said, "Goodbye and good riddance." Instead of "Please do have a nice day," he said, "I hope you get hiccups and fleas."

Ritchie now considered the sight before

him. He was thinking of something mean to say. The peculiar-looking girl just smiled at him.

Ritchie Tick blurted out once more, "Just *who* are you anyway?"

ALULA-BELLE MAKES
A FRIEND

A hush fell over the people. Clara Clearhead moved in for some more clicking of her camera. The entire town stood there watching, holding its breath and waiting for an answer. Les Fussbucket dropped his apples.

The tiny girl grinned at the crowd and called out another "Hi-dee-hi-hi." When nobody spoke or moved, she said, "Can anyone give me a hi-dee-hi-hi back? It's the polite thing to do, you know."

She had a small button nose that almost looked sewn on. Her thick hair fell in Popsicle-shaped curls around her face, and it flew in all directions at once. She wore a brightly colored dress with several pockets and trimmed in gold. On her feet were two colorful satinlike boots with brightly painted lightning designs on them. She clicked her toes together and kept smiling at Ritchie.

Ritchie frowned. "I think you're ugly, so there," he said in his unlikable way.

"Really?" She was genuinely delighted. "You are observant, aren't you? But come closer. Are you ugly, too?"

Ritchie's Aunt Rosie, who had a voice like a truck, shouted, "This is ridiculous. Ugly or not, tell us who you are! Tell us *now!*"

"Who am I?" the girl answered in the kindest voice you ever heard. "I'm glad you asked." She stood up and smoothed out her dress trimmed in gold with its many pockets and said proudly, "I am Alula-Belle Button-Top Paintbrush Softshoe Pucheeni Magrew. You can call me Alula-Belle Button-Top for short. Or Alula-Belle for shorter."

Nobody moved. Ritchie Tick licked his lips, then squinted his eyes. "You're still ugly," he sniveled, and he stomped back into the crowd.

Alula-Belle laughed. "Thank you. And now you must tell me who *you* are."

Nobody spoke. Mr. Fry-by-Night was very suspicious. "Are you armed?" he shouted.

Alula-Belle was delighted with the question. "Am I armed? Oh yes, indeed! And footed, too! And toed and elbowed and fingered as well."

With that she raised her arms like wings and lifted off the ground. As effortlessly as a bird or a butterfly, she twirled in the air and flew over the heads of the crowd.

"Anybody else armed—or footed—or legged, perhaps?" she called down to the stunned townsfolk.

"That does it," said Mrs. Lefse, who was still sore from rolling down the street and winding up in a bunch of laurel bushes in the

"It's a beautimous day today, don't you agree?"

Patterplumps' driveway. "First a big wind that nearly does me in, and now this incredible *apparition*!"

"Oh, how nice," blushed Alula-Belle, flying low. "I am ugly, *and* I am an apparition. What does this mean?"

"Don't answer her," warned Rufus Chuck's mother. "Everyone knows an apparition is a thing-a-ma-bob, a goofus doofus, a something-or-other. We'd better call the police."

"Police!"

Officer Brickbat was the town's only policeman, and he was standing in the rear of the crowd chewing on one of Les Fussbucket's pears. He wasn't used to anyone calling for the police.

"Police? Well, that's me!" he smoothed his lapel, puffed out his chest, and looked important.

"Police! Help! Do something!" screamed Mrs. Chuck.

Officer Brickbat blew his whistle.

"Everyone stay calm! Don't panic! Law and order is on the scene!" And he swallowed pear, core, seeds, stem, and all. He began to cough.

"Are you going to just stand there choking on a pear, Hank Brickbat?!" cried Mrs. Butterwork. "*Shoot it!*"

"What?" sputtered Officer Brickbat. "Shoot a little girl flying in the air laughing and clicking her toes? Whatever for?"

The crowd began to cheer

and wave their arms. Ritchie Tick shouted and jumped up and down insulting everyone he could.

Ed Frisley had an idea. "I say we capture her and put her in jail. Slap her in the ole slammer."

There was a good deal of commotion, and then everyone agreed. Well, almost everyone. There had not been a complete agreement in the town of Kneebend since it was founded back in the olden days when grandmas and grandpas ran things.

"I say we chase her out of town!" yelled Russell Clearhead.

Then something surprising happened. Ritchie Tick, who had been standing around frowning and grumbling and insulting people, stepped forward. The look on his face was changed. His gaze was fixed on the gentle smile of the little girl.

He started to stammer. "I say...we..." His voice cracked. "I say we...leave her alone! I say she's only a silly girl...who can"—and he added with disbelief—"*fly.*"

It was about as close to being nice or decent that Ritchie Tick had ever come. It would not have been unusual if he had thrown eggs at Alula-Belle. He was that mean.

The rest of the folk glared up at the girl who was flapping around in the sky. Ritchie wasn't the only one with a mean face. They all had mean faces! Every one!

Alula-Belle grinned from above and called down, "Anyone for a song or three? How about I make one up for you just as a sort of welcome gesture?"

"It's a trick!" screamed Mrs. Lefse.

"Oh, you like tricks?" exclaimed Alula-Belle. "So do I. Especially the ones where the white birds pop out of the hats of dancing clowns. Here's a good one for you! Can you do this?" And she did a triple somersault and two flipovers in the air while singing a song:

It's a beautimous day today,
don't you agree?
To make a new friend,
maybe several or three!

Then she landed on her feet with a big finale. *Tah-Duhm!*

"Want to see more?" she asked with a little hop and a skip.

Tony Cannoli, the baker, sighed, "This is all making me dizzy in the head. I've got to return to my oven. My biscuits may burn. My popovers may pop. I've got to check on my rigga-ma-rolls." He peered up at Alula-Belle.

"I must be dreaming," he mumbled into his apron.

The townsfolk prattled and screaked. "Yes, that's it. We're dreaming," they cried. "We're all having the same dream!"

Most everyone knew it wasn't likely that

the whole town could be having the same dream at the same time, especially when they weren't asleep. But nobody knew how else to explain the astounding presence of Alula-Belle Button-Top, so they let it go at that.

One by one the people turned away and went back to their homes and their places of business.

Only Ritchie Tick remained.

He glared at Alula-Belle, who was flapping around in the air again. He took a deep breath. "Hi-dee-hi-hi yourself—silly old ugly girl-person!"

Alula-Belle flapped off to the right of him. "Thank you very much," she said. "And who are you?"

"For your information, my name is Ritchie!" he yelled after her.

"Well, well, of course it is," replied Alula-Belle. "You're Ritchie, every bit of you. Yes, I can see that."

"You're silly!" screamed Ritchie. "You're a silly old girl-person! Ha!"

"Thank you so much, but you're repeating yourself," chuckled Alula-Belle.

Ritchie Tick could not think of another

insult offhand, so he slumped his shoulders the way angry people do when they've run out of words, and he started to walk away.

"Ritchie!" Alula-Belle called after him, "I'm starved. How about joining me for a yummer or two?"

Ritchie could hardly believe his ears. "*What* was that? *What* did you say?"

"Yummers, old boy. You know, vittles, munchels, nibbies, snackments—take your pick. I'm starved. Bite or banquet, it's all the same to me. Let's eat!"

Unlikable Ritchie Tick was amazed. Nobody ever invited him anywhere.

"Who...me?"

"Rightee-ho, Ritchie. Hurry up. I'm getting hungrier by the second. Do you like ice cream?"

"I hate ice cream. And I hate yummers."

Alula-Belle laughed and laughed and laughed. Ritchie Tick could not have begun to imagine, even in his most wild imaginings, the incredible adventure that lay ahead for him.

RITCHIE'S INCREDIBLE ADVENTURE

Ritchie scowled. "You're silly. I've never heard of yummers or munchels or nibbies or snackments. And besides, I'm not an 'old boy'. I'm ten years old, and that is not exactly old by any standard."

"You're right, old boy. Come on, hop aboard. Let's be on our way. I'm as hungry as a blue jay. How those fellows eat! Eat, eat eat, eat—that's all they think about. Well, are you coming or not?"

She rolled out a colorful winglike apparatus that made for a comfortable passenger seat.

"Hop aboard!"

Ritchie was horrified. "You mean *fly*? On *that*?"

"Rightee-ho, Ritchie. It's my Wing-a-Ling. All aboard!"

Ritchie was so afraid, his teeth clinked. But he didn't want to appear frightened, so he did as he was told. He stepped onto Alula-Belle's Wing-a-Ling.

It was like stepping onto a cloud. Immediately, they rose into the air and flew high up into the sky.

"Hang on, Ritchie!"

Away they went. They flew high over the trees, above the River Limber and beyond the town of Kneebend, leaving far behind all the grouchiness below.

They flew into the blue of the sky. "What was that name you had for me a moment ago?" asked Alula-Belle.

Ritchie turned pale. He remembered calling

Immediately they rose into the air and flew high up into the sky.

Alula-Belle a silly old ugly girl-person. She wasn't that at all. Oh no, she was a smart girl-person, very nice and not at all ugly—not in the least.

"I didn't mean it, Alula-Belle," he blubbered. "I am truly sorry. Don't drop me! Please don't drop me. I promise I won't call you anything but your real name from now on. Honest!"

"Drop you? Why ever would I do that? I'd only have to zoom around to catch you—unless, of course, you happen to have a Wing-a-Ling of your own. Do you?"

"Help!" screamed Ritchie. Now he was terrified. He was certain Alula-Belle intended to get back at him for calling her names and being insulting. He was ready to start crying when he noticed his hands were blue. In fact, he noticed all of him was blue. *Everything* was blue.

"Alula-Belle!" he shouted. "Blue! All is blue! Look at me! I'm blue!"

"Rightee-ho," laughed Alula-Belle. She wasn't at all surprised. "You see, Ritchie old boy, the sky is just a big upside-down bowl of blue. Didn't they tell you that in school? Everything gets smeared with a little blue up here.

But never mind, as soon as you get back to earth, the blue will go away, and it will be as though you were never covered with sky at all."

"Are you going to drop me?"

"Of course not. No, thank you. I'm busy enough as it is."

All Ritchie could get out was a frightened mumble that sounded like "Wubba-wubba."

"Isn't it so much better up here than being *out* of the blue, Ritchie? Tell you what. Since I met so many of your friends, I'd like to introduce you to a friend of mine."

"A f-friend?" asked Ritchie.

"Yes, how would you like to meet the wind?"

"Th-the *wind?*" asked Ritchie.

"Sure. The wind is a friend of mine," said Alula-Belle. "Her name is Wanda. Wanda Wind. She's really very friendly if you take the time to get to know her. She can be temperamental at times, however."

Ritchie was in such a state of bewilderment, he didn't know what to say.

"Umbrgg moomp" was all he could answer.

"Hi-dee-hi-hi, Wanda!" called Alula-Belle.

The loveliest voice floated out from behind a cloud. "Hello, my little friend!"

"How are things up here this afternoon, Wanda?"

"Oh, it's been quiet since I saw you last, Alula-Belle," said the voice. "By the way, how do you like your new home?"

"I like it just fine, thank you," answered Alula-Belle. "I'm sure I will be quite content there. This is my new friend Ritchie."

The wind said hello to Ritchie. He sput-

The loveliest voice floated out from behind a cloud. "Hello, my little friend!"

tered something back that sounded like "Mum-umummuh." (He was in shock.)

The wind gave a soft sigh, which created a gentle breeze. "I'm thinking of having a little storm down south in a few weeks," she confided to Alula-Belle. "Nothing fancy. Just a pure and hearty wind to kind of clean things up a bit—you know, blow some dust around."

"Wish I could be there,"said Alula-Belle, "but being I just moved to Kneebend-on-Limber, I'll have to get settled."

"Good luck to you, dear Alula-Belle," whistled Wanda Wind, and she blew her a kiss. Alula-Belle dove into the kiss, which landed on her nose and Ritchie's nose, too. It made Ritchie feel awfully good to be kissed by the wind.

"The wind is always blowing kisses. If people checked with their noses more often, they'd realize that," explained Alula-Belle.

They soared through the air a while longer. "Having fun, Ritchie?" Ritchie was now certain he was imagining everything.

He thought to himself, *All this can't be real. It just can't be true that I am covered with the blue of the sky, and that I am flying around*

*the air on a Wing-a-Ling with a girl who talks
to the wind.*

Out loud he muttered, "I have never known
anyone who could talk to the wind."

"That's because you may not know too
many folks whose mother is a butterfly."

At that news, Ritchie almost fell right off
his comfortable perch. He was absolutely bum-
buzzled, which is to say he was farummped.
What if this wasn't his imagination at all?
What if these things were really happening to
him? He didn't know whether to laugh or
faint.

"Your mother is a *butterfly*?"

"I'll tell you another secret, Ritchie. My
name Alula means Winged One. Isn't that a
corker? Because, as you can see, I don't have
any wings! Just a Wing-a-Ling." And she laughed
and laughed while dipping and flipping
through the air.

At last they landed at a clearing in the
woods by the edge of the River Limber. It took
about an hour for Ritchie to gather his wits,
which seemed to have scattered over hither and
yon. He tried to calm down. All he could say
for the longest time was, "Me fly sky trees

Wanda Wind flubba-flubba."

"So, do you have a favorite vittle, old boy? A special nibbie or munchel, a delicious yummer or two you'd like about now?" Alula-Belle's stomach was rumbling with hunger.

"Help!" sniffled Ritchie. (As it turned out, that boy didn't have a favorite anything.)

"Who, me? Favorite food?"

"We'll just have to invent a nice little snackment for you. Ever have peach nectar unmeat balls and rose petal noodles? How about clover and dandelion pie? Now there's a feast for you. If you just sit tight, I'll gather the ingredients and whip you up something absolutely yummerly."

So, as the sun was setting quietly overhead, Ritchie Tick and Alula-Belle Button-Top sat in the woods eating Alula-Belle's delicious cooking. After the first eight or twelve bites, Ritchie found his voice again and felt almost normal. "Yummer. Good food. Yummer," he warbled.

Ritchie Tick became thoughtful. Something odd was happening to him. Something unusual, different. He sensed an honest thought creeping into his head.

"No one likes me," he confessed. "I have

never had a real friend. You won't like me, either. I assure you of that."

"Well, old boy," said Alula-Belle to cheer him up. "It wouldn't hurt to clean your finger-nails once in a while. I always clean mine every January. Yes, that's what my dear mom taught me. Every January do your nails, she told me. My mother has lots of hands and feet, so she has to clean hers *twice* a year."

"I don't believe your mother is a butterfly. It's not possible. So there!" said Ritchie Tick with his mean, unlikable look. "But then, it's not possible for little girls to fly, is it? And it is not possible to have a conversation with the *wind*...oh-oh! This is a *very* weird dream!"

"Everything is possible," laughed Alula-Belle. My motto is:

If you can remember those words, you'll never be disappointed or frightened, Ritchie. Believe me. Here, have some more primrose tea."

"Be brave and do hard things?" repeated Ritchie Tick. He wasn't sure he understood what that meant.

Alula-Belle was concentrating on yummers, munchels, nibbies, and snackments. "Wait until winter comes," she said with a wistful sigh. "I create scrumptious snow vittles! My snow pudding is the yummerest best."

"Ha!" said Ritchie Tick. "That proves it! Your mother can't be a butterfly because butterflies don't come around in the snow. It's too cold."

"You are right!" replied Alula-Belle. "I'm glad you're up on your butterflies. Ever since I can remember, my mom and all the family either went into hibernation for the cold winter months, or they flew south where it's warmer.

"Anyway, that always left me to make my own way in the world. So the first thing I learned how to do is cook. I specialize in peaches, but you're going to love my blueberry stew. My begonia pie is also terrific."

By the end of the day, Ritchie Tick was actually behaving in a pleasant manner. He didn't call anyone a bad name, he didn't tell one lie, and he didn't give out any more insults. He felt like a very changed ten-year-old boy. Best of all, he thought maybe, just maybe, he had made an honest-to-goodness real friend.

C H A P T E R

4

THE WORLD'S
SMARTEST TURTLE

The next day Alula-Belle sat beside the River Limber reading a book. Ritchie Tick was at home trying to explain to his Aunt Rosie how he talked to the wind and rode on a Wing-a-Ling. Of course, that Rosie didn't believe a word and grounded him in his room without supper. Ritchie didn't mind—his tummy was

"Excuse me, but would you happen to have any peach jam with you?"

still full with a yummer of clover and dande-lions and unmeatball pie.

Alula-Belle took every opportunity to read a book, and this was a perfect day for it.

The sun was shining, the river was bub-bling along to wherever it bubbled along to, and things were quite peaceful. At least for now.

She was reading a book about train repair. Alula-Belle had never ridden on a train. In fact, she had never even seen a train. She just thought you never knew when a train might come along in your life, and there you'll be, as help-less as a mouse on a rug if you didn't know how to fix one.

As she read, she heard an unusual scratch-ing sound. She wondered what it was, but then became so interested in axles and steam and cow catchers and junctions that she ignored it.

A head poked up from behind a log. It was small and green and had two narrow eyes focus-ed on her. "Excuse me," said a scratchy voice.

Alula-Belle looked up from her book.

"Excuse me," repeated the voice belonging to the green head, "but would you happen to have any peach jam with you?"

And that is how Alula-Belle Button-Top Paintbrush Softshoe Pucheeni Magrew met Jo-Jo Peach Jam.

That turtle just popped up from the other side of a log. *Pop!* and there he was. He immediately noticed the book Alula-Belle was reading.

"Oh! I see you're reading one of my favorite books!" exclaimed the turtle. "In my opinion, *The Train Repair Manual* is a classic right up there with Shakesturtle and Hans Christian Turtleson."

Alula-Belle smiled at the turtle.

"Well?" he repeated. "Do you have any peach jam?"

Alula-Belle gave a little laugh. "It just so happens that I am an excellent peach jam maker. Probably the best in the westeastern north of south." Then she leaned forward to examine the turtle more closely.

"And you, sir, you should be wearing a hat. All this sun is turning you positively *green*." With that, she drew a picture of a hat and placed it on his head.

The instant the drawing of the hat reached the turtle's head, it became a real hat.

"Now the sun won't keep greening your face," said Alula-Belle. "You can thank me if you like."

"Thank you ever so much," said the turtle as he sat down beside her. "But you see, I am in

terrible need of some peach jam. Peach jam is what keeps me going, and I have absolutely run out. By the way, my name is Jo-Jo."

"Jo-Jo Peach Jam!" exclaimed Alula-Belle. "You don't look like anybody else but a Jo-Jo Peach Jam! And that's a truth."

The turtle sighed a droopy sort of sigh. "Do you know why turtles move about so slowly? It's because they don't get enough peach jam, that's why."

They sat for a while and felt the sun on

their toes. Alula-Belle was getting an idea. She reached her hand out to the turtle and propped him safely on top of her head. "You shall have your peaches," she said.

Alula-Belle drew a picture of a peach tree and showed it to Jo-Jo Peach Jam. "That ought to do for starters," she laughed, and immediately the picture became a real peach tree.

Jo-Jo Peach Jam clapped his little turtle flippers. "Hooray!" he shouted. "Peaches!"

"We have lots of work to do, Jo-Jo," said

Alula-Belle. I will make your peach jam, and then I must build a house for my family to come and visit. And there isn't much time. Soon the weather will be cold.

"I am going to build the most beautimous tree house you ever saw."

"Beautimous, yes indeed, absolutely," agreed the turtle. "And now, what about my peach jam?"

Alula-Belle patted the turtle's new hat. "I've been thinking," she said as she drew a picture of a gigantic pot of peach jam. "From this day

on, it shall be known in the here-abouts as the land of peaches. Everywhere the eye looks there will be peach trees. And in every home there will be peach jam. After all, my motto is: BE BRAVE AND DO HARD THINGS.

"I think I understand," sighed Jo-Jo. "But in case I don't totally catch on, perhaps you will show me."

The hard things were about to begin.

ALULA-BELLE BUILDS HER TREE HOUSE

Alula-Belle and Jo-Jo Peach Jam started gathering wood to build her tree house in the forest. Alula-Belle sang a little song.

With a widgiddy wudgiddy
wollobee woo,
and a hubbala hoobala hullaba-loo
building a tree house is not hard to do!

She explained to Jo-Jo Peach Jam that she planned to paint the new tree house many wonderful colors.

Widgiddy wudgiddy
wollobee wink
Blue and yellow and green and pink...

Being a very musical turtle, Jo-Jo Peach Jam sang along.

Binkiddy bonk and a wumpiddy doo.
Are you quite certain
we have enough blue?

As they were laughing and singing and working away, they heard a grumperly noise. It was a loud *grumperly-grumperly-grump* sort of noise. Then, all at once, a girl appeared from behind a tree. She had the grumpiest grumperly face Alula-Belle or Jo-Jo Peach Jam had ever seen.

"Just what is all this racket you're making?" grumped the grumperly grumpy-faced person, who actually turned out to be a girl about the same age as Alula-Belle.

Her name, she said, was Pearl Pox, and she lived next door just down the road from where Alula-Belle was building her tree house.

"Hi-dee-hi-hi," greeted Alula-Belle. Jo-Jo

She had the grumpiest grumperly face…

Peach Jam tipped his hat.

The girl frowned and stamped her foot. "You better stop making all that racket. And you better get out of this forest. It's mine! Go on! Scat! Shoo!"

Alula-Belle thought Pearl Pox was making up a new song, so she started to dance.

Go on! Scat! Shoo!

I don't mind if you do—

Pearl Pox became very angry. She was the daughter of Mr. and Mrs. Pox, who argued regularly over who the girl took after—Uncle Sniff or Aunt Snitt.

"Go home, you!" screeched Pearl Pox. Everybody in Kneebend knew about Pearl Pox's nasty temper. That girl was nasty. She was nine years old and didn't like anything. She was disagreeable from the inside out. She fed cat food to the dog and dog bones to the bird. She didn't know one song by heart and always interrupted when adults were talking.

That Pearl Pox was yawping and grumpering, and Alula-Belle and Jo-Jo Peach Jam were singing and dancing.

Which is when Mr. Fussbucket happened by. He was immediately irritated with what he saw.

Mr. Fussbucket asked
Alula-Belle in his irritated voice,
"What do you think you're
doing, *young lady*?"

Pearl Pox made a nasty face.
"Why do grownups always say
'young lady' or 'young man'
when it's obvious they're talking to a *child*?" She stuck her
tongue out at Alula-Belle and
Les Fussbucket.

Les Fussbucket made a face right back at
her. "Pearl Pox, you mind your own beeswax.
Mwaw!" (The *mwaw* part was when he made
the face.) "Mwaw!" he said again.

"Mwaw yourself!" screaked Pearl Pox,

and she made another face, this one more horrible than the last.

"How inspiring!" said Alula-Belle. "Exercising the facial muscles! Do you see that, Jo-Jo Peach Jam? Our neighbors' faces are fit as fiddles. Yes, I'd say their faces are in tip-top shape! Ever try this one?" And she made the biggest, cheesiest smile you ever saw. Jo-Jo laughed out loud.

"What is *that* supposed to be?" grunted

Pearl Pox.

Alula-Belle went right on grinning the most gigantic grin she had ever grinned.

"Terrific exercise," she said, breathing through her teeth. "Try it. You don't need special equipment, clothes, or gym shoes. Go for it!" And she grinned even bigger and wider.

"That's disgusting!" snarled Pearl Pox.

"Ghastly," said Les Fussbucket.

"Despicable," grunted Pearl.

"Despicable? What's that?" asked Les Fussbucket.

Pearl Pox scowled. "Adults are supposed to know what words mean."

Jo-Jo Peach Jam, who happened to read a great many books, said, "I believe despicable means the opposite of likeable."

"Of course," snipped Les Fussbucket. "I knew that!" And he made another *mwaw* face at Pearl Pox.

Alula-Belle had to break in. "Excuse me, kind neighbors," she said. "But I'm in the process of settling, if you please. Building my nest, so to speak."

"High in the treetop," added Jo-Jo Peach Jam.

"Yup!" said Alula-Belle. "Have either of you ever lived in a tree house?"

"I'm getting out of here," shrieked Pearl Pox.

"But first you must have some peach jam," smiled Alula-Belle.

Pearl Pox was exceptionally grumperly. "I don't like girls with turtles on their heads. I don't like tree houses. I don't like yucky, icky peach jam, and I don't like you. Or you. Or you! And that goes for everyone else!" She stomped off with her nose in the air.

"Thanks for coming by," called Alula-Belle with a merry wave. "It's nice to make a new friend."

When Pearl Pox heard that, she snapped around in a rage. "*Friend?* did you say *friend*? I'll never be your friend, you horrible girl! You're... you're *despicable*!"

"Such an intelligent friend," smiled Alula-Belle.

Pearl Pox became furious. "Don't think I will ever, ever, ever in twenty skillion jillion quadrillion zillion years be your friend!" And with that, she was gone, returned to her big house next door, slamming its door behind her.

"Be sure to come back soon," Alula-Belle called after her. "Don't be a stranger now, hear?"

Les Fussbucket was fussing.

"Alula-Belle, who gave you permission to build a house here in the forest? How do you think you're going to—that is, what kind of nest are you talking about? I...I *never*!" Then he pointed to the huge pot of peach jam sitting by the tree. "Is that *real*?"

"Help yourself if you like," answered Alula-Belle. "Peach Jam is very nice on a day such as this. Rub some on your chin. That's what butterflies like to do. Much better than beeswax. I'm sorry Pearl Pox didn't stay around for a little peach jam on the chin."

"I never heard of such a thing! Real! Real peach jam!" He was positively gushing. "Peach jam on the chin! Carrying lumber around in the woods! A turtle wearing a top hat! A *turtle*! I just...*never* blub! blub...er ub!"

He blubbered away so foolishly, Alula-Belle couldn't understand a thing he was trying to say.

"What's that, Mr. Fussbucket?" Alula-Belle

blinked her eyes. "I can't follow your drift. Be plain. Be simple. Now, try again."

Les Fussbucket went on blubbering. "You...created peach jam out of—I...uh, well—you can't just go around with a turtle on your head and building a—what did you say?"

"A nest, if you please. Some people call it a tree house," explained Alula-Belle. "I'm building it extra-beautimous so my relatives will fly by for visits—and I'm doing it all by myself. Tell you what, you can give me a hand if you'd like. How about hoisting that bit of wood over here to me?"

Les Fussbucket couldn't say a word. It was

all such a new experience. The people of Knee-bend-on-Limber were not used to new experiences.

Alula-Belle built that house high in the trees. She sang as she worked.

Hi-dee-ho and whoop dee dah!
What every girl needs is
a hammer and saw!
With a bonk-der bonk-bonk
and a boom-der boom-boom,
I'll have me a house with a family room.

Jo-Jo Peach Jam joined in on the last line.

Peach jam here and peach jam there,
peach jam on the chin and the hair!

Alula-Belle hammered and nailed and sawed, and before long, she had built the most wonderful tree house you ever saw. She then brought out paint and paintbrushes and began to paint the whole thing. But not just one color—oh no. Alula-Belle painted her house so many colors it would take a very smart soul to count them all.

"Well, I never!" fussed Les

Alula-Belle's House Beautimous

Fussbucket as he surveyed the awesome house high in the trees.

"I thank you for your help," said Alula-Belle, although Les had barely lifted a finger to help out. He had merely stood watching her work with his mouth hanging open.

"You must come up some time for a hatful of peach lemonade," she said politely.

Les Fussbucket felt as if he needed to blow his nose.

"Peaches indeed! I happen to know there are absolutely no peaches in Kneebend-on-Limber. Everyone knows that. There hasn't been a peach in Kneebend since olden days, since before who-knows-when. The boys and girls of Kneebend have never even *seen* a peach. You are one crazy girl."

Les Fussbucket was perplexed. He grunted. He grunted again. He peered at Alula-Belle with his wormy little eyes. "You think you can do really hard things, and that's ridiculous! You are daffy wacky," he charged.

"Thank you," said Alula-Belle happily. "And the same to you. Now, tell me, if you please, how would you like your peaches? Juicy and melting in the mouth? Or slurpy and syrupy for pudding and soup?"

Something like a smile crossed the face of Les Fussbucket. "Peaches! Peaches!" he yodeled. Then he couldn't help himself. He actually grinned.

That grouchy, fussy man started to laugh!

CHAPTER

THE CLEARHEADS GET INTO THE ACT

Russell and Clara Clearhead happened to be passing by. They spotted Les Fussbucket laughing away. They could hardly believe their eyes.

"That man hasn't laughed in a dog's age," gasped Clara Clearhead.

"Dog's age? Did you say 'dog's age'?" repeated Alula-Belle, who can hear things from a mile away. She gave Les Fussbucket an understanding look. "How old is the poor thing?"

Russell Clearhead scratched his head. "Old? Who?"

"The dog. What's its age?"

"I don't have a dog," said Les.

"Why, Les Fussbucket, I'm surprised. You have a dog's age and no dog!"

"Dog's age? What dog? It's a joke! A dog's age, but no dog! Hey, that's funny!" sputtered Clara Clearhead. Although she didn't mean to, she started to laugh.

Russell Clearhead groaned. "What are you doing, Clara? What is that on your face? Oh my! Oh my! It's a...*smile!*"

"And would you take a gander at that...that *turtle* on her head! What a funny girl!" giggled Clara, trying to cover her mouth. "A barrel of fun!"

"Fascinating!" said Alula-Belle. "I was not aware that fun came in barrels. I've always preferred my fun to come in peach pots."

Russell Clearhead nudged his wife in the rib with his elbow. "Did you hear that? 'Peach pots' of fun! There's not a peach around here

Russell and Clara Clearhead

for miles and miles!" And he let out a big guffaw (which is a wheezy kind of chuckle that sounds sort of like a whuckle).

"But look!" cried Clara. "Peach trees! Everywhere!" The peach trees were multiplying like mad.

Clara and Russell Clearhead were stunned. Besides that, they were chuckling and whuckling. When you have not chuckled or whuckled for an awfully long time, your face can nearly split in two with the shock of it. A guffaw can really stretch and pull the skin. Your ears twitch; your eyes water; your mouth spreads up and flaps out like flags in the breeze. Your throat feels tickly, and the hairs on your head start to itch.

Les Fussbucket and Clara and Russell Clearhead were now giggling out loud and jabbing one another like crazy with their elbows.

After that, everything happened so fast it's hard to remember what happened first and what happened eleventh. It started, I think, when Clara tripped over her own foot and stumbled bottom first into Alula-Belle's enormous tub of peach jam. It made a huge mess of things.

Les Fussbucket let out a howl of delight. He thought Clara looked comical sitting there up to her neck in slurpy, glurpy peach jam. He laughed so hard, he plopped down onto the

ground, which sent his hat flying. Well, that hat flew right into the pocket-book of Mrs. Lefse, who was on her way to the doctor for her sore knee.

Russell Clearhead shouted, "I got it, Les!" as if he were catching a baseball or a Frisbee, and he made a dive for Mrs. Lefse's purse. But Russell Clearhead was a bit nearsighted or farsighted, and he piled right into Mrs. Lefse herself, who went rolling down the riverbank and landed nose last in the River Limber, sore knee and all.

Clara started laughing out loud again. She thought her husband looked pretty ridiculous rolling down the bank after Mrs. Lefse, who was up to her sleeves in river. Clara began waving her arms and splashing peach jam all over the place.

Les, looking for his hat, accidently stepped in a big blob of peach jam and *boom!* Down he went, sliding down a slope of moss on the seat of his pants. Down he fell, slipping and sliding until he landed right in a bramble of sticks and tall weeds at the river's edge. Mrs. Lefse saw it all from her shallow spot in the river and burst

into laughter. Les Fussbucket looked even funnier than she did. The sticks and weeds stuck to the peach jam, and he looked like a prickly pile of safety pins.

At that exact moment, Ritchie Tick happened by. Now things *really* begin to happen.

"You must come up to visit some time."

WHEN THINGS REALLY BEGIN TO HAPPEN

R itchie Tick hopped across the road toward the commotion in the forest. "Hi-dee-hi-hi!" he called to Alula-Belle.

"Ritchie! I thought you were grounded!" answered a happy Alula-Belle.

"Aunt Rosie sent me to the store for macaroni. I hate macaroni."

"I am glad to see you," said Alula-Belle.

"Me too," said Jo-Jo Peach Jam.

Ritchie stopped short and mumbled to himself. "Er...did a turtle just speak to me?"

"Everyone loves my peach jam, old boy," Alula-Belle continued. "And I want you to have some, too. Be my guest."

"Dig right in," added Jo-Jo Peach Jam.

"I...I've never eaten a peach," said Ritchie. "What do they taste like?"

"Taste for yourself," said Alula-Belle, pointing to the drawing of the peach tree.

"But they're not real peaches," argued Ritchie.

"Oh? What do they teach you in school, Ritchie, old boy? Do they teach you that peaches are pears? Or that apples are carrots? Do they teach you that potatoes are elephants and socks are shoes?"

With that, she picked one of the painted peaches on the paper tree and began munching on it. Peach

juice ran down her chin and between her fingers.

"Now *that's* what I call a peach," she said happily and hopped off into the forest, peach juice dripping after her.

"Please, do have some peach jam!" called Jo-Jo Peach Jam.

Ritchie sat down on the grass. "Yes, I think a turtle *did* just speak to me," he muttered to himself. But nothing could surprise Ritchie anymore, so he decided to have himself a handful of peach jam. Anyhow, Aunt Rosie would no doubt ground him for thirty years when she heard about this.

That was when the Butterworks came by. They were out taking their daily walk, which involved sitting in their car and poking their heads out the window. They liked to look for coins along the road. They hoarded their finds at home in wooden boxes with huge locks.

(One day about a week ago they found seven pennies and four bottle caps in only eighty or twenty hours of driving around with their heads out the window.)

Mr. and Mrs. Butterwork couldn't believe their eyes when they saw Ritchie Tick sitting in the grass with a pleasant smile eating peach jam and getting it all over his chin. And a soaked Mrs. Lefse stuck in the river. And a Clara Clearhead covered with peach jam like a sandwich. And Russell Clearhead's feet poking out of the river weeds. And a Les Fussbucket stuck with prickly sticks.

Those Butterworks forgot all about looking for coins and hopped right out of the car. They wanted to laugh, too. They hadn't laughed since they were in the third or second grade, about two centuries ago.

What the Butterworks didn't know was that their car didn't feel like stopping. No, the Butterwork car had other things on its mind. Along it went, careening down the road. It just kept going on its jolly way until it finished its not-stopping right in front of Tony Cannoli's bakery. That crazy car came to a halt there.

Tony Cannoli looked out his window and saw the not-stopping Butterwork car had stopped smack in front of his door. He saw there was no driver. "Eeeek!" he screamed and threw his hands in the air.

When that Tony Cannoli threw his hands in the air, he knocked over a shelf filled with pastries. Cookies and tarts and dumplings bounced onto the floor. Another shelf fell down. Flour went flying everywhere. Down went another shelf. Strudel and biscotti flopped and flipped out the door. Rye bread and the sixty-grain bread tripped from their shelves.

Doughnuts with frosting and muffins with raisins rolled right out the door.

And where do you suppose everything was toppling in such a hurry? You guessed it. Right into the Butterwork car! The pies and cakes flopped into the Butterworks' backseat and stayed there waiting, as though they were on their way to camp or Aunt Liza's.

All of a sudden that car started moving. Guess where? Backward.

Tony Cannoli was whooping and bellowing and spreading flour and nuts all over the place. He didn't know *what* he was doing. Never had all his baked goods taken off on their own accord in a car with no driver.

He was so upset he ran down the street yammering, "Bring back my eclairs, my napoleons! My chocolate crullers!" He passed Jim Scrapnail's garage. Jim was inside working on his whatcha-ma-callit, but when he heard Tony's shouting, he put down the wrench and the doohickey he was working with and ran out to see what was going on.

What do you suppose that

Jim Scrapnail saw? He saw Tony Cannoli spreading clouds of flour and running and babbling along the street with doughnuts and cookies tumbling alongside him. He saw the shiny Butterwork car driving backward and packed to the top with Cannoli's yummerly pastries.

"Why, Tony, how generous of you!" shouted Jim Scrapnail with a big smile that nearly broke his two cheeks. He hadn't smiled with his whole face for sixteen years and eight months.

Everybody knew Tony Cannoli wasn't generous at all. Until today you couldn't get a free stale crumb out of that fat little man. Now his baked goods were rolling around everywhere free of charge. What could he be thinking?

The children of Kneebend came running out of their houses. They ran alongside the Butterwork car and grabbed at the free pies and cakes and jelly-

The children of Kneebend came running out of their houses.

filled rolls and cinnamon buns.

They ran and the backward-going car rolled all the way to the woods, where Alula-Belle was putting the finishing paint touches on her tree house high in the sky.

Before long, the entire town of Kneebend was laughing like hyenas.

They were wriggling around in powdered sugar and gobbling up pastries a mile a minute.

They were sliding down hills covered in peach jam. They were singing and dancing. Clara Clearhead was snapping pictures with her camera for the *Kneebend Gazette.*

Mrs. Lefse forgot all about her sore knee. Tony Cannoli sat down and ate a loaf of his own pumpersnicker bread.

The Butterworks were laughing so hard they dropped their precious coins and bottle caps everywhere and didn't mind one bit.

Rufus Chuck and his mother sat hunched over a big strawberry pie eating as fast as they could. Next they wanted to start chomping on the chocolate chip cookies.

"Stop chewing so loud," wailed Mrs. Chuck. "You horrible boy, you're chewing too loud! It's hurting my tender ears." She had no sooner uttered those words when Clara Clearhead, quite accidentally, splattered a huge clump of peach jam in her direction.

Rufus saw it coming and hopped up just in time so the gooey stuff wouldn't strike his mother. It hit him right in the face. *Splat!*

"Why, Rufus! You saved me!" clucked

Mrs. Rufus like a hen. You darling, precious boy! You're covered all over with peach jam! And you did it just for me!" She was overcome with joy. She kissed Rufus on the peachy cheek. She kissed him on top of his peachy head. "What a good boy!"

Then she started laughing. She had peach jam all over her face. So did Rufus. They looked like two lollipops.

Chuck Rufus and his mother were laughing for the first time ever. They happily gobbled up the peach jam together.

Ritchie Tick's Aunt Rosie Tick rushed through the trees looking for her nephew.

"Where's my macaroni?" she demanded. "I want my macaroni!" She saw Ritchie stuffing himself with peach jam.

"Here, Auntie dearest, try this," and he gave her a walloping dollop of peach jam.

"But how is it possible?" squealed Rosie. "There has been nothing peachy in Kneebend for years! Oh, delicious!" She ate another dollop and then gave Ritchie a big squeeze.

"What a darling nephew you are, Ritchie. Never mind the macaroni. Forget all about the macaroni. Who needs macaroni?" And she ungrounded the boy on the spot.

Alula-Belle was pleased. She felt like flying, so she lifted her arms and floated over the jolly, hilarious town.

"Quick! Take more pictures!" cackled Russell Clearhead to his wife. "This could be an historical event."

"Allow me," said Alula-Belle, and she snapped about six or eighteen aerial photographs as she glided above the town.

She looked over toward the home of the Poxes. Pearl Pox was watching everything from her patio. She was making bad wishes and expecting the worst. She had a snooty, grumperly scowl on her face. When Alula-Belle waved her cheerful hi-dee-hi-hi, Pearl stuck her nose up and kept grumpering on.

Pearl Pox's nose was stuck up so high in the air and her attitude was so grumperly, she completely missed out on what happened next.

At that moment, there was a brilliant fluttering of bright color sparking down from the sky. It was like a silken sheet sweeping downward, glittering with many colors. The colors were alive—they were butterflies!

The sky was *filled* with millions of butterflies, and they were all laughing and singing and dancing in the air.

The town of Kneebend-on-Limber looked up in astonishment. They were goggled, boggled, and shpoggled.

Alula-Belle grinned at them with her little arms outstretched. A breathtaking host of butterflies surrounded her.

But the music was really what shpoggled them. There came to their ears a lovely, gentle humming sound. It was the most enchanting music they had ever heard. It was the song of the butterflies.

A magnificent butterfly of many colors fluttered forward and hovered above Alula-Belle's shoulder. She was the most wondrous butterfly anyone had ever seen in the whole wide world. A gasp went up from the crowd.

"I want you all to meet my mother," announced

Alula-Belle proudly. The ravishing butterfly twirled and dipped and swooped over the heads of the townsfolk.

Everyone felt so happy. They knew, they positively *knew*, the town of Kneebend-on-Limber would never be the same.

And it wasn't.

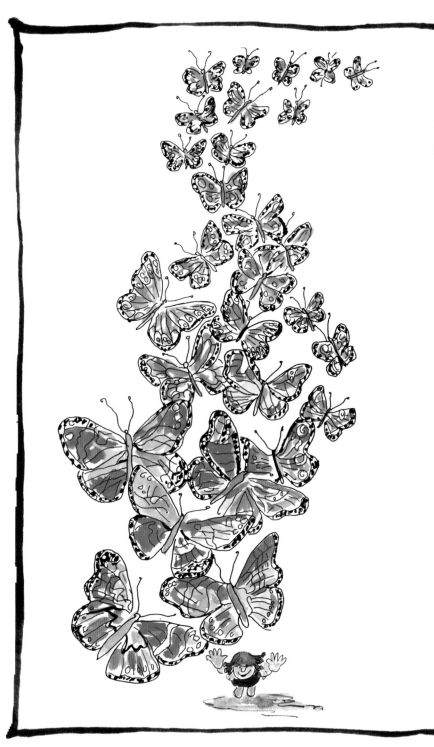

…there was a brilliant fluttering of bright color sparking down from the sky.

ABOUT THE AUTHOR

Marie Jordan Chapian is well loved around the world as an inspirational author and speaker. Her books have sold over two million copies. The Alula-Belle series was inspired by Marie's performances, stories and puppet shows for children, which she presents both live and for television and radio. As an artist, Marie's paintings have been shown in galleries in the United States and Europe and her whimsical illustrations have appeared in major magazines. She has won several awards as an author, playwright, poet, and designer, including the Cornerstone Book of the Year Award, the Gold Medallion, and the Chicago News Book of the Year Award. She currently lives in southern California.

THE GROLIER LIBRARY
OF
SCIENCE BIOGRAPHIES

VOLUME 10

Tsvet–Zworykin

Grolier Educational

Sherman Turnpike, Danbury, Connecticut 06816

Published 1997 by
Grolier Educational
Danbury Connecticut 06816

Copyright © 1996 by Market House Books Ltd.
Published for the School and Library market exclusively
by Grolier Educational, 1997

Compiled and Typeset by Market House Books Ltd, Aylesbury, UK.

General Editors
    John Daintith BSc, PhD
    Derek Gjertsen BA

Market House Editors
    Elizabeth Martin MA
    Anne Stibbs BA
    Fran Alexander BA
    Jonathan Law BA
    Peter Lewis BA, DPhil
    Mark Salad

Picture Research
    Linda Wells

Contributors
    Eve Daintith BSc
    Rosalind Dunning BA
    Garry Hammond BSc
    Robert Hine BSc, MSc
    Valerie Illingworth BSc, MPhil
    Sarah Mitchell BA
    Susan O'Neill BSc
    W. J. Palmer MSc
    Roger F. Picken BSc, PhD
    Carol Russell BSc
    W. J. Sherratt BSc, MSc, PhD
    Jackie Smith BA
    B. D. Sorsby BSc, PhD
    Elizabeth Tootill BSc, MSc
    P. Welch DPhil
    Anthony Wootton

Published by arrangement with
The Institute of Physics Publishing
Bristol BS1 6NX
UK

ISBN   Volume 10   0-7172-7636-8
           Ten-Volume Set   0-7172-7626-0
Library of Congress Catalog Number: 96-31474
Cataloging Information to be obtained directly from Grolier Educational.
First Edition
Printed in the United States of America

CONTENTS

PREFACE

ABOUT THE GROLIER LIBRARY OF SCIENCE BIOGRAPHIES

The 19th-century poet and essayist Oliver Wendell Holmes wrote:

Science is a first-rate piece of furniture for a man's upper chamber, if he has common sense on the ground floor.

The Poet at the Breakfast-Table (1872)

While it has been fashionable in this century to assume that science is capable of solving all human problems, we should, perhaps, pause to reflect on Holmes's comment. Scientific knowledge can only be of value to the human race if it is made use of wisely by the men and women who have control of our lives.

If this is true, all thinking people need a solid piece of scientific furniture in their upper chambers. For this reason the editors and publishers of this series of books have set out to say as much about science itself as about the scientists who have created it.

All the entries contain basic biographical data – place and date of birth, posts held, etc. – but do not give exhaustive personal details about the subject's family, prizes, honorary degrees, etc. Most of the space has been devoted to their main scientific achievements and the nature and importance of these achievements. This has not always been easy; in particular, it has not always been possible to explain in relatively simple terms work in the higher reaches of abstract mathematics or modern theoretical physics.

Perhaps the most difficult problem was compiling the entry list. We have attempted to include people who have produced major advances in theory or have made influential or well-known discoveries. A particular difficulty has been the selection of contemporary scientists, in view of the fact that of all scientists who have ever lived, the vast majority are still alive. In this we have been guided by lists of prizes and awards made by scientific societies. We realize that there are dangers in this – the method would not, for instance, catch an unknown physicist working out a revolutionary new system of mechanics in the seclusion of the Bern patent office. It does, however, have the advantage that it is based on the judgments of other scientists. We have to a great extent concentrated on what might be called the "traditional" pure sciences – physics, chemistry, biology, astronomy, and the earth sciences. We also give a more limited coverage of medicine and mathematics and have included a selection of people who have made important contributions to engineering and technology. A few of the entries cover workers in such fields as anthropology and psychology, and a small number of philosophers are represented.

A version of this book was published in 1993 by the Institute of Physics, to whom we are grateful for permission to reuse the material in this set. Apart from adding a number of new biographies to the Institute of Physics text, we have enhanced the work with some 1,500 photographs and a large number of quotations by or about the scientists themselves. We have also added a simple pronunciation guide (the key to which will be found on the back of this page) to provide readers with a way of knowing how to pronounce the more difficult and unfamiliar names.

Each volume in this set has a large biographical section. The scientists are arranged in strict alphabetical order according to surname. The entry for a scientist is given under the name by which he or she is most commonly known. Thus the American astrophysicist James Van Allen is generally known as Van Allen (not Allen) and is entered under V. The German chemist Justus von Liebig is commonly referred to as Liebig and is entered under L. In addition, each volume contains a section on "Sources and Further Reading" for important entries, a glossary of useful definitions of technical words, and an index of the whole set. The index lists all the scientists who have entries, indicating the volume number and the page on which the entry will be found. In addition scientists are grouped together in the index by country (naturalized nationality if it is not their country of origin) and by scientific discipline. Volume 10 contains a chronological list of scientific discoveries and publications arranged under year and subject. It is intended to be used for tracing the development of a subject or for relating advances in one branch of science to those in another branch. Additional information can be obtained by referring to the biographical section of the book.

JD
DG 1996

PRONUNCIATION GUIDE

A guide to pronunciation is given for foreign names and names of foreign origin; it appears in brackets after the first mention of the name in the main text of the article. Names of two or more syllables are broken up into small units, each of one syllable, separated by hyphens. The stressed syllable in a word of two or more syllables is shown in **bold** type.

We have used a simple pronunciation system based on the phonetic respelling of names, which avoids the use of unfamiliar symbols. The sounds represented are as follows (the phonetic respelling is given in brackets after the example word, if this is not pronounced as it is spelled):

a *as in* bat
ah *as in* palm (pahm)
air *as in* dare (dair), pear (pair)
ar *as in* tar
aw *as in* jaw, ball (bawl)
ay *as in* gray, ale (ayl)
ch *as in* chin
e *as in* red
ee *as in* see, me (mee)
eer *as in* ear (eer)
er *as in* fern, layer
f *as in* fat, phase (fayz)
g *as in* gag
i *as in* pit
I *as in* mile (mIl), by (bI)
j *as in* jaw, age (ayj), gem (jem)
k *as in* keep, cactus (**kak**-tus), quite (kwIt)
ks *as in* ox (oks)
ng *as in* hang, rank (rangk)
o *as in* pot

oh *as in* home (hohm), post (pohst)
oi *as in* boil, toy (toi)
oo *as in* food, fluke (flook)
or *as in* organ, quarter (**kwor**-ter)
ow *as in* powder, loud (lowd)
s *as in* skin, cell (sel)
sh *as in* shall
th *as in* bath
th *as in* feather (**feth**-er)
ts *as in* quartz (kworts)
u *as in* buck (buk), blood (blud), one (wun)
u(r) *as in* urn (but without sounding the "r")
uu *as in* book (buuk)
v *as in* van, of (ov)
y *as in* yet, menu (**men**-yoo), onion (**un**-yon)
z *as in* zoo, lose (looz)
zh *as in* treasure (**tre**-zher)

The consonants b, d, h, l, m, n, p, r, t, and w have their normal sounds and are not listed in the table.

In our pronunciation guide a consonant is occasionally doubled to avoid confusing the syllable with a familiar word, for example, -iss rather than -is (which is normally pronounced -iz); -off rather than -of (which is normally pronounced -ov).

Ts

Tsvet, Mikhail Semenovich

(1872–1919)

RUSSIAN BOTANIST

Tsvet (tsvyayt), who was born at Asti in Italy, entered Geneva University in 1891 and followed courses in physics, chemistry, and botany. In 1896, having presented his thesis on cell physiology, he moved to the biological laboratory at St. Petersburg, where he began working on plant pigments.

Before Tsvet started applying chemical and physical methods to pigment analysis it was thought that only two pigments, chlorophyll and xanthophyll, existed in plant leaves. Following established procedures, Tsvet soon demonstrated the existence of two forms of chlorophyll. However, the isolation of pigments became a much simpler matter once he had developed, in 1900, the technique of adsorption analysis. By 1911 Tsvet had found eight different pigments.

His technique involved grinding leaves in organic solvent to extract the pigments and then washing the mixture through a vertical glass column packed with a suitable adsorptive material (e.g., powdered sucrose). The various pigments traveled at different rates through the column due to their different adsorptive properties and were therefore separated into colored bands down the column. Tsvet first described this method in 1901 and in a publication of 1906 suggested it should be called "chromatography."

The technique is extremely useful in chemical analysis, being simple, quick, and sensitive, but it was not much used until the 1930s. Tsvet died when only 47 from overwork and the stress of the war, during which he was frequently transferred from one institute to another. He thus did not live to see the fruits of the wider application of chromatography in the hands of such scientists as Richard Kuhn.

Tull, Jethro

(1674–1741)

BRITISH AGRICULTURALIST, WRITER, AND INVENTOR

I am told that some pretenders to making the hoe-plow have fix'd its bottom to the plank immoveable, which makes it as useless for hoeing betwixt rows, as a violin with but one peg to its four strings would be for playing a sonata.
—*The New Horse-Hoeing Husbandry* (1731)

Born at Basildon in the eastern English county of Essex, Tull trained in law at Oxford University and was called to the bar in 1699 but gave this up to farm. He developed farming methods that became the basis of modern British agriculture. In about 1701 he invented a seed drill that sowed in regular straight rows. He also introduced a system of plowing that increased the water supply to plant roots and reduced the need for fallow land.

Tull's techniques were published in *The New Horse-Hoeing Husbandry: Or an Essay on the Principles of Tillage and Vegetation* (1731). At first they encountered opposition in Britain but they were more readily accepted in France, where Voltaire supported them.

Turing, Alan Mathison

(1912–1954)

BRITISH MATHEMATICIAN

> We do not need to have an infinity of different machines doing different jobs. A single one will suffice. The engineering problem of producing various machines for various jobs is replaced by the office work of "programming" the universal machine to do these jobs.
> —Quoted by A. Hodges in *Alan Turing: the Enigma of Intelligence*

Turing, who was born in London, saw little of his parents in his early years. His father served in the Indian Civil Service before retiring in 1926; thereafter they lived in France to eke out a small pension. Turing was educated at Cambridge University, where he gained a fellowship at King's College in 1935. He spent the period from 1936 to 1938 at Princeton. During this time he published one of the most significant mathematical papers of the century, *On Computable Numbers* (1937).

He began by describing a hypothetical universal computer, since known as a *Turing machine*. It consists of an infinite length of tape divided into cells, a movable scanner/printer capable of reading the tape, printing, erasing, moving to the left and right, and halting. In each cell the tape has a symbol taken from a finite set of symbols (in a simple case 0 and 1). The control unit of the machine can be in one of a finite set of internal states (states S_1, S_2, S_3, etc.). The machine has a "program," which is a set of groups of five symbols. For example, one set of five symbols might be S_101XS_2, where X is R, L, or N. This is interpreted as meaning that the machine is in state S_1 (the first symbol of the five) and reading 0 (the second symbol). In this state it replaces the 0 by 1 (third symbol). If X = R it moves to the next cell on the right, if X = L it moves to the next on the left, and if X = N it does not move (it halts). Finally it goes into state S_2. The program, which can be used to do calculations, consists of a set of such quintuples (e.g., S_100RS_1, S_110RS_2, S_201RS_3, etc.).

Turing went on to define a set of integers N as computable if there was a Turing machine which, given any number m as input, will halt on 1 if *m* is a member of *N*, and halt on 0 otherwise. Using a variant of Cantor's diagonal argument Turing proved, echoing earlier work by Kurt Godel and Alonzo Church, that some sets of integers are not computable.

Soon after the outbreak of war in 1939 Turing joined the government Code and Cypher School at Bletchley Park, Buckinghamshire. The Germans were known to be using a coding device called "Enigma." The basic model looked like an electric typewriter; the keyboard (input) was connected to the typed output by three rotors which changed position after each letter. This was equivalent to a polyalphabetic system with a periodicity of $26^3 = 17,576$. The military version of Enigma added a number of complications. The positions of the rotors could be changed, increasing the periodicity to 105,456. Further improvements increased the periodicity to over a trillion. The Germans felt that the military Enigma was "very close to practical insolvability."

Turing, along with a motley collection of mathematicians, linguists, and chess grandmasters, worked initially on the naval version of Enigma. The key innovation was the development of a computer, known as a "Bombe," to handle the vast amounts of traffic. The name derived from the fact that early models designed by Polish analysts ticked very loudly. The Bombe allowed numerous possible solutions to be quickly checked against traffic and eliminated. By March 1940 they were reading some of the traffic and finding that it consisted of nursery rhymes sent as practice transmissions. By June 1941 they were reading operational naval traffic. This, however, was not the end of Turing's work. In early 1942 the German navy adopted a new Enigma system and added a fourth rotor to its design. The sinking of Allied shipping rapidly increased. The breakthrough came in December 1942. The Germans were transmitting weather reports daily by Enigma machines using only the first three rotors. Cribs of the weather reports were provided rapidly from other sources. It was therefore only necessary for the Bombes to work through the 26 possibilities of the fourth rotor to decipher fully encrypted traffic. By the new year Allied shipping could once more be diverted away from known U-boat positions. Shortly after this Turing left Bletchley Park for nearby Hanslope Park where he worked for the rest of the war on speech encipherment. Few individuals can have contributed so much to the war effort, or have saved so many lives, as Turing. In 1946 he was awarded an OBE for his services.

Turing was reluctant to return to Cambridge and a career in pure mathematics. Consequently he accepted a position at the National Physical Laboratory working on the design of a new computer, ACE (Automatic Computing Engine). He moved to Manchester University in 1948 to undertake similar work on the development of MADAM (Manchester Automatic Digital Machine).

During this period Turing produced two influential papers. In his *Computing Machinery and Intelligence* (1950) he challenged his critics to specify how computers could be distinguished from intelligent human beings. In the imitation game the interrogator posed questions to two "individuals" A and B; he was asked to determine from their written replies which answer came from a computer. Both can of course lie. The *Turing test*, as the procedure is now called, has been cited as a way of testing machine intelligence and still causes debate and experiment. Turing himself was in no doubt that one day computers would be able to think.

Turing's other paper, *The Chemical Basis of Morphogenesis* (1952), concerned the generation of form. How can an assemblage of cells develop, as with the case of a starfish, a five-fold symmetry? Or how does a sphere of cells, in the process of gastrulation, form a groove at a specific point? He argued that it was possible for differences in chemical concentration to develop, even though the original situation had a uniform concentration. Turing's original model was mathematical. Chemists have, however, since found that there are systems, namely reaction–diffusion models, which mimic Turing's "morphogens."

Before he could develop his ideas further Turing committed suicide. He was homosexual and, for the times, fairly open about his life. A friend of a casual pick-up had stolen a few items of no great value from Turing's house and Turing reported the theft to the police. The culprit was arrested and in the course of investigations it was revealed that Turing had been sexually involved with a 19-year-old man. He was charged with gross indecency. Reluctantly he allowed himself to be persuaded to plead guilty and the court placed him on probation on the condition that he undergo hormone treatment. Although he seemed to find the process no more than irritating, and although his job remained secure, to the surprise of his family and friends he took his own life in 1954 by eating an apple dosed with cyanide.

Turner, David Warren

(1927–1990)

BRITISH PHYSICAL CHEMIST

Born at Leigh-on-Sea in Essex, England, Turner was educated at Exeter University and began his research at Imperial College, London. In 1965 he moved to Oxford. He is noted for his development of the technique known as molecular photoelectron spectroscopy. In this a narrow beam of monochromatic ultraviolet radiation is directed into a sample of gas; usually helium radiation (584 Å) is used. The gas is ionized and the energies of the ejected electrons are analyzed by electrostatic deflection. The energy of a particular electron equals the energy of the radiation minus the binding energy (ionization potential) of the electron in the atom or molecule. The technique thus determines the outer energy levels of the molecule, as well as information about the ions formed. It can also be used with solid samples to determine the energy bands. It is similar to the technique of Kai Siegbahn, which uses higher-energy x-rays and measures the binding energies of inner electrons.

Turner also worked on nuclear magnetic resonance, ultraviolet spectroscopy, and on a form of electron microscopy in which the electrons are ejected from the sample by x-rays or ultraviolet radiation.

Turner, Herbert Hall

(1861–1930)

BRITISH ASTRONOMER

Turner, born the son of an artist in Leeds, England, studied mathematics at Cambridge University from which he graduated in 1882. On the recommendation of George Airy he was appointed chief assistant at the Royal Observatory, Greenwich, in 1884. He moved to Oxford in 1893 as professor of astronomy, a post he held until his death.

At Greenwich Turner did much to organize the Royal Observatory's contribution to the catalog and photographic chart of the sky, the Carte du Ciel, proposed in Paris by E. Mouchez in 1887. Once at Oxford he devoted much time and energy to the completion of Oxford's share in the project and the work was published shortly after Greenwich's contribution in 1909. Following the formation of the International Astronomical Union in 1919 he became president of the committee in charge of the Carte du Ciel and did much to try and get the chart and catalog finished.

Turner also became interested in seismology and after the death of his friend John Milne in 1913 took on the responsibility for the collection and dissemination of basic seismological data. He consequently started in 1918 and continued to edit until 1927 the quarterly *International Seismological Summary*, providing the origins and times of all detected earthquakes.

Tuve, Merle Antony

(1901–1982)

AMERICAN GEOPHYSICIST

Born at Canton in South Dakota, Tuve gained his BS degree in electrical engineering in 1922 from the University of Minnesota. He held posts at Princeton (1923–24) and Johns Hopkins (1924–26), receiving his PhD from the latter in 1926. From 1926 he was a staff member of the department of terrestrial magnetism of the Carnegie Institution of Washington.

Tuve is known principally for his techniques of radio-wave exploration of the upper atmosphere. In 1925 Tuve and Gregory Breit at Carnegie conducted some of the first experiments in range-finding using radio-waves in which they measured the height of the ionosphere. They transmitted a train of pulses of waves and determined the time each pulse took to return to Earth. Thereafter, pulse-ranging became the standard procedure for ionospheric research and laid the foundation for much of the later work on the development of radar.

In 1926 Tuve investigated long-range seismic refraction – the effect of different materials in the Earth's crust on the propagation of a seismic disturbance. He went on to construct an "upper-mantle velocities map" of America, which has been found to accord with theories of isostasy – a hydrostatic state of equilibrium in the distribution of materials of varying density in the Earth's interior.

During World War II Tuve worked for the Office of Scientific Research and Development, developing the proximity fuse, which stopped the "buzz bomb" attacks on Britain and Antwerp, among other projects. He returned to Carnegie in 1946 to become director of the department of terrestrial magnetism, a position he held up to 1966.

As well as seismic refraction and range-finding, Tuve also made studies of artificially produced beta and gamma rays, transmutations of atomic nuclei, and artificial radioactivity. He was for nine years editor of the *Journal of Geophysical Research*.

Twort, Frederick William

(1877–1950)

BRITISH BACTERIOLOGIST

Twort, a doctor's son from Camberley in England, qualified in medicine in 1900 and after various appointments in London hospitals became professor of bacteriology at London University. His most important discovery was made during an attempt to grow viruses in artificial media: he noticed that bacteria, which were infecting his plates, became transparent. This phenomenon proved to be contagious and was the first demonstration of the existence of bacteria-infecting viruses. These were later called "bacteriophages" by the Canadian bacteriologist Felix d'Herelle, who discovered them independently.

Twort was also the first to culture the causative organism of Johne's disease, an important intestinal infection of cattle.

Tyndall, John

(1820–1893)

BRITISH PHYSICIST

Watch the cloud-banner from the funnel of a running locomotive; you see it growing gradually less dense. It finally melts away altogether, and if you continue your observations, you will not fail to notice that the speed of its disappearance depends upon the character of the day. In humid weather the cloud hangs long and lazily in the air; in dry weather it is rapidly licked up. What has become of it? It has been converted into true invisible vapor.

—"The Forms of Water" (1872)

Tyndall was born at Carlow (now in the Republic of Ireland) and after leaving school began work as a draftsman and civil engineer in the Irish Ordnance Survey. He later became a railway engineer for a Manchester firm. His drive for knowledge caused him to read widely and attend whatever public lectures he could. In 1847 he became a teacher of mathematics, surveying, and engineering physics at the Quaker school, Queenwood College, Hampshire.

The following year Tyndall entered the University of Marburg, Germany, to study mathematics, physics, and chemistry; after graduating in 1850 he worked in H. G. Magnus's laboratory in Berlin on diamagnetism. He was appointed professor of natural philosophy at the Royal Institution in 1853 and became a colleague and admirer of Michael

Faraday; he succeeded Faraday as director of the Royal Institution in 1867 and held this position until his retirement in 1887.

Tyndall's activities were many-sided. His chief scientific work is considered to be his researches on radiant heat; these included measurements of the transmission of radiant heat through gases and vapors published in a series of papers starting in 1859. But he is perhaps better known for his investigations on the behavior of light beams passing through various substances; he gave his name to the *Tyndall effect* – the scattering of light by particles of matter in its path, thus making the light beam visible – which he discovered in 1859. Tyndall elucidated the blue of the sky following the work of John Rayleigh on the scattering of light. He also discovered the precipitation of organic vapors by means of light, examined the opacity of the air for sound in connection with lighthouses and siren work, demonstrated that dust in the atmosphere contained microorganisms, and verified that germ-free air did not initiate putrefaction.

Tyndall was especially noted in his day as a great popularizer of science and advocate of scientific education, rather than as a great scientist. Among his many books for the nonspecialist the famous *Heat Considered as a Mode of Motion* (1863), the first popular exposition of the mechanical theory of heat, went through numerous editions. He was a member of the "X" Club, a group of prominent British scientists formed to ensure that the claims of science and scientific education were kept before the government of the day. He also helped to inaugurate the British scientific journal *Nature*. In 1872 and 1873 he undertook public lecture tours in America, giving the proceeds to a trust set up to benefit American science.

Tyndall died in 1893, accidentally poisoned by his wife with an overdose of chloral hydrate. "You have killed your John," he is alleged to have told her shortly before he died the following day. Louisa Tyndall lived another 47 years.

Uhlenbeck, George Eugene

(1900–1988)

DUTCH–AMERICAN PHYSICIST

Uhlenbeck (**oo**-len-bek), who was born at Batavia (now Djakarta) in Indonesia, was educated at the University of Leiden, where he obtained his PhD in 1927. He then emigrated to America where he worked at the University of Michigan (1927–60), being appointed professor of theoretical physics in 1939. In 1960 he moved to the Rockefeller Medical Research Center at the State University of New York (now Rockefeller University) where he remained until his retirement in 1974.

Uhlenbeck's chief contribution to physics was made in 1925 when, in collaboration with Samuel Goudsmit, he discovered electron spin.

Ulam, Stanislaw Marcin

(1909–1986)

POLISH–AMERICAN MATHEMATICIAN

The son of a lawyer, Ulam (**oo**-lam) was educated at the polytechnic in his native city of Lwow, Poland, where he completed his doctorate in 1933. This was a golden age of Polish mathematics. At coffee houses in Lwow and Warsaw, Ulam reported, Banach, Sierpiński, and Tarski could be found discussing the latest advances in set theory. Problems too difficult for an immediate solution were entered in a large notebook known as "The Scottish Book." It survived the war, and the occupation of Lwow by the Soviet Union and Germany, and was eventually translated and published by Ulam as *The Scottish Book* (Los Alamos, 1957).

Ulam quickly developed a reputation as an original mathematician and in 1936 he was invited to visit the Institute for Advanced Study, Princeton, for a year. He decided to remain in the United States and spent the period from 1937 to 1940 at Harvard before being appointed professor of mathematics at the University of Wisconsin. He became a naturalized American citizen in 1943.

At the same time Ulam was invited to work on the development of the atom bomb at Los Alamos, New Mexico, and he remained associated with Los Alamos until 1967. Here he worked on the theory of nuclear reactions. When neutrons are released in a reactor some scatter, some are absorbed, others escape or collide, etc. The actual process is too complex for analytical calculation. If, however, the fate of a practical number of neutrons is followed, and if at each branch one outcome with a suitable probability is selected, it is possible to derive a reasonably accurate mathematical model of the process. Ulam's technique, which is known as the "Monte Carlo method" (after the casino), is a widely used numerical method in many different fields.

After the war Ulam worked with Teller on the development of the hydrogen bomb. He served as research adviser to the director of Los Alamos from 1957 to 1967, when he was appointed professor of mathematics at the University of Colorado, Boulder, a post he held until his retirement in 1977. He left an account of his life in his *Adventures of a Mathematician* (New York, 1976).

Ulugh Beg

(1394–1449)

PERSIAN ASTRONOMER

> It is the duty of every true Muslim, man and woman, to strive after knowledge.
> —Quoting from the Hadith, the body of received tradition about
> the teachings and lives of Mohammed and his followers

Ulugh Beg (oo-luug beg) was a grandson of Tamerlane. He was born at Soltaniyeh (now in Iran) and succeeded to the throne in 1447 but was killed by his rebellious son two years later. He began building an observatory at Samarkand in 1428. He was himself an observer and published planetary tables and a catalog of stars in 1437. They were published in Europe in 1665. The observatory was reported to have had a gnomon for measuring the elevation of the Sun as high as the dome of St. Sophia in Byzantium (180 feet).

Unverdorben, Otto

(1806–1873)

GERMAN CHEMIST

Born at Potsdam in Germany, Unverdorben (uun-fer-dor-ben) was a self-taught chemist who worked on the distillation of various organic compounds, publishing his results between 1824 and 1829. In 1826 he isolated a new substance from indigo, which he named "crystalline." Some years later August Hofmann isolated a substance from coal tar that he recognized as being the same as that obtained by Unverdorben from indigo. He called it aniline, from *al nīl*, the Arabic name for the indigo plant.

Urbain, Georges

(1872–1938)

FRENCH CHEMIST

Urbain (oor-**ban**) studied chemistry at the Sorbonne, in his native city of Paris, receiving his PhD in 1899. After working in industry for some years he returned to the Sorbonne in 1908 as professor of mineral chemistry and became, in 1928, professor of general chemistry.

He is noted for his work on the lanthanoid elements and discovered the element lutetium in a sample of ytterbium in 1907.

Ure, Andrew

(1778–1857)

BRITISH CHEMIST

Born in Glasgow, Scotland, Ure was educated at Edinburgh and Glasgow universities where he studied medicine. He succeeded George Birkbeck in 1804 as professor of chemistry and natural philosophy at Anderson's College, Glasgow. In 1830 he set himself up in London as an analytical and consultant chemist and in 1834 he became analytical chemist to the Board of Customs.

Ure's chief significance was as an educationalist and an apologist for the industrial revolution. In 1809 he started popular science lectures in Glasgow following the tradition established by George Birkbeck. He published a two-volume *Dictionary of Chemistry* (1821) and a *Dictionary of Arts, Manufactures, and Mines* (1839), which are in this popular tradition. Ure also wrote a more original and unusual work; in his *Philosophy of Manufactures* (1835) he portrayed a very different picture of the industrial revolution from that which is usually represented. In it he welcomed and praised the benefits of industrialization and the actual mode of life of the workers in the mines and factories. He argued, for example, that gaslight was an adequate replacement for sunlight and that machinery reduced the laborious work.

Ure's chemical studies included work on the specific gravity of solutions of sulfuric acid. He also invented a method of mercury extraction.

Urey, Harold Clayton

(1893–1981)

AMERICAN PHYSICAL CHEMIST

Urey, born the son of a teacher and lay minister in Walkerton, Indiana, was educated at the universities of Montana, where he studied zoology, and California, where he obtained a PhD in chemistry (1923). After a year at the Institute of Theoretical Physics in Copenhagen, he began his teaching career at Johns Hopkins in 1924. In 1929 he moved to Columbia University, remaining there until 1958 when he became a professor at the University of California.

He is best known as the discoverer of deuterium – the isotope of hydrogen containing one proton and one neutron in its nucleus. This followed the accurate measurement of the atomic weights of hydrogen and oxygen by Francis W. Aston and the discovery of oxygen isotopes by William Giauque.

To obtain deuterium Urey used the fact that it would evaporate at a slightly slower rate than normal hydrogen. He took some four liters of liquid hydrogen, which he distilled down to a volume of one cubic centimeter. The presence of deuterium was then proved spectroscopically. Urey went on to investigate differences in chemical-reaction rate between isotopes. During World War II he was in charge of the separation of isotopes in the atomic-bomb project. Urey's research also led to a large-scale method of obtaining deuterium oxide (heavy water) for use as a neutron moderator in reactors.

His interest in isotope effects in chemical reactions gave him the idea for a method of measuring temperatures in the oceans in the past. It depended on the fact that the calcium carbonate in shells contains slightly more oxygen–18 than oxygen–16, and the ratio depends on the temperature at which the shell formed.

For his discovery of heavy hydrogen Urey was awarded the 1939 Nobel Prize for chemistry.

Vallisneri, Antonio

(1661–1730)

ITALIAN PHYSICIAN AND
BIOLOGIST

Born at Trassilico, near Modena in Italy, Vallisneri (or Vallisnieri; val-eez-**nyair**-ee) studied medicine at Bologna under Marcello Malpighi and at Reggio where he obtained his MD in 1684. After practicing medicine in Reggio, Vallisneri was appointed to the chair of medicine at the University of Padua in 1700 where he remained until his death.

Francesco Redi in 1668 had performed a famous experiment proving that the maggots in rotten meat were not spontaneously generated but arose, in the normal manner, from eggs laid by flies. He did however spoil the force of his argument by conceding that the larvae found in galls, for which he could find no eggs, were spontaneously generated. In 1700 Vallisneri plugged this gap in his *Sopra la curiosa origine di molti insetti* (On the Strange Origin of Many Insects) in which he reported success in detecting eggs of the insects in plant galls.

In 1715 Vallisneri published *Origine delle fontane* (Origin of Fountains), which threw much light on another longstanding problem. Many ancient and medieval authorities were convinced that springs and rivers originated in the sea, and consequently the source of artesian wells, such as those at Modena, presented a problem. By exploring the local mountains, Vallisneri found that the rain and melting snow ran into fissures and formed subterranean rivers. Such rivers, passing under Modena at high pressure, would readily produce "fontane" if deep enough shafts were sunk.

As a biologist and anatomist Vallisneri also produced a number of treatises on such unfamiliar animals as the ostrich (1712) and the chameleon (1715). His studies of a group of aquatic plants led to the genus *Vallisneria* being named for him.

Van Allen, James Alfred

(1914–   )

AMERICAN PHYSICIST

Van Allen was born at Mount Pleasant, Iowa. After graduating from the Iowa Wesleyan College in 1935 he went on to the University of Iowa, where he gained his PhD in 1939. His subsequent career took him to the Carnegie Institution of Washington (1939–42), as a physics research fellow in the department of terrestrial magnetism, and to the applied physics laboratory at the Johns Hopkins University (1942 and 1946–50). In 1951 Van Allen returned to the University of Iowa as a professor of physics and head of the department of physics and astronomy, retiring in 1990.

During the war years (1942–46) he served as an ordnance and gunnery specialist and combat observer with the U.S. Navy and developed the radio proximity fuse, a device that guided explosive weapons, such as antiaircraft shells, close to their targets and then detonated them. He also gained considerable expertise in the miniaturization of electronics and rocket controls, which he later put to use in the scientific exploration of the Earth's upper atmosphere.

After the war Van Allen was able to use German V–2 rockets for atmospheric studies and was associated with the development of the Aerobee sounding rocket. He also used rocket–balloon combinations that could carry small rockets to higher altitudes. In the years 1949–57 he organized and led several scientific expeditions (to Peru, the Gulf of Alaska, Greenland, and Antarctica) to study cosmic rays – highly energetic particles arriving from space. The direction of all this work led to the launching in January 1958 of America's first satellite, Explorer I (as part of a major International Geophysical Year series of experiments), which carried experiments designed to measure cosmic rays and other energetic particles. Unexpectedly high radiation levels were found in certain regions of the Earth's atmosphere – so high that the satellite's Geiger counters jammed. This observation was contrary to the observation of the first Russian satellite, Sputnik I, launched five months earlier, and gave impetus to further satellite exploration. Subsequent observations by a succession of satellites (Explorer, Pioneer, Sputnik, Mechta, Lunik) have shown that the Earth's magnetic field traps high-speed charged particles in two zones girdling the Earth, with the greatest particle concentration above the equator. One zone lies roughly 600–3,000 miles (1,000–5,000 km) above the Earth's surface; the other is 9,000–15,000 miles (15,000–25,000 km) above the equator, curving down toward the magnetic poles. These regions were later to be named the *Van Allen belts*. The particles in the belts are electrons and protons (as suggested by F. Singer early in 1957) originating in cosmic-ray collisions or captured from the "solar wind" of particles that streams out from the Sun. In 1958 a controversial experiment, known as "Project Argus," was carried out – also as part of the International Geophysical Year. This involved the detonation of three small nuclear bombs, at altitudes over 300 miles (480 km) over the South Atlantic Ocean, to inject very energetic particles into the upper atmosphere. These were subsequently found to have been captured in the Van Allen belts.

Van Allen has produced over 200 scientific papers, has received a great number of scientific awards, and has been a member of several U.S. governmental committees concerned with space exploration.

Van de Graaff, Robert Jemison

(1901–1967)

AMERICAN PHYSICIST

Born in Tuscaloosa, Alabama, Van de Graaff studied engineering at the University of Alabama, gaining his BS in 1922 and his MS in 1923. He enrolled in 1924 at the Sorbonne in Paris where he was inspired by the lectures of Marie Curie to study physics. In 1928 he obtained a PhD from Oxford University for research into the motion of ions in gases. It was during these studies that he conceived of an electrostatic generator that could radically improve on existing types, such as the Wimshurst machine, by building up electric charge on a hollow insulated metal sphere. A year later he returned to America and started working as a research fellow at Princeton. In 1931 he moved to the Massachusetts Institute of Technology as a research associate, serving as associate professor of physics from 1934 until he resigned in 1960.

While at Princeton he constructed, in 1931, the first model of his generator, now known as the *Van de Graaff generator*. The charge was carried to the hollow sphere by means of an insulated fabric belt and once transferred could accumulate on the outer surface of the sphere, leading ultimately to potentials of 80,000 volts. This was eventually increased to over a million volts.

At MIT Van de Graaff developed the generator for use as a particle accelerator. This *Van de Graaff accelerator* used the generator as a source of high voltage that could accelerate charged particles, such as electrons, to high velocities and hence high energies. It was thus to be a major tool in the developing fields of atomic and nuclear physics. One of Van de Graaff's aims was to explore the possibility of uranium fission and to try to create elements with larger atoms than uranium.

In collaboration with John Trump, an electrical engineer, he adapted the generator to produce high-energy x-rays, which could be used in the treatment of cancer. The first x-ray generator began operation in a Boston hospital in 1937. During World War II Van de Graaff was director of the radiographic project of the Office of Scientific Research and Development in which the generator was developed for another use: the examination of the interior structure of heavy ordnance by means of x-rays.

In 1946 Trump and Van de Graaff formed the High Voltage Engineering Corporation to market Van de Graaff accelerators and x-ray generators to hospitals, industry, and scientific research establishments. Van de Graaff was director and chief physicist and in 1960 left MIT to work there full time as chief scientist.

van de Hulst, Hendrik Christoffel

(1918–   )

DUTCH ASTRONOMER

Van de Hulst (van de hoolst) studied at the university in his native city of Utrecht where he obtained his PhD in 1946. He spent two years at the University of Chicago as a postdoctoral fellow (1946–48) then took up an appointment at the University of Leiden. Following several years at different universities in America he became professor of astronomy at Leiden and director of the Leiden Observatory.

In the German-occupied Netherlands a group of astronomers began to think about the implications of Grote Reber's discovery of radio emission from the Milky Way. Jan Oort, then director of the Leiden Observatory, wondered whether the emission was merely a uniform noise or could the equivalent of the absorption and emission lines of light be detected. In 1944 van de Hulst came up with the answer.

He proposed that hydrogen atoms, which occur in diffuse but widespread regions in interstellar space, can exist in two forms. In ordinary hydrogen the proton and its orbiting electron spin in the same direction. There is a very small chance that the electron will spontaneously flip over and spin in the opposite direction to the proton and in the process emit radiation with a wavelength of 21 centimeters, i.e., at a frequency of 1,420.4 megahertz. Although emission from a single atom is a very rare event, there is such an abundance of hydrogen in the universe that the process should be taking place with sufficient frequency to be detectable.

It was not, however, until 1951 that van de Hulst's proposal was confirmed: the 21-centimeter hydrogen line emission was detected at Harvard by Edward M. Purcell and Harold Ewen who used equipment specially built for the purpose. It has since proved a crucial tool for the investigation of the distribution and movement of neutral hydrogen in our own Galaxy and in other spiral galaxies. Since the hydrogen lies in the spiral arms and since the 21-centimeter emission passes unimpeded through the dust that prevents optical observation, this has led to a greatly increased knowledge of galactic structure.

It was also felt that if intelligent life did exist outside the solar system and wished to communicate with other civilizations, then it would be highly rational to transmit signals at the hydrogen-emission wavelength of 21 centimeters. Although much expensive telescope time has been spent listening on this wavelength, nothing has yet been heard that does not come from hydrogen itself.

van de Kamp, Peter

(1901–)

DUTCH–AMERICAN ASTRONOMER

Van de Kamp, who was born at Kampen in the Netherlands, studied at the University of Utrecht, obtaining his PhD in 1922. He emigrated to America in 1923 and, after appointments at the Lick Observatory (1924–25) and the University of Virginia (1923–24, 1925–37), became director of the Sproul Observatory and professor of astronomy at Swarthmore College, Pennsylvania. Following his retirement in 1972 he became research astronomer there.

In the 1960s van de Kamp found strong evidence for a new celestial phenomenon: planets orbiting stars other than the Sun. Since 1937 he had been studying the motion of Barnard's star, a nearby red star with a very large proper motion of 10.3 seconds of arc per year. By 1969 he was able to state that the star was oscillating very slightly in position about a straight line and that this wobbling motion was caused by an unseen companion. This companion was orbiting Barnard's star in about 25 years and was only about 1.5 times the mass of Jupiter. As this is too small a mass for a star, van de Kamp concluded that it was a planet. After further calculations he said that it was more likely that there were two planets, both of a similar mass to Jupiter, one orbiting in about 12 years and the other in 26 years.

This was not the only search for planets. In 1943 K. A. Strand claimed that he had detected a planetary body in the binary star 61 Cygni. His evidence was not as good as van de Kamp's however, although more recent observations indicate a planet about eight times the mass of Jupiter orbiting the brighter component of 61 Cygni in 4.8 years. There are other stars that have also shown perturbed motions from planet-sized companions.

The planets belong to stars that are relatively close. It is unlikely that this is merely coincidental and consequently van de Kamp and others concluded that planetary systems are likely to be widespread. Such a conclusion implies that some form of life may well be present outside the solar system.

van der Meer, Simon

(1925–)

DUTCH ENGINEER AND PHYSICIST

Van der Meer (van der mayr) was educated at the Gymnasium in his native city of The Hague and at the Technical University, Delft, where he gained his PhD in 1956. He immediately joined the staff at the European Organization for Nuclear Research (CERN) and remained there until his retirement in 1990.

In 1979 the Nobel Prize for physics was awarded to Sheldon Glashow and two colleagues for their unification of the electromagnetic and weak forces. Although the neutral currents predicted by the theory were detected in 1973, it still remained to discover the charged W^+ and W^- and the neutral Z^0 bosons whose existence was a consequence of the theory. As the masses of the particles were about 80 times that of the proton, the energy required for their production outstripped the capacity of any existing accelerator. In 1978 Carlo Rubbia, a colleague at CERN, asked van der Meer if there was any way to conjure such high energies from the existing accelerators.

CERN's SPS (Super Proton Synchroton) could deliver about 450 billion electronvolts (450 GeV). One possible solution would be to convert the SPS into a colliding-beam machine, that is, protons and antiprotons would be accelerated, stored separately, and then induced to collide with each other head-on. Proton–antiproton collisions, it was calculated, with an energy of 270 GeV per beam were equivalent to a beam of 155,000 GeV colliding with a stationary target.

The problem facing van der Meer was how to concentrate the beams. Protons normally repel each other, as do antiprotons, and, consequently, charged particle beams tend to spread out in space. To maximize the colliding power of the beams van der Meer somehow needed to focus them. He proposed to use the technique of "stochastic cooling," first described by him in 1972 as a way of reducing random motion in the beam. To achieve this the exact center of the beam was calculated and correcting magnetic fields were applied by a system of "kickers" placed around the ring. By this means particles out of line were nudged back into position. The system was successfully tested in May 1979 and was used in 1983 to create the W and the Z particles. Van der Meer shared the 1984 Nobel Prize for physics with Rubbia for this work.

van der Waals, Johannes Diderik

(1837–1923)

DUTCH PHYSICIST

This at once put his name among the foremost in science.
—James Clerk Maxwell, on van der Waals's thesis *On the Continuity of the Liquid and Gaseous States* (1873)

Van der Waals (van der vahls or van der wahlz) was born at Leiden in the Netherlands. He was largely self-taught in science and originally worked as a school teacher. He later managed to study at the University of Leiden, having been exempted from the Latin and Greek entrance requirements. In 1877 he became professor of physics at the University of Amsterdam.

Van der Waals studied the kinetic theory of gases and fluids and in 1873 presented his influential doctoral thesis, *On the Continuity of the Liquid and Gaseous States*. His main work was to develop an equation (the *van der Waals equation*) that – unlike the gas laws of Robert Boyle and Jacques Charles – applied to real gases. The Boyle–Charles law, strictly speaking, applies only to "ideal" gases but can be derived from the kinetic theory given the assumptions that there are no attractive forces between gas molecules and that the molecules have zero volume.

Since the molecules do have attractive forces and volume (however small), van der Waals introduced into the theory two further constants to take these properties into account. Initially these constants had to be specific to each gas since the size of the molecules and the attractive force between them is different for each gas. Further work by van der Waals yielded the law of corresponding states – an equation that is the same for all substances. His valuable results enabled James Dewar and Heike Kamerlingh-Onnes to work out methods of liquefying the permanent gases.

In 1910 van der Waals was awarded the Nobel Prize for physics for his work on the equation of state of gases and liquids. The weak electrostatic attractive forces between molecules and between atoms are called *van der Waals forces* in his honor.

Vane, Sir John Robert

(1927–)

BRITISH PHARMACOLOGIST

Vane studied chemistry at the University of Birmingham and pharmacology at Oxford, where he obtained his DPhil in 1953. He then worked at the Royal College of Surgeons, serving as professor of experimental pharmacology from 1966 until 1973, when he moved to the Wellcome Foundation as director of research and development. In 1985 Vane left Wellcome to serve as director of the William Harvey Research Institute, St. Bartholomew's Hospital, London. He was knighted in 1984.

Vane has worked on hormonelike substances, the prostaglandins, first observed by Ulf von Euler in the 1930s. In the 1960s he began to explore their physiological roles. He extracted in 1969 a substance from the lung tissue of rats sensitive to an allergen. As it caused rabbit aortas to contract it was named "rabbit aorta contracting substance" (RCS). He also found that RCS caused blood platelets to clot. It was later shown by Bengt Samuelsson that RCS contained the prostaglandin PGH_2 as an active ingredient. But Vane had earlier shown that the effects of RCS could be inhibited by aspirin and other antiinflammatory drugs. This allowed Vane to propose a mechanism for both the effects of aspirin and prostaglandins. Aspirin, he argued, reduced pain, inflammation, and fever by blocking the action of prostaglandins which, at least in some cases, seemed to produce precisely these effects. For his work in this field Vane shared the 1982 Nobel Prize for physiology or medicine with Bengt Samuelsson and Sune Bergström.

He has also worked on the pharmacological effects of adrenaline (epinephrine) and edited the CIBA Foundation symposium on the subject, *Adrenergic Mechanisms* (1960).

van Maanen, Adriaan

(1884–1946)

DUTCH–AMERICAN ASTRONOMER

Van Maanen (van **mah**-nen), who was born at Sneek in the Netherlands, studied at the University of Utrecht, where he obtained his doctorate in 1911. He worked at the University of Groningen from 1909 to 1911 when he moved to America. After working briefly at the Yerkes Observatory he took up an appointment in 1912 at the Mount Wilson Observatory in California, where he remained for the rest of his career.

Van Maanen specialized in measuring the minute changes in position of astronomical objects over a period of time, from which he could determine their proper motion and parallax. These objects included stars, clusters of stars, and nebulae. Between 1916 and 1923 he produced a number of measurements of spiral nebulae from which he calculated their rotation rate. This was at the time of the controversy between astronomers as to whether such nebulae were island universes in their own right or part of our own Galaxy. Van Maanen's results were therefore of considerable significance, for whether one can detect rotation in a distant body and measure its rate of rotation partly depend on the distance of the object from the observer. The rotation of about 0.02 seconds of arc per year that he obtained from a number of nebulae over a period of seven years seemed to be indisputable evidence against the emerging view that such objects as the Andromeda nebula were really separate remote star systems. This was certainly the view that Harlow Shapley took in 1920 as he could see no reason to doubt the work of van Maanen, his close friend, who was known to be a careful and competent observer.

Van Maanen's work was, however, incompatible with the growing body of measurements produced by Edwin Hubble, also at Mount Wilson. These suggested that nebulae like Andromeda were as much as 800,000 light-years away, at which distance it was inconceivable that any internal motion should be detectable. As no one, including van Maanen himself, had any idea where he had gone wrong, his work became something of a curiosity and tended to be ignored. Other astronomers, like Knut Lundmark in 1923, failed to reproduce his results while in 1935 van Maanen was able to detect a displacement only about half that found in the 1920s. When in the same year Hubble also reported failure to detect the rotation, it became widely accepted that there was some unknown instrumental or personal error in van Maanen's work.

It is unlikely to have been an instrumental error as Hubble used the same instruments while a later computer analysis of his work has revealed no major computational errors. This only leaves unconscious personal error and recent work has shown that a systematic error of only 0.002 millimeter in the measurements of points on photographic plates would be sufficient to produce his results. The same systematic error also occurred in his work on the strength of the solar magnetic field, which he considerably overestimated.

He did however discover the second white dwarf, since named *van Maanen's star*, with a density some 400,000 times that of the Sun.

van't Hoff, Jacobus Henricus

(1852–1911)

DUTCH THEORETICAL CHEMIST

A Dr. J. H. van't Hoff, of the veterinary school at Utrecht, has as it seems, no taste for exact chemical investigation.
    —Hermann Kolbe attacking van't Hoff's theory of molecular structure in *Journal für praktische Chemie* (1877; Journal of Practical Chemistry)

Van't Hoff (vahnt hoff) was born at Rotterdam in the Netherlands, the son of a physician. He studied at Delft Polytechnic and the University of Leiden before going abroad to work with August Kekulé in Bonn

(1872) and with Charles Adolphe Wurtz in Paris (1874), where he met Joseph-Achille Le Bel. In 1878 he was appointed to the Amsterdam chair of chemistry where he remained until moving to the University of Berlin in 1896.

In 1874 van't Hoff published a paper entitled *A Suggestion Looking to the Extension into Space of the Structural Formulas at Present Used in Chemistry*, which effectively created a new branch of science – stereochemistry. The problem began with the discovery of optically active compounds. Louis Pasteur later established the asymmetry of crystals of tartaric acid: some would rotate polarized light to the right and others to the left. This was explained by the actual asymmetry of the crystal: the crystals were mirror images of each other. Pasteur thought that the molecules themselves were asymmetric but could offer no proof. This would explain the further problem of the optical activity of noncrystalline solutions. Van't Hoff solved these problems and offered an account of molecular asymmetry by concentrating on the structure of the carbon atom, newly established by Kekulé. He announced (1874) that the four chemical bonds that carbon can form are directed to the corners of a tetrahedron. With this structure, certain molecules can have left- and right-handed isomers, which have opposite effects on polarized light. It also explained why certain isomers do not occur.

Van't Hoff's account of molecular structure was attacked by Hermann Kolbe but a similar theory was put forward simultaneously by Joseph-Achille Le Bel, independently of van't Hoff. Despite the hostility, his ideas were soon vindicated by Emil Fischer's researches into sugars in the 1880s.

Major contributions were also made by van't Hoff to the thermodynamics and kinetics of solutions. Many of these results are reported in his book *Etudes de dynamique chimie* (1884; Studies in Chemical Kinetics). He had the central insight in 1886 that there is a similarity between solutions and gases provided that osmotic pressure is substituted for the ordinary pressure of gases, and derived laws for dilute solutions similar to those of Robert Boyle and Joseph Gay-Lussac for gases. This fundamental result could be used to determine the molecular weight of a substance in solution.

In 1901 van't Hoff was awarded the first Nobel Prize for chemistry.

Van Vleck, John Hasbrouck

(1899–1980)

AMERICAN PHYSICIST

Van Vleck was born at Middletown, Connecticut, and educated at the University of Wisconsin, where he graduated in 1920. Moving to Harvard University he gained his master's degree (1921) and his doctorate (1922) and stayed for a further year as an instructor. From Harvard he went to the University of Minnesota, where he became a full professor in 1927, returned to Wisconsin in 1928, and then went back to Harvard in 1934.

Van Vleck is regarded as the founder of the modern quantum mechanical theory of magnetism. His earliest papers were on the old quantum theory, but with the advent of wave mechanics pioneered by Paul Dirac he began to look at the implications for magnetism in particular. In the field of paramagnetism he introduced the concept of temperature-independent susceptibility, now known as *Van Vleck paramagnetism*. He also made calculations of molecular structure that shed new light on chemical bonding and he developed ways of describing the behavior of an atom or an ion in a crystal. Another important contribution of Van Vleck was to point out the importance of electron correlation – the interaction between the motion of electrons – for the appearance of local magnetic moments in metals.

During World War II Van Vleck worked on radar, showing that at about 1.25-centimeter wavelength water molecules in the atmosphere would lead to troublesome absorption and that at 0.5-centimeter wavelength there would be a similar absorption by oxygen molecules. This was to have important consequences not just for military (and civil) radar systems but later for the new science of radioastronomy.

In 1977, together with Nevill Mott and Philip Anderson, he shared the Nobel Prize for physics for "fundamental theoretical investigations of the electronic structure of magnetic and disordered systems." (Anderson was once a student of Van Vleck's at Harvard.) Van Vleck's work on electron correlation was mentioned specifically for the central role it played in the later development of the laser.

Varenius, Bernhard

(1622–1650)

GERMAN PHYSICAL GEOGRAPHER

Varenius (far-**ay**-nee-uus) was born at Hitzacker in Germany and educated at the Hamburg gymnasium and the universities of Königsberg and Leiden, where he studied medicine. In 1649 he published his first geographical work, *Descriptio Regni Japoniae* (Description of the Kingdom of Japan).

His main work was his *Geographia generalis* (1650), published only shortly before his death. Some idea of the importance the 17th century attached to the work can be discerned by noting that none less than Isaac Newton issued a revised and enlarged edition in 1672. It was first translated into English in 1693 and went into its last English edition in 1765. In this work Varenius laid down a framework for physical geography. He defined his universal geography as that which "considers the whole Earth in general, and explains its properties without regard to particular countries." He divided it into three parts, the first part consisting of facts about the Earth, such as its dimensions. The second part consisted of facts related to celestial events, such as the length of days and nights or the seasons, and the third part was comparative.

Varmus, Harold Eliot

(1939–   )

AMERICAN MICROBIOLOGIST

Born at Oceanside, New York, Varmus was educated at Amherst College, Harvard, and at Columbia University, where he studied medicine. After working at the Presbyterian Hospital, New York (1966–68), he joined the National Institutes of Health, Bethesda, as clinical associate (1968–70) before moving to the Department of Microbiology at the University of California at San Francisco. He was appointed full professor in 1979.

In the 1970s, working in collaboration with Michael Bishop, Dominique Stehelin, and Peter Vogt, Varmus made a crucial breakthrough in our understanding of cancer. The Rous sarcoma virus, which causes cancer in chickens, was known to have a particular gene (called an "oncogene") associated with its cancer-causing capability. Varmus and his colleagues prepared a molecular probe for this gene – a fragment of DNA with a base sequence complementary to the gene and capable of pairing with it – and demonstrated that the gene was present in the cells of normal chickens.

This showed for the first time that viral oncogenes are derived from genes of the virus's host, incorporated into the genetic material of the virus in a modified form. This breakthrough led to the discovery of a large number of similar cellular genes, subsequently termed "proto-oncogenes," that acted as a source of oncogenes. The key to understanding how viral oncogenes transform a normal cell into a cancerous one thus lies in determining how their equivalent proto-oncogenes function in normal cells. Several roles have been elucidated for these genes, principally the regulation of cell growth, division, and differentiation. Interference or disturbance in these processes, as may occur in the presence of an oncogene, could lead to uncontrolled cell proliferation, as in cancer.

The results of Varmus's work were published in 1976 and opened the door to a major new field in cancer research. For this work Varmus and Bishop were jointly awarded the 1989 Nobel Prize for physiology or medicine.

Varolio, Constanzo

(1543–1575)

ITALIAN ANATOMIST

Varolio (vah-**roh**-lee-oh) was educated at the university in his native city of Bologna where he qualified as a physician in 1567; he later served as professor of anatomy and surgery there from 1569 until 1572. He then moved to Rome and, although he is thought to have served as physician to Pope Gregory XIII and taught at the Sapienza or Papal University, there is no real documentary evidence for either claim.

He is mainly remembered for his *De nervis opticis* (1573; On the Optic Nerves) in which he described the part of the brain situated between the midbrain and the medulla oblongata, since known as the pons varolii. His work contains what has been called a "crude illustration" of the base of the brain clearly showing the pons. A far superior drawing had been made by Bartolommeo Eustachio 20 years previously but his work was lost to science for about 150 years.

Vauquelin, Louis Nicolas

(1763–1829)

FRENCH CHEMIST

The son of a farm laborer from Saint-André d'Hebertot in France, Vauquelin (voh-**klan**) began work as an apprentice to a Rouen apothecary. He became a laboratory assistant to Antoine-François Fourcroy (1783–91), with whom he later collaborated. Vauquelin became a member of the French Academy of Sciences in 1791 and professor of chemistry in the School of Mines in 1795. In 1799 he wrote *Manuel de l'essayeur* (An Assayer's Manual), which led to his being appointed assayer to the mint in 1802 and professor of chemistry at the University of Paris in 1809.

Vauquelin is best known for his discovery of the elements chromium and beryllium. In 1798, while working with a red lead mineral from Siberia known as crocolite, he isolated the new element chromium – so called because its compounds are very highly colored. Martin Klaproth made a similar discovery shortly afterward. In the same year Vauquelin also isolated a new element in the mineral beryl. It was initially called glucinum because of the sweetness of its compounds, but later given its modern name of beryllium. He was the first to isolate an amino acid: asparagine from asparagus.

Vavilov, Nikolai Ivanovich

(1887–1943)

RUSSIAN PLANT GENETICIST

> We shall go to the pyre, we shall burn, but we
> shall not renounce our convictions.
> —Quoted by Z. A. Medvedev in *The Rise
> and Fall of T. D. Lysenko* (1969)

Having graduated from the Agricultural Institute in his native city of Moscow, Vavilov (**vav**-i-lof) continued his studies firstly in England under William Bateson and then in France at the Vilmoren Institution. Back in Russia he was appointed, in 1917, both professor of genetics and selection at the Agricultural Institute, Voronezh, and professor of agriculture at Saratov University. Three years later he took over the directorship of the Bureau of Applied Botany, Petrograd (now St. Petersburg), which later became the All Union Institute of Plant Industry. The institute flourished under Vavilov's leadership, becoming the center for over 400 research institutes throughout the Soviet Union. In 1929 he became the first president of the Academy of Agricultural Sciences.

During the years 1916–1933 Vavilov led several plant-collecting expeditions to countries all around the globe. The purpose was to gather material of potential use in crop-breeding programs, particularly the wild relatives and ancestors of cultivated plants. He was highly successful in this, his collection numbering some 250,000 accessions by 1940. This was the first large-scale attempt to conserve and utilize the immensely valuable genetic resources upon which crop improvement relies.

A second important consequence of these travels was Vavilov's observation that the genetic diversity of crop relatives is concentrated in certain areas that he termed "gene centers," postulating that these correspond to regions where agriculture originated. The theory and the exact number of centers have since been modified but the recognition of such areas is an invaluable aid to other plant hunters. He also found certain regularities between unrelated genera in such centers, described in *The Law of Homologous Series in Variation* (1922).

Vavilov's excellent work was gradually stifled by the intrusion of politics into Soviet biology in the 1930s. His belief in the advances in genetics made by Mendel and T. H. Morgan brought him into conflict with the government-backed Trofim Lysenko, who was returning to a Lamarckian view of inheritance. The 1937 International Congress of Genetics, due to be held in Moscow in view of the strides made in Soviet genetics under Vavilov, was canceled by the Lysenkoists. Vavilov was arrested in 1940 while plant collecting and died three years later in a Siberian labor camp.

Today Vavilov is recognized in his own country as an outstanding scientist, the Vavilov Institute being named in his honor.

Veksler, Vladimir Iosofich

(1907–1966)

UKRAINIAN PHYSICIST

Veksler (**vyayks**-ler), who was born at Zhitomar in the Ukraine, graduated from the Moscow Energetics Institute in 1931. He first worked for the Electrochemical Institute (1930–36), then moved to the Lebedev Physics Institute of the Academy. In 1956 he was appointed director of the High Energy Laboratory of the Institute of Nuclear Physics. In 1944 Veksler invented the synchrocyclotron independently of Edwin McMillan.

Vening Meinesz, Felix Andries

(1887–1966)

DUTCH GEOLOGIST

The son of the burgomaster of Rotterdam, Vening Meinesz (**vay**-ning **mI**-nes) was born in the Dutch capital The Hague. He graduated from the University of Delft in 1910 and, after working on a gravimetric survey of the Netherlands, was appointed in 1927 to the chair of geodesy, cartography, and geophysics at Delft.

Vening Meinesz developed, in 1923, a method for measuring gravity below the oceans using instruments carried by submarine. Measurements of the Earth's gravitational field had been made since Jean Richer's pendulum measurements in Cayenne in 1671. Despite the sophistication of later expeditions the measurements all suffered from the limitation of being continental; it was not possible to obtain accurate pendulum recordings at sea. Vening Meinesz first used his new method in a submarine voyage to Java (1923) and collected significant new data. During the period 1923–39 he made 11 voyages throughout the oceans of the world making 843 observations.

One of his most significant findings was that there are areas of weak gravity extending in long arcs through both the East and West Indies and along the oceanic side of Japan. These areas appear to coincide with the deep ocean trenches. Vening Meinesz further developed a theory of convection currents within the Earth similar to that formulated by Arthur Holmes in 1929.

Vernier, Pierre

(*c.* 1580–1637)

FRENCH MATHEMATICIAN

Born at Ornans in France, Vernier (vair-**nyay** or **ver**-nee-er) was educated by his father, a scientist, and became interested in scientific instruments. He was employed as an official with the government of Spain and then held various offices under the French government.

In 1631 Vernier invented the caliper named for him, an instrument for taking very precise measurements. The principle of the vernier scale is described in his book *La Construction, l'usage, et les propriétés du quadrant nouveau de mathématique* (1631; The Construction, Uses, and Properties of a New Mathematical Quadrant), which also contained some of the earliest tables of trigonometric functions and formulas for deriving the angles of a triangle from the lengths of its sides.

Vesalius, Andreas

(1514–1564)

BELGIAN ANATOMIST

It was when the more fashionable doctors in Italy, in imitation of the old Romans, despising the work of the hand, began to delegate to slaves the manual attentions they deemed necessary for their patients...that the art of medicine went to ruin.
—Quoted by B. Farrington in *Science in Antiquity* (1936)

Vesalius (ve-**say**-lee-us), born the son of a pharmacist in Brussels, Belgium, was educated at the universities of Louvain, Paris, and Padua, receiving his MD from the last in 1537. He was immediately appointed professor of anatomy and surgery at Padua where he remained until 1543 when, at the age of 28, he joined the Hapsburg court. Here Vesalius successively served as physician to the Emperor Charles V and King Philip II of Spain. For reasons unknown, he left their service sometime after 1562 and died while on a pilgrimage to the Holy Land.

Vesalius thus completed his anatomical researches in the short period between 1538, when he produced his six anatomical plates the *Tabulae sex* (Six Tables), and 1543, when his masterpiece *De humani corporis fabrica* (On the Structure of the Human Body) was printed in Basel. With this work he gained the reputation of being the greatest of Renaissance anatomists.

The work generally followed the physiological system of Galen and repeated some traditional errors; for example, he described the supposed pores in the septum of the heart despite confessing his inability to detect them. Other parts, such as the female generative organs, were treated inadequately because of a lack of the appropriate cadavers. However Vesalius's main innovation was to insist on conducting, personally, dissections on human cadavers, which taught him that Galenic anatomy was not to be treated unquestioningly.

The work of Vesalius was of considerable significance in marking the departure from ancient concepts. The *Fabrica* presented in a single, detailed, comprehensive, and accessible work (superbly illustrated, probably at the Titian school in Venice), a basis for following generations of anatomists to compare with their own dissections. It has been said that after Vesalius medicine became a science.

Vidal de la Blache, Paul

(1845–1918)

FRENCH GEOGRAPHER

Vidal (vee-**dal**) was born at Pézenas in France and studied history and geography at the Ecole Normale Supérieure, Paris, graduating in 1865. After some time at the French School in Athens and teaching at Nancy he returned, in 1877, to the Ecole Normale Supérieure, remaining there until he became professor of geography at the Sorbonne (1898–1918).

He is recognized as being the founder of French human geography and virtually all chairs of geography in France were occupied by his students for the first half of the 20th century. His approach was to study the interaction of people's activities with the environment in which they lived, examining in particular small areas. He argued against physical determinism, pointing out that man is able to modify his environment to a certain extent.

Vidal founded, in 1891, the important journal *Annales de géographie* (Annals of Geography), which he edited until his death, and began the publication of an annual *Bibliographie géographique* (Geographical Bibliography). Some of his more important papers were collected in *Principes de géographie humaine* (1922), published in English in 1950 as *Principles of Human Geography*.

Viète, François

(1540–1603)

FRENCH MATHEMATICIAN

> I...do not profess to be a mathematician, but...whenever there is leisure, delight in mathematical studies.
> —Introduction to *Reply...to a Problem Posed by Adrian Romanus* (1595)

Viète (vyet), who was born at Fontenay-le-Comte in France, is also known by the Latinized form of his name, Franciscus Vieta (vI-**ee**-ta). He was educated at Poitiers where he studied law and for a time he practiced as a lawyer. He was a member of the *parlement* of Brittany but because of his Huguenot sympathies he was forced to flee during the persecution of the Huguenots. On Henry IV's accession, however, he was able to hold further offices and became a privy councillor to the king. He put his mathematical abilities to practical use in deciphering the code used by Spanish diplomats.

Viète's chief work was in algebra. He made a number of innovations in the use of symbolism and several technical terms still in use (e.g., co-efficient) were introduced by him. His work is important because of his tendency to solve problems by algebraic rather than geometric methods. By bringing algebraic techniques to bear on them Viète was able to solve a number of geometrical problems. A particularly longstanding problem – formulated by the Greek geometer Apollonius of Perga – namely, how to construct a circle that touches three given circles, was solved in this way by Viète.

Viète's major work is contained in his treatise *In artem analyticem isa-goge* (1591; Introduction to the Analytical Arts) and among other advances in algebra that it contains are new and improved methods for solving cubic equations. Among these are techniques that make use of trigonometric methods. Viète also developed methods of approximating the solutions to equations.

Villemin, Jean Antoine

(1827–1892)

FRENCH PHYSICIAN

Villemin (veel-**man**), a farmer's son from Prey in France, was educated at the military medical schools of Strasbourg and Val-de-Grâce, Paris. He later taught at the latter school holding the chair of hygiene from 1869 to 1873, when he succeeded to the chair of clinical medicine.

In 1865 Villemin made a major breakthrough in our understanding of tuberculosis. Before Villemin it was widely thought that tuberculosis arose from an inherited predisposition to develop the disease. Villemin, however, pointed out that, while the disease was rare in the sparsely populated areas of the countryside, in situations where people were living at close quarters, such as army barracks, the incidence was high. Concluding then that the disease must be contagious, he took fluid from the lungs of a dead patient and injected it into some rabbits. When he killed the rabbits three months later he found their bodies riddled with tuberculous lesions. He also showed that bovine tuberculosis could be transmitted to rabbits, in this case with fatal results.

Villemin published his views fully in his *Etudes sur la tuberculose* (1868; Studies on Tuberculosis). They seemed, however, to have little effect on the work of his contemporaries. Robert Koch in particular, who later actually discovered the causative bacillus, went out of his way to belittle the work of Villemin. Julius Cohnheim, however, confirmed Villemin's results using an elegant experimental technique on rabbits.

Vine, Frederick John

(1939–1988)

BRITISH GEOLOGIST

A sudden change in attitude towards the matter is generally attributed to the publication in 1963 of a scientific article by Fred Vine and Drum Matthews...in spite of a few serious contrarians and the waggish carping of a group that called itself the Stop Continental Drift Society, continental drift is now accepted as the explanation for the present configuration of the continents.
—Charles Officer and Jake Page, *Tales of the Earth: Paroxysms and Perturbations*

Vine was educated at Cambridge University. After a period in America teaching at Princeton University (1965–70) he returned to Britain, becoming reader (1970) and professor of environmental science (1974) at the University of East Anglia.

In 1963, in collaboration with his supervisor Drummond Hoyle Matthews, Vine produced a paper, *Magnetic Anomalies over Ocean*

Ridges, which provided additional evidence for, and modified, the sea-floor spreading hypothesis of Harry H. Hess, published in 1962. The fact that magnetic reversals had occurred during the Earth's history had been known since the work of Matonori Matuyama in the 1920s and B. Brunhes earlier in the century. Vine and Matthews realized that if Hess was correct, the new rock emerging from the oceanic ridges would, on cooling, adopt the prevailing magnetic polarity. Newer rock emerging would push it further away from the ridge and, intermittently, as magnetic reversals occurred, belts of material of opposing magnetic polarity would be pushed out.

From examining several ocean ridges in the North Atlantic, Vine and Matthews established that the parallel belts of different magnetic polarities were symmetrical on either side of the ridge crests. This provided crucial evidence for the sea-floor spreading hypothesis. Correlation between the magnetic anomalies of ocean ridges in other oceans was also established.

Vinogradov, Ivan Matveevich

(1891–1983)

SOVIET MATHEMATICIAN

Vinogradov (vye-no-**grah**-dof), who was born at Milolyub (now Velikiye Luki) in Russia, held a number of posts at various institutions in the Soviet Union. Initially he taught at the University of Perm (1918–20) until appointed professor of mathematics at the Leningrad Polytechnic Institute. In 1925 he became a professor at Leningrad State University and in 1932 was appointed chairman of the National Committee of Soviet Mathematicians of the Soviet Academy of Sciences. From 1934 he was professor of mathematics at Moscow State University.

Vinogradov has been preeminent in the field of analytical number theory, i.e., the study of problems posed in purely number-theoretic terms by means of the techniques of analysis. He published several books, chiefly on various aspects of number theory, which include *A New Method in the Analytical Theory of Numbers* (1937) and *The Method of Trigonometric Sums in the Theory of Numbers* (1947).

One of his most outstanding achievements was his solution in 1937 of a problem of Christian Goldbach's (not to be confused with Goldbach's famous conjecture about even numbers and primes, which is still undecided). Vinogradov showed that every sufficiently large odd natural number is a sum of three primes.

Virchow, Rudolf Carl

(1821–1902)

GERMAN PATHOLOGIST

Pathology is the science of disease, from cells to societies.
—*Archiv für pathologische Anatomie* (Archive of Pathological Anatomy)

There can be no scientific dispute with respect to faith, for science and faith exclude one another.
—*Disease, Life, and Man*

The son of a merchant from Schivelbein (now Świdwin in Poland), Virchow (**feer**-koh) graduated in medicine from the Army Medical School, Berlin, in 1843. He then worked at the Charité Hospital in Berlin where he wrote a classic paper on one of the first known cases of leukemia. In 1849 he moved to Würzburg as professor of pathological anatomy. He returned to Berlin in 1856 as director of the university's Institute of Pathology, where he remained until his death.

In 1858 Virchow published *Die Cellular-pathologie* (Cellular Pathology), in which he formulated two propositions of fundamental importance. The first, consciously echoing the words of William Harvey: "Omne vivum ex ovo" (All life is derived from an egg), declared "Omnis cellula e cellula" (Every cell is derived from a preexisting cell). Others, such as John Goodsir, had already advanced such ideas but Virchow differed in applying them to pathology, his second major thesis being that disease was a pathological cellular state. The cells are the "seat" of disease, or, disease is simply the response of a cell to abnormal conditions. This by itself immediately generated the immense research program of collecting, examining, and classifying different types of cells and noting their variety and development, both normal and abnormal.

Virchow consequently had little time for the emerging germ theory of disease, which later in the century would sweep all other theories out of the way. In fact after 1870 Virchow tended to pursue interests other than pure science. Dissatisfied not only with the new germ theory but also with the theory of evolution, which he tried to have banned from school curricula, Virchow seemed more interested in archeology and politics than science.

Thus Virchow encouraged his friend Heinrich Schliemann in his determination to discover the site of Homer's Troy and actually worked on the dig at Hissarlik in 1879. In politics he was a member of the Reichstag from 1880 to 1893 and, as a leading liberal, was a bitter opponent of Bismarck who went so far as to challenge him to a duel in 1865.

Virchow was also widely known for founding, in 1847, the journal *Archiv für pathologische Anatomie* (Archive of Pathological Anatomy), which he continued to edit for 50 years.

Virtanen, Artturi Ilmari

(1895–1973)

FINNISH CHEMIST

Virtanen (**veer**-ta-nen) was educated at the university in his native city of Helsinki, where he obtained his PhD in 1919, and at the universities of Zurich and Stockholm. He worked from 1921 to 1931 as director of the Finnish Cooperative Dairies Association Laboratory and from 1924 at the University of Helsinki where, in 1931, he became director of the Biochemical Institute.

In 1945 Virtanen was awarded the Nobel Prize for chemistry for his method of fodder preservation. This AIV method, as it became known, named for his initials, was designed to stop the loss of nitrogenous material in storage. By storing green fodder in an acid medium he hoped to prevent spoilage and still retain nutritious fodder. After much experimentation he finally found that a mixture of hydrochloric and sulfuric acid was adequate as long as its strength was kept within certain precise limits. Specifically, this demanded a pH of about four. In 1929 Virtanen found that cows fed on silage produced by his method gave milk indistinguishable in taste from that of cows fed on normal fodder. Further, it was just as rich in both vitamin A and C.

Viviani, Vincenzo

(1622–1703)

ITALIAN MATHEMATICIAN

Viviani (vee-**vyah**-nee), who was born at Florence in Italy, was an associate and pupil of Galileo, although his chief interest was in mathematics rather than in physics. After the condemnation of Galileo's ideas by the Catholic Church it was unsafe for Viviani to pursue his work on Galileo's mathematics. Accordingly Viviani devoted himself to the thorough study of the mathematics of the Greeks, in particular their geometry, and in this field of work he achieved wide fame. In 1696 he was elected a fellow of the Royal Society of London. Viviani was particularly interested in trying to reconstruct lost sections of works by ancient Greek mathematicians, such as the missing fifth book of Apollonius's *Conics*. He also published Italian translations of the works of classical mathematicians including Euclid and Archimedes. He was an associate of the physicist Evangelista Torricelli and collaborated with him in his work on atmospheric pressure and in the invention of the mercury barometer.

Vogel, Hermann Karl

(1842–1907)

GERMAN ASTRONOMER

Born at Leipzig in Germany, Vogel (**foh**-gel) began as an assistant at the observatory there. He later directed a private observatory and finally moved to Potsdam to work in the new astrophysical observatory, of which he became director in 1882. He was one of the earliest astronomers to devote himself almost exclusively to spectroscopy. His first discovery came in 1871 when he showed that the solar rotation could be measured using spectroscopic Doppler effects, obtaining identical results to those achieved using sunspots as markers.

In 1890 he came across some unusual stellar spectra – in particular that of the variable star Algol. He found that some stars seemed to be both advancing and receding, for their spectral lines periodically doubled showing both a red and a blue shift. He correctly interpreted this as indicating a binary system with two stars so close together that they could not be separated optically, with one star advancing and one receding. When one star is eclipsed by its companion just one spectra will be visible, but as the other emerges the spectral line will appear to double only to disappear again in the next eclipse. Such systems are known as eclipsing binaries.

Volta, Count Alessandro

(1745–1827)

ITALIAN PHYSICIST

Nothing good can be done in physics unless
things are reduced to degrees and numbers.
—*Works*, Vol. I

[Volta] understood a lot about the electricity of women.
—Georg Christoph Lichtenberg, quoted in Volta's *Letters*, Vol. II

Volta (**vohl**-ta), who was born at Como in Italy, grew up in an atmosphere of aristocratic religiosity with almost all his male relations becoming priests. However, Volta decided early that his life's work lay in the study of electricity and, by the age of 24, had developed his own version of Benjamin Franklin's electrical fluid theory. In 1774 he started teaching physics at the gymnasium in Como, where, a few months later, he invented the electrophorus – a device for producing electric charge by friction and, at the time, the most efficient way of storing electric charge. On the strength of this invention he was promoted, in 1775, to the position of professor of physics at Como and, three years later, took up a similar appointment at Pavia University. Here, stimulated by the experiments of his friend Luigi Galvani, he started investigating the production of electric current. In 1795 he was appointed rector of Pavia but his work was disturbed by the political upheavals in Lombardy at the time. The state was oscillating between French and Austrian control in the Napoleonic campaigns and in 1799–1800 the Austrians closed the university.

Volta chose this time to make public his great discovery that the production of electric current did not need the presence of animal tissue, as Galvani and others had supposed. Volta produced the famous *voltaic pile*, consisting of an alternating column of zinc and silver disks separated by porous cardboard soaked in brine. This instrument revolutionized the study of electricity by producing a readily available source of current, leading almost immediately to William Nicholson's decomposition of water by electrolysis and later to Humphry Davy's discovery of potassium and other metals by the same process.

In 1800 Napoleon returned in victory to Pavia, reopened the university, and invited Volta to Paris to demonstrate his pile. He awarded Volta the medal of the Legion of Honor and made him a count. In his honor the unit of electric potential (or potential difference or electromotive force) was called the volt.

Voltaire, François Marie Arouet

(1694–1778)

FRENCH WRITER

Facts must prevail.

—Motto

You have confirmed in these tedious places what Newton found out without leaving his room.

—On Maupertius's expedition to the Arctic circle to verify the flattening of the Earth at the poles

The son of a Parisian lawyer, Voltaire (vol-**tair**) was educated in a Jesuit seminary. He began to train as a lawyer but his progress was impeded by political and literary scandals, as well as the occasional indiscreet love affair. In 1726 he began a famous quarrel with the Chevalier de Rohan who, unable to compete against Voltaire's wit, had Voltaire imprisoned in the Bastille. Released on the condition that he keep out of trouble, he thought it prudent to leave the country.

Voltaire arrived in London during the last few months of Newton's life and, although they never met, he attended Newton's funeral and spoke to many of Newton's friends and disciples. The result was that his *Letters Concerning the English Nation* (London, 1733) contained a comparison between the science of Descartes and Newton. Although Voltaire did his best to present in a brief compass some of the main features of Newton's thought, the gossip in Voltaire frequently got the better of him and many now-familiar anecdotes made their first appearance in the *Letters*. It was here that the story of the falling apple first received wide publicity, as did the news of Newton's unitarianism and chastity.

Voltaire went on to publish a much longer and more comprehensive study with his *Les éléments de la philosophie de Newton* (1738; Rudiments of Newton's Philosophy). At the same time he was helping Madame du Châtelet complete her translation of Newton's *Principia* and actually contributed a preface and a poem. Also, in the late 1730s, with Madame du Châtelet at her chateau at Cirey, Voltaire engaged upon some genuine scientific research. The issue was the nature of fire, set by the Académie as a prize competition. He tackled the old problem of whether or not fire has weight. His results were variable, he complained, and "To discover the least scrap of truth entails endless labor." The prize went to the mathematician Leonhard Euler. Following the death of Madame du Châtelet in 1749, Voltaire's interests were directed elsewhere.

von Braun, Wernher Magnus Maximilian

(1912–1977)

GERMAN–AMERICAN ROCKET ENGINEER

> It [the rocket] will free man from the remaining chains, the chains of gravity which still tie him to this planet.
> —*Time*, 10 February 1958

> Basic research is when I'm doing what I don't know I'm doing.
> —Attributed remark

Von Braun (fon brown) came from an affluent background in Wirsitz (now Wyrzysk in Poland). His father, a high government official, had served as minister of education and agriculture in the Weimar Republic. He studied at the Federal Institute of Technology, Zurich, received his BS in 1932 from the Institute of Technology in Berlin, and obtained his PhD in 1934 from the University of Berlin. He had already shown his interest in rockets, joining the VfR (*Verein für Raumschiffahrt* or Society for Space Travel) in 1930. The society consisted of a group of enthusiasts, numbering 870 in 1929, and included such talented engineers as

Hermann Oberth, Willie Ley, and Rudolph Nebel, who took the problem of building rockets seriously.

By the early 1930s the VfR and von Braun had come to the attention of the German military. Barred from openly developing conventional weapons by the Versailles Treaty, military interest turned to unconventional forms of weaponry such as rockets. Von Braun was recruited by the German Ordnance Department in 1932 and by 1934 had already developed the A–2 rocket which, using liquid fuel, reached an altitude of 1.6 miles (2.6 km).

In 1937 von Braun moved to Peenemünde, on the Baltic Sea, as civilian head of the technical department of the German rocket development center. There in October 1942 he successfully tested his A–4 rocket by delivering the missile directly on its target some 120 miles away. It was this rocket that became known as "Vengeance weapon 2" – the supersonic ballistic V–2 missile used against Britain in 1944. Von Braun also developed the supersonic antiaircraft missile Wasserfall but this never became operational. Not all his efforts, however, were directed to military ends. Even in the limited atmosphere of Peenemünde, von Braun was drawing up plans for his A–9, A–10, and A–11 rockets with which he could launch a payload of some 30 tons into space "and, maintaining a regular shuttle service to the orbit...permit the building of a space station there." His commitments to the dreams of his old VfR colleagues never lapsed.

With the collapse of Germany, von Braun delivered his rocket team en masse to the American army. He was still only 33. Initially they worked with the U.S. Army Ordnance Corps at Fort Bliss in Texas and at the White Sands testing facility in New Mexico, studying potential ramjet and rocket missiles and developing the V–2 for high-altitude research. In 1950 the team moved to the Redstone Arsenal in Huntsville, Alabama, to form what was later to become the Marshall Space Flight Center of NASA and which von Braun was to direct from 1960 to 1970. It was here in the 1950s that von Braun headed the American ballistic weapons program and he and his team designed the Jupiter–C, Juno, and Redstone rockets used in the American space program: Jupiter–C launched Explorer I, the first American satellite, into orbit on 31 January 1958. This was followed by the successful Saturn I, IB, and V rockets. Saturn V was used to launch the Apollo craft that landed Americans on the Moon in 1969.

In 1970 von Braun left Huntsville for NASA headquarters in Washington to serve as deputy associate administrator for planning. It soon became clear to him that there no longer existed any deep commitment to space exploration at the highest levels of American government. He consequently resigned from NASA in 1972 and moved into private industry. He worked for Fairchild Industries in Germantown, Maryland as vice-president for engineering and research. After unsuccessful surgery for cancer he resigned in December 1976, shortly before his death.

Von Braun wrote several books, including *History of Rocketry and Space Travel* (1967) and *Moon* (1970).

von Buch, Christian Leopold

(1774–1853)

GERMAN GEOGRAPHER AND GEOLOGIST

Von Buch (fon book) was the son of a wealthy nobleman from Angermünde in Germany. He was educated in Berlin and at the Mining Academy, Freiberg (1790–93), where he studied under Abraham Werner and formed his lifelong friendship with Alexander von Humboldt. He worked briefly in the mining service of Silesia but resigned in 1797 to devote himself exclusively to geological investigation.

He became one of the great geological travelers of his day. Apart from working on the Alps and the other popular geological parts of western Europe he also spent two years in Scandinavia, worked in North Africa and the Canaries, and gave one of the first clear descriptions of the geology of central Europe.

Von Buch left Freiberg committed to Werner's neptunism. However, unlike Werner who rarely ventured beyond Saxony, von Buch traveled extensively and had the problem of fitting his numerous observations into the rigid system of his master. He realized after his travels through Italy and the Auvergne district of France that volcanoes were more numerous and much more significant than Werner allowed. Nor could he locate the coal beds that supposedly fueled the volcanoes. Thus he was gradually converted to the vulcanist school of thought, believing that many rocks, such as basalt, were of igneous origin.

von Euler, Ulf Svante

(1905–1983)

SWEDISH PHYSIOLOGIST

Von Euler (fon **oi**-ler) was the son of Karl von Euler-Chelpin, Nobel Prize winner in 1929. He was born in the Swedish capital of Stockholm and educated at the Karolinska Institute, where he obtained his MD in 1930. He taught there from 1930 onward becoming, in 1939, professor of physiology. In 1966 von Euler was elected to the powerful position of president of the Nobel Foundation, which he held until 1975.

In 1906 the idea that nerve cells communicate with each other and the muscles they control by the release of chemicals was first proposed by Thomas Elliott. Since then there had been much searching for the elusive neurotransmitters and it was not until 1946 that von Euler succeeded in isolating that of the sympathetic system and showed it to be noradrenaline (norepinephrine). For this work von Euler shared the 1970 Nobel Prize for physiology or medicine with Julius Axelrod and Bernard Katz.

Von Euler had earlier, in 1935, discovered a substance in human semen showing great physiological potency. As he assumed it came from the prostate gland he named it "prostaglandin." It later turned out that prostaglandins could be found in many other human tissues; however, his deduction that they were fatty acids has since been confirmed.

von Kármán, Theodore

(1881–1963)

HUNGARIAN–AMERICAN
AERODYNAMICIST

> Scientists as a group should not try to force or
> even persuade the government to follow their
> decisions.
> —*Collected Works of Dr. Theodore*
> *von Kármán* (1956)

The son of a distinguished educationalist, von Kármán (von **kar**-mahn)
studied engineering at the Polytechnic in his native city of Budapest.
After graduating in 1902 he taught at the Polytechnic until 1906 when
he moved to Göttingen, where he completed his PhD in 1908. At about
this time his interest in aeronautics was aroused when he saw Henri
Farman fly a biplane in Paris. He pursued his new interests further at
Göttingen when he was asked to help Ludwig Prandtl design a wind tunnel for research on airships. Von Kármán continued to work in aeronautics and in 1912 he was invited to establish and direct a new institute
of aerodynamics at the University of Aachen. Here he remained until
1930, apart from the war years spent in Austria working at the Military
Aircraft Factory, Fischamend. In 1930, unhappy with political conditions
in Germany, he moved to the California Institute of Technology to set up
and direct another new institute, the Guggenheim Aeronautic Laboratory at Pasadena, California. He became a naturalized American in 1936.

Von Kármán remained director of the Guggenheim Laboratory until
1949. During this time he contributed to many branches of aeronautics
and encouraged work on jet propulsion, rockets, and supersonic flight. At
von Kármán's insistence the world-famous Jet Propulsion Laboratory was
set up in 1938 and he served as its director until 1945. He also served as
a consultant to the U.S. Army Air Corps from 1939 onward. After his retirement from Pasadena he organized the Advisory Group for Aeronautical Research and Development to provide NATO with technical advice.

Among his many contributions to aerodynamics, von Kármán is
probably best known for his discovery in 1911 of what have since been
called *Kármán vortices* – the alternating vortices found behind obstacles
placed in moving fluids. The basic idea was drawn to his attention by a
graduate student in Prandtl's laboratory. He had been asked to measure

the pressure distribution around a cylinder placed in a steady flow. But, the student found, the flow refused to move steadily and invariably oscillated violently. Prandtl insisted the fault lay with the student who had not bothered to machine circular cylinders. Von Kármán would enquire of the student daily how the flow was behaving and was daily given the sad reply that the flow still oscillated. Eventually von Kármán came to see that the student had stumbled upon a genuine effect. Over a weekend he calculated that the wake should indeed separate into two periodic vortices. Further, there is a symmetric arrangement of vortices which is unstable; only an asymmetric arrangement of vortices persists when the conditions are changed.

Von Kármán went on to demonstrate that above a certain velocity v, where d is the cylinder's diameter, vibrations will be induced with a frequency v/d cycles per second. It was precisely these vibrations which were induced in 1940 in the Tacoma Narrows suspension bridge when v exceeded its critical velocity of 42 mph.

von Laue, Max Theodor Felix

(1879–1960)

GERMAN PHYSICIST

No matter how great the repression, the representative of science can stand erect in the triumphant certainty that is expressed in the simple phrase: And yet it moves!
—Alluding to Galileo's supposed defiance of the Inquisition. Address to the Physics Congress, Würzburg, 18 September 1933

The son of a civil servant, von Laue (fon **low**-e) was born in Pfaffendorf, Koblenz, and educated at the universities of Strasbourg, Göttingen, Munich, and Berlin, where he obtained his doctorate in 1903. He worked in various universities before his appointment as professor of theoretical physics at Berlin University in 1919. He remained there until 1943 when he moved to Göttingen as director of the Max Planck Institute.

Although von Laue began his research career working on relativity theory, his most important work was the discovery of x-ray diffraction in 1912 for which he was awarded the 1914 Nobel Prize for physics. From this discovery much of modern physics was to develop and, some forty years later, the new discipline of molecular biology was to emerge.

Von Laue put together two simple and well known ideas. He knew that x-rays had wavelengths shorter than visible light; he also knew that crystals were regular structures with their atoms probably lined up neatly in rows. Thus, he concluded, if the wavelength of x-rays was similar to the interatomic distance of the atoms in the crystal, then x-rays directed onto a crystal could be diffracted and form a characteristic and decipherable pattern on a photographic plate.

He passed the actual experimental work to two of his students, Walter Friedrich and Paul Kipping, who first tried copper sulfate (1912), which yielded a somewhat unclear pattern. When they changed to zinc sulfide they almost immediately obtained a clear photograph marking out the regular and symmetric arrangement of the atoms in the crystal.

Vonnegut, Bernard

(1914–   )

AMERICAN PHYSICIST

Born in Indianapolis, Indiana, Vonnegut was educated at the Massachusetts Institute of Technology, where he obtained his PhD in 1939. After working in the Research Laboratory of the General Electric Company under Vincent Schaefer (1945–52), he moved to the Arthur D. Little Company and remained there until 1967, when he was appointed professor of atmospheric science at the New York State University, Albany.

In 1947, while with the General Electric Research Laboratory, Vonnegut made a major advance in the rain-making techniques developed by Schaefer, when he found that he obtained much better results with silver iodide crystals for cloud seeding than the dry ice used by Schaefer.

von Neumann, John

(1903–1957)

HUNGARIAN–AMERICAN
MATHEMATICIAN

He [von Neumann] was a genius, in the sense that a genius is a man who has *two* great ideas.
—Jacob Bronowski, *The Ascent of Man* (1973)

In mathematics you don't understand things. You just get used to them.
—Quoted by G. Zukav in *The Dancing Wu Li Masters*

John (originally Johann) von Neumann (von **noi**-man) was born in Budapest, Hungary, and studied at the University of Berlin, the Berlin Institute of Technology, and the University of Budapest, where he obtained his doctorate in 1926. He was *Privatdozent* (nonstipendiary lecturer) at Berlin (1927–29) and taught at Hamburg (1929–30). He left Europe in 1930 to work in Princeton, first at the university and later at the Institute for Advanced Study. From 1943 he was a consultant on the atomic-bomb project.

Von Neumann may have been one of the last people able to span the fields of pure and applied mathematics. His first work was in set theory (the subject of his doctoral thesis). Here he improved the axiomatization given by Ernst Zermelo and Abraham Fraenkel. In 1928 he published his first paper in the field for which he is best known, the mathematical theory of games. This work culminated in 1944 with the publication of *The Theory of Games and Economic Behavior*, which von Neumann had coauthored with Oskar Morgenstern. Not all the results in this work were novel, but it was the first time the field had been treated in such a large-scale and systematic way.

Apart from the theory of games von Neumann did important work in the theory of operators. Dissatisfied with the resources then available for solving the complex computational problems that arose in hydrodynamics, von Neumann developed a broad knowledge of the design of computers and with his interest in the general theory of automata became one of the founders of a whole new discipline. He was much interested in the general role of science and technology in society and this led to his becoming increasingly involved in high-level government scientific committees. Von Neumann died at the early age of 54 from cancer.

von Ohain, Hans Joachim Pabst

(1911–   )

GERMAN–AMERICAN AERONAUTICAL ENGINEER

Born at Dessau in Germany, von Ohain (von **oh**-In) took his PhD in aerodynamics at Göttingen in 1935. He immediately joined the Heinkel Aircraft Company at Rostock. It had long been apparent to engineers that if planes were to fly faster they would have to fly higher and so benefit from the lower air resistance. But in a thinner atmosphere propellers and piston engines worked badly. The dilemma, von Ohain realized, could be resolved if turbojets were used. Thus in 1935, four years after Frank Whittle, von Ohain took out his first patent on the gas-turbine jet engine.

Backed by Ernst Heinkel (1885–1958) he began to work on the He 178. In September 1937 a hydrogen-fueled bench model produced a 250-kilogram thrust. The plane was ready for its test flight, the first jet flight ever, in August 1939 when it reached a top speed of about 350 miles per hour. Whittle's first jet, the Gloster E28/39 prototype, had its maiden flight in 1941.

Heinkel went on to develop the He 280 powered by two von Ohain engines. By this time, however, Heinkel had lost the confidence of the Nazis and the contract to develop a jet fighter was awarded to Messerschmitt. The Me 262, powered by Junkers-built jet engines, entered service in late 1944 with a top speed of 550 miles per hour. Although 1,430 were built, only about 400 actually saw combat and they arrived too late to influence the war's outcome.

Despite this von Ohain found himself in great demand when peace came and in 1947 he began work for the U.S. airforce on the design of a new generation of military jets at the Wright-Patterson base, where he remained until 1975. After a further spell as chief scientist at the Aero-Propulsion Laboratory, von Ohain retired in 1979.

In 1991 he shared with Whittle the Draper Prize – the engineering equivalent of the Nobel Prize – for their independent invention of the jet engine.

von Richthofen, Baron Ferdinand

(1833–1905)

GERMAN GEOGRAPHER

Von Richthofen (fon **rikt**-hoh-fen) was born at Karlsruhe (now in Poland) and educated at the University of Berlin. After extensive travels in southeast Asia, China, and America, he occupied chairs of geography at the universities of Bonn (1877–83), Leipzig (1883–86), and Berlin.

He was the author of a classic five-volume work on the geography of China, *China, Ergebnisse eigener Reisen und darauf gegründeter Studien* (1877–1912; China, the Results of My Travels and the Studies Based Thereon), based on his own intensive fieldwork.

In 1883 he gave a famous inaugural lecture at Leipzig, *Problems and Methods of Modern Geography*, in which he tried to construct a framework for the conduct of geographical research. This he defined widely as the study of the Earth's surface whether of small areas or a continent. He also contributed to the development of modern geography in teaching and directing many of the next generation of German geographers.

Waage, Peter

(1833–1900)

NORWEGIAN CHEMIST

Waage (**vaw**-ge), who was born at Flekkefjord in Norway, became professor of chemistry at the University of Christiania (now Oslo) in 1862, remaining there until 1900. He is remembered for his collaboration with his brother-in-law, Cato Guldberg, for their discovery of the law of mass action in 1864.

Waddington, Conrad Hal

(1905–1975)

BRITISH EMBRYOLOGIST AND
GENETICIST

> DNA plays a role in life rather like that played by the telephone directory in the
> social life of London: you can't do anything much without it, but, having it, you
> need a lot of other things – telephones, wires, and so on – as well.
> —Review of James Dewey Watson's *The Double Helix*,
> *The Sunday Times*, 25 May 1968

Waddington, the son of a tea planter in southern India, was born at Evesham in England and graduated in geology from Cambridge University. In 1933 he was appointed embryologist at the Strangeways Research Laboratory, Cambridge, and in 1947 he moved to the University of Edinburgh where he served as professor of animal genetics until his retirement in 1970.

As a geneticist and a Darwinian, Waddington introduced two important concepts into the discussion of evolutionary theory. The first dealt with developmental reactions that occur in organisms exposed to natural selection and proposed that such reactions are generally canalized. In other words, they adjust to bring about one definite end result notwithstanding small changes in conditions over the course of the reaction.

The second idea was introduced in his 1953 paper *Genetic Assimilation of an Acquired Character*, in which he tried to show that the inheritance of acquired characteristics, the "heresy" of Jean Lamarck, could in fact be incorporated into orthodox genetics and evolutionary theory. As an example Waddington quoted the calluses formed on the embryonic rump of an ostrich. If the Lamarckian explanation of the inheritance of an earlier acquired characteristic is rejected then what remains is the convenient but implausible appearance of a random mutation.

Waddington claimed to have demonstrated experimentally the process of genetic assimilation in normal fruit flies (*Drosophila*). He subjected the pupae of the flies to heat shock and noted that a small proportion developed lacking the posterior cross-vein in their wings. Careful breeding increased the proportion of such flies and eventually Waddington built up a stock of flies without cross-veins that had never been subjected to heat shock. The experiment has been criticized as differing from the calluses of the ostrich in dealing with nonadaptive traits. It also appears to be the case that other genetic mechanisms are available to explain the data without assuming the reality of genetic assimilation.

As an embryologist Waddington was the author of the standard textbook *Principles of Embryology* (1956). He had earlier worked on the powers of the "organizer" of Hans Spemann, showing that Spemann's results can be extended to warm-blooded animals. Waddington also showed that the action of certain embryonic tissues in inducing organ formation is retained even when the tissue is dead.

Waddington was a well-known popularizer of science and as well as his important works in embryology and genetics he also wrote more general texts, such as *The Ethical Animal* (1960) and *Biology for the Modern World* (1962).

Wagner-Jauregg, Julius

(1857–1940)

AUSTRIAN PSYCHIATRIST

Wagner-Jauregg (vahg-ner-**yow**-rek) was born at Wels in Austria and educated at the University of Vienna, where he gained his MD in 1880. Finding it difficult to obtain an academic post in orthodox medicine, he turned to psychiatry in 1883 and in 1889 succeeded Krafft-Ebbing as professor of psychiatry at the University of Graz. In 1893 he returned to Vienna as director of the Psychiatric and Neurological Clinic, where he remained until his retirement in 1928.

In 1917 he proposed a new treatment for general paralysis of the insane (GPI), then a relatively common complication of late syphilis. As early as 1887 he had noticed that rare cases of remission were often preceded by a feverish infection, suggesting that the deliberate production of a fever could have a similar effect. Consequently, in 1917 he inoculated nine GPI patients with tertian malaria – a form of malaria that gives a two-day interval between fever attacks. He later reported that in six of these patients extensive remissions had taken place. It was for this work that Wagner-Jauregg received the Nobel Prize for physiology or medicine in 1927. Although therapeutic malaria inoculations were used in the treatment of GPI for some time, demand for them ceased with the discovery of penicillin.

Wagner-Jauregg also proposed in 1894 that cretinism, a thyroid deficiency disease, could be successfully controlled by iodide tablets.

Waksman, Selman Abraham

(1888–1973)

RUSSIAN–AMERICAN BIOCHEMIST

Waksman (**waks**-man), who was born at Priluki in Russia, emigrated to America in 1910; he graduated from Rutgers University in 1915 and obtained his American citizenship the following year. He studied for his doctorate at California University, receiving his PhD in 1918, and then returned to Rutgers, where he became professor of soil microbiology in 1930.

A new area in the science of soil microbiology was opened up with the discovery by René Dubos, in 1939, of a bacteria-killing agent in a soil microorganism. This stimulated renewed interest in Fleming's penicillin and, with the value of penicillin at last established, Waksman began a systematic search for antibiotics among microorganisms. In 1943 he isolated streptomycin from the mold *Streptomyces griseus* and found that it was effective in treating tuberculosis, caused by Gram-negative bacteria. This was a breakthrough as previously discovered antibiotics had proved useful only against Gram-positive bacteria. This work gained Waksman the 1953 Nobel Prize for physiology or medicine; he donated the prize money to a research foundation at Rutgers.

Waksman isolated and developed many other antibiotics, including neomycin. From 1940 until his retirement in 1958 he was professor of microbiology and chairman of the department at Rutgers; from 1949 he also held the post of director of the Rutgers Institute of Microbiology.

Walcott, Charles Doolittle

(1850–1927)

AMERICAN PALEONTOLOGIST

Walcott was born into a poor family in Utica, New York State, and educated in the public schools there. He began work as a farm laborer and took to collecting the trilobites he found scattered around the farm, some of which he sold to Louis Agassiz. In 1876 he was taken as assistant to the New York state geologist. He moved to the U.S. Geological Survey in 1879 as a field geologist and by 1894 had risen to be its director. In 1907 he accepted the important post of secretary of the Smithsonian Institution, a position he held, along with a number of other offices in scientific administration, until his death in 1927.

Walcott specialized in the Cambrian, the period 550 million years ago when multicellular organisms first appeared. In this field he is best known for his discovery in 1909 of the much discussed Burgess Shale fossils. The shale lies 8,000 feet high in the Rockies on the eastern border of British Columbia. Within two strata he found thousands of fossils representing 120 species of marine invertebrates. Further, while most fossils preserve only such hard parts as shells, bones, and teeth, the Burgess specimens by some geological fluke had preserved their soft tissues.

Walcott shipped his material back to Washington. Between 1910 and 1912 he published a few preliminary reports on the "abrupt appearance of the Cambrian fauna." His initial view that his specimens were early forms of modern groups remained unchallenged. Walcott himself was too concerned with administering American science to have time to reconsider his early ideas. It was not until the 1970s when Harry Whittington began to review Walcott's specimens that it was appreciated that another, more radical, view was possible. Walcott's story is vividly told in S. J. Gould's popular work *Wonderful Life* (1989).

Wald, George

(1906–   )

AMERICAN BIOCHEMIST

We already know enough to begin to cope with all the major problems that are now threatening human life and much of the rest of life on earth. Our crisis is not a crisis of information; it is a crisis of decision of policy and action.
—*Philosophy and Social Action* (1979)

Born in New York City, Wald was educated at New York University and at Columbia where he obtained his PhD in 1932. After spending the period 1932–34 in Europe, where he worked under Otto Warburg in Berlin and Paul Karrer in Zurich, he returned to America where he took up an appointment at Harvard. Wald remained at Harvard for the whole of his career, becoming professor of biology in 1948 and emeritus professor in 1977.

Wald did fundamental work on the chemistry of vision. In 1933 he discovered that vitamin A is present in the retina of the eye, and thereafter tried to find the relationship between this vitamin and the visual pigment rhodopsin. The first clue came from the constitution of rhodopsin. It was found to consist of two parts: a colorless protein, opsin, and a yellow carotenoid, retinal, which is the aldehyde of vitamin A. Wald was now in a position to work out the main outlines of the story.

Rhodopsin is light sensitive and splits into its two parts when illuminated, with the retinal being reduced further to vitamin A by the enzyme alcohol dehydrogenase. In the dark the procedure is reversed. What was further needed was some indication of how the splitting of the rhodopsin molecule could somehow generate electrical activity in the optic nerve and visual cortex. Part of the answer came from Haldan Hartline and Ragnar Granit who shared the 1967 Nobel Prize for physiology or medicine with Wald.

Wald has speculated that since retinal is a carotenoid pigment, and such pigments are also found in plants, then it is possible that the phototropic responses of plants may rely on a similar mechanism. Wald later became widely known for his opposition to the Vietnam War.

Walden, Paul

(1863–1957)

RUSSIAN–GERMAN CHEMIST

The son of a farmer from Cēsis (now in Latvia), Walden (**vahl**-den) was educated at Riga Polytechnic, where he studied under Wilhelm Ostwald. Having become professor of chemistry in 1894, he remained at the polytechnic until the Russian Revolution, when he moved to Germany. From 1919 to 1934 he served as professor of chemistry at the University of Rostock.

In 1896 Walden found that if he took a sample of malic acid that rotated polarized light in a clockwise direction and allowed it to react in a certain way, then on recovery it would be found to rotate polarized light in a counterclockwise direction. The actual reaction involved first combining the malic acid with phosphorus pentachloride to give chlorosuccinic acid. This converts back into malic acid under the influence of silver oxide and water but the malic acid has an inverted configuration. Such inversions later became a useful tool for studying the detail of organic reactions. *Walden inversions*, as they are called, occur when an atom or group approaches a molecule from one direction and displaces an atom or group from the other side of the molecule.

Walden also worked on the electrochemistry of nonaqueous solutions and formulated *Walden's rule*, which relates conductivity and viscosity in such solutions. In later life he turned to the history of chemistry on which topic he is notable for having regularly lectured at the University of Tübingen while well into his nineties.

Waldeyer-Hartz, Wilhelm von

(1836–1921)

GERMAN ANATOMIST AND
PHYSIOLOGIST

Waldeyer-Hartz (vahl-dI-er-**harts**), who is better known by his original surname, Waldeyer, was born in Hehlen, Germany, the son of an estate manager. He studied at the universities of Göttingen and Griefswald and at Berlin, where he graduated in medicine, and later taught at the University of Breslau, where he was professor of pathology from 1864 until 1872; he then moved to the chair of anatomy at Strasbourg. In 1883 he returned to Berlin where he remained until his retirement in 1917.

Waldeyer is mainly remembered for the introduction of two basic scientific terms. In 1888 he proposed the term "chromosome" to refer to the rods that appear in the cell nucleus before division occurs and which readily take up stain. He followed this in 1891 by coining the term "neuron" to explain the work of Santiago Ramón y Cajal, although he did not contribute any original work on nerve cells.

Waldeyer is known to anatomists for his description of the lymphoid tissue encircling the throat, known since as *Waldeyer's ring*. The tissue is presumed to be part of the immune system.

In 1863 Waldeyer established that cancer begins as a single cell and spreads to the other parts of the body by cells migrating from the original site via the blood or lymphatic system. Such an observation carried with it the implication that if the original cells could somehow be removed the cancer would be completely cured, a more congenial view than the bleak alternative that cancer was such a generalized attack on the body that removal of a particular focus was pointless.

Walker, Sir James

(1863–1935)

BRITISH CHEMIST

Walker, the son of a flax merchant from Dundee in Scotland, was apprenticed to a flax spinner before attending Edinburgh University (1882–85). After a year in Germany under Johann von Baeyer and Wilhelm Ostwald he returned to Edinburgh as assistant to Alexander Crum Brown before taking a post at University College, London, in 1892. In 1894 he was appointed to the chemistry chair at Dundee, where he remained until he moved to a similar chair at Edinburgh in 1908.

Walker was a physical chemist and did much to popularize the new subject. He himself did valuable work on ionization constants and osmotic pressure but his main importance was as a channel for the ideas of Ostwald; his textbook *Introduction to Physical Chemistry* (1899) was significant in this respect. Walker was knighted in 1921 for his work on TNT during World War I.

Wallace, Alfred Russel

(1823–1913)

BRITISH NATURALIST

These checks – war, disease, famine and the like – must, it occurred to me, act on animals as well as man...and while pondering vaguely on this fact there suddenly flashed upon me the idea of the survival of the fittest – that the individuals removed by these checks must be on the whole inferior to those that survived. In the two hours that elapsed before my ague fit was over, I had thought out almost the whole of the theory: and the same evening I sketched the draft of paper, and in the two succeeding evenings wrote it out in full, and sent it by the next post to Mr. Darwin.
—Quoted by Basil Willey in *Darwin and Butler* (1960)

Wallace, who was born at Usk in Wales, received only an elementary schooling before joining an elder brother in the surveying business. In 1844 he became a master at the Collegiate School, Leicester, where he met the entomologist Henry Bates. Wallace persuaded Bates to accompany him on a trip to the Amazon, and they joined a scientific expedition as naturalists in 1848.

Wallace published an account of his expedition in his *A Narrative of Travels on the Amazon and River Negro* (1853). In 1854 he traveled to the Malay Archipelago, where he spent eight years and collected over 125,000 specimens, a journey described in his *Malay Archipelago* (1869). In this region he noted the marked differences between the Asian and Australian faunas, the former being more advanced than the latter, and proposed a line, still referred to as *Wallace's line*, separating the two distinct ecological regions. He suggested that Australian animals are more primitive because the Australian continent broke away from Asia before the more advanced Asian animals evolved and thus the marsupials were not overrun and driven to extinction. This observation, together with a reconsideration of Thomas Malthus's essay on population, led him to propose the theory of evolution by natural selection. He wrote an essay entitled *On the Tendency of Varieties to Depart Indefinitely from the*

Original Type, which he sent to Darwin for his opinion. On receipt, Darwin realized this was a summary of his own views and the two papers were jointly presented at a meeting of the Linnaean Society in July 1858.

Wallace continued to collect evidence for this evolutionary theory, making an important study on mimicry in the swallowtail butterfly and writing pioneering works on the geographical distribution of animals, including his *Geographical Distribution of Animals* (2 vols., 1876) and *Island Life* (1880). He was also an active socialist, having been introduced to the ideas of the reformer Robert Owen at an early age, and he campaigned for land nationalization and women's suffrage.

In addition to his scientific and political pursuits, Wallace also participated in many of the more dubious intellectual movements of the 19th century. He supported spiritualism, phrenology, and mesmerism. He testified in 1876 on behalf of Henry Slade, a professional medium, charged on evidence submitted by Ray Lankester with being a "common rogue." His views on these matters led Wallace to disagree with Darwin on the evolution of man. Man's spiritual essence, Wallace insisted, could not have been produced by natural selection. "I hope you have not murdered our child," Darwin commented. Wallace also campaigned persistently against the practice of vaccination. He published a pamphlet in 1885 claiming British and U.S. statistics showed it to be "both useless and dangerous." He testified in a similar manner before a Royal Commission in 1890 and published his evidence in a pamphlet, *Vaccination, a Delusion* (1895).

Throughout his career Wallace never held an academic appointment and after 1848 no appointment of any kind. He hoped to live on the sale of specimens collected during his Amazon and Malay expeditions. Unfortunately, however, the bulk of the Amazonian material was lost at sea, while funds gathered from the sale of his Malay collection were squandered in unwise investments and expensive disputes with builders. Wallace was therefore forced to earn his living by writing and lecturing. The award of a civil list pension of £200 a year from 1880 greatly eased Wallace's financial burdens.

Wallace also published a spirited account of his life in *My Life* (London, 1905).

Wallach, Otto

(1847–1931)

GERMAN CHEMIST

Born at Königsberg (now Kaliningrad in Russia), Wallach (**vahl**-ahk or **wol**-ak) studied at Berlin and at Göttingen, where he obtained his PhD in 1869. After a period in industry in Berlin he moved to Bonn (1870), becoming August Kekulé's assistant and later (1876) professor of chemistry. He remained at Bonn until 1889, when he moved to a similar chair at Göttingen.

When Wallach began to give regular classes in pharmacy he became interested in essential oils – oils removed from plants by steam distillation with wide uses in medicine and the perfume industry – and started research into determining their molecular structure. This study led to what was to become his major field of research, the chemistry of the terpenes.

These had hitherto presented considerable difficulties to the analytic chemist. Wallach succeeded in determining the structure of several terpenes, including limonene, in 1894. His greatest achievement, however, was his formulation of the isoprene rule in 1887. Isoprene, with the formula C_5H_8, had been isolated from rubber in the 1860s by C. Williams. Wallach showed that terpenes were derived from isoprene and therefore had the general formula $(C_5H_8)_n$; limonene is thus $C_{10}H_{16}$. Terpenes were of importance not only in the perfume industry but also as a source of camphors. It was also later established that vitamins A and D are related to the terpenes.

Wallach published 126 papers on the terpenes – work for which he was awarded the Nobel Prize for chemistry in 1910.

Wallis, Barnes Neville

(1887–1979)

BRITISH ENGINEER

Wallis was born at Ripley in England, the son of a doctor. Having served an apprenticeship with the Thames Engineering Company (1904–08), he moved to a marine engineering company at Cowes on the Isle of Wight. In 1913 Wallis joined the aeronautical company Vickers, initially to work on the development of the airship, and spent most of his professional career with this company working on a variety of projects. He served with them as chief designer of structures from 1930 and as assistant chief designer of aviation from 1937. After World War II until his retirement in 1971 he worked as head of the department of aeronautical research and development.

His first major success came with the R100 airship in which he displayed his originality of structural design. In 1930 he invented the geodetic construction (a lattice structure in which compression loads on any member are balanced by tension loads in a crossing member), which he applied to aircraft design during the 1930s. As a result he designed the Wellesley, the first geodetic aircraft to enter service in the Royal Air Force, and the Wellington bomber. These aircraft, with the new construction, were lighter and stronger than earlier designs.

Wallis's main war work has become widely known with the massive success of the book and the film about 617 Squadron, better known as the "Dam Busters." Wallis's original idea for a bouncing bomb was contained in his 1940 paper *A Note on a Method of Attacking the Axis Powers.* Using this weapon the successful raid by 617 Squadron on the Möhne and Eder dams took place on 16–17 May 1943.

Wallis's originality persisted throughout the postwar years, which were devoted to the design of an entirely new type of aircraft. He first described in 1945 a design so different from traditional aircraft that he gave it a new name, the "aerodyne." This was based on his realization that no conventional airplane could be efficient under the great variety of conditions encountered in subsonic and supersonic flight. His solution, the "wing controlled aerodyne," more popularly known as the swing-wing airplane or the plane with variable geometry, received some backing from Vickers and an experimental version, the Swallow, was built and tested in the 1950s. The project was, however, abandoned when the British government decided to withdraw its backing, but some of Wallis's ideas were nonetheless incorporated in the American fighter airplane, the F1-11.

Although Wallis was made a member of the Royal Society in 1945, then a rare honor for an engineer, it was not until 1968 when, over 80, he was belatedly knighted.

Wallis, John

(1616–1703)

ENGLISH MATHEMATICIAN AND
THEOLOGIAN

Born at Ashford in England, Wallis was educated at Cambridge University (1632–40), obtaining his MA in 1640. His early training was in theology and it was as a theologian that he first made his name. He took holy orders and eventually became bishop of Winchester. He moved to London in 1645 where he became seriously interested in mathematics and in 1649 he was appointed to the Savilian Chair in Geometry at Oxford University.

Wallis's most celebrated mathematical work is contained in his treatise the *Arithmetica infinitorum* (1655; The Arithmetic of Infinitesimals). In this work he gave his famous infinite series expression for π:

$$\frac{2}{\pi} = \frac{1.3.3.5.5.7. \ldots}{2.2.4.4.6.6. \ldots}$$

Generally the treatise took the development of 17th-century mathematics a significant step nearer Newton's creation of the infinitesimal calculus. Wallis was one of the first mathematicians to introduce the functional mode of thinking, which was to be of such importance in

Newton's work. He also did notable work on conic sections and published a treatise on them, *Tractatus de sectionibus conicis* (1659; Tract on Conic Sections), which developed the subject in an ingeniously novel fashion. His writings were certainly read by Newton and are known to have made a considerable impact on him. Before Newton, Wallis was probably one of the most influential of English mathematicians.

Wallis wrote a substantial history of mathematics. His other interests included music and the study of language. He was active in the weekly scientific meetings that eventually led to the foundation of the Royal Society in 1662. During the English Civil War he was a Parliamentarian and put his mathematical talents to use in decoding enciphered letters.

Walton, Ernest Thomas Sinton

(1903–1995)

IRISH PHYSICIST

Walton, who was born at Dungarvan in Ireland, studied at the Methodist College, Belfast, where he excelled at mathematics and science. In 1922 he entered Trinity College, Dublin, graduating in mathematics and experimental science in 1926. In 1927 he went to Cambridge University on a research scholarship and worked in the Cavendish Laboratory under Ernest Rutherford. It was here that he performed experiments, together with John Cockcroft, with accelerated particles. The experiments were to lead to the two men sharing the 1951 Nobel Prize for physics for "their pioneer work on the transmutation of atomic nuclei by artificially accelerated atomic particles," more commonly known as "splitting the atom."

In 1934 Walton gained his PhD from Cambridge and returned to Dublin as a fellow of Trinity College. He was appointed Erasmus Smith Professor of Natural and Experimental Philosophy in 1946 and was elected a senior fellow in 1960. In 1952 he became chairman of the School of Cosmic Physics of the Dublin Institute for Advanced Studies, where he remained until his retirement in 1974.

Wankel, Felix

(1902–1988)

GERMAN MECHANICAL ENGINEER
AND INVENTOR

Wankel (**vahng**-kel or **wang**-kel) was born at Lahr in Germany. The son of a civil servant who was killed in World War I, he left school early when the family savings were rendered valueless by the hyperinflation of the 1920s. He began work in 1921 in a Heidelberg bookshop while pursuing his engineering interests by attending night classes and by taking correspondence courses. In 1924 he began to consider the possibility of constructing a rotary engine and would spend the rest of his life trying to perfect one.

There was nothing new in the idea of a rotary engine; over 2,000 patents had been taken out in Britain before 1910. None, however, worked adequately, for none had solved the problem of designing a gas-tight seal. In a piston engine it is a simple matter to maintain a good seal with piston rings. In Wankel's rotary engine the whole rotor circumference has to be sealed. If the seal is too loose, power is lost as gas escapes; if too tight, friction increases, power falls, and rotors wear out.

While working on his own engine Wankel also designed a rotary disk valve consisting of a flat disk with a hole that revolves to allow air or gas entry into the cylinder at the appropriate time. The success of his design enabled Wankel to leave the bookshop in 1926 and to set up his own workshop. He also found a patron in Wilhelm Keppler, a prosperous businessman and economic adviser to Hitler. With Keppler's aid Wankel received commissions from Daimler in 1933 and BMW in 1934. In 1936, again at Keppler's behest, Wankel was installed by the German Air Ministry in a workshop in Lindau to work on rotary valves for aircraft engines.

Wankel had in fact been a member of the Hitler Youth and the Nazi party but, he later claimed, he had left the party in 1932, and after exposing a corrupt party official was actually imprisoned in 1933 for several months. Despite this, his workshop was occupied and destroyed by the French in 1945.

It was not until 1951 that Wankel was allowed to reopen his work-shop. During the interval he had worked intensively on rotary-engine design and by 1953 he had a workable model – a triangular rotor housed in a trochoid-shaped chamber fitted with both apex and side seals. As the rotor revolves in its housing three chambers of variable size are produced, in each of which the four-stroke cycle of intake, compression, ignition, and exhaust takes place. Compared with reciprocating piston engines, Wankel's design was much smaller, required half the number of moving parts, and was virtually free of vibrations.

Over the years rights to manufacture Wankel's engine were sold to NSU in Germany, Curtis-Wright in America, and Toyo Kogyo in Japan. While most major motor companies, including Ford, General Motors, and Rolls Royce, showed some interest in the rotary engine, none, with the exception of Mazda, pursued the matter further. In 1971 Mazda tried to break into the American market with their R-100 and RX-2. Initially sales were good and 42,000 models were sold in 1972, but this was to prove the high point. The oil crisis of 1973 was no time to introduce a revolutionary new model. Consequently, Mazda's rotary engine found a more durable niche in one of their low-volume high-priced sports cars.

Wankel subsequently became director of his own research establishment at Lindau, where he did further work on rotary engines.

While few seem to have profited from Wankel's design, he himself accumulated a fortune of $20 million from the sale of manufacturing rights, the bulk of which was spent building homes for cats and dogs.

Warburg, Otto Heinrich

(1883–1970)

GERMAN PHYSIOLOGIST

A scientist must have the courage to attack the great unsolved problems of his time.
—Attributed remark

Warburg (**var**-buurk or **wor**-burg), who was born at Freiburg im Breisgau in Germany, was the son of Emil Warburg, a distinguished professor of physics at Berlin. Otto was educated at the University of Berlin, where he obtained his PhD in 1906, and at Heidelberg, where he gained his MD in 1911. He joined the Kaiser Wilhelm Institute for Biology in 1913, attaining professorial status in 1918, and in 1931 became director of the Kaiser Wilhelm Institute for Cell Physiology, renamed after Max Planck following World War II. Here Warburg remained in charge until his death at the age of 86.

When the human body converts lactic acid into carbon dioxide and water it consumes oxygen. In the early 1920s Warburg began to investigate just how such aerobic metabolism works. To do this he designed, in 1923, the *Warburg manometer*, which is used to measure the rate of oxygen uptake by human tissue. It was clear to Warburg that such a reaction could only take place at normal temperatures with the aid of enzymes but, because of the tiny amounts involved, such enzymes would be impossible to isolate by orthodox analytical techniques. He suspected the respiratory enzymes to be the cytochromes discovered a decade earlier and consequently set out to explore their nature by noting which substances affected the rate of oxygen uptake. He first noted that intercellular respiration was blocked by hydrogen cyanide and by carbon monoxide. This suggested to Warburg that the respiratory enzymes contained iron on the analogy that carbon monoxide acts on hemoglobin by breaking the oxygen–iron bonds. Support for such a supposition was derived from the similarity between the spectrum of the carbon monoxide–hemoglobin complex and that of the carbon monoxide–respiratory enzyme complex.

Warburg also studied the metabolism of cancerous cells and in 1923 discovered that malignant cells use far less oxygen than normal cells and can in fact live anaerobically. This extremely interesting observation led him to speculate that cancer is caused by a malfunction of the cellular respiratory system. He advocated that cancer might be prevented by avoiding foods and additives that impair cellular activity and by ensuring a high level of respiratory enzyme in the body by taking plenty of iron and vitamin B.

Warburg also worked on other enzyme systems, particularly the flavoproteins, or yellow enzymes, active in cellular dehydrogenation. He found that the coenzyme flavin adenine dinucleotide (FAD) is the active part of flavoproteins and later demonstrated that nicotinamide is similarly the active part of nicotinamide adenine dinucleotide (NAD^+). Following these discoveries he showed that in alcohol fermentation a hydrogenated form of NAD^+ ($NADH_2$) reacts with acetaldehyde to give NAD^+ and ethyl alcohol.

For his contributions to biochemistry, Warburg was nominated three times for the Nobel Prize for physiology or medicine, in 1926, 1931, and 1944, although he only actually received the award in 1931.

Ward, Joshua

(1685–1761)

ENGLISH PHYSICIAN AND
CHEMIST

Ward, who was born in the eastern English county of Suffolk, was elected to parliament as member for Marlborough in 1717. However, he was prevented from taking his seat because of electoral irregularities and was forced to flee to France. He returned on being pardoned in 1733. Ward became the most famous (or notorious) of the pill peddlers. He won the protection of George II when he cured him of a dislocated thumb and treated many of the 18th-century notables, including Edward Gibbon and Henry Fielding. The contents of his pills were revealed in an unsuccessful legal suit brought by him in 1734. Most of his pills, including the "white drops," contained antimony and some also contained arsenic. His popularity was such, however, that he was specifically excluded from the Apothecaries Act of 1748 designed to prevent unlicensed prescribing.

One of the great problems facing 18th-century industry was the production of sulfuric acid in quantity. In 1736 Ward opened a factory in Surrey where he burned sulfur in 50-gallon glass globes together with a sodium nitrate catalyst to produce sulfuric acid. He was able to produce enough sulfuric acid in this way both to make his own fortune and to reduce the price of the acid to an eighth of its original cost. This increase in quantity and decrease in price contributed to the growth of such industries as dyeing and bleaching later in the century.

Wassermann, August von

(1866–1925)

GERMAN BACTERIOLOGIST

Wassermann (**vah**-ser-mahn or **wah**-ser-man), who was born at Bamberg in Germany, was educated at the universities of Erlangen, Vienna, Munich, and Strasbourg, where he graduated in 1888. From 1890 he worked under Robert Koch at the Institute for Infectious Diseases in Berlin, becoming head of the department of therapeutics and serum research in 1907. In 1913 he moved to the Kaiser Wilhelm Institute, where he served as director of experimental therapeutics until his death.

Wassermann is best remembered for the *Wassermann test* (or *reaction*), which he introduced in 1906 for the diagnosis of syphilis. The test depends upon an infected person producing in his or her blood the antibody to syphilis, which will combine with known antigens, such as beef liver or heart, to form a complex. The test is regarded as positive by the ability of the complex to fix complement, the serum protein discovered by Jules Bordet in the 1880s. The test is still widely used as a diagnostic tool.

Waterston, John James

(1811–1883)

BRITISH PHYSICIST

Waterston graduated from the university in his native city of Edinburgh, where he studied medicine and science. He worked as an engineer in London and the Far East before returning to Edinburgh.

Apparently he was stimulated by the works of Julius Mayer and James Joule to work out for himself the kinetic theory of gases, which later won great fame for James Clerk Maxwell and Rudolf Clausius. Waterston submitted a paper to the Royal Society in 1845 describing his great discovery but it was rejected by their referee as being "nothing but nonsense." Lord Rayleigh found the paper in the Royal Society archives and arranged for it to be published in 1892, nine years after Waterston's death.

Watson, David Meredith Seares

(1886–1973)

BRITISH PALEONTOLOGIST

Watson was born in Manchester, England, the son of a prosperous industrialist. He studied chemistry and geology at the university in his native city, obtaining his MSc in 1909. For some years he worked in unofficial posts at the British Museum and University College, London; he also traveled in Australia and South Africa studying both their geology and fossils. In 1921 he succeeded Peter Hill as Jodrell Professor of Zoology and Comparative Anatomy at University College, London, a post he held until his retirement in 1951.

Watson, originally trained as a geologist, began his career working with Marie Stopes, then famous as the first female science lecturer at Manchester, on fossil plants in coal mines. He soon turned, however, to the main work of his life, vertebrate paleontology, on which topic he published over a hundred papers. His views were published in less specialized form in his *Palaeontology and Modern Biology* (1951).

Watson, James Dewey

(1928–   )

AMERICAN BIOCHEMIST

> It is necessary to be slightly underemployed
> if you want to do something significant.
> —Quoted by H. Judson in *The Eighth
> Day of Creation*

Watson entered the university in his native city of Chicago at the early age of 15, graduating in 1947. He obtained his PhD (1950) for studies of viruses at the University of Indiana and continued this work at the University of Copenhagen. In Copenhagen he realized that one of the major unsolved problems of biology lay in identifying the structure of the nucleic-acid molecules making up chromosomes. In 1951 he moved to the Cavendish Laboratory in Cambridge, England, to study the structure of DNA.

Early in 1953 Watson and Francis Crick published a molecular structure of DNA having two cross-linked helical chains (*General Implications of the Structure of Deoxyribonucleic Acid*). They arrived at this by considering possible geometric models, which they based on two independent sets of experimental work: the x-ray crystallography of Maurice Wilkins and Rosalind Franklin at King's College, London, and the earlier work of Ernst Chargaff, which had established the relative quantities of the organic bases present in the nucleic acids. Watson and Crick were able to show that certain organic bases linked the chains together by hydrogen bonds.

The model explains the three basic characteristics of heredity. It shows how genetic information can be expressed in the form of a chemical code; it demonstrates the way in which genes replicate themselves – when the two chains separate each can serve as a template for the synthesis of a new chain; and finally it provides an explanation of how mutations occur in genes, in terms of changes in the chemical structure of DNA. Watson, Crick, and Wilkins shared the Nobel Prize for physiology or medicine for this work in 1962.

Watson left Cambridge in 1953 for the California Institute of Technology. From 1955 to 1968 he worked at Harvard, becoming professor of biology in 1961. Here he continued to study the genetic code. In 1968 he became director of the Cold Spring Harbor Laboratory, New York, where he concentrated effort on cancer research. The same year he published *The Double Helix*, an informal, highly personal, and somewhat controversial account of the discovery of the structure of DNA. He retired in 1993.

Watson, Sir William

(1715–1787)

BRITISH PHYSICIST, PHYSICIAN, AND BOTANIST

> Never indolent in the slightest degree...an exact economist of his time.
> —R. Pulteney, *Sketches of the Progress of Botany in England* (1790)

Watson, the son of a London tradesman, was apprenticed to an apothecary from 1731 to 1738. After working for many years at that trade, Watson was made a licentiate of the Royal College of Physicians. This was later followed in 1762 with an appointment as physician to the Foundling Hospital.

Watson had a great interest in natural history and was instrumental in introducing the Linnaean system of botanical classification into Britain. He is, however, mainly remembered for his account of the nature of electricity. This was based on a series of experiments with the Leyden jar, discovered by Pieter van Musschenbroek in 1746. Watson not only improved the device by coating the inside of it with metal foil but also realized that the pattern of discharge of the jar suggested that electricity was simply a single fluid or, as he termed it, an "electrical ether." Normally bodies have an equal density of this fluid so that when two such bodies meet there will be no electrical activity. If, however, their densities are unequal the fluid will flow and there will be an electric discharge. That is, electricity can only be transferred from one body to another; it cannot be created or destroyed. Such a theory was also developed with greater depth at about the same time by Benjamin Franklin and was to emerge as the orthodox position by the end of the century.

Watson also made an early and unsuccessful attempt in 1747 to measure the velocity of electricity over a four-mile (6.4-km) circuit. Although it appeared to complete its journey in no time at all Watson sensibly concluded that it probably traveled too fast to be measured.

Watson-Watt, Sir Robert Alexander

(1892–1973)

BRITISH PHYSICIST

The wings of an aeroplane act like a kind of horizontal wire in the air. When you aim a powerful wireless beam at them, they turn into a "secondary transmitter" and send the waves back at the angle of incidence, just as a mirror reflects light rays.

—On the principle of radar. Quoted by Egon Larsen in
A History of Invention (1969)

Watson-Watt was born Robert Watt at Brechin in Angus, Scotland. The Watson part of his name came from his mother's family and the hybrid Watson-Watt was adopted in 1942 on receipt of his knighthood. He was the son of a carpenter and was educated at the University of St. Andrews. After graduating in 1912 he immediately joined the faculty but found his academic career disrupted by World War I. He spent much of the war working as a meteorologist at the Royal Aircraft Establishment, Farnborough, attempting to locate thunderstorms with radio waves.

He remained in the scientific civil service after the war and in 1921 was appointed superintendent of the Radio Research Station at Slough. In 1935 he was asked by the Air Ministry if a "death ray" could be built – one capable of eliminating an approaching enemy pilot. Watson-Watt asked a colleague to calculate how much energy would be needed to raise a gallon of water from 98°F to 105°F at a distance of a mile, i.e., a significant rise in body temperature. He advised the Ministry that the energy needed outstripped the available technology.

Watson-Watt also pointed out that Post Office engineers had noted interference in radio reception as aircraft flew close to their receivers. Interference of this kind, he suggested, could perhaps be used to detect the approach of enemy aircraft. In 1935 he submitted an important paper, *The Detection of Aircraft by Radio Methods*, to Tizard at the Ministry. Watson-Watt was normally a man, it was said, who could never say in one word what could be said in a thousand. This time, however, the report was terse and to the point. Tizard asked for a demonstration. In February 1935 the BBC short-wave transmitter at Daventry was successfully used to identify the approach of a Heyford bomber eight miles away.

Tizard moved quickly. Watson-Watt was invited to set up a research station at Bawdsley in Suffolk to develop radio detection and ranging; the acronym "radar" was first recorded in use in the *New York Times* in 1941.

The principles behind radar are relatively simple. Radio waves are reflected strongly off large objects such as airplanes. The difficulty was that very little, something of the order of 10^{-12}, of the transmitted signal would be picked up by the receiving antennae. Both high transmitting power and high amplification would therefore be needed. Watson-Watt assembled a talented team at Bawdsley and by the outbreak of World War II an operational chain of eight stations, known as "Chain Home," defended Britain's eastern and southern coasts. They operated in the high-frequency bands and required very visible 360-foot-high transmitters and 240-foot-high receivers.

Watson-Watt left Bawdsley in 1938 for the Air Ministry and the post of director of communication development. His main task was to make radar workable, to ensure that it was acceptable to the RAF and that they could actually operate the new equipment. He also had to arrange for the manufacture of the relevant transmitters, receivers, and electron tubes.

He finally left the civil service in 1945 to set up as a consultant. He was also invited to give evidence before the Royal Commission on Inventors on behalf of his colleagues and himself. After speaking for six days Watson-Watt was awarded £52,000 for his work on radar.

Watt, James

(1736–1819)

BRITISH INSTRUMENT MAKER AND INVENTOR

I have now got an engine that shall not waste
a particle of steam. It shall be all boiling hot;
– aye, and hot water injected if I please.
—Quoted by John Robison in *A Narrative
of Mr. Watt's Invention of the
Improved Engine* (1796)

James Watt, who, directing the force of an original genius, Early exercised in
philosophic research to the improvement of THE STEAM ENGINE, enlarged the
resources of his country, increased the power of men, and rose to an eminent
place among the most illustrious followers of science and the real benefactors
of the World.

—Epitaph in Westminster Abbey, London

The son of a Clydeside shipbuilder and house builder, Watt was born
in Greenock, Scotland. At the age of 17 he started a career in Glasgow
as a mathematical-instrument maker. Through his shop, opened in 1757,
he met many of the scientists at Glasgow University.

In 1764 it occurred to Watt that the Newcomen steam engine, a model
of which he had been repairing, wasted a great deal of energy by dissi-
pating the latent heat given up by steam condensing to water. The solution was to build an engine with a separate condenser, so that there
was no need to heat and cool the cylinder at each stroke. In 1768 Watt
entered into partnership with John Roebuck, who had established an
iron foundry, to produce the steam engine but his duties as a land surveyor, taken up in 1766, left him little time to develop this and Roebuck
went bankrupt in 1772. A second partnership (1775) with Matthew Boulton proved more productive although it took Watt until 1790 to perfect
what became known as the *Watt engine*.

This engine, throughout its various stages of improvement, was one
of the main contributors to the Industrial Revolution. Early reciprocating versions were used for pumping water out of Cornish copper and
tin mines. A rotating engine with the sun-and-planet gearing system invented by Watt in 1781 was used in flour mills, cotton mills, and paper
mills. An automatic speed control mechanism, the centrifugal governor
invented in 1788, was another improvement.

Watt made a great deal of money from the sale of his engines and became accepted into the scientific establishment. He retired from the business of steam-engine manufacture in 1800 and spent his time traveling, working as a consultant, and working on minor inventions in his workshop at home. Watt was the first to use the term horsepower as a unit of power and the *watt*, a unit of power, was named for him.

Weber, Ernst Heinrich

(1795–1878)

GERMAN PHYSIOLOGIST AND PSYCHOLOGIST

Weber was the eldest of three brothers who all made important contributions to science. He was born at Wittenberg in Germany and became a professor at the University of Leipzig in 1818, a position he held until his death.

Weber is best known for his work on sensory response to weight, temperature, and pressure. In 1834 he conducted research on the lifting of weights. From his researches he discovered that the experience of differences in the intensity of sensations depends on percentage differences in the stimuli rather than absolute differences. This is known as the just-noticeable difference (j.n.d.), difference threshold, or limen. The work was published in *Der Tastsinn und das Gemeingefühl* (1851; The Sense of Touch and the Common Sensibility) and was given mathematical expression by Weber's student Gustav Theodor Fechner as the *Weber–Fechner* law.

Weber is regarded as a founder of experimental psychology and psychophysics. He also conducted important anatomical work.

Weber, Joseph

(1919–)

AMERICAN PHYSICIST

Born in Paterson, New Jersey, Weber graduated from the U.S. Naval Academy in 1940 and served in the Navy until 1948, when he joined the faculty of the University of Maryland, College Park. He completed his doctorate at the Catholic University of America, Washington DC, in 1951 and was appointed professor of physics at Maryland in 1959, a post which he held for the remainder of his career.

Einstein's general theory of relativity predicts that accelerated masses should radiate gravitational waves. Like electromagnetic waves, these should carry energy and momentum and should be identifiable with a suitable detector. For gravitational waves, this would be an object of large mass with a method of detecting any disturbance of it. In 1958 Weber began the design and construction of just such a device. By 1965 he had built a solid aluminum cylinder detector, 3 feet in diameter and weighing 3.5 tons. Bonded around the cylinder were a number of piezo-electric crystals, which generate a voltage when the bar is compressed or extended. Weber claimed that his instruments could detect deformations corresponding to 1 part in 10^{16}, a difference of about 1/100th the diameter of an atomic nucleus.

Weber was aware of the problems involved in this kind of design. To rule out causes other than gravitational – acoustic, thermal, seismic, etc. – he suspended the cylinder in a vacuum. More significantly he built a second detector 600 miles away from Maryland at the Argonne National Laboratory in Chicago, and only recognized coincident readings as evidence for gravitational waves. He reported the first coincident readings in 1968. He also noted, in 1970, that such readings reached a peak when the cylinders were both oriented in the direction of the galactic center.

Unfortunately, although there were several attempts to replicate Weber's work in the 1970s, none proved successful. Work has, however, continued with more sensitive antennas. Supercooled niobium rods have been installed at the European Laboratory for Particle Physics in Geneva, at Stanford, and at the Louisiana State University for a three-way coincidence experiment. Despite recognizing 60–70 events a day, none have yet conclusively proved to be coincidental.

Attempts to resolve Weber's conjecture were also begun in 1991 with the announcement of the LIGO project (Laser Interferometer Gravitational-Wave Observatory). At a cost of $200 million, the California Institute of Technology and the Massachusetts Institute of Technology on opposite sides of the United States plan to use a different type of detector. This will have two intense laser beams traveling back and forth along a four-kilometer path and interfering with each other as they meet at a point. Any passing gravitational wave will slightly alter the interference patterns of the laser beams at the two locations. Theorists involved with the project are convinced that by the year 2000 they will have detected gravitational waves.

Weber, Wilhelm Eduard

(1804–1891)

GERMAN PHYSICIST

Weber (**vay**-ber) was the son of a professor of divinity and brother of the noted scientists Ernst Heinrich Weber and Eduard Friedrich Weber, both of whom worked in anatomy and physiology. He was born in Wittenberg in Germany and studied physics at Halle, where his early research concerned acoustics. He obtained his PhD in 1826 for a thesis on reed organ pipes. He remained teaching at Halle until 1831 when he was made professor of physics at Göttingen on the recommendation of the mathematician Karl Friedrich Gauss.

Some of Weber's research was done in collaboration with his brothers. Thus in 1824 he published work on wave motion with Ernst, and in 1833 he and Eduard investigated the mechanism of walking. However, most of his academic life was spent working with Gauss. In 1833 they built the first practical telegraph between their laboratories to coordinate their experiments on geomagnetism. In 1837 Weber lost his post for opposing the new king of Hannover's interference with the State constitution. Nevertheless, he stayed in Göttingen for a further six years until he was appointed professor at Leipzig. Here, he improved the tangent galvanometer invented by Hermann von Helmholtz and built an electrodynamometer suitable for studying the force produced by one electric current on another.

His main work was the development of a system of units that expressed electrical concepts in terms of mass, length, and time. Gauss had previously done this for magnetism. Since force was expressed in these dimensions, he was then able to find his law of electric force. The principle was not very satisfactory because it did not conserve energy, but with it Weber publicized the view that matter was made up of charged particles held together by the force. This inspired the direction that physics took in the latter half of the century. The units of Gauss and Weber were adopted at an international conference in Paris in 1881. The unit of magnetic flux (the *weber*) is named in his honor.

In 1849 he returned to his post in Göttingen and collaborated with R. H. A. Kohlrausch in measuring the ratio between static and dynamic units of electric charge. This turned out to be the speed of light; this unexpected link between electricity and optics became central to James Clerk Maxwell's great development of electromagnetic field theory.

Wegener, Alfred Lothar

(1880–1930)

GERMAN METEOROLOGIST AND GEOLOGIST

Wegener (**vay**-ge-ner), who was born in Berlin, was educated at the universities of Heidelberg, Innsbruck, and Berlin, where he obtained his doctorate in astronomy in 1905. In 1906 he went on his first meteorological research trip to Greenland and, on his return (1908), was ap-

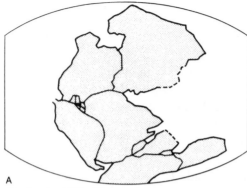

A
Permian about 225 million years ago

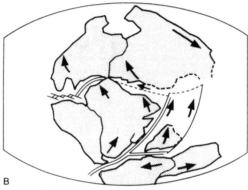

B
Late Triassic about 180 million years ago

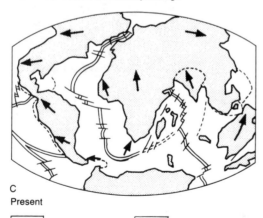

C
Present

| | midoceanic rift ℓ | | island arch-trench |

CONTINENTAL DRIFT Originally the present continents formed a single landmass – a super-continent called "Pangaea." This probably began to break up during the Mesozoic era. The stages are shown above.

pointed to a lectureship in astronomy and meteorology at the University of Marburg. After World War I he moved to a special chair of meteorology and geophysics at the University of Graz, Austria, in 1924. He made further expeditions to Greenland, where he died on his fourth visit.

In 1915 Wegener produced his famous work *Die Enstehung der Kontinente und Ozeane* (translated as *Origin of Continents and Oceans*, 1924), in which he formulated his hypothesis of continental drift. In this he proposed that the continents were once contiguous, forming one super-continent, Pangaea, which began to break up during the Mesozoic Era and drifted apart to form the continents we know today.

To support his theory Wegener produced four main arguments. He first pointed to the obvious correspondence between such opposite shores as those of Atlantic Africa and Latin America. An even better fit was evident if the edges of the continental shelves were matched instead of the coastlines. Secondly he argued that geodetic measurements indicated that Greenland was moving away from Europe. This supported his third argument that a large proportion of the Earth's crust is at two separate levels, the continental and the ocean floor, and that the crust is made of a lighter granite floating on a heavier basalt. His final argument was that there were patterns of similarities between species of the flora and fauna of the continents.

Wegener's theory at first met with considerable hostility. However, in 1929 Arthur Holmes was able to suggest a plausible mechanism to account for continental movement and this, together with advances in geomagnetism and oceanography, was to lead to the full acceptance of Wegener's theory and the creation of the new geophysical discipline of plate tectonics after World War II.

Wegener's meteorological works include *Die Klimate der Geologischen Vorzeit* (1924; Climates in Geological Antiquity) published in association with his father-in-law, Wladimir Köppen.

Weierstrass, Karl Wilhelm Theodor

(1815–1897)

GERMAN MATHEMATICIAN

> A mathematician who is not somewhat of a poet will never be a true mathematician.
> —Attributed remark

> The general theories [of Weierstrass] answer all our possible questions; unfortunately they answer them far too readily, without requiring any effort on our part.
> —H. Lebesgue, *Notes on the History of Mathematics* (1958)

Weierstrass (vI-er-shtrahs or vI-er-strahs), who was born at Ostenfelde in Germany, spent four years at the University of Bonn studying law to please his father. After abandoning law he trained as a school teacher and spent nearly 15 years teaching at elementary schools in obscure German villages. However, he found time to combine his mathematical researches with his school teaching and in 1854 he attracted considerable favorable attention with a memoir on Abelian functions, which he published in Crelle's journal. The fame this work brought him resulted in his obtaining a post as professor of mathematics at the Royal Polytechnic School in Berlin and he soon moved on to the University of Berlin.

Weierstrass's work on Abelian functions is generally considered to be his finest, but he made numerous other contributions to many other areas of mathematics. He was one of the first to make systematic use in analysis of representations of functions by power series. He was a superb and very influential teacher, an excellent fencer, and, unlike many mathematicians, he intensely disliked music. His work in "arithmetizing" analysis led him into a fierce controversy with the constructivist Leopold Kronecker, who thought that Weierstrass's widespread use of nonconstructive proofs and definitions was unsound.

It is to Weierstrass together with Augustin Cauchy that modern analysis is indebted for its high standards of rigor. Weierstrass gave the first truly rigorous definitions of such fundamental analytical concepts as limit, continuity, differentiability, and convergence. He also did very important work in investigating the precise conditions under which infinite series converged. Tests for convergence that he devised are still in use.

Weil, André

(1906–   )

FRENCH MATHEMATICIAN

Weil (vIl) studied at the Ecole Normale Supérieure in his native city of Paris and at the universities of Rome and Göttingen. He held teaching posts in many countries, including posts at the Aligarh Muslim University in India and at the universities of Strasbourg, São Paulo in Brazil, and Chicago. In 1958 he moved to the Institute for Advanced Study at Princeton, where he has been professor emeritus since 1976.

Weil's mathematical work has centered on number theory, algebraic geometry, and group theory. He proved one of the central results in the theory of algebraic fields. His publications include *Foundations of Algebraic Geometry* (1946).

The religious philosopher and mystic Simone Weil, who died in 1943, was his sister.

Weinberg, Steven

(1933–)

AMERICAN PHYSICIST

Born in New York, Weinberg was educated (as was Sheldon Glashow) at the Bronx High School of Science, at Cornell, and at Princeton, where he gained his PhD in 1957. Following appointments at Columbia (1957–59), Berkeley (1959–69), the Massachusetts Institute of Technology (1969–73), and Harvard (1973–83), he was appointed professor of physics at the University of Texas, Austin.

In 1967 Weinberg published a paper, *A Model of Leptons*, which proposed a unification of the weak and electromagnetic interactions since known as the "electroweak theory." In modern particle physics forces operate through the interchange of particles: the electromagnetic force by interchanging photons, and the weak force by the interchange of the W and Z bosons. The claim that the forces had been united into a single force would imply that photons and bosons belonged to the same family of particles. But it is only too clear that this could not be the case; the photon was virtually massless, while the bosons were even more massive than the proton.

The difference was explained by Weinberg in terms of spontaneous symmetry breaking (SSB). At the extremely high temperatures present shortly after the big bang photons and bosons would have been indistinguishable. At some point during the cooling the initial symmetry was spontaneously broken, and during this breakage some particles acquire different properties. Weinberg likens the process to what happens when a piece of iron is cooled below a temperature of 770°C. Below this point the material becomes ferromagnetic and a magnetic field pointing in some unpredictable direction can appear, spontaneously breaking the symmetry between different directions.

The question of the origin of the mass of the bosons remained. Weinberg proposed that the Higgs mechanism, described by Peter Higgs in

1964, though hypothetical, would suffice. As a consequence of Weinberg's theory the existence of "neutral weak currents" was predicted. It has previously been supposed that weak interactions invariably involved a transfer of electric charge carried by the bosons W^+ and W^-. In electromagnetic interactions the photon is exchanged setting up a neutral current. The weak interaction should be able to proceed in the same way with the transfer of the neutral boson Z^0. Neutral weak currents were first observed in 1973, and the bosons of the electroweak theory were detected by Carlo Rubbia at the European Laboratory for Particle Physics in 1983. It was for this work that Weinberg shared the 1979 Nobel Prize for physics with his schoolmate from the Bronx, Sheldon Glashow, and with Abdus Salam.

Weinberg has also worked in the field of cosmology, publishing in 1972 a substantial treatise on the subject, *Gravitation and Cosmology*. This was followed by *The First Three Minutes* (1977), an extremely popular account of the three minutes following "about one hundredth of a second after the beginning when the temperature had cooled to a mere hundred thousand million degrees Kelvin."

In a later work, *Dreams of a Final Theory* (1993), Weinberg argued that in today's theories we are already beginning to catch glimpses of the outlines of a final theory. Whether or not the glimpses are of shadows or something more substantial, Weinberg suggests, depends upon whether the U.S. Government goes ahead and constructs the 8-billion-dollar Superconducting Super Collider in Ellis County, Texas. When complete and running the SSC should be sufficiently powerful to reveal the Higgs boson.

Weismann, August Friedrich Leopold

(1834–1914)

GERMAN BIOLOGIST

> He has done more than any other man to focus attention on the mechanism of inheritance.
> —Citation on the award of the Royal Society's Darwin Medal to Weismann in 1908

Born at Frankfurt am Main in Germany, Weismann (**vIs**-mahn) studied medicine at Göttingen, graduating in 1856. He took several temporary jobs before joining the medical faculty of the University of Freiburg in 1863.

In his early work Weismann made much use of the microscope, but failing eyesight forced him to abandon microscopy for theoretical biology. His microscopic observations, especially those on the origin of the germ cells of hydrozoans, were nevertheless put to good use in the formulation of his theory of the continuity of the germ plasm, which he published in 1886 (English translation, 1893; *The Germ-Plasm: A Theory of Heredity*). Weismann had noted that germ cells can be distinguished from somatic cells early in embryonic development, and from this he visualized the protoplasm of the germ cell (germ plasm) as being passed on unchanged through the generations and therefore responsible for inheritance. Although the body might be modified by environmental effects, the germ plasm – well protected within it – could not be. This insulation of the germ plasm from environmental influences – the so-called *Weismann barrier* – is one of the fundamental tenets of modern Darwinian theory. Weismann himself argued strongly against the Lamarckian theory of the inheritance of acquired characteristics. His publication *Studies in the Theory of Descent* (1882) contained a preface by Darwin.

Weismann closely followed Edouard van Beneden's work on meiosis (reduction division of cells) and arrived at the correct explanation for this process – that a reduction division is necessary to prevent chromosome numbers doubling at fertilization. Weismann became director of the new museum and zoological institute built at Freiburg and remained at the university until his retirement in 1912.

Weizmann, Chaim Azriel

(1874–1952)

RUSSIAN–BRITISH–ISRAELI
CHEMIST

Born in Motol (now in Belarus), the son of a timber merchant, Weizmann (**vIts**-mahn or **wIts**-man) was brought up in an orthodox segregated Jewish community. His early promise was recognized but, owing to difficulties placed in the way of Jews seeking higher education in Russia, Weizmann was sent to Germany instead. In Germany he received a PhD from the University of Freiburg in 1899 and was also converted to the Zionist doctrines of Theodor Herzl. After three years working at the University of Geneva, Weizmann decided to settle in England in 1904, eventually becoming naturalized in 1910.

Weizmann entered Manchester University, first as a student, but in 1907 he was appointed lecturer in biochemistry. Now began his most creative period as a scientist. He started by attempting to develop a synthetic rubber, which produced a need for the alcohol butanol. Butanol was not available commercially so Weizmann began searching for a ferment that would produce as much butanol as he needed from a cheap source. Eventually he came up with the bacterium *Clostridium acetobutylicum*, which turns cooked corn into butanol and acetone.

It happened to be the acetone which made Weizmann's name rather than the butanol as acetone is an important ingredient in the manufacture of cordite. With the start of World War I in 1914, cordite became a valuable commodity and consequently factories were set up in several countries to manufacture acetone by Weizmann's method.

With the commitment to a national home in Palestine clearly stated in the Balfour Declaration of 1917, Weizmann became almost exclusively concerned with Zionist politics. He was apppointed head of the World Zionist Movement in 1920 and of the Jewish Agency for Palestine in 1929. Finally, when Israel was created in 1948, Weizmann was elected its first president.

Weizsäcker, Baron Carl Friedrich von

(1912–   )

GERMAN PHYSICIST

Those reductionists who try to reduce life to physics usually try to reduce it to primitive physics – not to good physics.
—*Theoria to Theory* (1968)

Classical physics has been superseded by quantum theory: quantum theory is verified by experiments. Experiments must be described in terms of classical physics.

—Attributed comment

Weizsäcker (**vIts**-zek-er), who was born at Kiel in Germany, studied at the universities of Berlin, Göttingen, and Leipzig, obtaining his PhD from Leipzig in 1933. Between 1933 and 1945 he taught successively at the universities of Leipzig, Berlin, and Strasbourg. In 1946 he returned to Göttingen as director of physics at the Max Planck Institute where he remained until 1957, when he was appointed professor of philosophy at Hamburg. In 1970 he moved to Starnberg as director of the Max Planck Institute on the Preconditions of Human Life in the Modern World, a post he occupied until his retirement in 1980.

Weizsäcker proposed solutions to two fundamental problems of astrophysics. In 1938 he tackled the problem of how stars like the Sun can continue to radiate colossal amounts of energy for billions of years. Independently of Hans Bethe, he proposed a chain of nuclear-fusion reactions that could proceed at the high temperatures occurring in the dense central cores of stars. In this sequence, called the "carbon cycle," one carbon nucleus and four hydrogen nuclei, or protons, undergo various transformations before ending the cycle as one carbon nucleus and one helium nucleus. The process involves the release of an immense amount of energy that is eventually radiated from the star's surface mainly as heat, light, and ultraviolet radiation. As the stars are rich in hydrogen, it was now clear that they could continue radiating until their core hydrogen was consumed.

In 1944 Weizsäcker proposed a variation of the nebular hypothesis of Pierre Simon de Laplace to account for the origin of the planets. Beginning with the Sun surrounded by a disk of rotating gas he argued that such a mass would experience turbulence and break up into a number of smaller vortices and eddies. Where the eddies met, conditions were supposed to be suitable for planets to form from the continuous aggregation of progressively larger bodies. The system did not, however, explain the crucial point of how the planets managed to acquire so much angular momentum, a property that is conserved and cannot just be created out of nothing. Modifications and additions later proposed by Hannes Alfvén and Fred Hoyle on this issue used forces generated by the Sun's magnetic field as the means of transmitting momentum and won a fair amount of support for the theory.

Welch, William Henry

(1850–1934)

AMERICAN PATHOLOGIST AND BACTERIOLOGIST

Medical education is not completed at the medical school: it is only begun.
—Attributed comment

Welch was born in Norfolk, Connecticut. With a father, grandfather, and great-grandfather all physicians, it is not surprising that he too studied medicine at the College of Physicians and Surgeons, New York. After obtaining his MD in 1875, he spent some time in Germany working with Carl Ludwig and Julius Cohnheim, learning techniques in pathology and microscopic anatomy. On his return to America in 1879 he became professor of pathology and anatomy at the Bellevue Hospital Medical College, New York. He was then appointed professor of pathology at Johns Hopkins University, Baltimore, in 1884 even though the medical school there was not actually opened until 1893. Following his retirement in 1916, Welch founded and became director of the Baltimore School of Hygiene and Public Health attached to Johns Hopkins University. From his second retirement in 1926, he served as professor of the history of medicine at the University until 1931.

Welch did much to establish Johns Hopkins as a major center for medical research. To it, and thus to America also, he introduced the new techniques for the culture and investigation of microbes that he had learned in Germany.

He achieved his own personal triumph in 1892 with the discovery and identification of the organism responsible for gas gangrene, *Clostridium perfringens*, later named *Clostridium welchii*.

Weldon, Walter

(1832–1885)

BRITISH INDUSTRIAL CHEMIST

Weldon, born the son of a manufacturer at Loughborough in Leicestershire, England, traveled to London at the age of 22 to become a journalist. There he founded the short-lived journal *Weldon's Register of Facts and Occurrences in Literature, Science, and Art* (1860–64). Weldon had no formal training in chemistry although he acquired a working knowledge of it. He became interested in how manganese used in the production of chlorine could be recovered. One of the major problems facing heavy chemical industries during the 19th century was the wastage of expensive ingredients, which were converted to unusable waste products.

During the period 1866–69 he took out six patents covering the *Weldon process*. In the Scheele process of chlorine production, hydrochloric acid and manganese dioxide yield chlorine and the waste product, manganese chloride. Weldon's method was to regenerate manganese dioxide by treating the manganese salt with milk of lime (calcium hydroxide in water) and blowing air through it. The liberated manganese dioxide could be pumped straight back into the chlorine stills. This considerably reduced the price of chlorine and quadrupled its production. His achievement was described by the great French chemist Jean Dumas: "By Mr. Weldon's invention, every sheet of paper and every yard of calico has been cheapened throughout the world."

Weldon became a fellow of the Royal Society (1882) and was active in founding the Society of Chemical Industry, becoming its president during the period 1883–84.

Weller, Thomas Huckle

(1915–   )

AMERICAN MICROBIOLOGIST

Born in Ann Arbor, Michigan, Weller was educated at the University of Michigan, where his father was professor of pathology, and at Harvard, where he gained his MD in 1940. After serving in the U.S. Army Medical Corps from 1942 until 1945 Weller worked with John Enders at the Children's Medical Center, Boston. In 1954 he returned to Harvard as professor of tropical public health, becoming professor emeritus in 1985.

In 1948 Weller, in collaboration with Franklin Neva, succeeded in growing the German measles (rubella) virus in tissue culture. They later went on to grow and isolate the chickenpox virus in a culture of human embryonic muscle and skin. With Enders and Frederick Robbins, Weller successfully applied the same method to the culture of poliomyelitis virus. By making adequate supplies of polio virus available to laboratory workers, this opened the way for the development of a successful polio vaccine.

For this work Weller shared the 1954 Nobel Prize for physiology or medicine with Enders and Robbins.

Wells, Horace

(1815–1848)

AMERICAN DENTIST

Wells was born in Hartford, Vermont, and studied dentistry in Boston. Later, while in practice, he formed a brief partnership in Boston with William Morton.

In 1844 he attended a demonstration of the effects of nitrous oxide (laughing gas) staged by a visiting showman. Like Crawford Long before him, Wells noted that although the subjects fell about frequently they did not seem to feel their bumps and bangs. Wells quickly saw the significance of this and persuaded the showman to administer the gas to him while a colleague, John Riggs, removed Wells's troublesome wisdom tooth.

In January 1845, considerably excited by his discovery, Wells informed Morton and the well-known Boston chemist Charles Jackson of his success, asking them to use their influence to arrange a demonstration for the surgeons of Boston. In early 1845 Wells was invited to demonstrate his invention before the leading Boston surgeon, John Collins Warren. He presumably, however, got his dosage wrong for the student who volunteered for an extraction seemed to scream in pain as soon as his tooth was touched.

Wells gave up his practice and took to selling first canaries, later shower baths, to the citizens of Connecticut. However, when, in 1846, Morton achieved success with ether Wells made extravagant claims for his priority, which he could never hope to establish.

Few of the early workers in anesthesia gained from their labor and many were to lose much. Of these Wells lost the most. In 1848, addicted to chloroform and deranged, he threw vitriol in the face of a New York prostitute. Arrested and imprisoned in the Tombs of New York, he inhaled some chloroform and committed suicide.

Wendelin, Gottfried

(1580–1667)

BELGIAN ASTRONOMER

Wendelin (**vent**-e-lin), who was born at Herck-la-Ville in Belgium and educated at Tournai and Louvain, became an official at Tournai cathedral. He was much respected in his time as an astronomer, being referred to as the Ptolemy of his age. Wendelin was an early Copernican who has been credited with attempting to determine the solar parallax, in 1626. He is also remembered as the teacher of Marin Mersenne, Pierre Gassendi, and Christiaan Huygens.

Wenzel, Carl Friedrich

(*c.* 1740–1793)

GERMAN CHEMIST

Wenzel (**vent**-sel) was born in Dresden, Germany, the son of a bookbinder. He studied surgery and medicine at Amsterdam and served as a ship's surgeon in the Dutch naval service. He was made chemist to the Freiberg mines in 1780, becoming chief assessor in 1784. In 1786 he became metallurgical chemist at the Meissen porcelain factory in Saxony.

Wenzel published, in 1777–82, his *Lehre von der Verwandtschaft der Körper* (Principles of the Affinity of Solids), which went through three editions. In it he tackled, among other problems, that of the affinity of substances for each other. He measured the varying rates at which an acid will dissolve cylinders of different metals and tried to use these figures to calculate their relative attractive forces.

Werner, Abraham Gottlob

(1750–1817)

GERMAN MINERALOGIST AND GEOLOGIST

> It is Werner's great merit, to have drawn attention to this sequence [of rock formations] and to have looked at it throughout with correct eyes...To determine how things were millions of years ago...is not interesting, the real interest being confined to that which is now in existence – the system of different formations.
> —G. W. F. Hegel, *Encyclopädie der philosophischen Wissenschaften* (1830; Encyclopedia of Philosophical Sciences)

Werner (**vair**-ner) was born in the traditional mining town of Wehrau, which is now in Poland. Most of his ancestors had worked in some position or other in the industry and his father was inspector of the iron foundry at the town. He began work as an assistant to his father before entering the new Freiberg Mining Academy in 1769. He studied at the University of Leipzig (1771–75) before returning to teach at the Freiberg Mining Academy. There he established his neptunist views on the aqueous origin of rocks and attracted a considerable following.

Werner's neptunian theory explained the surface of the Earth and the distribution and sequence of rocks in terms of a deluge, which had covered the entire Earth, including the highest mountains. The rock formations were laid down when the flood subsided in a universal and specific sequence. The first layer consisted of primitive rocks, such as granite, gneiss, and slates, and contained no fossils. The next strata (the transitional) consisted of shales and graywacke and contained fossilized fish. Above this were the limestones, sandstones, and chalks of the secondary rocks and then the gravels and sands of the alluvial strata. Finally, after the waters had completely disappeared, local volcanic activity produced lavas and other deposits.

However, this fivefold scheme, while no doubt applicable in Werner's region of Saxony, presented great difficulties outside the area. There was much that Werner could not explain, such as where the enormous flood had gone to and the presence of large basalt tracts in Europe, which were found in areas free of volcanoes. For many years Werner's theories eclipsed those of the plutonists, led by James Hutton, who emphasized the origin of igneous rocks from molten material. But as knowledge of the strata of Europe increased it became clear that there were too many regions in which Werner's sequence bore no relation to reality.

Yet neptunism certainly had its attractions, with Werner's disciples distributed throughout Europe. The advantages of the theory were that it was theologically acceptable, it was simple, and it showed how the Earth could be formed in the short time available.

Werner was also a mineralogist and he constructed a new classification of minerals. There was a major split among 18th-century mineralogists as to whether minerals should be classified according to their external form (the natural method) or by their chemical composition (the chemical method). Werner finally adopted, in 1817, a mixed set of criteria by which he divided minerals into four main classes – earthy, saline, combustible, and metallic.

Werner, Alfred

(1866–1919)

FRENCH CHEMIST

He has thrown fresh light on old problems and opened new fields of research, particularly in inorganic chemistry.
—Citation on the award of the Nobel Prize for chemistry to Werner in 1913

Werner (**vair**-ner or **wer**-ner) was born the son of an ironworker at Mulhouse in France. He was educated at the University of Zurich, where he gained his PhD in 1890. After a year in Paris working with Marcellin Berthelot he returned to Zurich, where he was appointed professor of chemistry in 1895.

In 1905 Werner produced a work, later translated into English as *New Ideas on Inorganic Chemistry* (1911), which was to revolutionize inorganic chemistry and earn him the Nobel Prize for chemistry in 1913. Although the ideas introduced by August Kekulé had contributed greatly to organic chemistry, attempts to apply his valence theory to in-

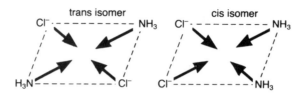

COORDINATION COMPOUNDS   *Simple coordination compounds according to Werner.*

organic molecules were much less successful. Many metals appeared to show variable valence and form complex compounds.

Werner proposed distinguishing between a primary and a secondary valence of a metal. The primary was concerned with binding ions, while the secondary valence applied not only to atoms but also to molecules, which can have an independent existence. Certain metals, such as cobalt and platinum, were capable through their secondary valences of joining to themselves a certain number of atoms or molecules. These were termed by Werner "coordination compounds" and the maximum number of atoms (or "ligands" as he called them) that can be joined to the central metal is its coordination number. This led Werner to make very detailed predictions about the existence of certain hitherto unsuspected isomers. He managed to resolve optical isomers of an inorganic compound in 1911.

Wernicke, Carl

(1848–1905)

GERMAN NEUROLOGIST AND PSYCHIATRIST

Wernicke (**vair**-ni-ke) born at Tarnowitz (now Tarnowskie Gory in Poland) and studied medicine at the University of Breslau, qualifying in psychiatry in 1875. He later taught neurology and psychiatry in various institutions in Berlin, Breslau, and Halle.

In 1874 he published his *Der aphasische Symptomencomplex* (The Complex of Aphasic Symptoms) in which he described a new type of aphasia. In 1861 Paul Broca had shown that damage to a particular part of the frontal cerebral cortex produced an aphasia characterized by abnormally slow and labored speech but, he went on to show in 1865, only if the damage was located in the left-hand side of the brain.

Wernicke identified a second area, also in the left part of the brain, but this time in the temporal lobe, damage to which had no effect on the mode of articulation but did seem to effect comprehension. This allowed him to define, rather neatly, three types of aphasia. Damage to Wernicke's area would produce sensory aphasia characterized by difficulty in comprehending, while damage to Broca's area would produce motor aphasia, i.e., difficulty in articulating. As he assumed the two areas to be connected, damage to the connecting area should produce a third type of disturbance later known as conduction aphasia. It was thus the work of Wernicke that opened up the modern study of the various aphasias.

Wernicke also described, in 1881, a condition involving disorders of gait and consciousness and paralysis of the eye muscles, later to be known as *Wernicke's encephalopathy* and shown to be due to thiamine deficiency.

West, Harold Dadford

(1904–1974)

AMERICAN BIOCHEMIST

West was educated at the University of Illinois, Urbana, graduating in 1925 and gaining his PhD in 1937. After working initially at Morris Brown College, Atlanta, he moved to Meharry Medical College, Nashville, in 1927. West spent his entire career at Meharry serving as professor of biochemistry from 1938 until his retirement in 1973, apart from a break between 1952 and 1963, when he held the position of college president.

Although West worked in a number of fields and conducted research on the biochemistry of various bacilli, the B vitamins, and antibiotics, he is best known for his studies of the amino acids. In particular it was West who first synthesized the essential amino acid threonine.

Westinghouse, George

(1846–1914)

AMERICAN INVENTOR

Westinghouse, who was born at Central Bridge in New York, served in both the army and the navy during the American Civil War. After the war he began to design and patent several devices, the most important of which was an air brake for trains, patented in 1869. This was widely used throughout Europe and America and later formed the basis of a standardized air-brake system, also devised by Westinghouse, that could be used on different types of train. Later he applied his knowledge of hydraulics to the development of an electrical and compressed-air railroad signaling system.

In the 1880s Westinghouse played a central role in the development of energy-supply systems. Not only did he design equipment for the safe piping of natural gas, but he was also instrumental in the introduction of alternating-current (a.c.) electricity supply to America. At this time a.c. electricity, which permits voltage changes by transformers, was being developed in Europe, but the American electrical systems were direct current (d.c.). Westinghouse imported and improved European a.c. generators and transformers and set up an a.c. electrical supply in Pittsburgh.

Westinghouse founded, in 1886, the Westinghouse Electric Company, which successfully used the patents that it received or bought to develop a profitable business. Although he gave up all connections with his companies a few years before his death, Westinghouse's name has continued to be associated with developments in energy technology, particularly in the nuclear-power industry.

Wexler, Nancy

(1946–)

AMERICAN CLINICAL
PSYCHOLOGIST

Wexler was born in New York, the daughter of the well-known psychoanalyst Milton Wexler. She was educated at Harvard and the University of Michigan where she completed her doctorate. In 1968 her mother developed Huntington's disease (HD), an untreatable and incurable condition that leads inevitably to the destruction of the mind. The disease usually appears between the ages of 35 and 50 and, as it is caused by a dominant gene, Nancy and her sister had a 50% chance of inheriting the condition. Milton Wexler's response was to set up the Hereditary Disease Foundation to stimulate and organize research into Huntington's disease and other hereditary complaints.

After completing her doctorate, Nancy Wexler moved to Columbia University as professor of clinical psychology. Following the death of her mother in 1978 she began to devote more of her time to work on HD. In 1981 she heard from a Venezuelan biochemist, Americo Negrette, of an extended family on the shores of Lake Maracaibo in which HD was rife. Wexler sought to trace the gene through the family tree, which began with Maria Concepcion and a presumed encounter with a European seaman in about 1800. Of her 9,000 living descendants Wexler traced 371 with HD and found 1,200 with a 50% chance of contracting the disease and a further 2,400 with a 25% chance. Wexler realized that, given the current state of molecular biology, the material she had gathered could be used to identify the gene responsible for HD.

The key step in this process had been the discovery by Ray White and his colleagues of RFLPs, DNA sequences that could be used as genetic markers. Blood samples were taken and sent immediately to James Gusella at Massachusetts General Hospital and he began what he thought would be a lengthy search for the appropriate RFLP. But Gusella was extremely lucky and the twelfth probe he tried seemed to be linked with HD. Further work established that the gene was on the short arm of chromosome 4.

Wexler and Gusella announced their results in 1983. They continued to home in on the gene and by 1992 had restricted it to a segment of 500,000 bases. More precisely, a stretch of DNA had been identified in which the nucleotide triplet C–A–G is repeated. In people without HD there seem to be 11–34 copies of the triplet, while those affected by HD have 42–86 triplets.

Weyl, Hermann

(1885–1955)

GERMAN MATHEMATICIAN

> Symmetry, as wide or as narrow as you may define its meaning, is one idea by which man through the ages has tried to comprehend and create order, beauty, and perfection.
> —*Symmetry*

Born at Elmshorn in Germany, Weyl (vIl) studied at Göttingen, where he was one of David Hilbert's most oustanding students. He became a coworker of Hilbert, who influenced his particular interests and his general outlook on mathematics. Weyl taught at the Federal Institute of Technology in Zurich from 1913, and this too had a decisive influence in directing his mathematical interests through the presence there of Albert Einstein. In 1930 he returned to Göttingen to take up the chair vacated by Hilbert. With the Nazis' rise to power in 1933, Weyl, with many other members of the Göttingen scientific community, went into exile in America. Weyl found a post at the Institute for Advanced Study in Princeton along with other exiles, such as Einstein and Kurt Gödel.

Weyl's mathematical interests, like those of Hilbert, were exceptionally wide, ranging from mathematical physics to the foundations of mathematics. He worked on two areas of pure mathematics: group theory and the theory of Hilbert space and operators, which, although developed for purely mathematical purposes, later turned out to be precisely the mathematical framework needed for the revolutionary physical ideas of quantum mechanics. Weyl also wrote a number of books on the theory of groups and he was particularly interested in symmetry and its relation to group theory. One of his most important results in group theory was a key theorem about the application of representations to Lie algebras. Weyl's work on Hilbert space had grown out of his interest in Hilbert's work on integral equations and operators. The theory of Hilbert space (infinite-dimensional space) was recognized by Erwin Schrödinger and Walter Heisenberg in the mid-1920s as the necessary unifying systematization of their theories of quantum mechanics.

Weyl's contact with Einstein at Zurich was responsible for an interest in the mathematics of relativity, and especially Riemannian geometry, which plays a central role. Weyl initiated the whole project of trying to generalize Riemannian geometry. He himself worked chiefly on the geometry of affinely connected spaces, but this was only one of many generalizations that resulted from his work. Weyl also did similar work on generalizing and refining the basic concepts of differential geometry. All this work was to be of importance for relativity. Weyl's views on relativity were expounded in his book *Raum-Zeit-Materie* (1919; Space-Time-Matter).

Weyl, like his teacher Hilbert, was always interested in the philosophical aspects of mathematics. However, in contrast to Hilbert, his general attitude was similar to that of L. E. J. Brouwer with whom he shared constructivist leanings developed from work in analysis. Weyl expounded his philosophical ideas in another book, *Philosophy of Mathematics and Natural Sciences* (1949). Unlike Brouwer, however, Weyl was less rigorous in avoiding nonconstructive mathematics, and doubtless his interest in physics contributed to this.

Wharton, Thomas

(1614–1673)

ENGLISH PHYSICIAN

A man of great learning and experience, and of equal freedom to communicate it.
—Izaak Walton, *The Compleat Angler* (1653)

Wharton was born at Winson-on-Tees in England and educated at the universities of Cambridge and Oxford, obtaining his MD from Oxford in 1647. He later spent much of his life in private practice in London, being appointed in 1659 physician at St. Thomas's Hospital. During the Great Plague (1665) he remained in London, unlike most physicians, to treat his patients.

In 1656 he published *Adenographia* (Textbook on Glands), the first comprehensive survey of the glands of the body. In it he named the thyroid, from the Greek "thyreos," a shield. He also described, for the first time, the duct of the submaxillary salivary gland, since known as *Wharton's duct*.

Wheatstone, Sir Charles

(1802–1875)

BRITISH PHYSICIST

After a private education in his native city of Gloucester, Wheatstone began business in London as a musical-instrument maker (1823). His early scientific researches were in acoustics and optics and his contributions were numerous. Thus he devised a "kaleidophone" to illustrate harmonic motions of different periods; he suggested a stereoscope (1838) that, using two pictures in dissimilar perspective, could give the appearance of solidity; he showed that every Chladni figure was the resultant of two or more sets of isochronous parallel vibrations; and he demonstrated how minute quantities of metals could be detected from the spectral lines produced by electric sparks.

Perhaps his most important work, however, was to produce, with William Cooke, the first practical electric telegraph system. In 1837, in conjunction with the new London and Birmingham Railway Company, Cooke and Wheatstone installed a demonstration line about one mile long. Improvements rapidly followed and, with the needs of the railroads providing the impetus and finance, by 1852 more than 4,000 miles of telegraph lines were in operation throughout Britain. Wheatstone constructed the first printing telegraph (1841) and a single-needle telegraph (1845). He made contributions to the development of submarine telegraphy and to dynamos. The *Wheatstone bridge*, a device for comparing electrical resistances, was not invented by Wheatstone but brought to notice by him.

Wheatstone was appointed professor of experimental philosophy at King's College, London, in 1834 and was knighted in 1868. At his death he held about 40 awards and distinctions. He was prolific in his inventions and had an extraordinary ability to turn his theoretical knowledge to practical account.

Wheeler, John Archibald

(1911–)

AMERICAN THEORETICAL
PHYSICIST

Time is what prevents everything from happening at once.
—*American Journal of Physics* (1978)

We shall call this completely collapsed gravitational object a "black hole."
—Address given at a conference on relativity, 1967

Born in Jacksonville, Florida, Wheeler was educated at Johns Hopkins University, where he obtained his PhD in physics in 1933. After spending the period 1933–35 in Copenhagen working with Niels Bohr, he returned to America to take up a teaching position at the University of North Carolina. In 1938 he went to Princeton, where he served as professor of physics from 1947 until his move to the University of Texas in 1976 to become professor of physics. He retired in 1986.

Wheeler has been active in theoretical physics. One of the problems tackled by him has been the search for a unified field theory. His earlier papers on the subject were collected in 1962 in his *Geometrodynamics*. It was here that he introduced the geon (gravitational–electromagnetic entity), with which he aimed to achieve the unification of the two fields. He also collaborated with Richard Feynman in two papers in 1945 and 1949 on the important concept of action at a distance. They formulated a problem that arises when it is accepted that such action cannot take place instantaneously. If X and Y are at rest and one light-minute apart, then any electromagnetic signal emitted by X will reach Y one minute later. This is described by saying X acts on Y by a retarded effect. But by Newton's third law, to each action there corresponds an opposite and equal reaction. This must mean that from Y to X there should also be an advanced effect acting backward in time. Feynman and Wheeler demonstrated how the advance wave could be eliminated from the model to account for the fact that the universe displays only retarded effects.

Wheeler also made important contributions to nuclear physics. With Niels Bohr he put forward an explanation of the mechanism of nuclear fission. He joined the Los Alamos group exploring the possibility of producing an explosive device using heavy hydrogen in 1949–50. Wheeler has provided a popular account of his work in his *Journey into Gravity and Spacetime* (1990); he has also published his autobiography, *At Home in the Universe* (1993).

Whewell, William

(1794–1866)

BRITISH SCIENTIST, HISTORIAN, AND PHILOSOPHER

We need very much a name to describe a cultivator of science in general. I should incline to call him a scientist.
—The first recorded use of the word.
The Philosophy of the Inductive Sciences, Vol. 1 (1840)

Whewell was the son of a master carpenter from Lancaster in northwest England; his talents were recognized by a local schoolmaster. In 1812 he won a £50 exhibition to Trinity College, Cambridge, where he remained for the rest of his life – as a fellow from 1817 and as master from 1841 until his death in 1866 from a horse-riding accident. He also served as professor of mineralogy (1828–32) and as professor of moral philosophy (from 1838).

Whewell was one of the great Victorian polymaths, the subject of Sydney Smith's aphorism that "Science was his forte, omniscience his foible." He published works on dynamics, mineralogy, chemistry, architecture, moral philosophy, history, political economy, geometry, and the theory of the tides, as well as translating German verse and Greek philosophy into English.

His most original scientific work can be found in the 14 memoirs on tides published between 1833 and 1850. Here he collected a vast amount of data in an attempt to establish cotidal lines (points of simultaneous high tide). He also investigated the diurnal inequality, that is, the differences found between the heights and times of tides at the same place on the same day. Whewell found the whole system so complex that he despaired of ever constructing a general theory of the tides.

Two other works of Whewell are still read today, namely, his *History of the Inductive Sciences* (3 vols., 1837) and his *Philosophy of the Inductive Sciences* (3 vols., 1840). In the former he presented the growth of science as the development of theories of ever-increasing generality. He spoke of development in terms of a prelude in which old theories began to face difficulties, an inductive epoch where new theories were established, and a final sequel in which the new theory was refined and applied to nature.

As a philosopher of science Whewell dismissed the view that induction was merely reasoning from the particular to the general. It also involves a process of "colligation" in which ideas are best understood by being placed in a common framework. In addition he spoke of the highest form of induction, "consilience," in which inductions from different fields are united, as when Newton demonstrated that the same law could describe both the vertical fall of an apple and the circular orbit of the moon.

Whewell has also left a permanent mark on the language of science. In 1834 he proposed to Michael Faraday the terms "anode" and "cathode" to distinguish between negative and positive electrodes. Other words proposed to Faraday include "anion," "cation," "ion," and "dielectric." To Charles Lyell he offered the terms "Eocene," "Miocene," and "Pliocene" to describe Tertiary epochs. As a final contribution Whewell in 1840 introduced into English the two terms "physicist" and "scientist."

Whipple, Fred Lawrence

(1906–   )

AMERICAN ASTRONOMER

Born in Red Oak, Iowa, Whipple graduated from the University of California in Los Angeles in 1927 and obtained his PhD from Berkeley in 1931. He then moved to Harvard where he became professor of astronomy in 1945, Philips Professor of Astronomy in 1950, and director of the Smithsonian Astrophysical Observatory from 1955 until his retirement in 1973.

He described his research as centering on "physical processes in the evolution of the solar system" and produced in this field a much admired work, *Earth, Moon and Planets* (1941 and many subsequent editions).

Whipple is also well known for his work on comets. In 1950 he proposed an icy-nucleus model in which he described the nucleus of a comet as a "dirty snowball," made from a mixture of water ice and dust, plus carbon dioxide, carbon monoxide, methane, and ammonia ices, and only becoming active when passing close to the Sun. The main advantage of this model is that it can account for such distinctive features of comets as their orbital motion. It had been long known that some comets, such as Encke's, persist in returning earlier than Newtonian theory would predict while others, such as Halley's, arrive over four days later than expected. Whipple proposed that solar radiation would cause the ices on the outside of the cometary nucleus to evaporate, leaving a thin insulating layer of dust particles, and that this would set up a delayed jet reaction. The radiation has the effect of pushing further out those comets that are rotating in the same direction as their orbit. This will increase their orbit and delay their return. The radiation will produce a drag force on those comets rotating counter to their orbit, causing them to drift in toward the Sun, reducing their period and thus hastening their return.

As there should be no preferred direction of rotation, Whipple predicted that about half the comets should appear to be retarded and half accelerated in their orbit, an effect since confirmed.

Whipple, George Hoyt

(1878–1976)

AMERICAN PHYSICIAN AND
PHYSIOLOGIST

Whipple, born the son of a physician in Ashland, New Hampshire, was educated at Yale and Johns Hopkins University, where he obtained his MD in 1905. After working at the University of California he moved in

1921 to the University of Rochester, where he served as professor of pathology until his retirement in 1955.

Whipple began his research career by working on bile pigments but went on to study the formation and breakdown of the blood pigment, hemoglobin, of which bile pigments are the breakdown products. To do this he bled dogs until he had reduced their hemoglobin level to a third, then measured the rate of hemoglobin regeneration. He soon noted that this rate varied with the diet of the dogs and by 1923 reported that liver in the diet produced a significant increase in hemoglobin production.

It was this work that led George Minot and William Murphy to develop a successful treatment for pernicious anemia and earned all three men the Nobel Prize for physiology or medicine in 1934.

Whiston, William

(1667–1752)

BRITISH MATHEMATICIAN AND GEOLOGIST

Whiston, the son of a parish priest from Norton in England, was educated at Cambridge University, where he came to the attention of Isaac Newton. He was selected, on Newton's recommendation, to succeed him as Lucasian Professor of Mathematics (1703) and to edit his *Arithmetica universalis* (1707; Universal Arithmetic). In 1710 he was dismissed from the university for his unorthodox religious belief in the Arian heresy, after which time he supported himself by giving public lectures on popular science.

Whiston's chief scientific work, *A New Theory of the Earth* (1696), was praised by Newton and by John Locke. In this Whiston followed the tradition recently established by Thomas Burnet in attempting to explain biblical events, such as the Creation, scientifically. The Flood, he believed, was caused by a comet pasing close to the Earth on 28 November 2349 BC. This put stress on the Earth's crust, causing it to crack and allow the water to escape and flood the Earth.

White, Gilbert

(1720–1793)

BRITISH NATURALIST

A more delightful, or more original work than Mr. White's *History of Selborne* has seldom been published...The book is not a compilation from former publications, but the result of many years' attentive observations to nature itself, which are told not only with the precision of a philosopher, but with that happy selection of circumstances, which mark the poet.
—*The Topographer* (1789)

White was educated at Oxford University but returned to his native village of Selborne to become a curate. He soon began making detailed observations on the flora and fauna in his garden and the surrounding countryside, concentrating particularly on the behavior and habitats of birds. His letters to friends on these matters provided the material for his book *The Natural History and Antiquities of Selborne* (1789), which collected together more than 20 years' work.

The book won immediate recognition from contemporary naturalists who praised White's meticulous observations and scientific procedure. Many important discoveries were recorded, such as the addition of the noctule bat and the harvest mouse to the list of British mammals. He also recognized the three different kinds of British leaf warblers by the differences in their song and recorded the migration of swallows.

The book has become a natural-history classic, going through several editions and still selling well today.

White, Ray

(1943–   )

AMERICAN MOLECULAR BIOLOGIST

Born in Eugene, Oregon, the son of a dentist, White originally intended to follow a medical career. However, while a student at the University of Oregon he became more interested in molecular biology and genetics. Consequently he moved to the Massachusetts Institute of Technology, where he completed his PhD in molecular biology in 1971. After a postdoctoral period at Stanford, he joined the staff of Massachusetts University Medical School, Worcester, in 1975. In 1980 he was appointed to the faculty at the Hughes Medical Institute, Utah.

During the 1970s scientists had begun to ask whether ways could be found to determine which of the 100,000 human genes scattered along 23 chromosomes are responsible for a large number of inherited diseases. A possible answer was proposed to White in 1978 by David Botstein. Biologists knew that while most of the sequences of nucleotides found in human DNA were identical, there were also stretches which varied from person to person. If "polymorphisms" of this kind were widely scattered throughout the genome, then it was possible that some of them could be reasonably close to a defective gene and that the presence or absence of the polymorphism could be used to indicate the presence or absence of a defective gene. As the polymorphisms varied in length, and as they were normally isolated by the use of a restriction enzyme, they soon became known as restriction fragment length polymorphisms, or RFLPs, pronounced "**rif**-lips."

The first test of the theory would be to see if RFLPs were actually collectable. White began the search in collaboration with Arlene Wyman in 1979. They began by eliminating sequences of repetitious DNA widely scattered throughout the genome. After much effort they were left with five unique sequences of about 15–20,000 bases. Complementary copies of unique sequences were made (cDNA) and mixed with a donor's DNA. If the donor also carried the unique RFLP, the cDNA, radioactively labeled, would coordinate with the RFLP and be easily detectable. White and Wyman worked with blood cells from 56 subjects and identified eight distinct RFLPs.

Having shown that RFLPs could be found, it remained for White to show that they could be used as genetic markers. If the RFLP was close enough to a gene it would be inherited along with the gene. This was shown in 1981 when Davies and Murray at St. Mary's Hospital, London, discovered a RFLP linked with Duchenne muscular dystrophy on the X chromosome. Since then several other links have been identified.

The situation was sufficiently promising, White argued, to make it worthwhile constructing a complete RFLP map of the human genome. White and his colleagues in Utah spent much of the 1980s on this project. By 1988 White could announce that "preliminary maps for most of the human chromosome" had been completed. He then began work upon a higher resolution map, which would indicate the location of RFLPs and genes with greater precision.

Whitehead, Alfred North

(1861–1947)

BRITISH MATHEMATICIAN AND
PHILOSOPHER

A science which hesitates to forget its found-
ers, is lost.
—Attributed remark. Quoted by Alan L.
Mackay in *A Dictionary of Scientific
Quotations* (1991)

Whitehead, who was born at Ramsgate on the south coast of England, obtained his PhD from Cambridge University in 1884. For the next few years he taught there and met Bertrand Russell, who was one of his students and with whom he was later to collaborate. Whitehead was one of a growing section of philosophers of science who criticized the deterministic and materialistic views prevalent in 19th-century science. The main theme of this critique was that scientific theories were patterns derived from our way of measuring and perceiving the world and not innate properties of the underlying reality. While in Cambridge his mathematical work reflected this viewpoint, developed in his book *Treatise of Universal Algebra* (1898), which treated algebraic structures as objects worthy of study in their own right, independent of their relationship to real quantities. In 1910 he published, with Russell, the first volume of the vast *Principia Mathematica* (Mathematical Principles) which was an attempt, inspired by the work of Gottlob Frege and Guiseppe Peano, to clarify the conceptual foundations of mathematics using the formal methods of symbolic logic.

Whitehead then moved to London, where he taught at University College and later became professor at Imperial College. Here he developed his action-at-a-distance theory of relativity, which challenged Einstein's field-theoretic viewpoint but never gained wide acceptance. In 1924 he emigrated to America and worked at Harvard, developing his antimechanistic philosophy of science and a system of metaphysics, until he retired in 1937.

Whittaker, Sir Edmund Taylor

(1873–1956)

BRITISH MATHEMATICIAN AND PHYSICIST

Born at Birkdale in northwest England, Whittaker studied at Cambridge and taught there from 1896. In 1906 he became Astronomer Royal for Ireland. From 1912 until 1946 he was professor of mathematics at Edinburgh.

Whittaker was primarily a mathematical physicist and was appropriately much interested in the theory of differential equations. In this field he obtained the general solution of Laplace's equation in three dimensions. This led Whittaker to finding the general integral representation of any harmonic function, which greatly simplified potential theory as well as opening up new areas of research. He also did notable work on the theory of automorphic functions. One of Whittaker's other great interests was in relativity theory. He wrote a number of influential textbooks on analysis, on quantum mechanics, and on dynamics, including his *History of the Theories of Aether and Electricity* (1910; revised 1941 and 1951), a comprehensive history of theories of electromagnetism and atomism. Whittaker was known as a superb and highly effective teacher. He was also a deeply religious man with an interest in the philosophical and religious importance of contemporary physics and wrote a number of books on these questions.

Whittington, Harry Blackmore

(1916–)

BRITISH GEOLOGIST

Whittington was born at Handsworth in Yorkshire, England. After gaining his PhD from the University of Birmingham, he spent the years of World War II teaching in the Far East, first at the University of Rangoon, Burma, and for the rest of the war at Ginling College, West China. He returned to Birmingham in 1945 but moved to Harvard as curator of vertebrate paleontology at the Museum of Comparative Zoology. In 1966 Whittington left America for the post of Woodward Professor of Geology at Cambridge, a position he held until his retirement in 1983.

Since the early 1960s Whittington has devoted the bulk of his time to the study of the Burgess Shale fossils, discovered and described by C. D. Walcott earlier in the century. He made two expeditions to the site in 1966 and 1967 and recruited two assistants, Derek Briggs and Simon Conway Morris, to help him reexamine the entire collection.

Whittington's first report, published in 1971, was devoted to *Marella splendens*, identified by Walcott as a trilobite, a primitive and long-extinct arthropod. Whittington, after four years' work on several thousand specimens, found too many uncharacteristic trilobite features to be happy with Walcott's classification. He compromised by calling it *Trilobitoidea* (trilobite-like). His suspicion that many of Walcott's arthropods had been wrongly classified were increased when Whittington next looked at the subject of his 1975 monograph, *Opabinia*. As he could find no jointed appendages it was clear to Whittington that *Opabinia* was not an arthropod. What its affinities were, however, remained uncertain.

By the time he came to deal in 1985 with *Anamalocaris* he could state confidently that it was no arthropod but "the representative of a hitherto unknown phylum." Whittington and his colleagues went on to identify ten invertebrate genera "that have so far defied all attempts to link them with known phyla."

Whittington's labors thus presented a dramatic new picture. The Cambrian is now seen as a period in which many new complex species suddenly appear. Further, relatively few of these seemingly advanced groups lasted beyond the Cambrian. The full significance of Whittington's work has yet to be worked out.

Whittle, Sir Frank

(1907–1996)

BRITISH AERONAUTICAL ENGINEER

Jet-propelled fighter aircraft have successfully passed experimental tests and will soon be in production...The greatest credit should be given to Group Captain Whittle for this fine performance, for it was his genius and energy that made this possible.

—*The Engineer*, 14 January 1944

Whittle, the son of a mechanic from Coventry in the English Midlands, joined the Royal Air Force as an apprentice in 1923. He was trained at the RAF College, Cranwell, and Cambridge University, where he studied mechanical sciences (1934–37).

While still a student at Cranwell, Whittle had expressed his prediction that there would soon emerge a demand for high-speed high-altitude aircraft. He recognized the inadequacies of the conventional airscrew to meet these needs and took out his first patent for the turbojet engine in 1930. He gained little government backing but with the assistance of friends he formed, in 1936, the company Power Jets. By the following year, his first engine, the W1, was ready for testing. With the advent of World War II government funds were rapidly awarded to develop this and the jet engine was fitted to the specially built Gloster E28/39 aircraft. It made its first flight on 15 May 1941 and by 1944 was in service with the RAF.

For his work Whittle was made a fellow of the Royal Society in 1947, knighted in 1948, and awarded a tax-free gift of £100,000 by the British government. He left the RAF in 1948 and served as a consultant with the British Overseas Airways Corporation (1948–52), the Shell Group (1952–57), and Bristol Siddeley Engines (1961–70). In 1977 Whittle accepted the post of research professor at the U.S. Naval Academy, Annapolis.

Whitworth, Sir Joseph

(1803–1887)

BRITISH ENGINEER

The son of a schoolmaster and congregational minister from Stockport in northwest England, Whitworth left school at fourteen to work with his uncle, a cotton spinner, in Derbyshire. He soon gained an intimate knowledge of the available machinery and was immediately struck by its crudity. Four years later he moved to London to gain further experience with machine tools working for Henry Maudslay (1771–1831), one of the great engineers of the day. During this period Whitworth also worked on the mechanical calculating machine being constructed by Charles Babbage.

In 1833 he returned to Manchester to set up his own machine-tool factory and at once sought to introduce new standards of accuracy into tool manufacture. He introduced sets of standard gauges and measures and these soon gained wide use. By 1859 he had built a measuring machine capable of detecting a difference of one millionth of an inch.

Earlier, in 1841, he had argued for a uniform system of screw threads. Before Whitworth, nuts and bolts were so individually matched that once separated they might as well be thrown away. Whitworth proposed that bolts of a given size would have threads of identical pitch and depth and a common thread angle of 55°. The Whitworth system rapidly became the standard for British engineering. Unfortunately the United States adopted in 1864 a different system based on a thread angle of 60° as proposed by William Sellers. Despite the difficulties imposed on the

Allied forces in two world wars the two standards persisted until 1948 when the Unified Thread System was adopted by the United States, Canada, and Britain. It incorporated features of both the Whitworth and Sellers systems.

In the wake of the Crimean War Whitworth was invited by the War Office to redesign the British army's ordnance. After much research and testing he produced a rifle with a smaller bore, a hexagonal barrel, an elongated projectile, and a more rapid twist. The War Office rejected Whitworth's work, although many features of Whitworth's designs subsequently found their way into the army's ordnance.

Whytt, Robert

(1714–1766)

BRITISH PHYSICIAN AND
ANATOMIST

Whytt graduated in arts at St. Andrews University and then studied medicine at the university in his native city of Edinburgh. He also spent some time pursuing medical studies in London, Paris, Rheims – where he obtained his MD in 1736 – and Leiden. He later returned to the University of Edinburgh where he served as professor of medicine from 1747 until his death.

In 1743 Whytt published his *Virtues of Lime Water in the Cure of the Stone*, a work that basically proposed the treatment of stones (calculi) with alkaline solutions and was probably the starting point for Joseph Black's discovery of carbon dioxide in 1756.

His most important work, however, was his *On the Vital and Other Involuntary Motions of Animals* (1751) in which, though not the first to talk of reflex actions (both René Descartes and Stephen Hales had preceded him), he was the first to accord them a proper prominence. Whytt argued that such "vital motions" as he called them were not dependent on the brain, for a decapitated frog continued for some time to move in a coordinated way when receiving the appropriate stimulation. The cause of such motions must then be in the spinal cord, for when particular parts were removed the reflexes could no longer be elicited. Individual reflexes described by Whytt included the pupillary response to light, sometimes known as *Whytt's reflex*.

The idea that actions could be mediated by parts of the body other than the brain or rational soul was a difficult one for the vitalistic and theologically based physiology of the 18th century. Incapable of seeing the "vital motion" in a mechanical way, Whytt actually went so far as to introduce the idea of an unconscious sentient principle in the spinal cord as the vital cause.

Wieland, Heinrich Otto

(1877–1957)

GERMAN CHEMIST

Wieland (**vee**-lahnt) was born in Pforzheim, Germany, the son of a chemist in a gold and silver refinery. He was educated at the University of Munich where he obtained his PhD in 1901. After teaching at the Munich Technical Institute and the University of Freiburg, Wieland succeeded Richard Willstätter in 1925 as professor of chemistry at the University of Munich, a post he retained until his retirement in 1950.

In 1912 Wieland began work on the bile acids. These secretions of the liver had been known for the best part of a century to consist of a large number of substances. He began by investigating three of them: cholic acid, deoxycholic acid, and lithocholic acid, finding that they were all steroids, very similar to each other, and all convertible into cholanic acid.

As Adolf Windaus had derived cholanic acid from cholesterol, an important biological sterol, this led Wieland to propose a structure for cholesterol. For his contributions to steroid chemistry Wieland was awarded the 1927 Nobel Prize for chemistry.

After 1921 Wieland worked on a number of curious alkaloids including toxiferin, the active ingredient in curare, bufotalin, the venom from toads, and phalloidine and amatine, the poisonous ingredients in the deadly amanita mushroom.

Wien, Wilhelm Carl Werner Otto Fritz Franz

(1864–1928)

GERMAN PHYSICIST

The son of a farmer from Gaffken in Eastern Europe, Wien (veen) studied mathematics and physics for a brief period in 1882 at the University of Göttingen. Having recommenced his studies in 1884 at the University of Berlin, he received a doctorate in 1886 for a thesis on the diffraction of light. At various times he considered becoming a farmer but after his parents were forced to sell their land he decided on an academic career in physics. In 1890 he joined the new Imperial (now Federal) Institute for Science and Technology in Charlottenburg, Berlin, as assistant to Hermann von Helmholtz, under whom he had studied. From 1896 to 1899 he worked at the technical college in Aachen and in 1900 was appointed professor of physics at the University of Würzburg. In 1920 he became professor at the University of Munich.

Wien was highly competent in both theoretical and experimental physics. His major research was into thermal or black-body radiation. In 1893 he showed that the wavelength at which the maximum energy is radiated from a source is inversely proportional to the absolute temperature of the source. Thus in heating an object it first glows red hot, emitting most of its energy at the wavelengths of red light; as the temperature is increased, the wavelength at which maximum energy is emitted becomes shorter, and the body becomes white hot. This behavior is known as *Wien's displacement law*. In 1896 Wien derived a formula, now known as *Wien's formula*, for the distribution of energy in black-body radiation for a whole range of wavelengths. Its importance for future research lay in the fact that although successful at short wavelengths it disagreed with experiments at longer wavelengths. The discrepancy, which is sometimes known as the "ultraviolet catastrophe," highlighted the inadequacies of classical mechanics and inspired Max Planck to develop the quantum theory. Wien was awarded the Nobel Prize for physics in 1911 for his discoveries regarding the laws governing the radiation of heat.

Wien also studied the conduction of electricity in gases and, while teaching in Aachen, confirmed that cathode rays consisted of high-velocity particles (1897) and were negatively charged (1898). In addition he showed that canal rays were positively charged particles. He later conducted research into x-rays.

Wiener, Norbert

(1894–1964)

AMERICAN MATHEMATICIAN

Born in Columbia, Missouri, Wiener was a child prodigy in mathematics who sustained his early promise to become a mathematician of great originality and creativity. He is probably one of the most outstanding mathematicians to have been born in the United States. Such was Wiener's precocity that he took his degree in mathematics, from Tufts University, at the age of 14 in 1909.

Throughout his life Wiener had many extramathematical interests, especially in biology and philosophy. At Harvard his studies in philosophy led him to an interest in mathematical logic and this was the subject of his doctoral thesis, which he completed at the age of 18. Wiener went from Harvard to Europe to pursue his interest in mathematical logic with Bertrand Russell in Cambridge and with David Hilbert in Göttingen. After he returned from Europe, Wiener's mathematical interests broadened but, surprisingly, he was unable to get a suitable post as a professional mathematician and for a time tried such unlikely occupations as journalism and even writing entries for an encyclopedia. In 1919 Wiener finally obtained a post in the mathematics department of the Massachusetts Institute of Technology, where he remained for the rest of his career.

After his arrival at MIT Wiener began his extremely important work on the theory of stochastic (random) processes and Brownian motion.

Among his other very wide mathematical interests at this time was the generalization of Fourier's work on resolving functions into series of periodic functions (this is known as harmonic analysis). He also worked on the theory of Fourier transforms. During World War II Wiener devoted his mathematical talents to working for the military – in particular to the problem of giving a mathematical solution to the problem of aiming a gun at a moving target. In the course of this work Wiener discovered the theory of the prediction of stationary time series and brought essentially statistical methods to bear on the mathematical analysis of control and communication engineering.

From here it was a short step to his important work in the mathematical analysis of mechanical and biological systems, their information flow, and the analogies between them – the subject he named "cybernetics." It allowed full rein to his wide interests in the sciences and philosophy and Wiener spent much time popularizing the subject and explaining its possible social and philosophical applications. Wiener also worked on a wide range of other mathematical topics, particularly important being his work on quantum mechanics.

Wieschaus, Eric

(1947–)

AMERICAN BIOLOGIST

While working in the late 1970s in the European Molecular Biology Laboratory, Heidelberg, Wieschaus collaborated with Christiane Nüsslein-Volhard on a study of the genetic factors producing segmentation in the fruit fly *Drosophila melanogaster*. Flies were exposed to mutagenic chemicals and thousands of their larval descendants examined to see if particular types of mutants emerged. Their work, published in 1980, established 15 mutant loci that radically altered the segmental pattern of the *Drosophila* larvae. It allowed the main development sequences to be marked out – to show, in effect, how the embryo becomes increasingly segmented. At first the gap genes divide the embryo into its main regions. Pair-rule genes then subdivide these regions into segments and, finally, polarity genes mark out repeating patterns in each segment. This has proved to be especially significant as it is suspected that the same development pattern may be found in other organisms. It has even been suggested that Waardenburg's syndrome, a rare disease in humans that leads to deafness and albinism, is caused by mutations in the human version of the pair-rule gene.

Wieschaus shared the 1995 Nobel Prize for physiology or medicine with his collaborators Nüsslein-Volhard and Edward Lewis.

Wiesel, Torsten Nils

(1924–   )

SWEDISH NEUROPHYSIOLOGIST

Wiesel (**vee**-sel), who was born at Uppsala in Sweden, obtained his MD from the Karolinska Institute, Stockholm. He moved to America shortly afterward, working first at Johns Hopkins before moving to Harvard (1959), where he was appointed professor of neurophysiology in 1974. In 1983 he moved to Rockefeller University, New York, where he served as head of the neurobiology laboratory.

Since his arrival in America Wiesel has been engaged upon a most productive investigation with David Hubel, into the mammalian visual system. Their 20-year collaboration led to the formulation of the influential hypercolumn theory. Wiesel and Hubel received the 1981 Nobel Prize for physiology or medicine for their work, sharing the prize with Roger Sperry. Wiesel has gone on to investigate the chemical transmitters involved in the nerve cells of the visual system.

Wigglesworth, Sir Vincent Brian

(1899–1994)

BRITISH ENTOMOLOGIST

Born at Kirkham in England, Wigglesworth was educated at Cambridge University and at St. Thomas's Hospital, London. He subsequently held posts as lecturer in medical entomology at the London School of Hygiene and Tropical Medicine and as reader in entomology at the universities of London and Cambridge. He was director of the Agricultural Research Council Unit of Insect Physiology at Cambridge (1943–1967) and from 1952 was Quick Professor of Biology. Wigglesworth's main line of research was in insect physiology, much of his work being done using the bloodsucking bug *Rhodnius prolixus*. He carried out research on hormonal stimulation in insect ecdysis (molting of the cuticle), glandular growth and reproductive secretions, external stimuli perception (e.g., heat receptors on antennae, and body hairs), and insects' perception of time, due to metabolic rate and daily rhythm. His most important publications are *The Physiology of Insect Metamorphosis* (1954), *The Control of Growth and Form* (1959), and *The Principles of Insect Physiology* (1939; 6th edition, 1965).

Wigner, Eugene Paul

(1902–1995)

HUNGARIAN–AMERICAN
PHYSICIST

The simplicities of natural laws arise through the complexities of the languages we use for their expression.
—*Communications on Pure and Applied Mathematics* (1959)

Born the son of a businessman in Budapest, Hungary, Wigner (**wig**-ner) was educated at the Berlin Institute of Technology, where he obtained a doctorate in engineering in 1925. After a period at Göttingen he moved to America in 1930 and took a part-time post at Princeton. He became a naturalized American citizen in 1937 and in 1938 was appointed to the chair of theoretical physics. Wigner remained at Princeton until his retirement in 1971 apart from leave of absence when he served at the Metallurgical Laboratory, Chicago (1942–45), and at Oak Ridge as director of the Clinton Laboratories (1946–47).

Wigner made many fundamental contributions to quantum and nuclear physics. He did some early work on chemical reactions and on the spectra of compounds. In 1927 he introduced the idea of parity as a conserved property of nuclear reactions. The basic insight was mathematical and arose from certain formal features Wigner had identified in transformations of the wave function of Erwin Schrödinger. The function $\Psi(x,y,z)$ describes particles in space, and parity refers to the effect of changes in the sign of the variables on the function: if it remains unchanged the function has even parity while if its sign changes it has odd parity. It was proposed by Wigner that a reaction in which parity is not conserved is forbidden.

In physical terms this meant that a nuclear process should be indistinguishable from its mirror image; for example, an electron emitted by a nucleus should be indifferent as to whether it is ejected to the left or the right. Such a consequence seemed natural and remained unquestioned until 1956 when Tsung Dao Lee and Chen Ning Yang shocked the world of physics by showing that parity was not conserved in the weak interaction.

In the 1930s Wigner made major contributions to nuclear physics. Working particularly on neutrons he established early on that the nuclear force binding the neutrons and protons together must be short-range and independent of any electric charge. He also with Gregory Breit in 1936 worked out the *Breit–Wigner formula*, which did much to explain neutron absorption by a compound nucleus. Wigner was involved in much of the early work on nuclear reactors leading to the first controlled nuclear chain reaction.

Wigner shared the 1963 Nobel Prize for physics with Maria Goeppert Mayer and J. Hans Jensen for "systematically improving and extending the methods of quantum mechanics and applying them widely."

Wilcke, Johan Carl

(1732–1796)

GERMAN–SWEDISH PHYSICIST

Wilcke (**vil**-ke) was born at Wisman in Germany but moved to Stockholm with his parents in 1739. His father was a priest. After studying at Uppsala he spent the period 1751–57 traveling on the Continent. On his return to Sweden he was appointed lecturer in physics at the Military Academy in Stockholm in 1759. He later became professor and in 1784 was made the secretary of the Stockholm Academy of Sciences.

Although he was a prolific and inventive physicist who worked in many fields he is best known for his work on latent and specific heat – ideas that he developed independently of Joseph Black. Wilcke started with a formula given by G. W. Richmann for calculating the final temperature of a mixture obtained by mixing liquids of different temperatures. In 1772 he found that the formula worked reasonably well with most mixtures but that if he took snow and water the mixture would not have the temperature predicted.

Wilcke calculated the amount of heat that was needed to melt the snow before any heat could be used to raise the temperature (i.e., the latent heat) and produced a new formula for such conditions. He followed this by producing tables of specific heats in 1781, which were calculated by mixing various hot substances with snow.

He had earlier, in 1757, published an important work on electricity, *De Electricitatibus Contrariis* (On Opposing Types of Electricity), in which he demonstrated that it was too simplistic to suppose that there were two absolutely distinct types of electricity – the vitreous and resinous types of Charles Dufay – which repel their own kind and attract the other. It was certainly true that two pieces of material rubbed on glass would repel each other and attract a piece rubbed on silk or amber, but Wilcke showed that these classifications were not absolute, for friction could produce both kinds of charge.

He also demonstrated other electrical effects, collaborating with Franz Aepinus. Together they established the phenomenon of pyroelectricity, finding that certain crystals would take opposite electric charges on opposite faces on being heated.

Wild, John Paul

(1923–   )

BRITISH–AUSTRALIAN RADIO ASTRONOMER

Wild, who was born at Sheffield in England, studied at Cambridge University. After service with the Royal Navy as a radar officer from 1943 to 1947, he joined the Commonwealth Scientific and Industrial Research Organization (CSIRO) in New South Wales, Australia, to work in the new field of radio astronomy. He later served as director of the CSIRO Solar Observatory at Culgoora from 1966, as chief of the radiophysics division from 1971 until 1977, and as chairman of the CSIRO from 1979 until 1985.

Wild first worked on solar bursts – intense outbursts of radio waves that frequently accompany solar flares. Normal radio telescopes measure radio noise over a narrow band of frequencies, making them of little use in the study of solar bursts with their rapid frequency drifts of in some cases 20 megahertz. Wild overcame this difficulty, in collaboration with L. McCready, with the design (1950) of a radio spectrometer capable of sweeping rapidly across a wide frequency band. With this "panoramic receiver" he investigated and classified the complicated pattern of solar outbursts.

He went on to construct at Culgoora an enormous radio heliograph, consisting of 96 dish antennas, equally spaced around the circumference of a 1.8-mile (3-km) diameter circle. When completed in 1967 it was capable of providing a practically instantaneous moving display of radio activity in the Sun's atmosphere.

Wildt, Rupert

(1905–1976)

GERMAN–AMERICAN ASTRONOMER

Wildt (vilt) was born in Munich, Germany, and studied at the University of Berlin, obtaining his PhD there in 1927. After a period of teaching at Göttingen he emigrated to America in 1934 and worked at various institutions including the Mount Wilson Observatory (1935–36), Princeton University (1937–42), and the University of Virginia (1942–46). In 1948 he took up an appointment at Yale University where he served as professor of astrophysics from 1957 until his retirement in 1973.

Wildt worked in stellar spectroscopy, theoretical astrophysics, and geochemistry, but his main interest lay in planetary studies. Since much of his work was done before the start of the space program it is not surprising that many of his speculations have since been rejected. Thus his claim that the Venusian clouds contained formaldehyde (CH_2O) formed under the influence of ultraviolet rays has not been confirmed by space probes.

He was, however, successful in his identification in 1932 of certain absorption bands observed by Vesto Slipher in the spectrum of Jupiter as being due to ammonia and methane. He also, in 1943, proposed a model of the constitution of Jupiter based on its density of 1.3 arguing that it consisted of a large metallic rocky core surrounded by ice and compressed hydrogen above which lies a thick layer of atmosphere. Saturn, Uranus, and Neptune were thought to have a similar constitution, but more recent models, together with the Pioneer and Voyager space flights, have suggested that the giant planets are made mainly of hydrogen in various forms with much smaller cores than Wildt proposed.

Wiles, Andrew John

(1953–   )

BRITISH MATHEMATICIAN

The son of a theology professor, Wiles was educated at Cambridge University, where he gained his PhD in 1980. He immediately took up an appointment as professor of mathematics at Princeton.

Wiles worked on the most famous of all mathematical problems, namely, "Fermat's last theorem" (FLT). Pierre Fermat claimed in 1637 that he had proved that there are no numbers $n > 2$ such that:

$$a^n + b^n = c^n$$

It was, of course, well known that where $n = 2$ there were many solutions to the equation as when $a = 3$, $b = 4$, and $c = 5$. Fermat had merely stated the theorem, as was his custom, in the margins of a book, in this case the *Arithmetica* of Diophantus. He simply added that there was insufficient room in the margin to record the details of the proof.

As over the years all Fermat's other marginalia have turned out to be accurate and proofs found, mathematicians were optimistic that the one unproved proposition – the last theorem – would also succumb. Yet 300 years later not only had no proof been found, but mathematicians seemed unaware in which direction a proof could be found. They could, of course, simply show the proposition to be false by finding an $n > 3$ which does satisfy the equation. But that was going to be no easy matter either, for it had been shown that any such number n must be very large – by 1992 all exponents up to 4 million had been tested and failed.

An alternative approach was suggested by some work in 1954 on elliptic curves by the Japanese mathematician Yutaka Taniyama. An elliptic curve is a set of solutions to an equation relating a quadratic in one variable to a cubic in another as in:

$$y^2 = ax^3 + bx^2 + cx + d$$

The Taniyama conjecture asserts that associated with every elliptical curve was a function with certain very precise specific properties. The German mathematician Gerhard Frey argued in 1985 that the Taniyama conjecture had important implications for Fermat's last theorem. He demonstrated that any possible solution to the theorem would give rise to a class of elliptical curves, referred to as Frey curves, which could not satisfy the conditions of the Taniyama conjecture. Thus a proof of the Taniyama conjecture would show that there could be no solutions to Fermat's last theorem.

In 1986 Wiles set out to show that Frey curves could not exist. Seven years later he had established a 200-page proof, which he revealed to the public for the first time at a mathematical conference in Cambridge, England, in 1993. Although Wiles's proof made headline news around the world it soon became evident that gaps still existed. After a further year the gaps had been eliminated and the 200-page paper had been accepted for publication.

Wilkes, Maurice Vincent

(1913–)

BRITISH COMPUTER SCIENTIST

Wilkes was born at Dudley in Worcestershire, England, and educated at Cambridge University. After working on operational research during World War II, he returned to Cambridge where he was appointed professor of computing technology in 1965, a post he held until his retirement in 1980.

In 1946 Wilkes attended a course on the design of electronic computers at the Moore School of Electrical Engineering at the University of Pennsylvania. Here Wilkes learned of the direction modern computers would have to follow. Earlier models, such as the Moore School's ENIAC, were really designed to deal with one particular type of problem. To solve a different kind of problem thousands of switches would have to be reset and miles of cable rerouted. The future of computing lay with the idea of the "stored program," as preached by John von Neumann at the Moore School.

Consequently Wilkes returned to Cambridge to begin work on EDSAC (Electronic Delay Storage Automatic Computer). In order to store a program, the computer must first have a memory, something lacking from ENIAC and earlier devices. Wilkes chose to adopt the mercury delay lines suggested by J. P. Eckert to serve as an internal memory store. In a delay tube an electrical signal is converted into a sound wave traveling through a long tube of mercury with a speed of 1,450 meters per second. It can be reflected back and forth along the tube for as long as necessary. Thus assigning the number 1 to be represented by a pulse of 0.5 microsecond, and 0 by no pulse, a 1.45-meter-long tube could retain 1,000 binary digits.

EDSAC came into operation in May 1949, gaining for Wilkes the honor of building the first working computer with a stored program; it remained in operation until 1958. The future, however, lay not in delay lines but in magnetic storage, and EDSAC soon became as obsolete as ENIAC. Wilkes provided a lively account of his work in his *Memoirs of a Computer Pioneer* (1985).

Wilkins, John

(1614–1672)

ENGLISH MATHEMATICIAN AND SCIENTIST

Perhaps there may be some other means invented for a conveyance to the Moon...We have not now any Drake or Columbus to undertake this voyage, or any Daedalus to invent a conveyance through the aire. However, I doubt not but that time...will also manifest to our posterity that which we now desire but cannot know.

—*The Discovery of a World in the Moon* (1638)

Born at Fawsley in Northamptonshire, England, Wilkins was educated at Oxford University, graduating in 1631. He was a parliamentarian during the English Civil War and became warden of Wadham College, Oxford University. In 1659 he was appointed master of Trinity College, Cambridge University. After the Restoration he lost his post but regained favor to become bishop of Chester.

Wilkins's chief contribution to the development of science was his part in founding the Royal Society. His influence can be traced back to his student days at Oxford when he collected around him a lively group of philosophers and scientists who later became founder members of the society in 1662. His own writings covered a wide range of fields and although he had a certain amount of mathematical knowledge he was more a practical scientist. His *Discovery of a World in the Moon* (1638) is a fantasy in which he speculated about the structure of the Moon. A later semimathematical work, *Mathematical Magick*, deals with the principles of machine design and in it Wilkins argued that perpetual motion is a theoretical possibility. One nonscientific interest to which Wilkins devoted much time was his project of devising a universal language.

Wilkins, Maurice Hugh Frederick

(1916–   )

NEW ZEALAND–BRITISH
BIOPHYSICIST

Wilkins was born at Pongaroa in New Zealand. After graduating in physics from Cambridge University in England in 1938, he joined John Randall at Birmingham University to work on the improvement of radar screens. He received his PhD in 1940 for an electron-trap theory of phosphorescence and soon after went to the University of California, Berkeley, as one of the British team assigned to the Manhattan project and development of the atomic bomb. The results and implications of this work caused him to turn away from nuclear physics and in 1945 he began a career in biophysics, firstly at St. Andrews University, Scotland, and from 1946 at the Biophysics Research Unit, King's College, London.

The same year that Wilkins joined King's College, scientists at the Rockefeller Institute announced that genes consist of deoxyribonucleic acid (DNA). Wilkins began studying DNA molecules by optical measurements and chanced to observe that the DNA fibers would be ideal material for x-ray diffraction studies. The diffraction patterns showed the DNA molecule to be very regular and have a double-helical structure. The contributions of Wilkins's colleague, Rosalind Franklin, were especially important in showing that the phosphate groups are to the outside of the helix, so disproving Linus Pauling's theory of DNA structure.

Wilkins passed on his data to James Watson and Francis Crick in Cambridge who used it to help construct their famous molecular model of DNA. For their work in elucidating the structure of the hereditary material, Wilkins, Watson, and Crick were awarded the 1962 Nobel Prize for physiology or medicine.

Wilkins went on to apply his techniques to finding the structure of ribonucleic acid (RNA). From 1955 he was deputy director of the Biophysics Research Unit and from 1963 he was professor at King's College, firstly of molecular biology and from 1970 of biophysics. He retired in 1981.

Wilkins, Robert Wallace

(1906–   )

AMERICAN PHYSICIAN

Born at Chattanooga in Tennessee, Wilkins was educated at the University of North Carolina and at Harvard Medical School, where he obtained his MD in 1933. He then held various posts at Harvard and Johns Hopkins University before moving to Boston University in 1940, where he served as professor of medicine from 1955 until his retirement in 1972.

Wilkins investigated means of relieving the condition of hypertension (high blood pressure). He demonstrated that the disease is reversible, at least in its early stages, and in searching for suitable hypotensive drugs he helped to introduce the drug reserpine into the modern pharmacopoeia. The drug, an alkaloid derived from the tropical plant *Rauwolfia serpentina*, had been used extensively in India for a wide variety of complaints for many centuries. It was originally tested for its ability to reduce high blood pressure and has since been used as a hypotensive.

It was, however, soon noted that on some patients it had a marked calming effect without actually sending them to sleep. It was in fact the first of the "tranquilizers." Once widely used in the treatment of schizophrenia, it has been largely replaced by the phenothiazine drugs, such as chlorpromazine, because of its serious side effects.

Wilkinson, Sir Denys Haigh

(1922–   )

BRITISH PHYSICIST

Wilkinson, who was born at Leeds in England, was educated at the University of Cambridge, where he obtained his PhD in 1947. He remained at Cambridge, serving as professor of experimental physics and head of the Nuclear Physics Laboratory from 1957 until 1976, when he was appointed vice-chancellor of Sussex University. He retired in 1987.

Wilkinson has worked mainly in the field of elementary-particle physics. In particular he has investigated the phenomenon of charge independence found in the so-called strong force, which holds together the particles of the atomic nucleus. Following the collapse of parity in weak interactions as reported by Chen Ning Yang and Tsung Dao Lee he has also investigated the validity of parity conservation in strong nuclear interactions. He was knighted in 1974.

Wilkinson, Sir Geoffrey

(1921–)

BRITISH INORGANIC CHEMIST

Wilkinson was born at Todmorden in Yorkshire, England, and educated at Imperial College, London; after spending World War II working in North America on the development of the atomic bomb, he finally obtained his PhD in 1946. He later worked at the Massachusetts Institute of Technology and at Harvard, before being elected to the chair of inorganic chemistry at Imperial College, a post he held from 1956 until 1988. He was knighted in 1976.

Wilkinson is noted for his studies of inorganic complexes. He shared the Nobel Prize for chemistry in 1973 with Ernst Fischer for work on "sandwich compounds." A theme of Wilkinson's work in the 1960s was the study and use of complexes containing a metal–hydrogen bond. Thus complexes of rhodium with triphenyl phosphine ($(C_6H_5)_3P$) can react with molecular hydrogen. The compound $RhCl(P(C_6H_5)_3)$, known as *Wilkinson's catalyst*, was the first such complex to be used as a homogeneous catalyst for adding hydrogen to the double bonds of alkenes (hydrogenation). This type of compound can also be used as a catalyst for the reaction of hydrogen and carbon monoxide with alkenes (hydroformylation). It is the basis of industrial low-pressure processes for making aldehydes from ethene and propene.

Williams, Robert R.

(1886–1965)

AMERICAN CHEMIST

The son of a Baptist missionary, Williams was born at Nellore in India and educated at the universities of Ottawa, Kansas, and Chicago. He began his career in government service, serving as chemist to the Bureau of Science in Manila before returning to America, where he worked at the Bureau of Chemistry in the agriculture department until 1918. He then moved into industry, working first for Western Electric before joining the Bell Telephone Laboratories in 1924, where he directed the chemistry laboratory until 1945.

With considerable single-mindedness Williams, early in his career, set himself the task of isolating the cause of beriberi. As early as 1896 Christiaan Eijkman had shown that it was a deficiency disease while Casimir Funk had demonstrated that the vitamin whose absence caused the disease was an amine. Beyond that nothing was known when Williams began his work in the Philippines.

Working mainly in his spare time, in 1934 he managed to isolate, from several tons of rice husks, enough of the vitamin, B_1, to work out its formula. In 1937 he succeeded in synthesizing it.

His brother Roger, also a chemist, discovered pantothenic acid, another important vitamin in the B complex.

Williams, Robley Cook

(1908–)

AMERICAN BIOPHYSICIST

Williams, who was born in Santa Rosa, California, received a PhD in physics from Cornell University in 1935 and then went on to teach astronomy at the University of Michigan, transferring to the physics department in 1945. He remained there until 1950, when he transferred to a lecturing post in the biochemistry department at the University of California, Berkeley. In 1964, when a department of molecular biology was established at Berkeley, Williams became its chairman.

As an astronomer Williams worked on the estimation of stellar surface temperatures. Military research during World War II turned his attention to electron microscopy, and an insight drawn from his knowledge of astronomical techniques led to a fruitful collaboration with the crystallographer Ralph Wyckoff. The early electron microscopes were transmission microscopes, i.e., the beam of electrons passes through the sample, giving a two-dimensional image. Working with Ralph Wyckoff at Michigan, Williams developed a technique of preparing specimens so that they could be observed with reflected beams of electrons. The technique involves depositing metal obliquely on the specimen. This effectively "casts shadows" and creates a vivid three-dimensional effect in the image.

Williams turned to the study of viruses, using his shadowing technique, and made important contributions to an understanding of viral structure. In 1955 (in collaboration with Heinz Fraenkel-Conrat) he achieved, with the tobacco mosaic virus, the first reconstitution of a biologically active virus from its constituent proteins and nucleic acids.

Williamson, Alexander William

(1824–1904)

BRITISH CHEMIST

Williamson's father was a clerk in the East India Company in London. After his retirement in 1840 the family lived on the Continent, where Williamson was educated. He studied at Heidelberg and at Giessen (under Justus von Liebig), where he received his PhD in 1846. He also studied mathematics in Paris. In 1849 he took up the chair of chemistry at London University, a post he occupied until 1887.

Between 1850 and 1856 Williamson showed that alcohol and ether both belong to the water type. Type theory, developed by Charles Gerhardt and Auguste Laurent, was based on the idea that organic compounds are produced by replacing one or more hydrogen atoms of inorganic compounds (which form the types) by radicals. Using the correct formula for alcohol (which he had recently established) Williamson represented the water type as: H_2O (water); C_2H_5OH (alcohol); $C_2H_5OC_2H_5$ (ether), where the H of water is progressively replaced by C_2H_5.

A further contribution to chemical theory was his demonstration (in 1850) of reversible reactions: two substances, A and B, react to form the products X and Y, which in turn react to produce the original A and B. Under certain conditions the system could be in dynamic equilibrium, when the amount of A and B reacting to form X and Y is equal to the amount of A and B produced by X and Y. He is remembered for what is now known as *Williamson's synthesis*, a method of making ethers by reacting a sodium alcoholate with a haloalkane.

Williamson, William Crawford

(1816–1895)

BRITISH PALEOBOTANIST

The son of a gardener and naturalist, Williamson was born in Scarborough in northeast England and was apprenticed in 1832 to an apothecary. In 1835, however, Williamson left for Manchester to take up the appointment of curator of the newly formed Museum of the Natural History Society. He later completed his medical training at University College, London, and after some years in private practice in Manchester entered academic life in 1851 as professor of natural history at Owens College, in which post he remained until his retirement in 1890.

In the 1850s Williamson's interest in the plants of the Carboniferous was aroused when he was presented with a number of coal balls – aggregates of petrified plants found in the coal itself. To their study he devoted the rest of his career, publishing his results in his *On the Organization of Fossil Plants of the Coal Measures* (19 parts; 1871–93). The work contains much information on the early pteridophytes and seed plants.

Willis, Thomas

(1621–1675)

ENGLISH ANATOMIST AND PHYSICIAN

Willis, who was born at Great Bedwin in England, entered Oxford University in 1636 and graduated firstly in arts before returning to take his MB in 1646. He fought for the royalists in the siege of Oxford during the English Civil War and afterwards he was a member of the "Invisible College," the informal group of scientists from whose meetings the Royal Society emerged in 1660. With the Restoration of Charles II the loyalty of Willis was rewarded with his appointment to the chair of natural philosophy at Oxford in 1660. Willis resigned in 1666 and moved to London where he set up in private practice.

It was as an anatomist that Willis made his most significant contribution to medicine. In 1664 he published his *Cerebri anatome* (Anatomy of the Brain), a work still in use a century later. It contains a much improved treatment of the cranial nerves, being in complete agreement with modern neurology on the first six and giving the first description of the eleventh cranial nerve. It also contains the first account of the so-called *circle of Willis* at the base of the brain.

This arose out of an observation at an autopsy of a body with a completely occluded right carotid artery in the neck. Surprisingly this appeared not to have obstructed the blood supply to the brain nor to have produced any obvious symptoms during the life of the deceased. Careful dissection revealed an interconnected ring of arteries at the base of the brain. The effect of this, Willis saw, would be to preserve a continuous supply of blood to both sides of the brain even if there had been a failure on one side.

Willis also made an attempt to apply the advances in chemistry and atomic theory to the problems of disease. His attempt was premature but nevertheless he was the first to describe a number of diseases, such as diabetes mellitus, puerperal fever, and general paralysis of the insane (a late effect of syphilis).

Willstätter, Richard

(1872–1942)

GERMAN CHEMIST

Willstätter (**vil**-shtet-er) was the son of a textile merchant from Karls-ruhe in Germany. He was educated at the University of Munich, re-ceiving his PhD in 1894 for work on cocaine. He was professor of chemistry in Zurich from 1905 to 1912, when he left to work in the Kaiser Wilhelm Institute in Berlin. In 1916 he succeeded Adolf von Baeyer to the chemistry chair at Munich. He resigned in 1924 in protest at the growing anti-Semitism in Germany but remained in his homeland until he felt his own life was no longer safe, going into exile in Switzer-land in 1939.

His early work was mainly on the structure of alkaloids – he managed to throw light on such important compounds as cocaine, which he syn-thesized in 1923, and atropine. In 1905 he began work on the chemistry of chlorophyll. By using the chromatographic techniques developed by Mikhail Tsvet, he was soon able to show that it consists of two com-pounds, chlorophyll a and b, and to work out their formulas. One of the significant features he noted was that chlorophyll contains a single atom of magnesium in its molecule, just as hemoglobin contains a single iron atom. He also investigated other plant pigments, including the yellow pigment carotene and the blue pigment anthocyanin. His work on chlorophyll was justified in 1960 when Robert Woodward succeeded in synthesizing the compounds described by his formulas and came up with chlorophyll.

Willstätter was less successful with his enzyme theory. In the 1920s he claimed to have isolated active enzymes with no trace of protein. His views were widely accepted until protein was restored to its rightful place in enzyme activity by the work of John Northrop in 1930.

For his work on plant pigments Willstätter was awarded the Nobel Prize for chemistry in 1915.

Wilson, Alexander

(1766–1813)

SCOTTISH–AMERICAN ORNITHOLOGST

> The achievement of this man is little short of
> marvelous.
> —Frances Herrick on Wilson's publication of
> *The American Ornithology*

Wilson was born at Paisley in Scotland and spent his early life as a weaver and peddler. He was also a poet, but the nature of his poems, championing the weaver's cause in Scotland, led to fines and imprisonment. In 1894 he emigrated to America, where he spent most of the remainder of his life compiling his monumental *American Ornithology*, seven volumes of which he completed from 1808 to 1813, others being added after his death. He made extensive and often arduous travels throughout America and listed, described, and illustrated a total of 264 species, many of them new to science. Wilson also made many contributions to knowledge of bird calls and songs, egg numbers, plumage and sexual differences, behavior, migration numbers, and so on. His analyses of bird stomach contents produced new information about food preferences and requirements, while he also demonstrated, by means of dissection, the stereoscopic vision of owls. Characterized by accuracy and great attention to detail, Wilson's *American Ornithology* has been described as probably the most important pioneering contribution to ornithological science in America.

Wilson, Allan Charles

(1934–1991)

NEW ZEALAND BIOCHEMIST

Born at Ngaruawakia in New Zealand, Wilson was educated at the University of Otago, Dunedin, and at Washington State University before completing his PhD in 1961 at the University of California, Berkeley. After working at the Weizmann Institute in Israel and at universities in Nairobi, Kenya, and Harvard, he returned to Berkeley serving as professor of biochemistry until his death from leukemia in 1991.

In 1967, in collaboration with Vincent Sarich, Wilson, following the work of Emile Zuckerandl, argued that molecular clocks could reveal much about the early history of man. Against the opposition of paleontologists they claimed that the divergence between man and the great apes began only 5 million years ago. Their view seems to have prevailed.

In the 1980s Wilson sought to challenge the paleontologists once more, this time on the issue of the emergence of modern man. While anthropologists favored a date of 1 million years, Wilson's work suggested a time no later than 200,000 years ago.

He chose to work with mitochondria, the cellular organelles which convert food into energy. Like a cell nucleus, mitochondria also contain DNA. It encodes, however, only 37 genes as opposed to the 100,000 of nuclear DNA. Further, mitochondrial DNA evolved rapidly and regularly and, surprisingly, it is inherited from the mother alone. It follows, Wilson pointed out, that "all human mitochondrial DNA must have had an ultimate common female ancestor." Where and when, he went on to ask, could she be found?

Wilson adopted the parsimony principle that subjects are connected in the simplest possible way. That is, the fewer differences found in mitochondrial DNA, the closer they were connected. Mitochondria from 241 individuals from all continents and races were collected and analyzed. The tree constructed had two branches, both of which led back to Africa.

What was the date of this "African Eve" as she was quickly dubbed by the press? Wilson measured the ratio of mitochondrial DNA divergence between humans to the divergence between humans and chimpanzees. The ratio was found to be 1:25 and, as human and chimpanzee lineages diverged 5 million years ago, human maternal lineages must have separated by 1/25 of this time, namely, 200,000 years ago.

Wilson's hypothesis, first presented in 1987, has provoked considerable opposition. Those who prefer a multiregional explanation of human evolution have questioned most of Wilson's assumptions and have argued that until it is backed up by unequivocal fossil evidence it must remain speculative.

Wilson, Charles Thomson Rees

(1869–1959)

BRITISH PHYSICIST

In September 1894 I spent a few weeks...on the summit of Ben Nevis. The wonderful optical phenomena shown when the sun shone on the clouds surrounding the hill-top, and especially the coloured rings surrounding the sun...made me wish to imitate them in the laboratory.

—*Weather* (1954)

Charles Wilson was the son of a sheep farmer from Glencorse in Scotland but his father died when he was four and Charles and his mother moved to Manchester. He was educated there and started to specialize in biology but moved to Cambridge University to study physics. There he started work with J. J. Thomson.

Wilson began experiments to duplicate cloud formation in the laboratory by letting saturated air expand, thus cooling it. He found that clouds seemed to need dust particles to start the formation of water droplets and that x-rays, which charged the dust, greatly speeded up the process. Inspired by this, he showed that charged subatomic particles traveling through supersaturated air also formed water droplets. This was the basis of the cloud chamber, which Wilson perfected in 1911 and for which he received the Nobel Prize for physics in 1927. The cloud chamber became an indispensable aid to research into subatomic particles and, with the addition of a magnetic field, made different particles distinguishable by the curvature of their tracks.

Returning to the study of real clouds, Wilson also investigated atmospheric electricity and developed a sensitive electrometer to measure it. A result of this work was his determination of the electric structure of thunder clouds.

Wilson, Edward Osborne

(1929–   )

AMERICAN ENTOMOLOGIST,
ECOLOGIST, AND
SOCIOBIOLOGIST

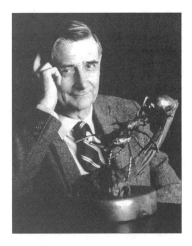

> Marxism is sociobiology without biology...Although Marxism was formulated as the enemy of ignorance and superstition, to the extent that it has become dogmatic it...is now mortally threatened by the discoveries of human sociobiology.
> —*On Human Nature* (1978)

Wilson, who was born in Birmingham, Alabama, graduated in biology from the University of Alabama in 1949 and obtained his PhD from Harvard in 1955. He joined the Harvard faculty the following year, becoming professor in 1964 and curator of entomology at the Museum of Comparative Zoology in 1971.

Much of Wilson's entomological work was with ants and other social insects and was comprehensively surveyed in his massive *Insect Societies* (1971). He has also worked on speciation and with William Brown introduced the term "character displacement" to describe the process that frequently takes place when closely related species that have previously been isolated begin to overlap in distribution. The differences that do exist between the species become exaggerated to avoid competition and hybridization.

Wilson collaborated with Robert MacArthur in developing a theory on the equilibrium of island populations from which emerged their *Theory of Island Biogeography* (1967). To test such ideas Wilson conducted a number of remarkable experiments with Daniel Simberloff in the Florida Keys. They selected six small mangrove clumps and made a survey of the number of insect species present. They then fumigated the islands to eliminate all the 75 insect species found. Careful monitoring over the succeeding months revealed that the islands had been recolonized by the same number of species, thus confirming the prediction that "a dynamic equilibrium number of species exists for any island."

It was, however, with his *Sociobiology* (1975) that Wilson emerged as a controversial and household name. He argued that "a single strong thread does indeed run from the conduct of termite colonies and turkey brotherhoods to the social behavior of man." Using the arguments of William Hamilton and Robert Trivers, Wilson had little difficulty in showing the deep biological and genetic control exercised over many apparently altruistic acts in insects, birds, and mammals. He also proposed plausible mechanisms to explain much of the social behavior and organization of many species. Many believe, however, that he is on very shaky ground when he extends such arguments to human social evolution. Wilson has continued to produce a large number of popular, personal, and technical works. Among these are a work on ecology, *The Diversity of Life* (1992); his Pulitzer prize-winning *The Ants* (1988, written in collaboration with B. Hölldobler); and his revealing autobiography, *Naturalist* (1994).

Wilson, John Tuzo

(1908–1993)

CANADIAN GEOPHYSICIST

Born in Ottawa, Canada, Wilson was educated at the University of Toronto and at Princeton, where he obtained his PhD in 1936. After working for the Canadian Geological Survey (1936–39) and war service, he was appointed professor of geophysics at the University of Toronto (1946) where he remained until his retirement in 1974.

Wilson did much to establish the new discipline of plate tectonics during the early 1960s and was the first to use the term "plate" to refer to the rigid portions (oceanic, continental, or a combination of both) into which the Earth's crust is divided. In 1963 he produced some of the earliest evidence in favor of the sea-floor spreading hypothesis of Harry H. Hess when he pointed out that the further away an island lay from the midocean ridge the older it proved to be.

His most significant work, however, was contained in his important paper of 1965, *A New Class of Faults and Their Bearing on Continental*

Drift, in which he introduced the idea of a transform fault. Plate movement had been identified as divergent, where plates are being separated by the production of new oceanic crust from the midocean ridges, and convergent, where plates move toward each other with one plate sliding under the other. Wilson realized a third kind of movement was needed to explain the distribution of seismic activity and the way in which the ocean ridges do not run in continuous lines but in a series of offsets joined by the transform faults. Here the plates slide past each other without any creation or destruction of material.

Wilson replied to critics of the plate tectonics theory, such as Vladimir Belousov, in his *A Revolution in Earth Science* (1967).

Wilson, Kenneth G.

(1936–   )

AMERICAN THEORETICAL
PHYSICIST

Wilson was educated at Harvard and Cal Tech where he gained his PhD in 1969. He taught at Cornell University from 1963, serving as professor of physics there from 1970 to 1988, when he moved to a similar post at Ohio State University, Columbus.

Wilson received the 1982 Nobel Prize for physics for theoretical work on critical phenomena in connection with phase transitions. He first applied his methods to the problem of ferromagnetic materials. Above a certain temperature, known as the Curie point, such materials become paramagnetic. This behavior results from the individual magnetic moments of the atoms. In the ferromagnetic state numbers of individual atoms "couple" together so that their spins are aligned, and there is a resulting long-range interaction over a region of the solid. Above the critical point (the Curie point) this long-range order breaks down. Wilson's achievement was to develop a theory that could apply to the system near the critical point.

He did this using an idea first suggested by Leo Kadanoff. He took a block of atoms and calculated the effective spin of the block, then took a number of blocks and calculated the value for the larger block, and so on. The method involves a mathematical technique known as renormalization.

Using such methods Wilson could go from the properties of individual atoms to properties characteristic of many atoms acting together, and the resulting theory could be applied to properties other than magnetism. Thus it can be used for the critical state observed in the change between liquid and gas and to changes in alloy structure. Wilson is now applying his methods to the strong forces between nucleons.

Wilson, Robert Woodrow

(1936–   )

AMERICAN ASTROPHYSICIST

Wilson studied initially at Rice University in his native city of Houston, where he gained his BA in physics in 1957; he went on to obtain his PhD from the California Institute of Technology in 1962. He joined the Bell Laboratories, Holmdel, New Jersey, in 1963 and served as head of the radiophysics research department from 1976 to 1990.

It was at the Bell Laboratories that he and his coworker Arno Penzias found the first evidence in 1964 of the cosmic microwave background radiation, which is now widely interpreted as being the remnant radiation from the "big bang" creation of the universe several billion years ago. The two men were jointly honored with the 1978 Nobel Prize for physics, which they shared with Pyotr L. Kapitza for his (unrelated) discoveries in low-temperature physics.

Wilson is continuing his astrophysics work with Penzias, looking for interstellar molecules and determining the relative abundances of interstellar isotopes.

Windaus, Adolf Otto Reinhold

(1876–1959)

GERMAN CHEMIST

Windaus (**vin**-dows) studied medicine at the university in his native city of Berlin and at Freiburg University, where he changed to chemistry under the influence of Emil Fischer. After holding chairs in Freiburg and Innsbruck he became, in 1915, professor of chemistry at Göttingen, where he remained until his retirement in 1944.

In 1901 Windaus began his study of the steroid cholesterol, a compound of considerable biological significance. Over the years he threw considerable light on its structure and in 1928 was awarded the Nobel Prize for chemistry for this work and for showing the connection between steroids and vitamins.

It was known that cod-liver oil prevents rickets because it contains vitamin D. It was also known that sunlight possesses antirachitic properties and, further, that mere exposure of certain foods to sunlight could make them active in preventing rickets. Clearly something in the food is converted photochemically into vitamin D but nobody knew what.

As vitamin D is fat soluble, the precursor of vitamin D (the provitamin) was not surprisingly found to be a steroid. In 1926 Windaus succeeded in showing that the provitamin is present as an impurity of cholesterol, ergosterol, which is converted into vitamin D by the action of sunlight.

Winkler, Clemens Alexander

(1838–1904)

GERMAN CHEMIST

Winkler (**vingk**-ler) was born at Freiberg in Germany and studied at the School of Mines there. He was later appointed to the chair of chemical technology and analytical chemistry at Freiberg in 1871.

In 1885 a new ore – argyrodite – was discovered in the local mines. Winkler, who had a considerable reputation as an analyst, was asked to examine it and to his surprise the results of his analysis consistently came out too low. He discovered that this was due to the presence of a new element, which, after several months' search, he isolated and named germanium after his fatherland. The properties of germanium matched those of the eka-silicon whose existence had been predicted in 1871 by Dmitri Mendeleev. Winkler's discovery completed the detection of the three new elements predicted by Mendeleev nearly 20 years before.

Winograd, Terry Allen

(1946–)

AMERICAN COMPUTER SCIENTIST

Born at Tacoma Park in Maryland, Winograd was educated at the University of Colorado and at the Massachusetts Institute of Technology, where he obtained his PhD in 1970. He remained at MIT until 1973 when he moved to Stanford, California, as professor of computer science and linguistics.

Much of Winograd's work has been concerned with artificial intelligence (AI). In this field he developed in 1970 the successful program SHRDLU; the name is taken from the letters SHRDLU ETAOIN, which appear on the keyboard of a typesetting machine and are used by printers to mark something unintelligible. One pervasive problem facing AI programs is that of background knowledge. For example, in translating technical texts between Russian and English, readers were puzzled to find frequent references to a "water sheep" – the computer was doing its best to cope with "hydraulic ram." To avoid semantic problems of this kind Winograd created a simple closed world that could be completely described. It consisted of a small number of differently shaped colored bricks. The computer was then instructed to perform such simple tasks as "put a small cube onto the green cube which supports a pyramid," and to answer correctly questions of the form: "How many things are on top of green cubes?" The actions and answers took place only within the confines of a computer program, thus avoiding the problem of designing a robotic arm. Despite this SHRDLU worked effectively. It was described by Winograd in his *Understanding Natural Languages* (1972).

He noted, further, in 1984 that there is too much deep ambiguity in a natural language to permit unrestricted machine translation. Such sentences as "the chickens are ready to eat," and "he saw that gasoline can explode," with their deep structural ambiguity, are common in a natural language and still tend to defeat any computer. The solution, to preedit and postedit the text, is expensive and time-consuming. But, Winograd notes, such a system was used by the Pan American Health Organization to translate a million words from Spanish into English between 1980 and 1984. Winograd has concluded, however, that there is no software currently capable of dealing with meaning over a significant subset of English.

Wislicenus, Johannes

(1835–1902)

GERMAN CHEMIST

Wislicenus (vis-lee-**tsay**-nuus) was born in Klein-Eichstadt, Germany, the son of a Lutheran pastor who was forced to flee Europe in 1853 because of his political views. Wislicenus accompanied his father to America, where he attended Harvard until returning to Europe in 1856. He continued his education at Halle and at Zurich, where he was appointed professor of chemistry in 1870. In 1872 he moved to Würzburg, where he stayed until he succeeded Adolph Kolbe as professor of chemistry at the University of Leipzig (1885).

In 1872 Wislicenus showed that there were two forms of lactic acid having the formula $CH_3CH(OH)COOH$. One, derived from sour milk by Carl Scheele in 1870, was optically inactive; the other, discovered by Jöns Jacob Berzelius in 1808, was active. Wislicenus suggested that this was caused by different arrangements of the same atoms in space producing different properties in the compounds. Wislicenus's findings and similar work led Jacobus van't Hoff and Joseph Le Bel to establish the new discipline of stereochemistry a few years later. Wislicenus went on to study "geometrical isomerism" – the existence of isomers because of different arrangements of groups or atoms about a double bond in the molecule.

Withering, William

(1741–1799)

BRITISH PHYSICIAN

Time will fix the real value upon this discovery.
—On his discovery of the medicinal
properties of the foxglove

Withering was born at Wellington in England and educated at the University of Edinburgh, where he obtained his MD in 1766. He then practiced in Stafford but in 1775 moved to a more prosperous practice in Birmingham where, as a member of the Lunar Society, he met such eminent scientists as Joseph Priestley and Erasmus Darwin. Withering retired in 1783 as he was then suffering from tuberculosis. His house, like that of his friend Priestley, was sacked in 1791 by the Birmingham mob for his sympathy with the French Revolution.

Withering was an expert botanist and in 1776 began the publication of his *Botanical Arrangement*. Because of his reputation his advice was sought on a mixture of herbs an old Shropshire woman was using to cure dropsy. He realized that the active herb was the foxglove and began a more careful study of its properties in 1775. He decided that the leaves were preferable to the root of the plant and set about establishing a standardized dose. He recommended its use as a diuretic but was in error in supposing that the foxglove acted directly as a diuretic. In fact it acted directly on the heart, whose beat it both slowed and strengthened. He published a full report of his work in his *An Account of the Foxglove* (1785). Since then drugs derived from digitalis, an extract of foxglove leaves, have come to have an important role in the treatment of heart failure. They are, however, no longer used for "dropsy" as such because more powerful and specialized diuretics are now available.

Withering was also an authority in mineralogy and the ore witherite (barium carbonate) is named for him.

Witten, Ed(ward)

(1951–   )

AMERICAN MATHEMATICAL PHYSICIST

Witten was born in Baltimore, Maryland. Having graduated from Brandeis College, Massachusetts, in 1971 with a degree in history, he intended to pursue a career in journalism. However, after working on George McGovern's 1972 presidential campaign, he realized that he was ill-suited to the world of political journalism and returned to university to study physics at Princeton. After completing his PhD in 1976 Witten remained at Princeton, where he was appointed professor of physics – a post he occupied until 1987 when he moved to the Institute for Advanced Study.

Witten has worked mainly in the development of string theory. In the 1960s Yoichipo Nambu and others had shown that elementary particles could be treated as strings of a certain kind, but it was soon shown that the theory only worked satisfactorily in 26 dimensions. A more ambitious theory of superstrings was promoted by Mike Green and others in the 1970s. When Witten came across the theory in 1975 he saw that it could throw light on what he termed "the single biggest puzzle in physics," namely, how to unify general relativity, which deals with gravity and space, with quantum mechanics, which explains events at the nuclear level. The realization in 1982 that superstring theory demanded the presence of gravity in its working was, for Witten, "the greatest intellectual thrill of my life." In the early 1980s Witten ruled out string theories in 11 dimensions derived from models based on the approach of Theodor Kaluza and Oskar Klein. Further, he argued that a number of mathematical anomalies would emerge in spaces with two, six, or ten dimensions. In 1984, however, Green and John Schwarz were able to show that, under certain special assumptions, a theory of ten dimensions could be developed that avoided the anomalies and explained the existence of particles with a built-in handedness (chirality).

Witten then began work showing how, in a ten-dimensional universe, the hidden extra six dimensions could be compacted and how they could interact with particles in detectable ways. He has sought for an analysis, based on geometric foundations, and has attempted to develop a topological quantum-field theory that gives due regard to the fundamental geometrical properties of matter. Witten's work is important in pure mathematics as well as in physics. In 1990 he was awarded the Fields Medal (regarded as the mathematics equivalent of a Nobel prize).

Some critics, including the Nobel laureate Sheldon Glashow, have objected that Witten's work has nothing to do with physics and is merely mathematical, while being impenetrable at the same time. Witten has replied that the theory has not been fully worked out yet and that it may well be many years before a precise description of nature can be offered. He has described string theory as "a 21st-century theory that has dropped by accident into the 20th century." Glashow replied:

"Please heed our advice that you too are not smitten;
The book's not finished, the last word is not Witten."

Wittig, Georg

(1897–1987)

GERMAN ORGANIC CHEMIST

Born in Berlin, Germany, Wittig (**vit**-ik) was educated at the university of Marburg. He worked at Braunschweig (1932–37), at Freiburg im Breisgau (1937–44), and at Tubingen (1944–65). In 1965 he became director of the Chemical Institute at Heidelberg, a post he held until his retirement in 1967.

Wittig worked extensively in organic chemistry, in particular on the chemistry of carbanions – negatively charged organic ions such as $C_6H_5^-$. In this work he discovered a class of reactive phosphorus compounds of the type $(C_6H_5)_3P{:}CH_2$. Such compounds (known as ylides) are able to replace the oxygen of a carbonyl group C=O by a CH_2 group, to give C=CH_2. This reaction, known as the *Wittig reaction*, is of immense importance in the synthesis of certain natural compounds, such as prostaglandin and vitamins A and D_2. Wittig also discovered a useful directed form of the aldol condensation. He was awarded the Nobel Prize for chemistry in 1979.

Wöhler, Friedrich

(1800–1882)

GERMAN CHEMIST

Organic chemistry just now is enough to drive one mad. It gives one the impression of a primeval, tropical forest full of the most remarkable things, a monstrous and boundless thicket, with no way of escape, into which one may well dread to enter.
—Letter to J. J. Berzelius, 28 January 1835

Wöhler (**vu(r)**-ler), who was born at Eschersheim near Frankfurt, acquired from his father, the master of horse of the crown prince of Hesse-Cassel, an interest in mineralogy – he actually met the aged poet Johann Wolfgang von Goethe, another devotee, in the shop of a Frankfurt mineral dealer. He began training as a physician at Marburg and Heidelberg but was persuaded by Leopold Gmelin to change to chemistry. After a year in Sweden with Jöns Jacob Berzelius he taught chemistry in Berlin and Cassel before his appointment to the chair of chemistry at Göttingen (1836), where he remained for the rest of his life.

Wöhler's most famous discovery occurred in 1828, when he synthesized crystals of urea while evaporating a solution of ammonium cyanate. He wrote excitedly to Berzelius, "I must tell you I can prepare urea without requiring a kidney of an animal, either man or dog." The significance of his achievement was that urea is an organic substance, which it was hitherto thought could be synthesized only by a living organism. If the constituents of a living body can be put together in the laboratory like common salt or sulfuric acid then there is apparently nothing left to distinguish the living from the nonliving. For this reason Wöhler's work is frequently cited as marking the death of vitalism, although at the time Wöhler was probably more concerned with the chemical reactions involved.

However, it was not seen by Wöhler's contemporaries as having that significance. Just because one substance had been synthesized, no one was prepared to claim that all organic substances could be so created. Justus von Liebig, who knew Wöhler's work well and collaborated with him over a long period of time, was a vitalist and vitalism was too complex and deep-seated an idea to disappear as a result of one experiment. Wöhler's work was more important in opening up whole new dimensions of biochemistry, stimulating work on the chemistry of digestion, respiration, growth, and reproduction.

Wöhler made other contributions to organic chemistry. In 1832, in collaboration with Liebig, he showed that the benzoyl radical (C_6H_5CO) could enter unchanged in a series of compounds: the hydride, chloride, cyanide, and oxide. Thus organic chemistry became, for a time, the chemistry of compound radicals. With the theories of Berzelius, this approach led to a great increase in the knowledge of organic compounds without a corresponding understanding of their chemistry.

In fact organic chemistry became so confusing that Wöhler returned to inorganic chemistry. In later years he tended to concentrate on the chemistry of metals, in particular the production of pure samples of some of the less common metals. He succeeded, at great expense, in obtaining pure aluminum (1827) and beryllium (1828).

With Liebig he was partly responsible for the discovery of isomerism. In 1823, while working in the laboratory of Berzelius, he prepared silver cyanate; at the same time Liebig produced silver fulminate, a compound with very different properties. To their surprise they found both compounds had identical formulas. Berzelius named the phenomenon "isomerism."

One final achievement of Wöhler was the creation of one of the first great teaching laboratories of Europe at Göttingen. From the 1830s nearly all creative chemists of the 19th century spent some time at Göttingen; students came not just from the Continent but also from America and Britain. The tradition persisted until the time of Hitler.

Wolf, Johann Rudolf

(1816–1893)

SWISS ASTRONOMER

Wolf (volf), the son of a minister from Fällenden in Switzerland, studied at the universities of Zurich, Vienna (1836–38), and Berlin (1838). He began his career in 1839 at the University of Bern where he served as director of the observatory from 1847 and professor of astronomy from 1844 until 1855, when he moved to Zurich. He there held chairs of astronomy at the university and the Institute of Technology as well as serving as director of the newly opened Federal Observatory.

It was not until 1851 that the work of Heinrich Schwabe on sunspot cycles became widely known. Wolf immediately began a study of solar observations dating back to the 17th century from which he was able to demonstrate that the cycle had a mean period of 11.1 years. He further recorded the maxima and minima from 1610 onward. With the announcement in 1851 by Johann von Lamont of an approximately 10-year variation in the terrestrial magnetic field, it occurred to Wolf, as it did independently to Edward Sabine and Alfred Gautier, that the two cycles were in fact connected.

Under Wolf the Federal Observatory became the world center for sunspot information and from 1855 daily counts of sunspots were made. To establish some kind of common statistical basis, Wolf proposed the "Zurich relative sunspot number" that is still used to indicate the level of sunspot activity. It is calculated from a formula that takes into account the number of sunspot groups, the total number of component spots in the groups, and in addition the competence of the observer and the quality of the instrument used.

Wolf, Maximilian Franz Joseph Cornelius

(1863–1932)

GERMAN ASTRONOMER

The son of a wealthy physician, Wolf studied at the university in his native city of Heidelberg, where he obtained his PhD in 1888. After spending two years in Stockholm he returned to the University of Heidelberg, where he was appointed to the chair of astronomy and astrophysics in 1901 and where he remained until his death in 1932.

Wolf is best known for his discovery of hundreds of new asteroids or minor planets. These are small rocky bodies that orbit the Sun, mainly in a belt between the orbits of Mars and Jupiter. The first to be discovered was Ceres by Giuseppe Piazzi in 1801 and by 1891 a further 300 had been identified. It was then that Wolf introduced his "labor-saving photographic method." A camera was attached to a telescope that moved at the same speed as the stars and thus gave point images on the photographic plate; asteroids, moving at a different speed relative to the stars, showed up on the plates as streaks. Wolf worked first in his private observatory in the center of Heidelberg and then at a new observatory, the Baden Observatory, built for him on the Königstuhl. He managed to discover over 500 new asteroids including, in 1906, Achilles, the first of the Trojan asteroids, which lie in two groups in Jupiter's orbit and form an equilateral triangle with Jupiter and the Sun.

Wolf also drew attention to dark regions of the Milky Way that appeared to be devoid of stars. He argued that they were caused by the presence of obscuring clouds of dust and gas and in 1923 devised the *Wolf diagram* – a method for determining the distance and absorption characteristics of the dark nebulae. By 1911 he had established the means of differentiating between spiral nebulae, later shown to be star systems lying far beyond our Galaxy, and the dark and the luminous nebulae within the Galaxy. These methods were soon widely adopted.

Wolff, Kaspar Friedrich

(1733–1794)

GERMAN ANATOMIST AND PHYSIOLOGIST

Wolff, who served as a surgeon during the Seven Years' War, studied in his native city of Berlin and at Halle, presenting in 1759 his thesis *Theoria generationis* (Theory of Reproduction). In this he destroyed the preformation or homunculus theory of development, which had postulated that the embryo contained all the adult organs preformed in miniature. In its place Wolff advanced the now accepted idea that organs develop from undifferentiated tissue. His theories were initially based on philosophical grounds but he later carried out research at St. Petersburg that substantiated his claims. While examining chick embryos Wolff also discovered an embryonic form of the kidney – now called the *Wolffian body* – that precedes the true organ in developing animals.

Wolfram, Stephen

(1959–   )

BRITISH THEORETICAL PHYSICIST

The son of a novelist father and philosopher mother, Wolfram showed an early passion for and understanding of science. Born in London, he entered Oxford University when he was sixteen, having already written several papers in particle physics. As he could find no one at Oxford capable of teaching him anything interesting, he attended no lectures and pursued his own interests. At the suggestion of Murray Gell-Mann he moved to the California Institute of Technology in 1978 and completed his PhD within a year. He immediately joined the Institute staff and began work on the development of a new computer language, SMP, capable of manipulating algebraic formulas as well as numbers. In 1983 Wolfram moved to the Institute for Advanced Studies, Princeton, where he remained until 1986, when he was appointed professor of physics at the University of Illinois where he set up the Center for Complex Systems Research. He is also the founder and president of the Wolfram Research Company, Champaign, Illinois.

In 1982 Wolfram became interested in cellular automata (CA), a subject devised by John von Neumann in the 1940s, and has worked almost entirely in this field ever since. One-dimensional cellular automata begin with a horizontal line of cells with each cell in one of two states, blank or filled. Further states displayed below each other are generated by a rule; for example, the rule that a cell is filled if and only if one and only one of the three cells immediately above is also filled.

With the aid of a computer the outcome of various rules can be examined over hundreds of generations. Wolfram has claimed to be able to distinguish between four classes of one-dimensional automata:

1. The starting pattern dissolves to a uniform, homogenous state, e.g., all cells filled or all cells blank.
2. The pattern evolves to a fixed finite size or oscillates endlessly between two fixed patterns.
3. Patterns continue to grow at a fixed rate and often produce self-similar fractal patterns.
4. Patterns show apparently chaotic behavior; they grow and contract unpredictably and irregularly.

Behind Wolfram's manipulation of CA on computer screens is the hope that it will lead to a greater insight into the development of complex systems.

Wollaston, William Hyde

(1766–1828)

BRITISH CHEMIST AND PHYSICIST

[At a] distance from the misrepresentations of narrow-minded bigots.
—Referring to his choice of astronomy as a specialty. *The Secret History of a Private Man* (1795)

Wollaston, the son of a clergyman from East Dereham in Norfolk, England, was educated at Cambridge University, England, where he graduated in 1788. He practiced as a physician before moving to London (1801) to devote himself to science, working in a variety of fields, including chemistry, physics, and astronomy, and making several important discoveries, both theoretical and practical.

Wollaston made himself financially independent by inventing, in 1804, a process to produce pure malleable platinum, which could be welded and made into vessels. He is reported to have made about £30,000 from his discovery, as he kept the process secret until shortly before his death, allowing no one to enter his laboratory. Working with platinum ore, he also isolated two new elements: palladium (1804), named for the recently discovered asteroid Pallas, and rhodium (1805), named for the rose color of its compounds. In 1810 he discovered the second amino acid, cystine, in a bladder stone.

In optics Wollaston developed the reflecting goniometer (1809), an instrument for the measurement of angles between the faces of a crystal. He also patented the camera lucida in 1807. In this device an adjustable prism reflects light from the object to be drawn and light from the paper into the draftsman's eye. This produces the illusion of the image on the paper, allowing him to trace it. Wollaston was a friend of Thomas Young and a supporter of the wave theory of light. One opportunity he missed occurred when, in 1802, he observed the dark lines in the solar spectrum but failed to grasp their importance, taking them simply to be the natural boundaries of colors. He missed a similar chance in 1820 when he failed to pursue the full implications of Hans Oersted's 1820 demonstration that an electric current could cause a deflection in a compass needle. Although he performed some experiments it was left to Michael Faraday in 1821 to discover and analyze electromagnetic rotation. Wollaston was successful in showing that frictional and galvanic electricity were identical in 1801. In 1814 he proposed the term "chemical equivalents."

Wolpert, Lewis

(1929–)

BRITISH EMBRYOLOGIST

Wolpert, who was born at Johannesburg in South Africa, trained initially as an engineer at the University of Witwatersrand. After working as an engineer in Britain and Israel, Wolpert's interests turned to biology and he began to study for a PhD in embryology at King's College, London. He taught there from 1958 until 1966, when he was appointed professor of biology at the Middlesex Hospital Medical School. From 1987 he has worked at University College, London.

Wolpert has worked mainly on the problem of pattern formation in biological development. How is it, for example, that the same differentiated cells – muscle, cartilage, skin, connective tissue – arrange themselves as legs in one place and arms in another. Francis Crick proposed in 1970 that patterns could be produced through the action of a "morphogen," a substance whose concentration throughout the field could be sensed by individual cells. Wolpert illustrated the mechanism with his flag analogy.

Imagine a line of cells capable of turning blue, red, or white. What simple mechanism could generate the pattern of the French tricolor? One way would be to have a chemical whose concentration, while fixed at one end of the line, decreased along the line. Cells could respond to a certain concentration of the morphogen and turn blue, red, or white accordingly.

Wolpert found that in such a system it should be possible to specify some 30 different cell states along a line of about 100 cells. The limiting factor was the accuracy with which cells can identify thresholds of concentration.

Wolpert identified a second positional system, one dependent upon time. Wing growth in chicks, for example, is mainly due to cell multiplication at the tip of the limb in a region known as the "progress zone." The cells learn their position by responding to the length of time they remain in the progress zone. Thus the cells which stay in the progress zone the shortest time form the humerus, and those that stay in the longest develop into digits.

Much recent work in developmental biology was described by Wolpert in his *The Triumph of the Embryo* (Oxford, 1991), material that was originally presented in his 1986 Royal Institution Christmas Lectures. Wolpert has also taken it upon himself to speak for science in such works as his *The Unnatural Nature of Science* (London, 1993), against what he sees as increasingly philistine attacks from journalists and politicians against the aims and methods of modern science.

Wood, Robert Williams

(1868–1955)

AMERICAN PHYSICIST

Wood was born in Concord, Massachusetts, and majored in chemistry at Harvard, graduating in 1891. However, during his postgraduate research (1891–96) at Johns Hopkins University, Baltimore, and the universities of Chicago and Berlin, he turned toward physics. In 1897 he started teaching at the University of Wisconsin and four years later was appointed professor of experimental physics at Johns Hopkins. On his retirement in 1938 he was reappointed research professor.

Wood had wide-ranging interests in science and technology but his major contributions were in optics and spectroscopy. At Johns Hopkins he started his lifelong study of the optical properties of fluorescent gases and his spectroscopic data formed much of the experimental foundation of the model of the atom put forward by Niels Bohr in 1913.

Wood liked experimenting with slightly mysterious things that would grip the public imagination. This predilection led to his work on infrared and ultraviolet photography and he invented a filter, since named *Wood's glass*, that is almost opaque to visible light but lets through the ultraviolet. As well as investigating "invisible light" during World War I, he became interested in "inaudible sounds," especially in the biological effects of these ultrasonic vibrations. His work on ultrasonics aroused considerable interest in the subject. His book *Physical Optics* (1905) became a standard work on the subject and he was also well known as a popular writer and lecturer.

Woodward, Sir Arthur Smith

(1864–1944)

BRITISH PALEONTOLOGIST

Woodward, the son of a silk dyer from Macclesfield in northwest England, was educated at Owens College, Manchester. In 1882 he was appointed to the staff of the department of geology at the British Museum (Natural History), where he remained until 1924, being made keeper in 1901.

Woodward was a most conscientious worker with over six hundred publications to his credit. His most substantial work was on the topic of fossil fish, with his catalog of the Natural History Museum collection (4 vols., 1889–1901) his most solid achievement. However, despite his devotion to such an esoteric subject, he became known to a wide public for a discovery made by him and some friends in 1912.

While exploring the gravels of the Sussex Ouse with Charles Dawson they discovered the remains of Piltdown man. By the end of the year Woodward was ready to describe the skull to a meeting of the Geological Society. It possessed, he declared, a cranium like that of modern man with a jaw similar to an ape's, in which were found two molar teeth with a marked regular flattening that had not been observed among apes. Without the molars, Woodward stated, it would be impossible to tell the jaw was human. The evidence of geology made Piltdown older than Neanderthal man, thus leading Woodward to his main conclusion that *Eoanthropus dawsoni*, as he named it, was the true ancestor of modern man.

Woodward never wavered in his view. He in fact died some years before the exposure of the Piltdown fraud by Keith Oakley in 1953.

Woodward, John

(1665–1728)

BRITISH GEOLOGIST

Little is known of Woodward's early life except that he was born in England and apprenticed to a draper; he later came to the attention of a physician to Charles II who organized his education. In 1692 he was appointed professor of physics at Gresham College, London.

In 1695 Woodward published his *Essays Toward a Natural History of the Earth*. Following Thomas Burnet, he attempted to give a clear and naturalistic account of the Earth's history in keeping with the Creation as told in Genesis. Unlike the universal decay that Burnet proclaimed, Woodward saw the deluge as creating the Earth very much as we now know it. Woodward thus had the problem of explaining the facts of geological change. He denied that earthquakes and volcanoes altered the topography and would not accept that valleys and mountains could be worn away. His answer to the obvious signs of denudation was to propose a compensating mechanism by which the materials eroded would be washed into the rivers, picked up by the winds, and fall back onto the mountains.

In other fields Woodward conducted a series of experiments on plant nutrition in 1691 and was the first to show that much of the moisture absorbed by plants is transpired. He also, from 1704 until his death, worked on systems of mineral classification. His final achievement was the creation of a chair of geology at Cambridge University named for him.

Woodward, Robert Burns

(1917–1979)

AMERICAN CHEMIST

Born in Boston, Massachusetts, Woodward was educated at the Massachusetts Institute of Technology, obtaining his PhD in 1937. His whole career was spent at Harvard where, starting as a postdoctoral fellow in 1937, he became Morris Loeb Professor of Chemistry in 1953.

In 1944 Woodward, with William von Eggers Doering, synthesized quinine from the basic elements. This was an historic moment for it was the quinine molecule that William Perkin had first, somewhat prematurely, attempted to synthesize in 1855.

Woodward and his school later succeeded in synthesizing an impressive number of molecules, many of which are important far beyond the field of chemistry. Thus among the most important were cholesterol and cortisone in 1951, strychnine and LSD in 1954, reserpine in 1956, chlorophyll in 1960, a tetracycline antibiotic in 1962, and vitamin B_{12} in 1971. The work on the synthesis of B_{12} led Woodward and Roald Hoffman to introduce the principle of conservation of orbital symmetry. This major theoretical advance has provided a deep understanding of a wide group of chemical reactions.

He received the Nobel Prize for chemistry in 1965. Woodward's death in 1979 deprived him of a second Nobel award, namely, the chemistry prize awarded to his colleague Hoffmann in 1981 for their work on orbital theory.

Woolley, Sir Richard van der Riet

(1906–1986)

BRITISH ASTRONOMER

Woolley was born in Weymouth on the south coast of England. The son of a rear-admiral, he was educated at the University of Cape Town, where his father had moved on retirement, and at Cambridge. After spending two years at Mount Wilson Observatory, California, he returned to Cambridge in 1931. Shortly afterward he was appointed for the first time to the Royal Observatory, Greenwich, as chief assistant.

From 1933 to 1937 Woolley worked mainly in the solar department and published jointly with F. Dyson *Eclipses of the Sun and Moon* (London, 1937). After a second spell at Cambridge he moved to Australia in 1939 as director of the Commonwealth Solar Observatory, Mt. Stromlo, Canberra. During his long stay he sought to move the observatory into astrophysics and to concentrate its observational work on the southern stars. To this end he installed a 74-inch reflector in 1950.

In 1956 Woolley returned to Greenwich as the 11th Astronomer Royal, the last one to be in charge of the Royal Observatory, which, by 1958, had completed its move from Greenwich to Herstmonceaux, Sussex. One of Woolley's first tasks was to revive plans to build the 100-inch Isaac Newton telescope first proposed in 1946. Under Woolley the telescope was eventually opened in 1967. Woolley retired as Astronomer Royal in 1971 but served a further period in South Africa as Director of the Cape Observatory (1972–76).

For many Woolley will always be remembered for his 1956 judgment that space travel was "utter bilge," just one year before Sputnik 1 was launched.

Worsaae, Jens Jacob Asmussen

(1821–1885)

DANISH ARCHEOLOGIST

> The actual founder of antiquarian research as an independent science.
> —Johannes Brøndsted, describing Worsaae

Worsaae (**vor**-saw), the son of a government official, was born at Vejle in Denmark. Although he was initially trained as a law student his real interest, going back to his schooldays, lay in the collection of antiquities. He consequently joined Christian Thomsen as an unpaid assistant at the Danish National Museum in 1836 and in 1847 he was appointed inspector of Danish historic and prehistoric monuments. In 1854, as professor of archeology at the University of Copenhagen, he became the first ever paid full-time archeologist. In 1865 he succeeded Thomsen as director of the National Museum, a post he occupied until his death in 1885.

With his *Danmark's Oldtid oplyst ved Oldsager og Gravhøie* (1843), translated into English in 1849 as *Primeval Antiquities of Denmark*, Worsaae made the first application of Thomsen's three-age system to actual excavations in the field as opposed to exhibits in museums. He was thus able to show that the Danish grave-hills are usually divisible into three classes, corresponding to the Stone, Bronze, and Iron age periods.

He further argued for the importance of comparative studies, emphasizing the necessity of studying similar monuments in other countries to gain a satisfactory knowledge of Danish memorials. In general, Worsaae is regarded as one of the people responsible for establishing scientific standards in the field of archeology.

Wright, Sir Almroth Edward

(1861–1947)

BRITISH PHYSICIAN

Wright was born in Richmond, England, and educated at Trinity College, Dublin, where he received a BA in modern literature (1882) and his bachelor of medicine (1883). He completed his medical studies in London, Europe, and at the University of Sydney, Australia, before being appointed to an army medical school. Here he developed a vaccine against typhoid fever. This later proved to be of considerable strategic importance in combat.

In 1902 Wright began his long association with St. Mary's Hospital, London, as professor of pathology. In 1911 he went to South Africa to develop an antipneumonia inoculation. During World War I he served in France, investigating techniques for treating infected wounds. Several of Wright's students at St. Mary's subsequently achieved fame, including the discoverer of penicillin, Alexander Fleming. Wright was also noted as a vehement antifeminist and received a public rebuke for this failing from the writer George Bernard Shaw. He was knighted in 1906.

Wright, Orville

(1871–1948)

AMERICAN AERONAUTICAL
ENGINEER

Wright, Wilbur

(1867–1912)

AMERICAN AERONAUTICAL
ENGINEER

> For some years I have been afflicted with the belief that flight is possible to man. My disease has increased in severity and I feel that it will soon cost me an increased amount of money if not my life. I have been trying to arrange my affairs in such a way that I can devote my entire time for a few months to experiment in this field.
>
> —Wilbur Wright, letter to Octave Chanute, 13 May 1900

The sons of a bishop in the United Brethren Church, Wilbur Wright was born in Millville, Indiana, and Orville in Dayton, Ohio. Neither brother received more than a high-school education. They had, however, shown a certain inventiveness and an interest in things mechanical. They were the kind of boys who having seen a woodcut in a magazine would immediately make their own woodcut. Thus on leaving school they first experimented with printing, publishing the weekly *West Side News* for over a year. By 1892 they had lost their interest in printing and decided instead to open a bike shop in which they not only sold and repaired bikes but made them themselves.

They later reported that their interest in flight had been stimulated by reading in 1896 of the death of the German engineer Lilienthal in a gliding accident. They first devoured the available literature describing the machines and flights of Lilienthal, Samuel Langley, and others. Above all they were struck by the lack of control mechanisms in the early machines. The early designers had merely sought to maintain equilibrium, but the Wrights saw that flying meant directing and upsetting equilibrium in a carefully controlled manner. A specific control mechanism was suggested to them by observing the flight of pigeons, and how they maintained their balance by twisting their wing tips. A comparable effect could be achieved in a plane by warping the wings' ends. But how could this be produced? The answer came to Wilbur when, while fiddling with a narrow rectangular box, he noted how easily the ends could be twisted in opposite directions.

The principle was incorporated in a biplane kite which they tested in 1900 on the sandhills at Kitty Hawk, North Carolina. A larger kite was tested in 1901 and in 1902 further data was collected from trials in a wind tunnel constructed by the brothers. One result of this work was the installation of a vertical tail on the 1902 glider. At this point they considered converting their kite-glider to a powered aircraft. Characteristically they designed and built their own 12 horsepower model and fitted two propellers with a diameter of 8.5 feet. Wilbur piloted the first flight on 14 December 1903 but induced a stall; during the second flight, on 17 December, Orville covered 120 feet at an average speed of 7 miles per hour. The plane, known as "the Flyer," was damaged in a later flight that day and was never flown again; it was later placed as a permanent exhibit at the Smithsonian, Washington DC.

The brothers continued to work on their design and only when completely satisfied with a new version of the Flyer were they prepared to demonstrate powered flight to the public. Wilbur first flew publicly near Le Mans in France in August 1908, and Orville a few days later at Fort Meyer, Virginia.

In 1909 they set up the Wright Company, with considerable financial backing, to build versions of the Flyer. They also received license fees from European manufacturers. Much of their time, however, must have been spent in patent disputes which dragged on in one form or another until 1928. Wilbur died from typhoid fever in 1912. Orville sold the business in 1915 for a sum said to be $1.5 million, while remaining as a consultant for $25,000 a year. Much of his later life was spent ensuring the contribution of the Wright brothers to the early history of aviation was properly recognized. He died of a heart attack in 1948.

Wright, Sewall

(1889–1988)

AMERICAN STATISTICIAN AND GENETICIST

Born in Melrose, Massachusetts, Wright graduated from Lombard College in 1911; he gained his master's degree from the University of Illinois the following year and his doctorate from Harvard in 1916. He then worked as senior animal husbandman for the U.S. Department of Agriculture and began his researches into the population genetics of guinea pigs. His first work aimed to find the best combination of inbreeding and crossbreeding to improve stock, this having practical application in livestock breeding. From this he also developed a mathematical theory of evolution.

His name is best known, however, in connection with the process of genetic drift, which is also termed the *Sewall Wright effect*. He demonstrated that in small isolated populations certain forms of genes may be lost quite randomly, simply because the few individuals possessing them happen not to pass them on. The loss of such characters may lead to the formation of new species without natural selection coming into operation. Wright held professorial positions at the University of Chicago and Edinburgh University and was emeritus professor at the University of Wisconsin.

Wrinch, Dorothy

(1894–1976)

BRITISH–AMERICAN
MATHEMATICIAN AND BIOCHEMIST

Wrinch was born at Rosario in Argentina and educated at Cambridge University, where she held a research fellowship from 1920 to 1924. She then taught physics at Oxford until 1939, when she moved to America to take up an appointment as lecturer in chemistry at Johns Hopkins University. In 1942 she moved to Smith College, remaining there until her retirement in 1959.

In 1934 Wrinch tackled the important problem of identifying the chemical carriers of genetic information. In common with other scientists at that time, she argued that chromosomes consisted of sequences of amino acids; these were the only molecules thought to possess sufficient variety to permit the construction of complex molecules. She proposed a model of the gene in the form of a T-like structure with a nucleic-acid stem and a sequence of amino acids as the cross bar.

In actual fact there were many such models in the 1930s. If it was not accepted that genes were made from specific sequences of amino acids then it became very difficult to see what they could come from. The trouble with all these models was that the experimentalists quickly found serious defects in them. Thus W. Schmidt in 1936 was able to show that Wrinch's model was incompatible with the known optical properties of nucleic acid and the chromosomes. The first suggestion that there might be an alternative to the protein structure of the gene came with the famous experiment of Oswald Avery in 1944.

Wróblewski, Zygmunt Florenty von

(1845–1888)

POLISH PHYSICIST

Wróblewski (vroo-**blef**-skee), who was born at Grodno (now in Belarus), was a student at Kiev. However, his education was interrupted when he was exiled to Silesia for his part in the 1863 uprising against Russia. On his release he studied abroad with Hermann von Helmholtz in Berlin and at Strasbourg before being appointed to the chair of physics at the University of Cracow in 1882. He died in the flames of his laboratory, apparently having knocked over a kerosene lamp while working late.

Wróblewski was one of the 19th-century physicists who worked on the liquefaction of gases following the success of Raoul Pictet and Louis Cailletet. In 1883 Wróblewski and K. Olszewski developed a method of making liquid oxygen in usable quantities.

Wu, Chien-Shiung

(1912–   )

CHINESE–AMERICAN PHYSICIST

Now one of the world's leading experimental physicists, Wu (woo), who was born in Shanghai, China, gained her BS from the National Central University of China before moving to America in 1936. Here she studied under Ernest O. Lawrence at the University of California, Berkeley. She gained her PhD in 1940, then went on to teach at Smith College, Northampton, Massachusetts, and later at Princeton University. In 1946 she became a staff member at Columbia University, advancing to become professor of physics in 1957.

Her first significant research work was on the mechanism of beta disintegration (in radioactive decay). In particular, she demonstrated in 1956 that the direction of emission of beta rays is strongly correlated with the direction of spin of the emitting nucleus, showing that parity is not conserved in beta disintegration. This experiment confirmed the theories advanced by Tsung Dao Lee of Columbia and Chen Ning Yang of Princeton that in the so-called "weak" nuclear interactions the previously held "law of symmetry" was violated. Yang and Lee later received the Nobel Prize for physics for their theory, and the discovery overturned many central ideas in physics.

In 1958 Richard Feynman and Murray Gell-Mann proposed the theory of conservation of vector current in beta decay. This theory was experimentally confirmed in 1963 by Wu, in collaboration with two other Columbia University physicists.

Wu's other contributions to elementary-particle physics include her demonstration that the electromagnetic radiation from the annihilation of positrons and electrons is polarized – a finding in accordance with Dirac's theory, proving that the electron and positron have opposite parity. She has also undertaken a study of the x-ray spectra of muonic atoms. More recently she has become interested in biological problems, especially the structure of hemoglobin.

Wu, Hsien

(1893–1959)

CHINESE BIOCHEMIST

Born into a scholarly family in Fouchow, China, Wu won a scholarship to the Massachusetts Institute of Technology in 1911 to study naval architecture. A reading of T. H. Huxley's "On the physical basis of life" diverted him to the study of biology and chemistry at Harvard, where he completed his PhD in 1919.

While at Harvard, working under Otto Folin, Wu developed important analytical techniques that allowed most clinical tests to be carried out with blood samples as small as 10 milliliters. In 1920 he returned to

China to the Peking Union Medical College, being appointed in 1928 professor of biochemistry, a post he continued to hold until the Japanese occupation in 1942. Much of Wu's work was carried out in the field of nutrition. He produced a textbook on the subject, *The Principles of Nutrition* (1929). After the war Wu was appointed director of the Nutrition Institute in Peking. But, soon after, with the rise of communism, Wu decided to settle in America and spent the latter part of his life as professor of biochemistry at the University of Alabama.

Wunderlich, Carl Reinhold August

(1815–1877)

GERMAN PHYSICIAN

The son of a physician, Wunderlich (**vuun**-der-lik) was born in Sulz, Germany. He studied medicine at the University of Tübingen, qualifying as a doctor in 1837. After a few years' further study in Paris and Vienna he took up an appointment at the Tübingen clinic in 1839. Wunderlich moved in 1850 to Leipzig University where he served as professor of anatomy until his death.

In 1868 Wunderlich published one of the classic works of modern medicine, *Das Verhalten der Eigenwärme in Krankheiten*, translated into English in 1871 as *On the Temperature in Disease*. He had begun in 1848 to record systematically the temperature of his patients, a most unusual event at the time if only because the thermometers of his day were bulky, uncomfortable, and required a good deal of time to register accurately.

Wunderlich demonstrated two basic principles; constant temperature in health but variation in disease, and the normal range of temperature. More importantly, however, he noted that certain diseases are characterized by a given pattern of changes in temperature. He had thus shown that clinical thermometry could be used as an important additional diagnostic technique.

Wurtz, Charles Adolphe

(1817–1884)

FRENCH CHEMIST

Wurtz (voorts) was educated at the university in his native city of Strasbourg. He worked under Justus von Liebig in Giessen and under Jean Dumas in Paris. In 1853 he was appointed professor of chemistry at the Ecole de Médicine until he moved to the chair of organic chemistry at the Sorbonne in 1874.

Wurtz contributed to the development of the type theory of Charles Gerhardt and Auguste Laurente by introducing the ammonia type in 1849. He synthesized ethylamine from ammonia and constructed his ammonia type by substituting the carbon radical C_2H_5 for one or more of the hydrogen atoms in ammonia (NH_3). He thus produced the series ammonia (NH_3); ethylamine ($C_2H_5NH_2$); diethylamine (($C_2H_5)_2NH$); triethylamine (($C_2H_5)_3N$). Other types were added by Gerhardt.

In 1855 Wurtz developed a method of synthesizing hydrocarbons by reacting alkyl halides with sodium (still known as the *Wurtz reaction*). With Rudolf Fittig he developed a similar reaction for synthesizing aromatic hydrocarbons. In 1860 Wurtz was involved, with August Kekulé, in initiating the first conference of the International Chemical Congress at Karlsruhe. He was also involved in the Couper tragedy. In 1858 Archibald Couper had apparently anticipated Kekulé in working out the structure of the carbon atom and asked Wurtz to present his paper to the Académie des Sciences. Wurtz delayed and Kekulé published. When Couper remonstrated with Wurtz he was expelled from Wurtz's laboratory. Couper had a breakdown on his return to Scotland and never did any serious chemistry again.

Wurtz was a prolific author, his *La Théorie atomique* (1879; Atomic Theory), being his best-known work.

Wyckoff, Ralph Walter Graystone

(1897–1994)

AMERICAN CRYSTALLOGRAPHER AND ELECTRON MICROSCOPIST

Wyckoff was born in Geneva, New York, and graduated from Hobart College. He obtained his PhD from Cornell in 1919. Between 1919 and 1938 Wyckoff worked first in the Geophysical Laboratory, New York, and then at the Rockefeller Institute before transferring to the Lederle Laboratories in 1938. He then worked at the University of Michigan (1943–45) and the National Institute of Health (1945–59). He was appointed to the chair of physics and microbiology at the University of Arizona in 1959.

While at the Rockefeller Institute Wyckoff managed to purify various viruses, including that causing equine encephalomyelitis, using an ultracentrifuge. The pure preparations of encephalomyelitis virus were used to develop a killed-virus vaccine which proved effective against the epidemic that was affecting horses in America. This success led to a program for producing typhus vaccine.

In 1944 Wyckoff entered into an unusual and profitable collaboration with the astronomer-turned-biophysicist Robley Williams. Wyckoff was using the electron microscope to photograph viruses but found, as did other virologists of the time, that the amount of information conveyed about the size and shape of the virus was strictly limited.

Wyckoff discussed with Williams the problem of determining the size of a speck of dust that had fallen onto a specimen and been photographed with it. To an astronomer the solution was obvious, for it is a standard procedure to measure the heights of lunar mountains from the length of the shadow cast by them and knowledge of the angle of the incident light source. The problem was to make viruses cast shadows. They placed the specimen in a vacuum together with a heated tungsten filament covered with gold. This vaporized and coated the side of the specimen nearest the filament, leaving a "shadow" on the far side.

This technique of "metal shadowing" opened a new phase in the study of viruses allowing better estimates to be made of their size and shape, as well as revealing details of their structure.

Wynne-Edwards, Vero Copner

(1906–)

BRITISH ZOOLOGIST

Wynne-Edwards, who was born at Leeds in England, graduated in natural science from Oxford University in 1927. After leaving Oxford in 1929 he taught zoology at Bristol University (1929–30) and at McGill University, Montreal (from 1930). He returned to Britain in 1946 and served as professor of natural history at Aberdeen University until his retirement in 1974.

In 1962 Wynne-Edwards published his *Animal Dispersion in Relation to Social Behaviour*, one of the most influential zoological works of the postwar years. Much of it became known to a wider public through the popular writings of Robert Ardrey. In it he put the strongest possible case for group selection, the view that animals sacrifice personal survival and fertility to control population growth, that is, for the good of the group as a whole. They behave, in fact, altruistically.

Thus for Wynne-Edwards all such animal behavior as territoriality, dominance hierarchies, and grouping in large flocks (epideictic behavior) were simply devices for the control of population size. Such views stimulated a strong reaction, forcing his opponents to develop alternative accounts of altruism and population control in as much depth as his own.

It was from this dispute that theorists such as William Hamilton and Robert Trivers began to develop the concepts that emerged as one of the strains of sociobiology developed by Edward O. Wilson.

Xenophanes of Colophon

(*c.* 560 BC–*c.* 478 BC)

GREEK PHILOSOPHER

Xenophanes (ze-**nof**-a-neez) appears to have moved from his birthplace, Colophon (which is now in Turkey), when the Persians invaded Asia Minor in about 546 BC. First he went to Sicily and then to Elea in southern Italy. Although Parmenides is usually considered the founder of the Eleatic school, Xenophanes anticipated his views.

It is Xenophanes who made the first explicit and comprehensive attack on the anthropomorphic view of nature so prevalent in the ancient world. Drawing attention to the relativity of belief he commented that: "The Ethiopians say their gods are snub-nosed and black, the Thracians that theirs have light-blue eyes and red hair." More radical, however, was his claim that if horses and cattle had hands, "they would draw the forms of the gods like horses, and...like cattle." In place of the anthropomorphic polytheism of Homer he substituted the cryptic "the One is god."

Xenophanes also left a number of astronomical fragments, none of which, however, rise above his: "The Sun comes into being each day from little pieces of fire."

Yalow, Rosalyn Sussman

(1921–   )

AMERICAN PHYSICIST

Yalow was born in New York City and educated at Hunter College and at the University of Illinois, where she obtained her PhD in nuclear physics in 1945. Since 1947 she has worked at the Veterans Administration Hospital in the Bronx as a physicist and, since 1968, she has also held the post of research professor at the Mount Sinai School of Medicine.

In the 1950s, working with Solomon Berson, Yalow developed the technique of radioimmunoassay (RIA), which permits the detection of extremely small amounts of hormone. The technique involves taking a known amount of radioactively labeled hormone, together with a known amount of antibody against it, and mixing it with human serum containing an unknown amount of unlabeled hormone. The antibodies bind to both the radioactive and normal hormone in the proportions in which they are present in the mixture. It is then possible to calculate with great accuracy the amount of unlabeled hormone present in the original sample; using this technique, amounts as small as one picogram (10^{-12} g) can be detected.

This technique enabled Roger Guillemin and Andrew Schally to detect the hypothalamic hormones; Yalow, Guillemin, and Schally shared the Nobel Prize for physiology or medicine in 1977.

Yang, Chen Ning

(1922–   )

CHINESE–AMERICAN PHYSICIST

Yang, who was born the son of a mathematics professor at Hefei in China, graduated from the National Southwest Associated University in Kunming and received an MSc from Tsinghua. A fellowship enabled him to travel to America, where he studied for his PhD at the University of Chicago, under Enrico Fermi. After teaching at Chicago he joined the Institute for Advanced Study, Princeton, becoming professor of physics in 1955. In 1965 he was appointed Einstein Professor of Physics and director of the Institute of Theoretical Physics at the State University of New York, Stony Brook.

Yang collaborated with Tsung Dao Lee, and in 1956 they made a fundamental theoretical breakthrough in predicting that the law of conservation of parity would break down in the so-called weak interactions. Their startling prediction was quickly confirmed experimentally, by Chien-Shiung Wu, and in 1957 Yang and Lee were awarded the Nobel Prize for physics.

Yang has also made other advances in theoretical physics. In collaboration with R. L. Mills he proposed a non-Abelian gauge theory – also known as the *Yang–Mills theory* – a mathematical principle describing fundamental interactions for elementary particles and fields. Yang has also made contributions to statistical mechanics.

Yanofsky, Charles

(1925–)

AMERICAN GENETICIST

Born in New York City, Yanofsky graduated in chemistry from the City College of New York in 1948 and went on to gain his PhD in microbiology from Yale University in 1951. During three years' postdoctoral work at Yale on gene mutations, he demonstrated that the effect of one mutation may be compensated for by another "suppressor" mutation, which supplies the enzyme lacking, or rendered ineffective, in the original mutant. In 1958 Yanofsky joined Stanford University as associate professor in microbiology. His research at Stanford provided evidence that the linear sequence of amino acid molecules in proteins is determined by the order of nucleotide molecules in the hereditary material (DNA). This concept had been central to genetics since James Watson and Francis Crick proposed their molecular structure of DNA, but the theory still remained to be proved.

Yanofsky demonstrated the colinearity of DNA and proteins by using Seymour Benzer's strain of the bacteriophage T4 with the gene rII, rendering it incapable of multiplying on a certain type of the bacterium *Escherichia coli*. Many different mutants of the rII gene were isolated, and by recombination studies the positions of these mutations within the gene were mapped. The amino acid sequence of the enzyme produced by the rII gene was established, as were the sequences of the various mutant forms of the enzyme. It was then seen that the positions of amino acid changes corresponded to the mutant sites on the genetic map, indicating that proteins are indeed colinear with DNA.

Yanofsky has been professor of biology at Stanford University since 1961 and has received many awards for his research in molecular biology.

Yersin, Alexandre Emile John

(1863–1943)

SWISS BACTERIOLOGIST

Yersin (yair-**san**) was born at Aubonne, near Lausanne, in Switzerland. He studied medicine at the universities of Marburg and Paris and, in 1888, became an assistant to the bacteriologist Emile Roux, at the Pasteur Institute, Paris. They collaborated in investigating the toxins produced by the diphtheria bacterium. Yersin also briefly worked under Robert Koch in Berlin before making the first of several trips to Southeast Asia. In 1894, while based in Hong Kong, he discovered the bacterium responsible for causing bubonic plague, *Pasteurella pestis* (now renamed *Yersinia pestis*). Simultaneously and independently, the same discovery was made by the Japanese bacteriologist, Shibasaburo Kitasato. In the following year Yersin prepared the first antiplague serum.

Yersin made a great contribution to fighting disease in Indochina and helped to found a medical school in Hanoi. He also had a keen interest in the fauna and flora of the region, especially its agricultural crops.

Yoshimasu, Todu

(1702–1773)

JAPANESE PHYSICIAN

Yoshimasu, also known as Yoshimasu Shusuke (yoh-shee-**mah**-soo shuu-**soo**-ke), was actually named Tamenori; he was born at Hiroshima in Japan and studied medicine in Kyoto where he also practiced. As the 18th century began, Japanese medicine was derived almost entirely from traditional Chinese sources. The particular form prevalent in Japan has become known as "phase energetics" and involved correlating bodily states with the presence in the body of yin–yang and the five elements (earth, fire, wood, metal, and water), all against a background of calendrical and meteorological conditions.

Yoshimasu made clear his opposition to Chinese medicine. The yin and the yang, he insisted, were the "ch'i" (energy) of the universe and had nothing to do with medicine. In the place of such speculative theories, he insisted, observation should rule. Only then could we establish the important correspondence – that between specific symptoms and drugs capable of curing them. To this effect Yoshimasu published his *Ruijuho* (Classified Prescription; 1764); it contained 220 prescriptions, all derived from Chinese sources, reportedly based upon observation.

Yet despite his insistence upon observation in therapeutics, Yoshimasu could be as dogmatic as any traditionalist in his diagnostics. Thus in an earlier work, *Idan* (New Perspective on Medicine; 1759), Yoshimasu claimed that all disease originated in the abdomen and could be attributed to a single toxic principle.

Young, James

(1811–1883)

BRITISH CHEMIST

Young was the son of a carpenter from Glasgow in Scotland. He worked with his father by day and attended the classes of Thomas Graham at Anderson's College, Glasgow, by night. There he made friends with Lyon Playfair and the explorer David Livingstone, two fellow students. He became Graham's assistant in 1832 and moved with him when he took up a post at University College, London (1837).

Young started his industrial career as a manager with James Muspratt at his alkali factory in 1839, moving to Charles Tennant's factory in Manchester in 1844. While there he heard from Lyon Playfair of oil seepage at Alfreton, Derbyshire. In 1847 Young acquired the mineral rights and was soon producing 300 gallons daily for use in lubrication and lighting. The source was exhausted in 1851 when he moved to Lothian, where once more his source soon ran out.

Rather than rely on oil springs Young pioneered the low-temperature distillation of oil-rich shales and coals to produce yields of paraffin oil. He moved to Glasgow where he produced oils for use in lighting, heating, and lubrication. He sold his business in 1866.

Young's interest in science persisted and in 1881 he tried to determine the speed of light using Fizeau's technique, obtaining an answer in excess of that of Albert Michelson at a little over 300,000 kilometers per second. He also established that blue light travels faster than red.

He gave substantially to Livingstone to finance his travels and also endowed the Young Chair of Technical Chemistry at Anderson's College, becoming its president during the period 1868–77.

Young, Thomas

(1773–1829)

BRITISH PHYSICIST, PHYSICIAN, AND EGYPTOLOGIST

Acute suggestion was...always more in the line of my ambition than experimental illustration.
—Quoted by George Peacock in his *Life of Thomas Young* (1855)

Young, who was born at Milverton in southwest England, was a child prodigy. He could read with considerable fluency at the age of 2 and by 13 he had a good knowledge of Latin, Greek, French, and Italian. He had also begun to study natural history and natural philosophy and could make various optical instruments. A year later he began an independent study of the Hebrew, Chaldean, Syriac, Samaritan, Arabic, Persian, Turkish, and Ethiopic languages. When he was 19 he was a highly proficient Latin and Greek scholar, having mastered many literary and scientific works including Newton's *Principia* and *Opticks* and

Antoine Lavoisier's *Traité élémentaire de chimie* (Elementary Treatise on Chemistry).

In 1793 Young began a medical education, studying first at St. Bartholomew's Hospital, London, and then at the universities of Edinburgh (1794), Göttingen (1795), and Cambridge (1797). In 1800, after receiving a considerable inheritance, he set up a medical practice in London; this practice, however, never really flourished. In 1801 he was appointed professor of natural philosophy at the Royal Institution. Although his lectures were erudite, and remarkable for their scope and originality, they were not successful. They were too technical and detailed for popular audiences and compared unfavorably with those of his colleague, Humphry Davy. In 1803 Young resigned his post. From then until his death he held various medical appointments and several offices related to science.

Young's early scientific researches were concerned with the physiology of the eye. He was elected a fellow of the Royal Society in 1794 for his explanation of how the ciliary muscles change the shape of the lens to focus on objects at differing distances (accommodation); in 1801 he gave the first descriptions of the defect astigmatism and of color sensation.

Young's most lasting contribution to science was his work in helping to establish the wave theory of light. Between 1800 and 1804 he revived an interest in this theory and gave it strong support. He compared the ideas of Newton and Christiaan Huygens on the nature of light, criticizing the corpuscular theory for its inadequacy in explaining such phenomena as simultaneous reflection and refraction. He introduced the idea of interference of light, which he explained by the superposition of waves – a principle that he applied to a range of optical phenomena including Newton's rings, diffraction patterns, and the color of the supernumerary bows of the rainbow. In his best-known demonstration of interference he passed light first through a single pinhole, then through two further pinholes close together; the light then fell upon a screen and gave a series of

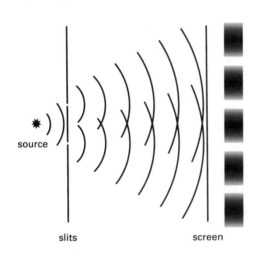

source

slits   screen

YOUNG'S SLITS The production of interference patterns from two slits. Note that in the original experiment, Young used pinholes rather than slits.

light and dark bands. The apparatus is known as *Young's slits*. Young's views were very badly received in England, where opposition to Newton's corpuscular theory was unthinkable. During this period Young was savagely and maliciously attacked by the writer and politician (and amateur scientist) Henry Brougham in the fashionable *Edinburgh Review*.

From about 1804 Young devoted himself more to medical practice and the study of philology, especially the decipherment of hieroglyphic writing. He made very important contributions to the latter field and, independently of Jean François Champollion, helped in translating the text of the Rosetta Stone. His interest in optics was revived in about 1816 by the work of François Arago and Augustin Fresnel. In a letter to Arago he suggested that light might be propagated as a transverse wave (in which the vibrations of the medium are perpendicular to the direction of propagation). This allowed polarization to be explained on the wave theory and gave a satisfactory explanation of the known optical phenomena. The decisive test on the nature of light came later when its speed in the air and water could be accurately measured. Young's other scientific contributions included researches into sound, capillarity, and the cohesion of fluids. Because he gave a physical meaning to the constant of proportionality (E) in Hooke's law, E is called *Young's modulus*.

Yukawa, Hideki

(1907–1981)

JAPANESE PHYSICIST

Yukawa (yoo-**kah**-wah) was born Hideki Ogawa at Kyoto in Japan, the son of the professor of geography at the university there; he assumed the name of his wife, Sumi Yukawa, on their marriage in 1932. He was educated at the university of Kyoto and at Osaka, where he joined the faculty in 1933 and where he completed his doctorate in 1938. In the following year Yukawa was appointed professor of physics at Kyoto University, a position he continued to hold until his retirement in 1970.

Yukawa was concerned with the force that binds the neutrons and protons together in the nucleus. At first sight, any nucleus containing more than one proton should be unstable since positively charged particles repel each other; squeezing a number of positively charged protons into the nucleus of an atom should generate powerful repulsive forces. The obvious answer is that there must be another, attractive, force that operates only at short range and holds the nucleons together. Such a force became known to physicists as the "strong interaction."

Yukawa sought to find the mechanism of the strong force and used the electromagnetic force as an analogy. Here the interaction between charged particles is seen as the result of the continuous exchange of a quantum or unit of energy carried by a "virtual particle" – in this case the photon. So, just as electrons and protons interact by exchanging photons, the nucleons interact by exchanging the appropriate particle. Yukawa could predict its mass from quantum theory as the range over which a particle operates is inversely proportional to its mass. The massless photon is thus thought to operate over an infinite distance; as the strong force operates over a distance of less than 10^{-12} cm it must be mediated by a particle, Yukawa predicted, with a mass of about 200 times that of the electron.

Yukawa made his prediction in 1935 and when two years later Carl Anderson found signs of such a particle in cosmic-ray tracks physicists took this as supporting Yukawa's hypothesis and named the particle a mu-meson (now called a muon). However, although the muon had the appropriate mass it interacted with nucleons so infrequently that it could not possibly be the nuclear "glue." Yukawa's theory was saved, however, by the discovery in 1947 by Cecil Powell, once more in cosmic-ray tracks, of a particle with a mass of 264 times that of the electron and of which the muons were the decay product. The pi-meson, or pion as it became known, interacted very strongly with nucleons and thus filled precisely Yukawa's predicted role.

For this work Yukawa was awarded the Nobel Prize for physics in 1949, the first Japanese person to be so honored.

Z

Zeeman, Pieter

(1865–1943)

DUTCH PHYSICIST

Born at Zonnemair in the Netherlands, Zeeman (**zay**-mahn) studied at Leiden University and received a doctorate in 1893. This was for his work on the Kerr effect, which concerns the effect of a magnetic field on light. In 1896 he discovered another magnetooptical effect, which now bears his name – he observed that the spectral lines of certain elements are split into three lines when the sample is in a strong magnetic field perpendicular to the light path; if the field is parallel to the light path the lines split into two. This work was done before the development of quantum mechanics, and the effect was explained at the time using classical theory by Hendrik Antoon Lorentz, who assumed that the light was emitted by oscillating electrons.

This effect (splitting into three or two lines) is called the *normal Zeeman effect* and it can be explained using Niels Bohr's theory of the atom. In general, most substances show an *anomalous Zeeman effect*, in which the splitting is into several closely spaced lines – a phenomenon that can be explained using quantum mechanics and the concept of electron spin.

Zeeman was a meticulous experimenter and he applied his precision in measurement to the determination of the speed of light in dense media, confirming Lorentz's prediction that this was related to wavelength. Also, in 1918, he established the equality of gravitational and inertial mass thus reconfirming Einstein's equivalence principle, which lies at the core of general relativity theory.

Zeeman and Lorentz shared the 1902 Nobel Prize for physics for their work on magnetooptical effects.

Zeno of Elea

(*c.* 490 BC–*c.* 430 BC)

GREEK PHILOSOPHER

Zeno (**zee**-noh) was born at Elea (now Velia in Italy) and in about 450 BC accompanied his teacher, Parmenides, to Athens. There he propounded the theories of the Eleatic school and became famous for his series of paradoxes and his invention of dialectic.

Little survives of Zeno's written work and this only in other authors' writings. He proposed that motion and multiplicity are unreal (thus supporting Parmenides's theories) since assumption of their existence gave rise to contradictory propositions. One of the most famous arguments against plurality and motion is that of Achilles and the tortoise: if the tortoise is given a start in a race against Achilles, when Achilles reaches the tortoise's starting position, the tortoise will have advanced a small way to a new position. Endless repetition of this argument means that Achilles can never overtake the tortoise.

Zeno's paradoxes remained unresolved for about 20 centuries, in fact until the advances in rigor of mathematical analysis (to the development of which these paradoxes may be said to have contributed). These advances included the study of convergent series (infinite series with a finite sum), the invention by Gottfried Leibniz and Isaac Newton of calculus, and Georg Cantor's theory of the infinite in the 19th century.

Following his return to Elea Zeno died while joining a coup against the tyrant Nearchus.

Zernike, Frits

(1888–1966)

DUTCH PHYSICIST

Zernike (**zair**-ni-ke), who was the son of mathematics teachers at Amsterdam in the Netherlands, studied at the university there, obtaining a doctorate in 1915. In 1913 he became assistant to the astronomer Jacobus Kapteyn at the University of Groningen, where he remained until his retirement in 1958, becoming professor of theoretical physics in 1920 and later of mathematical physics and theoretical mechanics.

Zernike's interest centered around optics and, more particularly, diffraction and in 1935 he developed the phase-contrast microscope. This uses the fact that light passing through bodies with a different refractive index from the surrounding medium has a different phase. The microscope contains a plate in the focal plane, which causes interference patterns and thus increases the contrast. For instance, it can make living cells observable without killing them by staining and fixing. The method of phase contrast also allows the detail in transparent objects or on metal surfaces to be observed.

Ziegler, Karl

(1898–1973)

GERMAN CHEMIST

Ziegler (**tsee**-gler or **zee**-gler) was born at Helsa in Germany, the son of a minister. He received his doctorate from the University of Marburg in 1923 and then taught at Frankfurt, Heidelberg, and Halle before becoming director of the Max Planck Institute for Coal Research in 1943. In 1963 he was awarded the Nobel Prize for chemistry with Giulio Natta for their discovery of *Ziegler–Natta catalysts*.

One of the earliest plastics, polyethylene, was simply made by polymerization of the ethylene molecule into long chains containing over a thousand ethylene units. In practice, however, the integrity of the chain tended to be ruined by the development of branches weakening the plas-

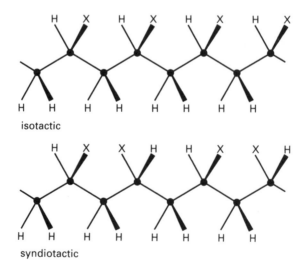

STEREOSPECIFIC POLYMERS   *Examples of stereospecific polymers produced by the Ziegler process.*

tic and endowing it with a melting point only slightly above the boiling point of water.

In 1953 Ziegler introduced a family of catalysts that prevented such branching and produced a much stronger plastic, one which could be soaked in hot water without softening. The catalysts are mixtures of organometallic compounds containing such metallic ions as titanium and aluminum. The new process had the additional advantage that it requires much lower temperatures and pressures than the old method.

Zinder, Norton David

(1928–   )

AMERICAN GENETICIST

Born in New York City, Zinder graduated from Columbia University and did graduate work with Joshua Lederberg at the University of Wisconsin. After obtaining his PhD in medical microbiology in 1952 he moved to the Rockefeller Institute (now Rockefeller University), where he has served as professor of genetics since 1964.

While working under Lederberg, Zinder attempted to extend Lederberg's observation of mating (conjugation) in the bacterium *Escherichia coli* to the closely related species *Salmonella*. He obtained large numbers of nutritional mutants of *Salmonella* by developing an effective new and much less laborious screening method involving the antibiotic penicillin. This method utilizes the fact that penicillin only kills growing bacteria and thus any mutant unable to grow on a certain medium would survive the application of penicillin while all the normal cells would succumb.

Having thus obtained his mutants, and maintained them on selectively enriched media, Zinder began looking for conjugation, but instead found a completely new means of genetic transfer in bacteria – bacterial transduction. Investigations revealed that small portions of genetic material are transferred from one bacterium to another via infective bacterial viruses or phage particles. This discovery allowed small portions of the bacterial genome to be investigated and enabled Milislav Demerec to show that the genes controlling sequential steps in a given biosynthetic pathway are clustered together in what are now termed "operons."

Zinder's group also discovered the F2 phage, a small virus that has RNA for its genetic material. Studies of the messenger RNA produced by this virus showed that, in addition to the codons for specific amino acids, there are "punctuation" points to signal the initiation and termination of protein chains.

Zinn, Walter Henry

(1906–)

CANADIAN–AMERICAN PHYSICIST

Born at Kitchener in Ontario, Canada, Walter Zinn moved to America in 1930 and received a PhD from Columbia University four years later. He continued research there in collaboration with Leo Szilard, investigating atomic fission. In 1938 he became a naturalized American citizen.

A year later, Zinn and Szilard demonstrated that uranium underwent fission when bombarded with neutrons and that part of the mass was converted into energy according to Einstein's famous formula, $E = mc^2$. This work led him, during World War II, into research into the construction of the atomic bomb. After the war Zinn started the design of an atomic reactor and, in 1951, he built the first breeder reactor. In a breeder reactor, the core is surrounded by a "blanket" of uranium–238 and neutrons from the core convert this into plutonium–239, which can also be used as a fission fuel.

Zozimus of Panopolis

(born *c.* 250)

GREEK–EGYPTIAN ALCHEMIST

Little seems to be known about the life of Zozimus (or Zosimos; **zoh**-si-mus or **zoh**-si-mos) except that he was born at Panopolis (now Alchmon in Egypt). He is best known for his writings – a 28-volume encyclopedia of chemical arts. Zozimus showed how alchemy had progressed since the time of Bolos of Mende, a hellenized Egyptian who lived in the Nile Delta. Sulfur, mercury, and arsenic were essential ingredients in this alchemy, mercury being alluded to variously as "divine dew" or "Scythian water." The main aim was the preparation of gold from base metals and its success depended on the production of a series of colors, usually from black to red, yellow, white, black, green, and finally purple. Although the search for the philosopher's stone had not yet begun Zozimus refers to "the tincture," a substance the alchemists believed to exist, that could instantly transform base metals to gold.

Zsigmondy, Richard Adolf

(1865–1929)

AUSTRIAN CHEMIST

A swarm of dancing gnats in a sunbeam will give one an idea of the motion of the gold particles in the hydrosol of gold.
—*Kolloidchemie* (1912; Colloidal Chemistry)

The son of a Viennese doctor, Zsigmondy (**zhig**-mon-dee) was educated at the universities of Vienna and Munich, where he acquired his PhD in 1890. After periods at the University of Graz and in a glass factory in Jena, in 1908 he became professor of inorganic chemistry at the University of Göttingen, where he remained until his death.

Zsigmondy's first interest was in the chemistry of glazes applied to glass and ceramics. Studies on colored glasses led him into the field of colloids, first distinguished and named by Thomas Graham. Little advance had been made since Graham's time as it was not clear how to study them; the conventional microscope was not powerful enough to detect the particles. In 1903 Zsigmondy remedied this when, in collaboration with Henry Siedentopf, he invented the ultramicroscope in which the particles were illuminated with a cone of light at right angles to the microscope. Although still too small to be seen the particles would diffract light shone on them and therefore appeared as disks of light against a dark background. The particles could be counted, measured, and have their velocity and path determined. Zsigmondy published his work in this field in his book *Kolloidchemie* (1912; Colloidal Chemistry). In 1925 he was awarded the Nobel Prize for chemistry for his work on colloids.

Zuckerandl, Emile

(1922–   )

AUSTRIAN MOLECULAR EVOLUTIONARY BIOLOGIST

Zuckerandl (**tsuuk-er-an-dl**) was born in the Austrian capital of Vienna and educated at the University of Illinois and at the Sorbonne, where he gained his PhD in 1959. He worked with Linus Pauling at the California Institute of Technology from 1959 until 1964, when he moved to the CNRS at Montpellier. In 1980 Zuckerandl returned to California to serve as head of the Linus Pauling Institute, Palo Alto, California.

Zuckerandl has examined the hemoglobin from a number of animal species. Human hemoglobin is composed of four chains. The beta-chain consists of 146 amino acids. When compared with the beta-chain of a gorilla it differs at just one point, containing arginine where the gorilla has lysine. In contrast horse-beta differs at 26 sites and fish hemoglobin has a total lack of overlap.

Zuckerandl went on to argue that comparison of hemoglobin chains offered a way to measure the rate at which evolution works. Thus variations between the alpha and beta hemoglobin chains of humans with those of horses, pigs, cattle, and rabbits produced a mean number of differences of 22. If the estimated time of their common ancestor is 80 million years then it can be estimated that there should be a change of one amino acid per seven million years.

Zuckerandl's approach has been adapted by other workers. Vincent Sarich in 1967 tried to use the protein albumin to establish a molecular clock, as did Finch and Margoliash with cytochrome c. More recently Allan Wilson has used mitochondrial DNA.

Zuckerman, Solly, Baron Zuckerman

(1904–1993)

BRITISH ZOOLOGIST AND EDUCATIONALIST

The nuclear world, with all its perils is the scientists' creation; it is certainly not a world that came about in response to any external demand.
—*Apocalypse Now?* (1980)

Zuckerman, who was born at Cape Town in South Africa, received his education at the university there and at University College Hospital, London. He then spent a year in America at Yale University before joining the faculty of Oxford University (1934) where he remained until the outbreak of World War II. During the war he investigated the biological effects of bomb blasts and later, as adviser to the RAF chief of combined operations, developed the plan for selective bombing of coastal defenses in Europe in preparation for D-Day. He then became Sands Cox Professor of Anatomy at Birmingham (1946–68) and was appointed secretary of the Zoological Society of London in 1955. Zuckerman served as scientific adviser to the secretary of state for defence (1960–66), working in collaboration with Lord Mountbatten, and was chairman of the United Kingdom Natural Resources Committee (1951–64).

Zuckerman did extensive research on vertebrate anatomy, zoology, and endocrinology. As anatomical research fellow of the Zoological Society he carried out important studies of the menstrual cycle of primates

(1930), while studies of captive apes, such as hamadryad baboons, resulted in such classic works as *The Social Life of Monkeys and Apes* (1932) and *Functional Affinities of Man, Monkeys, and Apes* (1933). His interest in ethology led him to oppose the Konrad Lorenz–Robert Ardrey view that man's aggressiveness is instinctive, his critique being published as a collection of essays entitled *Man and Aggression* (1968). From 1969 Zuckerman was professor-at-large of the University of East Anglia.

Zuse, Konrad

(1910–1995)

GERMAN COMPUTER ENGINEER

Zuse (**tsoo**-ze) graduated in engineering from the Technical College in his native city of Berlin in 1935. He immediately started work with the Henschel Aircraft Company in Berlin as a stress analyst. Part of his duties involved solving large numbers of linear equations, a tedious and time-consuming task. Consequently, as he later put it, he sat down one day in 1936 and invented the computer, "out of laziness."

Like George Stibitz, Zuse worked with binary rather than decimal numbers and abandoned wheels and gears in favor of electromagnetic relays. In this way he avoided the problem of how to carry and borrow numbers. His first model in 1938, the ZI, worked badly. The defects were eliminated in Zuse's second model, the ZII, which was completed in 1939. The models were originally named V1, V2, etc., where V stood for *Versuchsmodall*, or experimental model. He later renamed them ZI, ZII, etc., so that they would not become confused with the V1 and V2 rockets.

Before he could develop his work, war broke out and Zuse found himself drafted. When he offered his computing skills to the Luftwaffe to help design aircraft, he was told that German aircraft were already the best in the world and his services would not be needed. A few months later, however, he was released from military service to work as an engineer in the aircraft industry. He also worked on a new version of his machine, ZIII, completed in 1941, which he used to handle equations describing wing flutter. This was in fact the first "fully functional, program-controlled, general purpose, digital computer." It was also built two years before ENIAC, designed by J. V. Mauchly and J. P. Eckert, was even started. ZIII was destroyed in the bombing of 1944.

By this time Zuse was working on a larger version, the ZIV, completed in 1945. It was removed from Berlin in the final months of the war and hidden in the village of Hopferau in the Bavarian Alps. In 1950 it was installed at the Zurich Technical Institute where at the time it was the only modern computer in continental Europe.

Zuse had earlier attempted to develop an electronic computer, one operating with vacuum tubes. Although the idea was a clear advance on working with relays it had to be abandoned because of the shortage of electron tubes in wartime Germany.

After 1945 Zuse set up his own business, Zuse Apparatebau, a small computer company which was taken over by Siemens in 1956. He also sought from 1945 onward to devise Plankalkul – a universal algorithmic language. He left a full account of his work in his *Der Computer, mein Lebenswerk* (1970; The Computer, My Life's Work).

Zwicky, Fritz

(1898–1974)

SWISS–AMERICAN ASTRONOMER
AND PHYSICIST

Zwicky (**tsvik**-ee), who was born at Varna in Bulgaria, studied at the Federal Institute of Technology, Zurich, where he obtained his BS in 1920 and his PhD in 1922. He moved to America in 1925, working at the California Institute of Technology and the Mount Wilson and Palomar Observatories until his retirement in 1968. He was associate professor of theoretical physics from 1929 to 1942 and professor of astrophysics from 1942 to 1968.

Zwicky worked in various fields of physics, including jet propulsion and the physics of crystals, liquids, and gases. He is, however, better known for his astronomical research. In 1936 he began an important search for supernovas. These are celestial bodies whose brightness suddenly increases by an immense amount as a result of a catastrophic explosion. They had been observed over several centuries in our Galaxy and one had been detected in the Andromeda galaxy as long ago as 1885. But when Edwin Hubble showed in 1923 that the Andromeda galaxy was about 900,000 light-years away, the question arose as to how anything could appear so bright over such a vast distance.

Zwicky worked out their frequency as about three per millennium per galaxy. Although many have passed unobserved in our Galaxy, five supernovas have been reported since AD 1000, including one in 1054 that produced the Crab nebula, Tycho's star in 1572, and Kepler's star in 1604. Zwicky also showed that supernovas characteristically have an absolute magnitude of –13 to –15, which makes them up to 100 million times brighter than the Sun.

In 1932 Lev Landau introduced the concept of a neutron star into astronomy and in 1934 Zwicky and Walter Baade suggested that these compact superdense objects might be produced in the cores of supernovas. This was later developed by Robert Oppenheimer, G. M. Volkoff, and others in 1939 into an important theory of stellar evolution.

In more recent years Zwicky and his colleagues carefully studied both galaxies and clusters of galaxies. One result of this work is the so-called *Zwicky catalog*, which gives the positions and magnitudes of over 30,000 galaxies and almost 10,000 clusters lying mainly in the northern-hemisphere sky.

Zworykin, Vladimir Kosma

(1889–1982)

RUSSIAN–AMERICAN PHYSICIST

Born at Mouron in Russia, Zworykin (**zwor**-i-kin) studied electrical engineering at Petrograd (now St. Petersburg), graduating in 1912. During World War I he served as a radio officer in the Russian army. He moved to America in 1919 and joined the Westinghouse Electric Corporation in 1920. He did graduate research at Pittsburgh University, receiving a PhD in 1926. In 1929 he joined the Radio Corporation of America.

Zworykin made a number of contributions to electron optics and was the inventor of the first electronic-scanning television camera – the iconoscope.

The first such device was constructed at Westinghouse in 1923. The principle was to focus an image on a screen made up of many small photoelectric cells, each insulated, which developed a charge that depended on the intensity of the light at that point. An electron beam directed onto the screen was scanned in parallel lines over the screen, discharging the photoelectric cells and producing an electrical signal.

Zworykin also used the cathode-ray tube invented in 1897 by Karl Ferdinand Braun to produce the image in a receiver. The tube (which he called a "kinescope") had an electron beam focused by magnetic and electric fields to form a spot on a fluorescent screen. The beam was deflected by the fields in parallel lines across the screen, and the intensity of the beam varied according to the intensity of the signal. In this way it was possible to reconstruct the electrical signals into an image. In 1923 an early version of the system was made and Zworykin managed to transmit a simple picture (a cross). By 1929 he was able to demonstrate a better version suitable for practical use.

Zworykin also developed other electron devices, including an electron-image tube and electron multipliers. In 1940 he invited James Hillier to join his research group at RCA, and it was here that Hillier constructed his electron microscope.

Sources and Further Reading

ULAM

Ulam, S. M. *Adventures of a Mathematician*. New York: Scribners, 1973.

VESALIUS

Gjertsen, Derek. *The Classics of Science*. New York: Lilian Barber Press, 1984.

Saunders, J. B. de C. M., and Charles O'Malley. *The Anatomical Drawings of Andreas Vesalius*. New York: Bonanza Books, 1982.

VON NEUMANN

Macrae, Norman. *John von Neumann*. New York: Pantheon Books, 1992.

Poundstone, William. *Prisoner's Dilemma: John von Neumann, Game Theory and the Puzzle of the Bomb*. New York: Doubleday, 1992.

WAKSMAN

Waksman, Selman A. *My Life with the Microbes*. London: Hale, 1958.

WALLACE

Brackman, Arnold C. *A Delicate Arrangement: The Strange Case of Charles Darwin and A. R. Wallace*. New York: Times Books, 1980.

Darwin, C., and A. R. Wallace. *Evolution by Natural Selection*. New York: Cambridge University Press, 1958.

WALLIS, Barnes

Morpurgo, J. E. *Barnes Wallis: A Biography*. New York: St Martin's Press, 1972.

WARBURG

Krebs, J. *Otto Warburg: Cell Physiologist, Biochemist, and Eccentric*. New York: Oxford University Press, 1981.

WATSON, James Dewey

Watson, J. D. *The Double Helix: A Personal Account of the Discovery of the Structure of DNA*. New York: Atheneum, 1968.

——. *Molecular Biology of the Gene*. Menlo Park, CA: Cummings, 4th ed., 1988.

WATT

Robinson, Eric, and A. E. Musson. *James Watt and the Steam Revolution: A Documentary History*. London: Adams & Dart, 1969.

WEBER, Joseph

Collins, Harry, and Trevor Pinch. *The Golem: What Everyone Should Know About Science*. New York: Cambridge University Press, 1993.

WEGENER

Hallam, A. *A Revolution in the Earth Sciences: From Continental Drift to Plate Tectonics*. New York: Oxford University Press, 1973.

Wegener, Alfred. *The Origin of Continents and Oceans*. New York: Dover Publications, 1966.

WEINBERG

Weinberg, Steven. *The First Three Minutes*. New York: Basic Books, 1977.

——. *Dreams of a Final Theory*. New York: Pantheon, 1992.

WEXLER

Bishop, Jerry, and Michael Waldholz. *Genome*. New York: Simon and Schuster, 1991.

Kevles, Daniel, and Leroy Hood, eds. *Scientific and Social Issues in the Human Genome Project*. Cambridge, MA: Harvard University Press, 1992.

WEYL

Weyl, H. *Symmetry*. Princeton, NJ: Princeton University Press, 1952.

WHEELER

Wheeler, John. *A Journey into Gravity and Spacetime*. New York: Freeman, 1990.

WHIPPLE, Fred Lawrence

Brandt, John C., ed. *Comets*. San Francisco, CA: Freeman, 1981.

Whipple, Fred L. *The Mystery of Comets*. New York: Cambridge University Press, 1985.

WHITE, Ray

Bishop, Jerry E., and Michael Waldholz. *Genome*. New York: Simon and Schuster, 1991.

WHITTLE

Whittle, Frank. *Jet*. New York: Philosophical Library, 1954.

WIENER

Heims, Steve J. *John von Neumann and Norbert Wiener*. Cambridge, MA: MIT Press, 1980.

Wiener, Norbert. *I Am a Mathematician*. Cambridge, MA: MIT Press, 1964.

WILSON, Allan

Brown, Michael H. *The Search for Eve*. New York: Harper and Row, 1990.

WILSON, Edward

Wilson, Edward. *Sociobiology*. Cambridge, MA: Harvard University Press, 1975.

WILSON, John Tuzo

Sullivan, Walter. *Continents in Motion: The New Earth Debate*. New York: McGraw-Hill, 1974.

WINOGRAD

Gardner, Howard. *The Mind's New Science: A History of the Cognitive Revolution.* New York: Basic Books, 1987.

WITTEN

Davies, P. C. W., and J. Brown. *Superstrings: A Theory of Everything.* New York: Cambridge University Press, 1988.

Peat, F. David. *Superstrings: And the Search for the Theory of Everything.* New York: Scribners, 1988.

WÖHLER

Jaffe, Bernard. *Crucibles: The Story of Chemistry.* New York: Simon and Schuster, 1957.

WOLPERT

Wolpert, Lewis. *The Triumph of the Embryo.* New York: Oxford University Press, 1991.

WRIGHT, Sir Almorth

Cope, Zachary. *Almorth Wright: Father of Modern Vaccine-Therapy.* London: Nelson, 1966.

WRIGHT, Wilbur

Moolman, Valerie. *The Road to Kitty Hawk.* Alexandria, VA: Time-Life Books, 1980.

ZUCKERMAN

Zuckerman, Solly. *From Apes to Warlords 1904–46: An Autobiography.* London: Hamish Hamilton, 1978.

———. *Monkeys, Men and Missiles 1946–88: An Autobiography.* London: Collins, 1988.

Glossary

absolute zero The zero value of thermodynamic temperature, equal to 0 kelvin or –273.15°C.

acceleration of free fall The acceleration of a body falling freely, at a specified point on the Earth's surface, as a result of the gravitational attraction of the Earth. The standard value is 9.80665 m s^{-2} (32.174 ft s^{-2}).

acetylcholine A chemical compound that is secreted at the endings of some nerve cells and transmits a nerve impulse from one nerve cell to the next or to a muscle, gland, etc.

acquired characteristics Characteristics developed during the life of an organism, but not inherited, as a result of use and disuse of organs.

adrenaline (epinephrine) A hormone, secreted by the adrenal gland, that increases metabolic activity in conditions of stress.

aldehyde Any of a class of organic compounds containing the group –CHO.

aliphatic Denoting an organic compound that is not aromatic, including the alkanes, alkenes, alkynes, cycloalkanes, and their derivatives.

alkane Any of the saturated hydrocarbons with the general formula C_nH_{2n+2}.

alkene Any one of a class of hydrocarbons characterized by the presence of double bonds between carbon atoms and having the general formula C_nH_{2n}. The simplest example is ethylene (ethene).

alkyne Any one of a class of hydrocarbons characterized by the presence of triple bonds between carbon atoms. The simplest example is ethyne (acetylene).

allele One of two or more alternative forms of a particular gene.

amino acid Any one of a class of organic compounds that contain both an amino group ($-NH_2$) and a carboxyl group ($-COOH$) in their molecules. Amino acids are the units present in peptides and proteins.

amount of substance A measure of quantity proportional to the number of particles of substance present.

anabolism The sum of the processes involved in the synthesis of the constituents of living cells.

androgen Any of a group of steroid hormones with masculinizing properties, produced by the testes in all vertebrate animals.

antibody A protein produced by certain white blood cells (lymphocytes) in response to the presence of an antigen. An antibody forms a complex with an antigen, which is thereby inactivated.

antigen A foreign or potentially harmful substance that, when introduced into the body, stimulates the production of a specific antibody.

aromatic Denoting a chemical compound that has the property of aromaticity, as characterized by benzene.

asteroid Any of a large number of small celestial bodies orbiting the Sun, mainly between Mars and Jupiter.

atomic orbital A region around the nucleus of an atom in which an electron moves. According to wave mechanics, the electron's location is described by a probability distribution in space, given by the wave function.

ATP Adenosine triphosphate: a compound, found in all living organisms, that functions as a carrier of chemical energy, which is released when required for metabolic reactions.

bacteriophage A virus that lives and reproduces as a parasite within a bacterium.

bacterium (*pl.* **bacteria**) Any one of a large group of microorganisms that all lack a membrane around the nucleus and have a cell wall of unique composition.

band theory The application of quantum mechanics to the energies of electrons in crystalline solids.

baryon Any of a class of elementary particles that have half-integral spin and take part in strong interactions. They consist of three quarks each.

beta decay A type of radioactive decay in which an unstable nucleus ejects either an electron and an antineutrino or a positron and a neutrino.

black body A hypothetical body that absorbs all the radiation falling on it.

bremsstrahlung Electromagnetic radiation produced by the deceleration of charged particles.

carbohydrate Any of a class of compounds with the formula $C_nH_{2m}O_m$. The carbohydrates include the sugars, starch, and cellulose.

carcinogen Any agent, such as a chemical or type of radiation, that causes cancer.

catabolism The sum of the processes involved in the breakdown of molecules in living cells in order to provide chemical energy for metabolic processes.

catalysis The process by which the rate of a chemical reaction is increased by the presence of another substance (the catalyst) that does not appear in the stoichiometric equation for the reaction.

cathode-ray oscilloscope An instrument for displaying changing electrical signals on a cathode-ray tube.

cellulose A white solid carbohydrate, $(C_6H_{10}O_5)_n$, found in all plants as the main constituent of the cell wall.

chelate An inorganic metal complex in which there is a closed ring of atoms, caused by attachment of a ligand to a metal atom at two points.

chlorophyll Any one of a group of green pigments, found in all plants, that absorb light for photosynthesis.

cholesterol A steroid alcohol occurring widely in animal cell membranes and tissues. Excess amounts in the blood are associated with atherosclerosis (obstruction of the arteries).

chromatography Any of several related techniques for separating and analyzing mixtures by selective adsorption or absorption in a flow system.

chromosome One of a number of threadlike structures, consisting mainly of DNA and protein, found in the nucleus of cells and constituting the genetic material of the cell.

codon The basic coding unit of DNA and RNA, consisting of a sequence of three nucleotides that specifies a particular amino acid in the synthesis of proteins in a cell.

collagen A fibrous protein that is a major constituent of the connective tissue in skin, tendons, and bone.

colligative property A property that depends on the number of particles of substance present in a substance, rather than on the nature of the particles.

continental drift The theory that the Earth's continents once formed a single mass, parts of which have drifted apart to their present positions.

cortisone A steroid hormone, produced by the cortex (outer part) of the adrenal gland, that regulates the metabolism of carbohydrate, fat, and protein and reduces inflammation.

critical mass The minimum mass of fissile material for which a chain reaction is self-sustaining.

cryogenics The branch of physics concerned with the production of very low temperatures and the study of phenomena occurring at these temperatures.

cyclotron A type of particle accelerator in which the particles move in spiral paths under the influence of a uniform vertical magnetic field and are accelerated by an electric field of fixed frequency.

cytoplasm The jellylike material that surrounds the nucleus of a living cell.

dendrochronology A method of dating wooden specimens based on the growth rings of trees. It depends on the assumption that trees grown in the same climatic conditions have a characteristic pattern of rings.

dialysis The separation of mixtures by selective diffusion through a semipermeable membrane.

diffraction The formation of light and dark bands (diffraction patterns) around the boundary of a shadow cast by an object or aperture.

diploid Describing a nucleus, cell, or organism with two sets of chromosomes, one set deriving from the male parent and the other from the female parent.

DNA Deoxyribonucleic acid: a nucleic acid that is a major constituent of the chromosomes and is the hereditary material of most organisms.

dissociation The breakdown of a molecule into radicals, ions, atoms, or simpler molecules.

distillation A process used to purify or separate liquids by evaporating them and recondensing the vapor.

ecology The study of living organisms in relation to their environment.

eigenfunction One of a set of allowed wave functions of a particle in a given system as determined by wave mechanics.

electrolysis Chemical change produced by passing an electric current through a conducting solution or fused ionic substance.

electromagnetic radiation Waves of energy (electromagnetic waves) consisting of electric and magnetic fields vibrating at right angles to the direction of propagation of the waves.

electromotive force The energy supplied by a source of current in driving unit charge around an electrical circuit. It is measured in volts.

electromotive series A series of the metals arranged in decreasing order of their tendency to form positive ions by a reaction of the type $M = M^+ + e$.

electron An elementary particle with a negative charge equal to that of the proton and a rest mass of 9.1095×10^{-31} kilograms (about 1/1836 that of the proton).

electron microscope A device in which a magnified image of a sample is produced by illuminating it with a beam of high-energy electrons rather than light.

electroweak theory A unified theory of the electromagnetic interaction and the weak interaction.

enthalpy A thermodynamic property of a system equal to the sum of its internal energy and the product of its pressure and its volume.

entomology The branch of zoology concerned with the study of insects.

entropy A measure of the disorder of a system. In any system undergoing a reversible change the change of entropy is defined as the energy absorbed divided by the thermodynamic temperature. The entropy of the system is thus a measure of the availability of its energy for performing useful work.

escape velocity The minimum velocity that would have to be given to an object for it to escape from a specified gravitational field. The escape velocity from the Earth is 25,054 mph (7 miles per second).

ester A compound formed by a reaction between an alcohol and a fatty acid.

estrogen Any one of a group of steroid hormones, produced mainly by the ovaries in all vertebrates, that stimulate the growth and maintenance of the female reproductive organs.

ethology The study of the behavior of animals in their natural surroundings.

excitation A change in the energy of an atom, ion, molecule, etc., from one energy level (usually the ground state) to a higher energy level.

fatty acid Any of a class of organic acids with the general formula R.CO.OH, where R is a hydrocarbon group.

fermentation A reaction in which compounds, such as sugar, are broken down by the action of microorganisms that form the enzymes required to catalyze the reaction.

flash photolysis A technique for investigating the spectra and reactions of free radicals.

free energy A thermodynamic function used to measure the ability of a system to perform work. A change in free energy is equal to the work done.

free radical An atom or group of atoms that has an independent existence without all its valences being satisfied.

fuel cell A type of electric cell in which electrical energy is produced directly by electrochemical reactions involving substances that are continuously added to the cell.

fungus Any one of a group of spore-producing organisms formerly classified as plants but now placed in a separate kingdom (Fungi). They include the mushrooms, molds, and yeasts.

galaxy Any of the innumerable aggregations of stars that, together with gas, dust, and other material, make up the universe.

gene The functional unit of heredity. A single gene contains the information required for the manufacture, by a living cell, of one particular polypeptide, protein, or type of RNA and is the vehicle by which such information is transmitted to subsequent generations. Genes correspond to discrete regions of the DNA (or RNA) making up the genome.

genetic code The system by which genetic material carries the information that directs the activities of a living cell. The code is contained in the sequence of nucleotides of DNA and/or RNA (*see* codon).

genome The sum total of an organism's genetic material, including all the genes carried by its chromosomes.

global warming *See* greenhouse effect.

glycolysis The series of reactions in which glucose is broken down with the release of energy in the form of ATP.

greenhouse effect An effect in the Earth's atmosphere resulting from the presence of such gases as CO_2, which absorb the infrared radiation produced by the reradiation of solar ultraviolet radiation at the Earth's surface. This causes a rise in the Earth's average temperature, known as "global warming."

half-life A measure of the stability of a radioactive substance, equal to the time taken for its activity to fall to one half of its original value.

halogens The nonmetallic elements fluorine, chlorine, bromine, iodine, and astatine.

haploid Describing a nucleus or cell that contains only a single set of chromosomes; haploid organisms consist exclusively of haploid cells. During sexual reproduction, two haploid sex cells fuse to form a single diploid cell.

heat death The state of a closed system when its total entropy has increased to its maximum value. Under these conditions there is no available energy.

histamine A substance released by various tissues of the body in response to invasion by microorganisms or other stimuli. It triggers inflammation and is responsible for some of the symptoms (e.g., sneezing) occurring in such allergies as hay fever.

histology The study of the tissues of living organisms.

hormone Any of various substances that are produced in small amounts by certain glands within the body (the endocrine glands) and released into the bloodstream to regulate the growth or activities of organs and tissues elsewhere in the body.

hydrocarbon Any organic compound composed only of carbon and hydrogen.

hydrogen bond A weak attraction between an electronegative atom, such as oxygen, nitrogen, or fluorine, and a hydrogen atom that is covalently linked to another electronegative atom.

hysteresis An apparent lag of an effect with respect to the magnitude of the agency producing the effect.

ideal gas An idealized gas composed of atoms that have a negligible volume and undergo perfectly elastic collisions. Such a gas would obey the gas laws under all conditions.

immunology The study of the body's mechanisms for defense against disease and the various ways in which these can be manipulated or enhanced.

insulin A hormone that is responsible for regulating the level of glucose in the blood, i.e., "blood sugar." It is produced by certain cells in the pancreas; deficiency causes the disease diabetes mellitus.

integrated circuit An electronic circuit made in a single small unit.

interferon Any one of a group of proteins, produced by various cells and tissues in the body, that increase resistance to invading viruses. Some types are synthesized for use in medicine as antiviral drugs.

internal energy The total energy possessed by a system on account of the kinetic and potential energies of its component molecules.

ion An atom or group of atoms with a net positive or negative charge. Positive ions (cations) have a deficiency of electrons and negative ions (anions) have an excess.

ionizing radiation Electromagnetic radiation or particles that cause ionization.

ionosphere A region of ionized air and free electrons around the Earth in the Earth's upper atmosphere, extending from a height of about 31 miles to 621 miles.

isomerism The existence of two or more chemical compounds with the same molecular formula but different arrangements of atoms in their molecules.

isotope Any of a number of forms of an element, all of which differ only in the number of neutrons in their atomic nuclei.

ketone Any of a class of organic compounds with the general formula RCOR', where R and R' are usually hydrocarbon groups.

kinetic energy The energy that a system has by

virtue of its motion, determined by the work necessary to bring it to rest.

kinetic theory Any theory for describing the physical properties of a system with reference to the motion of its constituent atoms or molecules.

laser A device for producing intense light or infrared or ultraviolet radiation by stimulated emission.

latent heat The total heat absorbed or produced during a change of phase (fusion, vaporization, etc.) at a constant temperature.

lepton Any of a class of elementary particles that have half-integral spin and take part in weak interactions; they include the electron, the muon, the neutrino, and their antiparticles.

lipid An ester of a fatty acid. Simple lipids include fats and oils; compound lipids include phospholipids and glycolipids; derived lipids include the steroids.

liquid crystal A state of certain molecules that flow like liquids but have an ordered arrangement of molecules.

macromolecule A very large molecule, as found in polymers or in such compounds as proteins.

magnetohydrodynamics The study of the motion of electrically conducting fluids and their behavior in magnetic fields.

meiosis A type of nuclear division, occurring only in certain cells of the reproductive organs, in which a diploid cell produces four haploid sex cells, or gametes.

meson Any member of a class of elementary particles characterized by a mass intermediate between those of the electron and the proton, an integral spin, and participation in strong interactions. They consist of two quarks each.

metabolism The totality of the chemical reactions taking place in a living cell or organism.

mitosis The type of nuclear division occurring in the body cells of most organisms, in which a diploid cell produces two diploid daughter cells.

moderator A substance used in fission reactors to slow down fast neutrons.

monoclonal antibody Any antibody produced by members of a group of genetically identical cells (which thus constitute a "clone"). Such antibodies have identical structures and each combines with the same antigen in precisely the same manner.

morphology The study of the form of organisms, especially their external shape and structure.

muon An elementary particle having a positive or negative charge and a mass equal to 206.77 times the mass of the electron.

mutation Any change in the structure of a gene, which can arise spontaneously or as a result of such agents as x-rays or certain chemicals. It may have a beneficial effect on the organism but most mutations are neutral, harmful, or even lethal. Mutations affecting the germ cells can be passed on to the organism's offspring.

natural selection The process by which the individuals of a population that are best adapted to life in a particular environment tend to enjoy greater reproductive success than members which are less well adapted. Hence, over successive generations, the descendants of the former constitute an increasing proportion of the population.

neutrino An elementary particle with zero rest mass, a velocity equal to that of light, and a spin of one half.

nuclear fission The process in which an atomic nucleus splits into fragment nuclei and one or more neutrons with the emission of energy.

nuclear fusion A nuclear reaction in which two light nuclei join together to form a heavier nucleus with the emission of energy.

nuclear winter The period of darkness and low temperature, predicted to follow a nuclear war, as a result of the obscuring of sunlight by dust and other debris.

nucleic acid Any of a class of large biologically important molecules consisting of one or more chains of nucleotides. There are two types: deoxyribonucleic acid (DNA) and ribonucleic acid (RNA).

nucleotide Any of a class of compounds consisting of a nitrogen-containing base (a purine or pyrimidine) combined with a sugar group (ribose or deoxyribose) bearing a phosphate group. Long chains of nucleotides form the nucleic acids, DNA and RNA.

nucleon A particle that is a constituent of an atomic nucleus; either a proton or a neutron.

nucleus 1. The positively charged part of the atom about which the electrons orbit. The nucleus is composed of neutrons and protons held together by strong interactions. 2. A prominent body found in the cells of animals, plants, and other organisms (but not bacteria) that contains the chromosomes and is bounded by a double membrane.

oncogene A gene, introduced into a living cell by certain viruses, that disrupts normal metabolism and transforms the cell into a cancer cell.

optical activity The property of certain substances of rotating the plane of polarization of plane-polarized light.

osmosis Preferential flow of certain substances in solution through a semipermeable membrane. If the membrane separates a solution from a pure solvent, the solvent will flow through the membrane into the solution.

oxidation A process in which oxygen is combined with a substance or hydrogen is removed from a compound.

ozone layer A layer containing ozone in the Earth's atmosphere. It lies between heights of 9 and 19 miles and absorbs the Sun's higher-energy ultraviolet radiation.

parity A property of elementary particles depending on the symmetry of their wave function with respect to changes in sign of the coordinates.

parthenogenesis A form of reproduction in which a sex cell, usually an egg cell, develops into an embryo without fertilization. It occurs in certain plants and invertebrates and results in offspring that are genetically identical to the parent.

pathology The study of the nature and causes of disease.

peptide A compound formed by two or more amino acids linked together. The amino group ($-NH_2$) of one acid reacts with the carboxyl group (–COOH) of another to give the group –NH–CO–, known as the "peptide linkage."

periodic table A tabular arrangement of the elements in order of increasing atomic number such that similarities are displayed between groups of elements.

pH A measure of the acidity or alkalinity of a solution, equal to the logarithm to base 10 of the reciprocal of the concentration of hydrogen ions.

photocell Any device for converting light or other electromagnetic radiation directly into an electric current.

photoelectric effect The ejection of electrons from a solid as a result of irradiation by light or other electromagnetic radiation. The number of electrons emitted depends on the intensity of the light and not on its frequency.

photolysis The dissociation of a chemical compound into other compounds, atoms, and free radicals by irradiation with electromagnetic radiation.

photon A quantum of electromagnetic radiation.

photosynthesis The process by which plants, algae, and certain bacteria "fix" inorganic carbon, from carbon dioxide, as organic carbon in the form of carbohydrate using light as a source of energy and, in green plants and algae, water as a source of hydrogen. The light energy is trapped by special pigments, e.g., chlorophyll.

piezoelectric effect An effect observed in certain crystals in which they develop a potential difference across a pair of opposite faces when subjected to a stress.

pion A type of meson having either zero, positive, or negative charge and a mass 264.2 times that of the electron.

plankton The mass of microscopic plants and animals that drift passively at or near the surface of oceans and lakes.

plasma 1. An ionized gas consisting of free electrons and an approximately equal number of ions. **2.** Blood plasma: the liquid component of blood, excluding the blood cells.

plate tectonics The theory that the Earth's surface consists of lithospheric plates, which have moved throughout geological time to their present positions.

polypeptide A chain of amino acids held together by peptide linkages. Polypeptides are found in proteins.

potential energy The energy that a system has by virtue of its position or state, determined by the work necessary to change the system from a reference position to its present state.

probability The likelihood that an event will occur. If an event is certain to occur its probability is 1; if it is certain not to occur the probability is 0. In any other circumstances the probability lies between 0 and 1.

protein Any of a large number of naturally occurring organic compounds found in all living matter. Proteins consist of chains of amino acids joined by peptide linkages.

proton A stable elementary particle with a positive electric charge equal to that of the electron. It is the nucleus of a hydrogen atom and weighs 1,836 times the mass of the electron.

protozoa A large group of minute single-celled organisms found widely in freshwater, marine, and damp terrestrial habitats. Unlike bacteria they possess a definite nucleus and are distinguished from plants in lacking cellulose.

pulsar A star that acts as a source of regularly fluctuating electromagnetic radiation, the period of the pulses usually being very rapid.

quantum electrodynamics The quantum theory of electromagnetic interactions between particles and between particles and electromagnetic radiation.

quantum theory A mathematical theory involving the idea that the energy of a system can change only in discrete amounts (quanta), rather than continuously.

quark Any of six elementary particles and their corresponding antiparticles with fractional charges that are the building blocks of baryons and mesons. Together with leptons they are the basis of all matter.

quasar A class of starlike astronomical objects with large redshifts, many of which emanate strong radio waves.

radioactive labeling The use of radioactive atoms in a compound to trace the path of the compound through a biological or mechanical system.

radioactivity The spontaneous disintegration of the nuclei of certain isotopes with emission of beta rays (electrons), alpha rays (helium nuclei), or gamma rays.

radio astronomy The branch of astronomy involving the use of radio telescopes.

radiocarbon dating A method of dating archeological specimens of wood, cotton, etc., based on the small amount of radioactive carbon (carbon–14) incorporated into the specimen when it was living and the extent to which this isotope has decayed since its death.

radioisotope A radioactive isotope of an element.

recombination The reassortment of maternally derived and paternally derived genes that occurs during meiosis preceding the formation of sex cells. Recombination is an important source of genetic variation.

redox reaction A reaction in which one reactant is oxidized and the other is reduced.

redshift The displacement of the spectral lines emitted by a moving body towards the red end of the visual spectrum. It is caused by the Doppler effect and, when observed in the spectrum of distant stars and galaxies, it indicates that the body is receding from the earth.

reduction A process in which oxygen is removed from or hydrogen is combined with a compound.

reflex An automatic response of an organism or body part to a stimulus, i.e., one that occurs without conscious control.

refractory A solid that has a high melting point and can withstand high temperatures.

relativistic mass The mass of a body as predicted by the theory of relativity. The relativistic mass of a particle moving at velocity v is $m_0(1 - v^2/c^2)^{-1/2}$, where m_0 is the rest mass.

rest mass The mass of a body when it is at rest relative to its observer, as distinguished from its relativistic mass.

retrovirus A type of virus whose genome, consisting of RNA, is transcribed into a DNA version and then inserted into the DNA of its host. The flow of genetic information, from RNA to DNA, is thus the reverse of that found in organisms generally.

RNA Ribonucleic acid: any one of several types of nucleic acid, including messenger RNA, that process the information carried by the genes and use it to direct the assembly of proteins in cells. In certain viruses RNA is the genetic material.

semiconductor A solid with an electrical conductivity that is intermediate between those of insulators and metals and that increases with increasing temperature. Examples are germanium, silicon, and lead telluride.

semipermeable membrane A barrier that permits the passage of some substances but is impermeable to others.

serum The fraction of blood plasma excluding the components of the blood-clotting system.

sex chromosome A chromosome that participates in determining the sex of individuals. Humans have two sex chromosomes, X and Y; females have two X chromosomes (XX) and males have one of each (XY).

sex hormone Any hormone that controls the development of sexual characteristics and regulates reproductive activity. The principal human sex hormones are progesterone and estrogens in females, testosterone and androsterone in males.

simple harmonic motion Motion of a point moving along a path so that its acceleration is directed towards a fixed point on the path and is directly proportional to the displacement from this fixed point.

SI units A system of units used, by international agreement, for all scientific purposes. It is based on the meter-kilogram-second (MKS) system and consists of seven base units and two supplementary units.

soap A salt of a fatty acid.

solar cell Any electrical device for converting solar energy directly into electrical energy.

solar constant The energy per unit area per unit time received from the Sun at a point that is the Earth's mean distance from the Sun away. It has the value 1,400 joules per square meter per second.

solar wind Streams of electrons and protons emitted by the Sun. The solar wind is responsible for the formation of the Van Allen belts and the aurora.

solid-state physics The experimental and theoretical study of the properties of the solid state, in particular the study of energy levels and the electrical and magnetic properties of metals and semiconductors.

speciation The process in which new species evolve from existing populations of organisms.

specific heat capacity The amount of heat required to raise the temperature of unit mass of a substance by unit temperature; it is usually measured in joules per kilogram per kelvin.

spectrometer Any of various instruments used for producing a spectrum (distribution of wavelengths of increasing magnitude) and measuring the wavelengths, energies, etc.

speed of light The speed at which all electromagnetic radiation travels; it is the highest speed attainable in the universe and has the value 2.998×10^8 meters per second in a vacuum.

standing wave A wave in which the wave profile remains stationary in the medium through which it is passing.

state of matter One of the three physical states – solid, liquid, or gas – in which matter may exist.

stereochemistry The arrangement in space of the groups in a molecule and the effect this has on the compound's properties and chemical behavior.

steroid Any of a group of complex lipids that occur widely in plants and animals and include various hormones, such as cortisone and the sex hormones.

stimulated emission The process in which a photon colliding with an excited atom causes emission of a second photon with the same energy as the first. It is the basis of lasers.

stoichiometric Involving chemical combination in exact ratios.

strangeness A property of certain hadrons that causes them to decay more slowly than expected from the energy released.

strong interaction A type of interaction between elementary particles occurring at short range (about 10^{-15} meter) and having a magnitude about 100 times greater than that of the electromagnetic interaction.

sublimation The passage of certain substances from the solid state into the gaseous state and then back into the solid state, without any intermediate liquid state being formed.

substrate A substance that is acted upon in some way, especially the compound acted on by a catalyst or the solid on which a compound is adsorbed.

sugar Any of a group of water-soluble simple carbohydrates, usually having a sweet taste.

sunspot A region of the Sun's surface that is much cooler and therefore darker than the surrounding area, having a temperature of about $4,000°C$ as opposed to $6,000°C$ for the rest of the photosphere.

superconductivity A phenomenon occurring

in certain metals and alloys at temperatures close to absolute zero, in which the electrical resistance of the solid vanishes below a certain temperature.

superfluid A fluid that flows without friction and has extremely high thermal conductivity.

supernova A star that suffers an explosion, becoming up to 10^8 times brighter in the process and forming a large cloud of expanding debris (the supernova remnant).

surfactant A substance used to increase the spreading or wetting properties of a liquid. Surfactants are often detergents, which act by lowering the surface tension.

symbiosis A long-term association between members of different species, especially where mutual benefit is derived by the participants.

taxonomy The science of classifying organisms into groups.

tensile strength The applied stress necessary to break a material under tension.

thermal conductivity A measure of the ability of a substance to conduct heat, equal to the rate of flow of heat per unit area resulting from unit temperature gradient.

thermal neutron A neutron with a low kinetic energy, of the same order of magnitude as the kinetic energies of atoms and molecules.

thermionic emission Emission of electrons from a hot solid. The effect occurs when significant numbers of electrons have enough kinetic energy to overcome the solid's work function.

thermodynamics The branch of science concerned with the relationship between heat, work, and other forms of energy.

thermodynamic temperature Temperature measured in kelvins that is a function of the internal energy possessed by a body, having a value of zero at absolute zero.

thixotropy A phenomenon shown by some fluids in which the viscosity decreases as the rate of shear increases, i.e., the fluid becomes less viscous the faster it moves.

transducer A device that is supplied with the energy of one system and converts it into the energy of a different system, so that the output signal is proportional to the input signal but is carried in a different form.

transistor A device made of semiconducting material in which a flow of current between two electrodes can be controlled by a potential applied to a third electrode.

tribology The study of friction between solid surfaces, including the origin of frictional forces and the lubrication of moving parts.

triple point The point at which the solid, liquid, and gas phases of a pure substance can all coexist in equilibrium.

tritiated Denoting a chemical compound containing tritium (^{3}H) atoms in place of hydrogen atoms.

ultracentrifuge A centrifuge designed to work at very high speeds, so that the force produced is large enough to cause sedimentation of colloids.

unified-field theory A theory that seeks to explain gravitational and electromagnetic interactions and the strong and weak nuclear interactions in terms of a single set of equations.

vaccine An antigenic preparation that is administered to a human or other animal to produce immunity against a specific disease-causing agent.

valence The combining power of an element, atom, ion, or radical, equal to the number of hydrogen atoms that the atom, ion, etc., could combine with or displace in forming a compound.

valence band The energy band of a solid that is occupied by the valence electrons of the atoms forming the solid.

valence electron An electron in the outer shell of an atom that participates in the chemical bonding when the atom forms compounds.

vector 1. A quantity that is specified both by its magnitude and its direction. 2. An agent, such as an insect, that harbors disease-causing microorganisms and transmits them to humans, other animals, or plants.

virtual particle A particle thought of as existing for a very brief period in an interaction between two other particles.

virus A noncellular agent that can infect a living animal, plant, or bacterial cell and use the apparatus of the host cell to manufacture new virus particles. In some cases this causes disease in the host organism. Outside the host cell, viruses are totally inert.

viscosity The property of liquids and gases of resisting flow. It is caused by forces between the molecules of the fluid.

water of crystallization Water combined in the form of molecules in definite proportions in the crystals of many substances.

wave equation A partial differential equation relating the displacement of a wave to the time and the three spatial dimensions.

wave function A mathematical expression giving the probability of finding the particle associated with a wave at a specified point according to wave mechanics.

wave mechanics A form of quantum mechanics in which particles (electrons, protons, etc.) are regarded as waves, so that any system of particles can be described by a wave equation.

weak interaction A type of interaction between elementary particles, occurring at short range and having a magnitude about 10^{10} times weaker than the electromagnetic force.

work function The minimum energy necessary to remove an electron from a metal at absolute zero.

x-ray crystallography The determination of the structure of crystals and molecules by use of x-ray diffraction.

zero point energy The energy of vibration of atoms at the absolute zero of temperature.

zwitterion An ion that has both a positive and negative charge.

Chronology

c. **590** BC

Physics
Thales proposes that water is fundamental principle of all matter

c. **546** BC

Physics
Anaximenes proposes air as primal substance

c. **540** BC

Mathematics
Pythagorean mathematics

c. **500** BC

Physics
On Nature (Heraclitus) – doctrine of change

c. **480** BC

Physics
On Nature (Anaxagoras)

c. **465** BC

Mathematics
Zeno proposes his paradoxes

c. **450** BC

Physics
Empedocles proposes 4-element theory (earth, air, fire, water)

c. **400** BC

Medicine
Corpus Hippocraticum

Physics
Democritus expounds atomism

c. **387** BC

Philosophy
Plato founds Academy

c. **300** BC

Physics
Epicurus revives atomism

c. **3rd century** BC

Mathematics
Elements (Euclid)

c. **200** BC

Mathematics
Conics (Apollonius of Perga)

c. **100** BC

Earth Science
Poseidonius measures circumference of Earth

56 BC

General
De rerum natura (Lucretius)

c. AD **62**

Technology
Hero describes a simple steam engine

c. AD **77**

Medicine
De materia medica (Dioscorides)

c. **150**

Astronomy
Almagest (Ptolemy) – describes Ptolemaic system with Earth at center of universe

c. **175**

Biology
Galen shows that the arteries carry blood not air

c. **250**

Mathematics
Arithmetica (Diophantus) – contains Diophantine equations

c. 464

Mathematics

Ch'ung-Chih Tsu calculates the value of pi

628

Astronomy

Brahmasiddhanta (The Opening of the Universe; Brahmagupta)

c. 800

Chemistry

Geber introduces idea that all metals are formed from mercury and sulfur

c. 1020

Medicine

Al Qanun (The Canon; Avicenna)

c. 1086

Physics

Shen Kua describes discovery of magnetic compass

1459

Astronomy

Purbach publishes his table of lunar eclipses

1492

General

Columbus lands in Bahamas (Oct. 12)

1535

Mathematics

Tartaglia discovers a method to solve the general cubic equation

1536

Medicine

Paré shows that the practice of cauterizing wounds is harmful

1543

Astronomy

De revolutionibus orbium coelestium (Copernicus) – heliocentric system of universe

Medicine

De humani corporis fabrica (Vesalius)

1545

Mathematics

Ars magna (Cardano) – introduces the solutions for the general cubic and general quartic equations

1546

Medicine

Fracastoro publishes a work in which he anticipates the germ theory of disease

1553

Biology

Servetus describes the lesser circulation

1555

Biology

Belon publishes a work on birds in which he draws attention to homologies between bird and human skeletons

1556

Chemistry

De re metallica (Agricola)

1561

Biology

Observationes anatomicae (Fallopius) – describes the fallopian tubes

1564

Biology

Opuscula anatomica (Eustachio) – describes the eustachian tubes of the ear and also the first description of the adrenal glands

1569

Chemistry

De mineralibus (Albertus Magnus)

Earth Science

Mercator introduces a cartographic projection (Mercator's projection) that allows navigators to chart courses on a straight line

1570

Earth Science

Theatrum orbis terrarum (Ortelius) – first modern atlas of world

1572

Physics

Publication of Latin translation of Alhazen's work on optics as *Opticae thesaurus*

1573

Astronomy

De nova stella (Tycho Brahe)

1581

Physics

Norman publishes discovery of magnetic dip

1596

Astronomy

D. Fabricius discovers first variable star (Mira Ceti)

Medicine

Pen Tshao Kang Mu (The Great Pharmacopoeia; Shih-Chen Li) – published posthumously

1597

Biology

Herball (Gerard)

1600

Physics

De magnete (Gilbert) – introduces idea that Earth acts as a large bar magnet

1603

Biology

De venarum ostiolis (Fabricius ab Aquapendente) – describes the venous system

General

Accademia dei Lincei founded in Rome by Prince Federico Cesi

1604

Physics

Galileo proves falling bodies move with uniform acceleration

1605

General

Advancement of Learning (Bacon)

1606

Chemistry

Alchymia (Libavius)

1608

Physics

Lippershey makes first telescope

1609

Astronomy

Astronomia Nova (Kepler) – first two laws of planetary motion

(to 1610) Galileo makes astronomical observations using telescope – studies Moon and discovers satellites of Jupiter

1612

Medicine

Sanctorius constructs and describes a clinical thermometer

1613

Astronomy

Letters on Sunspots (Galileo)

1614

Biology

Sanctorius publishes results revealing the extent of water loss by perspiration

Mathematics

Mirifici logarithmorum (Napier) – introduction of logarithms

1619

Astronomy

De harmonices mundi (Kepler) – includes his 3rd law of planetary motion

1621

Physics
Snell discovers his law of refraction (not published until 1638 in a work by Descartes)

1622

Biology
Aselli discovers the lacteals

Mathematics
Oughtred invents the slide rule

1623

Astronomy
The Assayer (Galileo)

1627

Astronomy
Kepler publishes the Rudolphine Tables

1628

Biology
De motu cordis (Harvey) – describes the circulation of the blood

1631

Technology
Vernier invents the caliper and scale named for him

1632

Astronomy
Dialogo di Galileo Galilei (Galileo) – exposition of Copernican system of universe

1635

Mathematics
Cavalieri introduces his method of indivisibles

1637

Mathematics
La Géométrie (Descartes) – introduces coordinate geometry

1638

Physics
Discorsi e dimostrazioni...(Galileo) – describes work on motion

1644

Physics
Torricelli constructs first mercury barometer

1650

Earth Science
Geographia generalis (Toscanelli)

Physics
Guericke constructs first vacuum pump

1651

Biology
Rudbeck discovers the vertebrate lymphatic system
Pecquet publishes the first description of the thoracic duct

1654

Physics
Guericke demonstrates pressure of atmosphere using Magdeburg hemispheres

1655

Astronomy
Huygens discovers Titan (satellite of Saturn)

Mathematics
Arithmetica infinitorum (Wallis)

General
Philosophical and Physical Opinions (Margaret Cavendish)

1657

Physics
Huygens designs first pendulum clock

General
Accademia del Cimento founded by Ferdinand and Leopold de Medici

1658

Biology
Swammerdam discovers red blood corpuscles

1660

Biology
Malpighi describes blood capillaries in the lungs

Physics

New Experiments Physico-Mechanicall, Touching the Spring of the Air and its Effects (Boyle)

General

The Royal Society founded on November 29. Its first patron was Charles II and its first secretary was Henry Oldenburg

1661

Chemistry

The Sceptical Chymist (Boyle)

1662

Astronomy

Venus in Sole Vista (Venus in the Face of the Sun; Jeremiah Horrocks – published posthumously)

Physics

Explicit statement of Boyle's law concerning the effect of pressure on the volume of a gas

Incorporation of Royal Society

1665

Physics

Newton starts work on gravitation, calculus, and optics

Grimaldi publishes discovery of diffraction of light (posthumously)

Micrographica (Hooke)

General

The Philosophical Transactions, the first genuine scientific periodical, is published by the Royal Society

1668

Astronomy

Newton makes first reflecting telescope

Biology

Graaf describes the structure of the testicles

1669

Biology

Historia insectorum (Jan Swammerdam)

Physics

Bartholin announces his discovery of double refraction

c. 1669

Chemistry

Brand discovers phosphorus

1670

Mathematics

Lectiones geometricae (Isaac Barrow)

Methodis fluxionum (Isaac Newton) – published posthumously in 1736

1671

Astronomy

Cassini discovers Iapetus (satellite of Saturn)

1672

Astronomy

Cassini discovers Rhea (satellite of Saturn)

Cassegrain invents a reflecting telescope

Construction of Paris Observatory completed by the Académie des Sciences

Physics

New Theory about Light and Colours (Isaac Newton)

1673

Biology

Graaf describes the ovarian follicles

Physics

Horologium oscillatorium (Huygens)

1675

Astronomy

Cassini discovers Cassini's division of Saturn's rings

John Flamsteed appointed Astronomer Royal by Charles II and provided with an observatory at Greenwich

1676

Astronomy

Rømer discovers a procedure for measuring the speed of light

Royal Greenwich Observatory opened

Physics

Mariotte independently formulates, and refines, Boyle's law relating pressure and volume of gas

1678

Physics

Huygens advances his wave theory of light

1679

Biology

Antony van Leeuwenhoek announces his discovery of human spermatozoa

Physics

Hooke announces his law of elasticity (Hooke's law)

Papin invents pressure cooker (steam digester)

1682

Astronomy

Halley observes comet now named for him – calculates date of return

1683

Mathematics

Lectiones mathematicae (Isaac Barrow) – published posthumously

1684

Astronomy

Cassini discovers Dione and Tethys (satellites of Saturn)

Biology

Antony van Leeuwenhoek describes red blood cells

Mathematics

Nova methodus pro maximis et minimis (Leibniz) – publication of invention of calculus

1687

Physics

Principia (Newton) – theory of gravitation and laws of motion

Amontons invents hygrometer

1688

Earth Science

Halley produces meteorological map

1690

Physics

Traité de la lumière (Huygens)

1698

Technology

Savery's steam engine is patented

1699

Physics

Amontons does early work on variation of gas volume with temperature

c. 1701

Agriculture

Tull introduces a seed drill that sows in straight rows

Earth Science

Halley produces magnetic map

1702

Physics

Amontons invents constant-volume air thermometer

1704

Physics

Opticks (Newton)

1707

Physics

Papin publishes design for steam engine

1712

Technology

The first of Newcomen's piston-operated steam engines is installed

1714

Physics

Fahrenheit invents mercury thermometer

1715

Mathematics

Taylor publishes his work containing Taylor's theorem

1717

Medicine

Lancisi draws attention to the connection between swamps, mosquitoes, and malaria

1718

Medicine

Petit invents the screw tourniquet

1721

Astronomy

John Hadley produces his first reflecting telescope

1725

Astronomy

Historia coelestis Britannica (Flamsteed)

1727

Biology

Vegetable staticks (Hales) – observations on plant physiology

1729

Astronomy

Bradley discovers aberration of light

1733

Medicine

Haemastaticks (Hales) – observations on circulation of the blood, including measurements of blood pressure

Physics

Du Fay introduces two-fluid theory of electricity (vitreous and resinous)

1735

Biology

Systema Naturae (Linnaeus) – systematic classification of animal, plant, and mineral kingdoms

Earth Science

Concerning the Cause of the General Trade Winds (Hadley) – introduces idea of Hadley cell

c. 1740

Biology

Bonnet discovers parthenogenesis in aphids

1742

Chemistry

Brandt isolates cobalt

1743

Mathematics

Traité de dynamique (D'Alembert)

Simpson's rule formulated by Thomas Simpson

Physics

Théorie de la figure de la terre; Alexis Claude Clairaut – confirms that the Earth is shaped like an oblate spheroid

1744

Physics

Maupertuis formulates the principle of least action

1746

Physics

Musschenbroek reports his discovery of the Leyden jar

1747

Chemistry

Marggraf discovers sucrose in beet

1749

Biology

Linnaeus introduces binomial nomenclature in taxonomy

1751

Astronomy

Lacaille and Lalande observe lunar parallax

Biology

Whytt describes and emphasizes the importance of reflex reactions

Chemistry

Cronstedt discovers nickel

Earth Science

Guettard observes evidence for ancient volcanic activity

Technology

La Condamine first reports existence of rubber in Europe

1752

Physics

Franklin performs his electrical experiment with a kite in a thunderstorm

1753

Biology

Species Plantarum (Linnaeus)

1754

Medicine

Lind publishes a cure for scurvy

1756

Chemistry

Experiments upon Magnesia Alba, Quick-lime, and some other Alcaline Substances (Black)

1757

Biology

Monro publishes a work distinguishing clearly between the lymphatic and circulatory systems

Physics

Black introduces concept of latent heat
Carton observes fluctuations in Earth's magnetic field

1758

Physics

Dollond invents achromatic lens system
Alexis Claude Clairaut informs the Académie des Sciences in November that Halley's Comet would be at perihelion on April 13 1759 (the actual date within the margins of error was March 13)

1759

Biology

Wolff presents the thesis that destroyed the preformation theory of development and held instead that organs develop from undifferentiated tissue

c. 1760

General

The Lunar Society formed by Erasmus Darwin, Mathew Boulton, and William Small in Birmingham, England

1761

Astronomy

Nathaniel Bliss observes a transit of Venus

enabling him to calculate the horizontal parallax of the Sun as 10.3″

Medicine

Auenbrugger publishes his work on chest percussion
De sedibus et causis morborum (Morgagni)

Physics

Black measures latent heat of fusion of ice

1763

General

The Royal Society of Edinburgh is founded

1764

Technology

Watt repairs a model of a Newcomen steam engine and begins to develop his own improved engine
Hargreaves invents the spinning jenny

1765

Astronomy

Nevil Maskelyne, fifth Astronomer Royal, first publishes the *Nautical Almanac*, which uses Greenwich as its prime meridian

Physics

Cavendish formulates concept of specific heat (unpublished)

1766

Physics

Three Papers containing Experiments of Factitious Airs (Cavendish) – distinguishing hydrogen (inflammable air) and carbon dioxide (fixed air) from common air

1767

Biology

Spallanzani disproves theory of spontaneous generation in microorganisms

1768

Earth Science

Desmarest shows that not all rocks are sedimentary
James Cook sets sail in the *Endeavour* for the South Pacific to observe the planet Venus and chart the coast of New Zealand and E Australia

Mathematics

Lambert publishes his proof that π and e are irrational

1769

Technology

Arkwright patents his spinning machine

1770

Technology

Cugnot builds a two-piston steam boiler for military use, probably the first fuel-driven vehicle

1771

Earth Science

(to 1775) Werner develops his theory of neptunism

1772

Astronomy

Bode publishes Bode's law

Chemistry

Lavoisier experiments on combustion

1774

Chemistry

Gahn discovers manganese

Priestley discovers oxygen

1776

Anthropology

De generis humani variatate nativa (Blumenbach) – classifies humans into five races

Chemistry

(to 1777) *Eléments de chimie théorique et pratique* (Guyton de Morveau) – an attempt to quantify chemical affinity

1777

Chemistry

Chemical Observations and Experiments on Air and Fire (Scheele)

1779

Botany

Ingenhousz shows that plants absorb carbon dioxide and give off oxygen (i.e., photosynthesize) in the presence of light

1781

Astronomy

Herschel discovers Uranus

Chemistry

Experiments on Air (Cavendish) – showing that air is oxygen and nitrogen in ratio 1:4 and water is formed of hydrogen and oxygen in ratio 2:1

Hauy discovers the geometrical law of crystallization

1782

Astronomy

Goodricke proposes that Algol is an eclipsing binary

Chemistry

Hjelm discovers molybdenum

Müller first isolates the element tellurium

1783

Chemistry

Méthode de nomenclature chimique (Lavoisier and others) – proposes new names for elements

Lavoisier experiments on formation of water from hydrogen and oxygen

D. F. and J. J. D'Elhuyar discover tungsten

Physics

Saussure invents hair hygrometer

Technology

Cort patents method of rolling iron into bars using grooved rollers

The Montgolfier brothers demonstrate the first hot-air balloon on June 4 at Annonay

In October the first manned flight in a hot-air balloon is made by François de Rozier in Paris

1784

Astronomy

Messier publishes first nebula catalog

Earth Science

Elements of Mineralogy (Kirwan)

Technology

Cort patents dry-puddling process for converting pig iron into wrought iron

1785

Medicine

Withering publishes a report on the use of

the foxglove as a source of the drug digitalis

Physics

Coulomb publishes his inverse square law of electrical attraction and repulsion (Coulomb's law)

Technology

Cartwright's power loom is patented

1786

Astronomy

Discovery of Encke's Comet (orbit computed by Encke in 1819)

1787

Astronomy

Herschel discovers Titania and Oberon (satellites of Uranus)

Chemistry

Hope isolates strontium

Physics

Charles discovers law governing change in volume of a gas with temperature (Charles's law)

1788

Biology

Linnean Society founded

Chemistry

Blagden discovers that lowering of freezing point of a solution is proportional to amount of solute (Blagden's law)

Earth Science

Hutton first publishes his uniformitarian theory

Physics

Mécanique analytique (Lagrange)

1789

Astronomy

(to 1790) Herschel discovers Mimas and Enceladus (satellites of Saturn)

Biology

Genera Plantarum (Jussieu) – classification of plants

Chemistry

Klaproth discovers zirconium and uranium

Traité élémentaire de chimie (Lavoisier) – states law of conservation of mass

1791

Biology

Galvani publishes his findings in electrophysiology

Chemistry

Nicolas Leblanc patents his process for producing soda ash

Gregor discovers titanium (not identified as new element until 1795 when isolated by Klaproth)

Physics

Prévost puts forward his theory of exchanges for heat

1794

Biology

Young explains accommodation of the eye

Medicine

Dalton describes the condition of color blindness

1795

Chemistry

Klaproth rediscovers titanium

Earth Science

Theory of the Earth (Hutton)

1796

Medicine

Jenner first uses cowpox vaccine

1798

Biology

An Essay on the Principle of Population (Malthus)

Chemistry

Klaproth discovers chromium

Vauquelin discovers chromium and beryllium

Physics

Cavendish measures density of Earth by torsion-balance experiment

Enquiry concerning the Source of Heat excited by Friction (Rumford)

1799

Astronomy

(to 1825) *Traité de mécanique céleste* (Laplace)

Chemistry

Proust formulates his law of definite proportions

Mathematics

Gauss's proof of fundamental theorem of algebra

1799

General

The Royal Institution is founded by Count Rumford at 21 Albemarle St, London

1800

Chemistry

Nicholson discovers electrolysis

Physics

Volta invents voltaic pile – first battery

1801

Astronomy

Piazzi discovers Ceres (first minor planet)

Chemistry

Del Rio discovers vanadium (rediscovered by Sefström in 1830)

Dalton reads his paper on the constitution of gas mixtures, which contains the law of partial pressures

Clément and Désormes discover carbon monoxide

Hatchett discovers the element now known as niobium (originally named columbium)

Henry formulates his law for the solubility of gases (Henry's law)

Earth Science

Matthew Flinders sets sail in the *Investigator* to chart the coast of Australia

Mathematics

Disquisitiones arithmeticae (Gauss)

Physics

Ritter identifies ultraviolet radiation

Wollaston shows that frictional and galvanic electricity are the same

1802

Astronomy

Olbers discovers asteroid Pallas

Chemistry

Ekeberg discovers tantalum

Dalton compiles his first table of atomic weights

Gay-Lussac establishes Gay-Lussac's law

Earth Science

Illustrations of the Huttonian Theory (J. Playfair) – summarizes Hutton's uniformitarian theory of the Earth

1803

Chemistry

Klaproth discovers cerium oxide

Hisinger and Berzelius discover cerium

Dalton expounds his atomic theory

(to 1804) S. Tennant discovers iridium and osmium

Physics

Young provides evidence for the wave nature of light by demonstrating interference using Young's slits

1804

Chemistry

Wollaston discovers palladium

1805

Chemistry

Wollaston discovers rhodium

Medicine

Sertürner isolates morphine from opium

1806

Biochemistry

Vauquelin isolates the first amino acid – asparagine

Earth Science

Beaufort proposes scale for wind speed (Beaufort scale)

1807

Astronomy

Olbers discovers asteroid Vesta

1808

Biology

(to 1813) *American Ornithology* (Wilson)

Chemistry

A New System of Chemical Philosophy (Dalton)

Gay-Lussac formulates his law of combining volumes

Physics

Malus describes the polarization of light

1809

Biology

Philosophie zoologique (Lamarck) – includes theory of evolution by inheritance of acquired characteristics

Physics

Chladni demonstrates the patterns (Chladni's figures) formed by vibrations of a plate

1810

Chemistry

Davy establishes that chlorine does not contain oxygen and is an element in its own right

Physics

Zur Farbenlehre; Goethe

1811

Biology

New Idea of Anatomy of the Brain (Charles Bell)

Chemistry

Avogadro publishes the paper containing Avogadro's hypothesis

Courtois discovers iodine (published 1813)

Dulong discovers the gas nitrogen trichloride

Earth Science

Brongniart and Cuvier first identify rock strata by their fossil content

Medicine

Bell partly anticipates Magendie in showing functional differentiation of spinal nerve roots (Bell–Magendie law) but does not publish

Physics

Arago discovers chromatic polarization

1812

Earth Science

Mohs introduces a scale of hardness for minerals (Mohs scale)

Medicine

Parkinson establishes perforation as the cause of death in appendicitis

1813

Biology

Théorie élémentaire de la botanique (Candolle) – system of classifying plants

Chemistry

Clément and Désormes confirm Courtois's discovery of iodine

Physics

Brewster formulates Brewster's law for polarization by reflection

1814

Physics

Fraunhofer observes absorption lines (Fraunhofer lines) in the solar spectrum

1815

Biology

(to 1822) *Natural History of Invertebrates* (Lamarck) – reorganizes the classification of invertebrate animals

Chemistry

Biot shows that solutions (as well as solids) can show optical activity

Prout suggests that the atomic weight of any atom is an exact multiple of the atomic weight of hydrogen (Prout's hypothesis)

1816

Chemistry

The Davy lamp is produced

Medicine

Laënnec invents the stethoscope

Technology

Stirling invents the Stirling engine

1817

Biology

Pelletier and Caventou discover chlorophyll

Chemistry

Strohmeyer discovers cadmium

Berzelius discovers selenium

(to 1820) Caventou and Pelletier isolate the alkaloids strychnine, brucine, cinchonine, quinine, veratrine, and colchicine

Medicine

Parkinson publishes his description of Parkinson's disease

1818

Chemistry

Discovery of lithium

1819

Biology

Chamisso discovers the alternation of generations in mollusks and tunicates

Chemistry

Mitscherlich formulates his law of isomorphism

Dulong and Petit discover the law of atomic heats (Dulong and Petit's law)

Kidd and Garden obtain naphthalene from coal tar

Physics

Clément and Désormes publish paper on principal specific heats of gases

1820

Physics

Arago demonstrates electromagnetic effect to French Academy of Sciences

Oersted publishes his discovery of electromagnetism

Schweigger invents multiplier (galvanometer)

Ampère begins his work on electromagnetism

Faraday begins work on electromagnetism

1821

Physics

Faraday constructs simple electric motor

1822

Biology

Magendie (and, earlier, Charles Bell) discovers that the roots of the anterior nerves of the spinal cord control motion, while the roots of the posterior nerves control sensation

Mathematics

Théorie analytique de chaleur (Fourier) – introduces the use of Fourier series

Medicine

Magendie publishes his work on alkaloids, introducing such compounds as morphine, strychnine, and quinine into medical practice

Physics

Latour discovers the critical state

Seebeck discovers thermoelectric effect (Seebeck effect)

1823

Mathematics

Babbage designs his analytical engine (computer)

Technology

Macintosh produces a flexible waterproof material

1824

Biology

Flourens publishes his work demonstrating the major roles of different parts of the central nervous system

Physics

Réflexions sur la puissance motrice du feu (Carnot) – introduces Carnot cycle

1825

Chemistry

Faraday discovers benzene

Balard discovers bromine

Medicine

Bretonneau performs the first successful tracheotomy to treat diphtheria

Physics

Nobili invents astatic galvanometer

Ampère deduces law for force between current-carrying conductors (Ampère's law)

Technology

Stockton–Darlington railway opened (September 27)

1826

Astronomy

Olbers proposes his paradox

Discovery of Biela's comet

Biology

Müller shows that sensory nerves can only interpret stimuli in one way

Chemistry

Unverdorben synthesizes aniline (which he names crystalline)

Mathematics

Lobachevsky announces his non-Euclidean geometry

Technology

Niepce produces the first permanent camera photograph

General

Michael Faraday introduces the Christmas lectures for children at the Royal Institution, London. He also begins the Friday evening discourses, in which leading scientists speak about their work to Royal Institution members

1827

Biology

Baer publishes his discovery of the mammalian ovum within the Graafian follicle

(to 1838) *Birds of America* (Audubon)

Chemistry

Brownian motion first described, by Robert Brown

Wöhler synthesizes aluminum

Physics

Ohm publishes his law relating current and voltage (Ohm's law)

Mémoires sur la théorie mathématique des phénomènes electrodynamiques uniquement déduite de l'expérience (Ampère)

Technology

Fourneyron constructs his first outward-flow turbine, a six-horsepower unit

1828

Chemistry

Wöhler isolates beryllium

Berzelius discovers thorium

Wöhler synthesizes urea, the first organic compound to be synthesized from inorganic materials

Physics

Sturgeon constructs first electromagnet

Invention of Nicol prism

1829

Chemistry

Döbereiner formulates his law of triads

Graham publishes a paper on the diffusion of gases, which contains his law of diffusion

Physics

Nobili makes first thermopile

Babinet first suggests that wavelengths of spectral lines could be used as standards of length

Henry invents first practical electric motor

1830

Chemistry

Sefström discovers vanadium

Earth Science

The Principles of Geology (Lyell) – establishes Hutton and J. Playfair's uniformitarian theories

Physics

On the Improvement of Compound Microscopes (J. J. Lister) – showing how distortions can be reduced by use of achromatic lenses

Technology

Stephenson's *Rocket* wins the Rainhill trials in England

1831

Biology

Müller confirms the Bell–Magendie law distinguishing between motor and sensory nerves

(to 1836) Expedition of HMS *Beagle* to South America, with Darwin aboard as naturalist

Chemistry

Guthrie and Soubeiran independently discover chloroform

Physics

Mellini and Nobili publish a description of a sensitive thermopile

Experimental Researches in Electricity, 1st series (Faraday)

Technology

Philips patents the contact process for making sulfuric acid

General

The British Association for the Advancement of Science established in York, with Vernon Harcourt as its first chairman

1832

Astronomy

Henderson measures parallax of Alpha Centauri (but does not publish until 1839)

Biology

Dutrochet demonstrates that gas exchange in plants is via the stomata

Gideon Algernon Mantell discovers the first armored dinosaur, *Hylaeosaurus*

Mathematics

Bolyai publishes his version of non-Euclidean geometry

Galois outlines his ideas on group theory

Medicine

T. Hodgkin describes lymphadenoma (Hodgkin's disease)

Physics

Faraday performs experiments on electromagnetic induction

Henry discovers self-induction

1833

Medicine

Observations on the Gastric Juice and the Physiology of Digestion (W. Beaumont)

1834

Chemistry

Runge discovers quinoline

Dumas and Peligot discover methyl alcohol (methanol)

Physics

Peltier demonstrates thermoelectric effect (Peltier effect)

Lenz discovers law for magnetic induction (Lenz's law)

1835

Biology

Dujardin is able to refute the claim that microorganisms have the same organs as higher animals

Earth Science

Charpentier first presents his glaciation theory

Physics

Coriolis describes the inertial Coriolis force

Henry develops the electric relay

Technology

Morse produces a working model of the electric telegraph

1836

Anthropology

Lartet discovers fossil ancestors of the gibbon (Pliopithecus)

Astronomy

Baily observes Baily's beads during total eclipse

Biology

Schwann and Cagniard de la Tour independently discover the role of yeast in alcoholic fermentation

Schwann prepares the first precipitate of an enzyme (pepsin) from animal tissue

Chemistry

The Daniell cell is introduced

Gossage improves process for manufacture of alkali

Physics

Sturgeon designs moving-cell galvanometer and introduces commutator for electric motor

1837

Biology

Purkinje locates the Purkinje cells in the brain

Chemistry

Boussingault begins his experiments proving that leguminous plants are capable of using atmospheric nitrogen

Earth Science

A System of Mineralogy (Dana)

Mathematics

Recherches sur la probabilité des jugements (Poisson) – introduces law of large numbers and Poisson distribution

Technology

Wheatstone and Cooke produce first practical telegraph system

1838

Astronomy

Bessel announces detection of parallax of

61 Cygni – first determination of stellar distance

Biochemistry

Peligot and Bouchardat demonstrate glucose in the urine of diabetics

Biology

Beiträge zur Phytogenesis (Schleiden) – states that all structures of plants composed of cells or their derivatives

Remak shows that nerves are not hollow tubes

(to 1843) *Flora of North America* (A. Gray)

1839

Biology

A Naturalist's Voyage on the Beagle (Darwin)

Purkinje discovers the Purkinje fibers in the heart

Chemistry

Mosander discovers lanthanum

Technology

Nasmyth designs the steam hammer

Daguerre perfects the daguerreotype

1840

Chemistry

Hess formulates the law of constant heat summation

Schönbein discovers ozone

Earth Science

Etudes sur les glaciers (Agassiz) – postulates existence of ice ages

General

William Whewell introduces the terms "physicist" and "scientist" into the English language

1841

Earth Science

Essai sur les glaciers (Charpentier)

Technology

Sir Joseph Whitworth first argues for a unified system of screw threads – the Whitworth system, which becomes the standard for British engineering

1842

Biology

Naegeli publishes his observations on cell division during pollen formation, so disproving Schleiden's theory of cell formation by budding off the nuclear surface

Steenstrup publishes his observations of the alternation of generations in certain animals

Bowman publishes his work on the Malpighian bodies of the kidneys, which includes a description of the structure and role of the Bowman's capsules

Medicine

Braid suggests the use of hypnosis to treat pain, anxiety, and certain nervous disorders

Physics

Doppler discovers the Doppler effect for wave motions

Mayer's paper containing the law of conservation of energy is published

1843

Astronomy

Schwabe announces discovery of sunspot cycle

Biology

Du Bois-Reymond shows that applying a stimulus to a nerve causes a drop in electrical potential at the point of stimulus

Chemistry

Mosander discovers erbium and terbium

Medicine

Holmes publishes a paper on the contagious nature of puerperal fever

General

Women first admitted to membership of the British Association for the Advancement of Science

1844

Astronomy

Bessel announces that Sirius is a double star system

Biology

Remak discovers ganglion cells in the heart

Chemistry

Gerhardt develops his type theory of organic compounds

1845

Astronomy

J. C. Adams works out position of Neptune

Biology

(to 1848) *Viviparous Quadrupeds of North America* (Audubon)

Chemistry

Schröder discovers red phosphorus

Physics

Waterson's paper on the kinetic theory of gases is rejected by the Royal Society

Faraday discovers effect of magnetic field on polarized light (Faraday effect)

Kirchhoff formulates his laws for electric circuits (Kirchhoff's laws)

An Essay on the Application of Mathematics to Electricity and Magnetism (George Green), reissued by Lord Kelvin in *Crelle's Journal* thus introducing *Green's theorem*, *Green's function*, and the notion of electric potential into science

1846

Astronomy

Leverrier works out position of Neptune – discovered by Galle

Lassell discovers Triton (satellite of Neptune)

Harvard College Observatory founded with W. C. Bond as director at Cambridge, Massachusetts

Biology

Siebold and Stannius publish their textbook of comparative anatomy

Hugo von Mohl coins the term protoplasm for the substance surrounding the cell nucleus

Chemistry

Sobrero discovers nitroglycerine

Schönbein discovers guncotton

Earth Science

Loomis publishes first synoptic weather map

Medicine

Morton demonstrates the use of ether inhalation to produce general anesthesia

1847

Biology

The first volume of *Antiquités celtiques et antédiluviennes* (Boucher de Perthes)

Ludwig invents the kymograph

Chemistry

Babo formulates his law for the depression of vapor pressure by a solute (Babo's law)

Medicine

J. Y. Simpson introduces chloroform as an anesthetic in hospital operations

Semmelweis discovers the nature of puerperal fever and implements a successful preventative policy

Physics

Über die Erhaltung der Kraft (Helmholtz) – develops the law of conservation of energy

Kelvin draws an analogy between an electrostatic field and an incompressible elastic solid

1848

Astronomy

W. C. Bond and G. Bond discover Hyperion (satellite of Saturn)

Biology

Kölliker isolates cells of smooth muscle

(to 1854) *Untersuchungen über tierische Elektricität* (Du Bois-Reymond) – reports his work on nerve and muscle activity

Chemistry

Pasteur discovers molecular asymmetry (as cause of optical activity)

Physics

Joule publishes a paper on the kinetic theory of gases in which he makes the first estimate of the speed of gas molecules

Kelvin introduces the absolute temperature scale

General

American Association for the Advancement of Science founded with W. C. Redfield as its first president

1849

Chemistry

Wurtz synthesizes ethylamine from ammonia

Deville discovers nitrogen pentoxide

Medicine

Addison describes Addison's disease

Physics

Fizeau measures the speed of light by a toothed-wheel method

On the Mechanical Equivalent of Heat
(Joule)

1850

Astronomy

W. C. Bond makes first photograph of a
star (Vega) and discovers third ring of Saturn (crepe ring)
Roche proposes and calculates *Roche limit*
Lamont announces discovery of magnetic
cycle of Earth

Earth Science

Mallet begins precise experiments to determine speed of earthquake waves

Physics

Fizeau and Foucault provide experimental
support for the wave theory of light by
measuring the speed in air and in water
Über die bewegende Kraft der Wärme
(Clausius) – first formulates the second
law of thermodynamics

1851

Astronomy

Lassell discovers Ariel and Umbriel (satellites of Uranus)

Biology

Helmholtz invents the ophthalmoscope
Vergleichende Untersuchungen (Hofmeister) – describes discovery of alternation of
generations in lower plants and similarities
between seed-bearing and non-seed-bear-
ing plants

Chemistry

Thomas Anderson extracts pyridine from
bone oil

Physics

Foucault uses pendulum to demonstrate
rotation of Earth

1852

Chemistry

Frankland originates the theory of valence

Mathematics

Francis Guthrie first notices the map-
coloring problem

Physics

Kelvin sets out the law of conservation of
energy
(to 1862) Joule and Kelvin investigate the
Joule–Kelvin effect

1853

Aeronautics

Cayley constructs the first successful man-
carrying glider

Chemistry

Hittorf introduces idea of ionic mobility in
electrolysis
Cannizzaro discovers the reaction known
as Cannizzaro's reaction

Mathematics

Hamilton introduces quaternions

1854

Chemistry

Berthelot synthesizes fats from glycerin
and fatty acids

Mathematics

The Laws of Thought (Boole)
Reimann puts forward his general formulation of Reimannian geometry

1855

Biology

Pringsheim confirms the occurrence of sexuality in algae

Chemistry

Wurtz develops the Wurtz reaction for
synthesizing hydrocarbons
Deville develops a process for the large-
scale production of aluminum

1856

Anthropology

Lartet discovers fossil ancestor of apes
(Dryopithecus)

Biology

Pasteur declares that fermentation is
caused by living organisms

Chemistry

Perkin discovers first synthetic dye (mau-
veine)

Medicine

Brown-Séquard shows there is a connection between excising the adrenal glands
and Addison's disease

Technology

Bessemer announces his process for con-
verting pig iron into steel
Charles William Siemens and Friedrich
Siemens introduce the regenerator furnace

1857

Astronomy

G. Bond shows how stellar magnitude may be calculated from photographs

Earth Science

Buys Ballot formulates law concerning wind direction

1858

Biology

On the Tendency of Varieties to Depart Indefinitely from the Original Type (Wallace)

Joint paper by Darwin and Wallace, outlining their theory of evolution by natural selection, read at meeting of Linnean Society

Die Cellularpathologie (Virchow)

Chemistry

Kekulé publishes his paper on bonding in carbon compounds

1859

Astronomy

(to 1862) *Bonner Durchmusterung* (Argelander) – survey of northern stars

Biology

On the Origin of Species by Means of Natural Selection (Darwin)

Physics

Tyndall discovers scattering by colloidal suspension (Tyndall effect)

Planté invents Planté battery – the first storage battery

1860

Biology

Oxford meeting of the British Association for the Advancement of Science, in which T. H. Huxley and others defend Darwin's theory of evolution

Chemistry

Bunsen and Kirchhoff publish their paper on spectroscopy – spectroscopic methods enabled Bunsen to discover rubidium and cesium

First meeting of the International Chemical Congress at Karlsruhe

Graham distinguishes colloids

c. 1860

Physics

Illustrations of Dynamical Theory of Gases (Maxwell)

Technology

Lenoir takes out a patent for an internal combustion engine

1861

Astronomy

A. G. Clark discovers Sirius B

Schiaparelli discovers the asteroid Hesperia

Biology

H. W. Bates publishes his paper on Batesian mimicry in butterflies

Gegenbaur shows that all vertebrate eggs and sperm are unicellular

Chemistry

Bunsen and Kirchhoff discover rubidium

Crookes discovers thallium

Technology

Solvay patents his process for soda production

Massachusetts Institute of Technology (MIT) founded in Boston with William Barton Rogers as its first president

1862

Biology

(to 1883) *Genera Plantarum* (Bentham and Hooker)

Chemistry

Béguyer de Chancourtois proposes his periodic classification of the elements (telluric screw)

1863

Astronomy

Huggins shows the stars to be composed of known elements

Biology

Helmholtz publishes his theory of hearing

Chemistry

Reich and Richter discover indium

Earth Science

Galton publishes his work on weather systems, outlining the modern technique of weather mapping

Medicine

Leuckart publishes the first volume of his work on the parasites of man

Davaine shows that anthrax can be transmitted to healthy cattle by injecting them with the blood of diseased cattle

Waldeyer establishes that cancer begins as a single cell

General

National Academy of Sciences created

1864

Astronomy

Donati first observes spectrum of comet – discovers gaseous composition of tails

W. Huggins discovers some nebulae to be gaseous

Chemistry

Guldberg and Waage discover the law of mass action

Newlands publishes his law of octaves

Physics

Dynamical Theory of the Electric Field (Maxwell) – contains Maxwell's differential equations describing the propagation of electromagnetic waves

1865

Biology

Sachs shows that chlorophyll is confined to discrete bodies – chloroplasts

Chemistry

Kekulé proposes a ring structure for benzene

(to 1885) Baeyer researches indigo

Zur Gross der Loftmolecule; Loschmidt

Medicine

Villemin shows that tuberculosis is contagious

Physics

Clausius introduces the term entropy as a measure of the availability of heat

1866

Astronomy

Schiaparelli shows meteors follow cometary orbits

Biology

De Bary shows that a lichen is a close association between an alga and a fungus

Mendel publishes the results of his plant-breeding experiments, summarized later as the law of segregation and the law of independent assortment

His introduces the microtome

Medicine

Allbutt invents the short clinical thermometer

Physics

Kundt develops the Kundt tube to measure the speed of sound

Technology

Leclanché invents the electrical battery (dry cell)

1867

Biology

Handbuch der physiologische Optik (Helmholtz)

Medicine

Cohnheim publishes his work on inflammation, disproving Virchow's theory that pus corpuscles originate at the point of wounding, and demonstrating that swelling is due to the passage of leukocytes from the veins into the wound

Joseph Lister introduces the principles of antiseptic surgery into medicine

Technology

Nobel patents dynamite and the detonating cap in the UK

1868

Anthropology

Lartet discovers remains of Cro-Magnon man

Astronomy

W. Huggins discovers red shift in spectrum of Sirius

Lockyer identifies lines of helium in solar spectrum

Medicine

Wunderlich publishes his investigations into body temperature and disease, so introducing clinical thermometry as an important diagnostic technique

1869

Chemistry

Mendeleev proposes his periodic table of the elements

T. Andrews publishes his work on the liquefaction of gases, which includes the concept of critical temperature

Caro, Graebe, and Liebermann synthesize alizarin, the first natural dye to be synthesized

Medicine

Joseph Lister uses catgut ligatures instead of silk

1870

Biology

Hitzig and Fritsch publish a paper containing the first experimental evidence for cerebral localization

Chemistry

J. L. Meyer publishes his periodic classification of elements

1871

Biochemistry

Miescher announces the discovery of nuclein (later renamed nucleic acid) in cell nuclei

Biology

Hoppe-Seyler discovers the enzyme invertase

Ranvier describes the nodes of Ranvier

The Descent of Man (Darwin)

1872

Astronomy

H. Draper photographs first stellar spectrum (of Vega)

Biology

Untersuchungen über Bacterien (Cohn) – provides basis for modern bacterial nomenclature

Chemistry

Dewar devises the Dewar vacuum flask

Wislicenus demonstrates geometrical isomerism in lactic acid

Earth Science

(to 1876) C. W. Thomson collects evidence for the presence of the Mid-Atlantic Ridge

Medicine

George Huntington describes Huntington's chorea

Physics

E. Abbe invents Abbe condenser lens for microscopes

Amagat experiments on behavior of gases at high pressures

1873

Biology

Osler discovers the blood platelets

Chemistry

(to 1876) Gibbs develops the theory of chemical thermodynamics

On the Continuity of the Liquid and Gaseous States (van der Waals) – includes the van der Waals equation

Medicine

Billroth performs first laryngectomy

Hansen observes rod-shaped bacilli in the tissues of leprosy patients

1874

Chemistry

A Suggestion Looking to the Extension into Space of the Structural Formulae at Present Used in Chemistry (van't Hoff) – introduces idea of tetrahedral arrangement of bonds to carbon atom

Lecoq de Boisbaudran discovers gallium

Physics

Braun discovers use of semiconducting crystals as rectifiers

Technology

A. G. Bell's multiple telegraph is patented

General

The Cavendish laboratory opens in Cambridge, England, with Clerk Maxwell as its first director

1876

Biology

Geographical Distribution of Animals (Alfred Russell Wallace)

Chemistry

On the Equilibrium of Heterogeneous Substances (J. W. Gibbs) – work on chemical thermodynamics introducing phase rule

Medicine

Koch publishes the life cycle of the anthrax bacillus

Technology

A. G. Bell's invention of the telephone is patented

1877

Astronomy

A. Hall discovers Phobos and Deimos (satellites of Mars)

Chemistry

Friedel and Crafts discover the Friedel–Crafts reaction for the alkylation or acylation of aromatic hydrocarbons

Medicine

Manson demonstrates, from his investigations of elephantiasis, that certain diseases are transmitted by insects

Physics

Cailletet succeeds in producing liquid oxygen

Technology

Edison invents the phonograph

1878

Chemistry

Marignac isolates ytterbium

1879

Biology

De Bary coins the term symbiosis to describe the mutually beneficial association between two unrelated organisms

Chemistry

Cleve discovers thulium

Lecoq de Boisbaudran discovers samarium

Nilson discovers scandium

Fahlberg discovers saccharin

Medicine

Neisser discovers the gonococcus responsible for gonorrhea

Physics

Stefan formulates law for heat radiation (Stefan–Boltzmann law)

Swan invents carbon-filament incandescent electric lamp

Edwin Hall discovers the Hall effect

Technology

Edison demonstrates his electric light bulb

The Thomas–Gilchrist steel-making process is demonstrated

1880

Chemistry

Skraup synthesizes quinoline

Marignac discovers gadolinium

Earth Science

Milne invents seismograph

Medicine

Laveran discovers the causative agent of malaria – the *Plasmodium* parasite

Physics

P. Curie discovers piezoelectricity

Technology

Eadweard James Muybridge demonstrates the first moving picture in public using the "zoopraxiscope"

1881

Biology

T. W. Engelmann demonstrates chemotactic response of bacteria

Medicine

Finlay publishes a paper naming the mosquito as the vector of yellow fever

Physics

Ewing discovers hysteresis

1882

Biology

Ants, Bees and Wasps (Lubbock)

Zell-substanz, Kern und Zelltheilung (W. Flemming)

Chemistry

Raoult shows that the depression in freezing point of a solvent is proportional to the mass of substance dissolved divided by the substance's molecular weight (Raoult's rule)

Earth Science

Anthropogeographie (Ratzel, 2nd vol. 1891) – lays foundation for modern study of human geography

Medicine

Metchnikoff describes phagocytosis

Pasteur produces an attenuated vaccine for anthrax

Koch discovers the bacillus responsible for tuberculosis

Physics

Ritter builds first dry voltaic pile

Rowland designs diffraction grating for spectral photography

1883

Biology

Galton coins the term eugenics

Medicine

Kocher demonstrates that operative myxedema (cretinism) following removal of the thyroid, can be avoided by leaving a portion of the thyroid in the body

Physics

Wroblewski and Olszewski achieve liquefaction of large amounts of oxygen

1884

Biology

Gram discovers the Gram stain

Chemistry

Chardonnet's rayon, the world's first artificial fiber, is patented

Le Chatelier discovers Le Chatelier's principle

Tilden synthesizes isoprene, leading to the production of synthetic rubber

Mathematics

Die Grundlagen der Arithmetik (Frege) – defines cardinal number and derives properties of numbers

Medicine

Löffler isolates and cultivates the bacillus responsible for diphtheria

Gaffky obtains a pure culture of the typhoid bacillus

Koller publishes his experiments on the use of cocaine as a local anesthetic

Physics

Poynting introduces Poynting's vector

Technology

Parsons invents the multistage steam turbine

General

The International Meridian Conference in Washington adopts a single prime meridian passing through the center of the transit instrument at the Royal Greenwich Observatory

1885

Biology

Kossel isolates adenine from his newly discovered nucleic acids

Chemistry

Winkler discovers germanium

Medicine

Roux and Yersin show that diphtheria is caused by a toxin released from diphtheria bacteria

Pasteur successfully uses a rabies vaccine to cure a rabies victim

Physics

Balmer discovers formula for series of lines in hydrogen spectrum (Balmer series)

Technology

Daimler patents the first internal-combustion engine

1886

Biology

Eichler publishes his plant classification system

Weismann publishes his theory of the continuity of the germ plasm

Chemistry

Beckmann discovers the Beckmann rearrangement

Moissan isolates fluorine gas

C. M. Hall and Héroult independently discover a cheap process for extracting aluminum

Lecoq de Boisbaudran discovers dysprosium

Physics

Boltzmann derives distribution law for energies of gas molecules (Maxwell–Boltzmann distribution)

E. Abbe invents apochromatic lens system

Goldstein discovers canal rays

Technology

Benz patents his three-wheeled automobile, the first practical automobile powered by an internal-combustion engine

1887

Astronomy

Paris Observatory organizes a congress that decides to construct the *Carte du Ciel*, a photographic map of the whole sky

Biology

Henson introduces the term plankton

Petri introduces the Petri dish for cultures

Chemistry

Arrhenius publishes his theory on ionic dissociation in solution

Wallach characterizes the terpenes

Physics

Hertz discovers photoelectric effect

Michelson and Morley attempt to detect the ether and obtain negative result

(to 1888) Lodge discovers propagation of electromagnetic waves along conducting wires

Technology

Tesla invents the first alternating-current motor

1888

Astronomy

New General Catalogue of Nebulae and Clusters of Stars (NGC) (Dreyer)

Lick Observatory completed at a site on Mount Hamilton overlooking San José, California

Chemistry

Baeyer makes the first synthesis of a terpene

Earth Science

(to 1889) Nansen explores Greenland icecap

Mathematics

Was sind und was sollen die Zahlen (Dedekind) – the first formulation of the axioms of arithmetic

Physics

Hertz demonstrates propagation of electromagnetic waves (radio waves)

Technology

Eastman markets his hand-held box camera

1889

Biology

Pavlov shows the secretion of gastric juices is prompted by the sight of food

Intracellular Pangenesis (de Vries) – the theory that hereditary traits are determined by "pangenes" in the cell nucleus

Chemistry

F. A. Abel and J. Dewar introduce cordite

Mathematics

Peano presents axioms of arithmetic

Physics

Sur les trois corps et les equations de la dy-

namique (Henri Poincaré) – discusses the three-body problem

Technology

Otto Lilienthal publishes *Der Vogelflug als Grundlage der Fliegerkunst* and builds his first model glider

1890

Astronomy

Vogel discovers eclipsing binaries spectroscopically

Biology

Kitasato and von Behring announce the discovery of diphtheria and tetanus antitoxins

Koch formulates Koch's postulates for establishing that an organism is the cause of a disease

Chemistry

Guillaume begins work on nickel alloys (invar, elinvar)

Beilby patents a process for the synthesis of potassium cyanide

Commercial synthetic indigo is produced

Computing

Herman Hollerith invents a tabulating system using punched cards for the 1890 U.S. census

Medicine

Grassi, Marchiafava, and Celli show there are a number of protozoan species that can produce malaria

Physics

Rydberg discovers formula for spectral-line frequencies, using *Rydberg constant*

1891

Astronomy

Chandler announces discovery of Earth's Chandler wobble

Biology

Strasburger demonstrates that physiological rather than physical forces are responsible for the movement of liquids up the plant stem

Chemistry

E. H. Fischer deduces the configurations of the 16 possible aldohexose sugars

Physics

Poynting determines the mean density of the Earth

Stoney coins term electron

Lippmann produces the first color photograph

General

The Throop Polytechnic Institute, the forerunner of the California Institute of Technology, is founded in Pasadena, California

1892

Astronomy

E. E. Barnard discovers Amalthea (satellite of Jupiter)

Biology

Ivanovsky, working on tobacco mosaic disease, finds the first evidence of viruses

Chemistry

Bevan and Cross patent the viscose process of rayon manufacture

Crum Brown and Gibson propose Crum Brown's rule for reactions of benzene compounds

Medicine

Welch discovers the bacterium that causes gas gangrene

Physics

(to 1904) Lorentz develops his electron theory

1893

Astronomy

Maunder discovers Maunder minimum for sunspot activity

Chemistry

Kjeldahl develops the Kjeldahl method for determining the amount of nitrogen in compounds

Mathematics

(and 1903) *Grundgesetze der Arithmetik* (Frege)

Physics

Wien derives his displacement law for radiation from hot bodies

Poynting determines the gravitational constant

Technology

Diesel demonstrates his first engine

1894

Biology

Pfeiffer discovers bacteriolysis

Rubner demonstrates that human energy production can be explained by thermodynamics

Chemistry

Ramsay and Rayleigh discover argon

Sulfur is raised from deep underground by means of superheated water – the Frasch process

Medicine

Yersin and Kitasato discover the bacterium responsible for bubonic plague

Physics

Lodge develops his coherer for detecting radio waves

Technology

Marconi begins experiments on communicating with radio waves

1895

Astronomy

Keeler shows the rings of Saturn do not rotate uniformly

Chemistry

Ramsay and Crookes identify helium

Medicine

Bruce discovers the trypanosome parasite that causes sleeping sickness

Physics

Lorentz describes force (Lorentz force) on charged particle in electromagnetic field

P. Curie discovers transition temperature for change from ferromagnetic to paramagnetic behavior (Curie point)

Röntgen discovers x-rays

Psychology

Studien über Hysterie (Freud) – beginning of psychoanalysis

1896

Biology

The first observation of the fermentation of sugar by cell-free extracts of yeast, proving the process is purely chemical and does not require intact cells

Schäfer and Oliver discover that injecting an extract from the adrenal gland increases blood pressure

Chemistry

Walden discovers the Walden inversion in organic substitution reactions

Mathematics

Hadamard sets out his proof of the prime number theorem (independently of de la Vallée-Poussin)

Physics

Becquerel discovers radioactivity (in uranium salts)

Wien derives a formula for the distribution of energy in black-body radiation (Wien's formula)

Boltzmann introduces the equation relating entropy to probability

Zeeman discovers splitting of spectral lines in magnetic field (Zeeman effect)

Technology

Marconi patent on radio telegraphy

Popov in Russia experiments with radio communication

Sperry invents the gyrocompass

A plant using the Castner–Kellner process is opened at Niagara Falls

General

Alfred Nobel dies leaving a fortune and instructions in his will to set up the Nobel Foundation

1897

Astronomy

Yerkes Observatory opened under the directorship of G. Hale at Williams Bay, Wisconsin

Biology

J. J. Abel isolates a physiologically active substance from the adrenal gland – adrenaline (epinephrine)

Chemistry

Sabatier demonstrates hydrogenation of organic compounds

Medicine

Ross identifies malaria parasites (plasmodia) in the bodies of *Anopheles* mosquitoes fed on blood from infected patients

Eijkman discovers a cure for beriberi

Physics

Larmor predicts precession of electron orbits in atoms (Larmor precession)

J. J. Thomson discovers the electron

Boys determines the gravitational constant

1898

Biology

Bordet discovers alexin (complement)

Pflanzengeographie auf physiologischer Grundlage; Schimper)

Löffler and Frosch demonstrate that viruses can cause diseases in animals

Golgi describes the Golgi apparatus

Beijerinck coins the term filterable virus for the causative agent of tobacco mosaic disease

Chemistry

Lowry describes mutarotation of optically active compounds

E. H. Fischer synthesizes purine

Ramsay and Travers discover neon, krypton, and xenon

Caro discovers Caro's acid, a powerful oxidizing agent

J. Dewar produces liquid hydrogen

Medicine

Grassi demonstrates that only the *Anopheles* species of mosquito can transmit malaria to humans

Physics

M. Curie discovers radium and polonium

Townsend measures the charge of the electron

1899

Astronomy

W. H. Pickering discovers Phoebe (satellite of Saturn)

Chemistry

Thiele proposes the idea of partial valence in chemical compounds

J. Dewar produces solid hydrogen

Physics

Rutherford distinguishes alpha and beta rays in radioactivity

Technology

Marconi achieves first international radio transmission (England–France)

1900

Biology

Correns rediscovers Mendel's work and publishes his own work on crossing experiments confirming Mendel's results

Chemistry

The discovery of the Grignard reagents

Gomberg obtains triphenylmethyl – a stable free radical

Tsvet develops the technique of adsorption analysis, which he later named chromatography

Earth Science

Oldham clearly identifies primary (P) and secondary (S) seismic waves for the first time

Köppen first formulates his climatic classification

Mathematics

Hilbert presents list of 23 research problems at International Congress of Mathematicians in Paris

Medicine

Leishman discovers the protozoan parasite causing kala-azar (now known as leishmaniasis)

Grassi and Manson provide evidence that malaria is transmitted by mosquitoes

Physics

Debierne discovers actinium

Rutherford discovers gamma radiation

Dorn discovers that radium evolves radioactive gas (radon)

Planck publishes paper giving theory of energy distribution in black-body radiation, introducing the idea of quantized energy transfer

1901

Biology

Takamine achieves the first isolation and purification of a hormone (adrenaline) from a natural source

Hopkins discovers the amino acid tryptophan

J. N. Langley finds that extract from adrenal gland stimulates effect of sympathetic nervous system

(to 1903) *The Mutation Theory* (de Vries) – proposes that new species evolve by genetic mutations

Chemistry

Demarçay discovers europium

Earth Science

(to 1909) *Die Alpen im Eiszeitalter* (Penck) – identification of four ice ages

Medicine

Einthoven develops the electrocardiogram

Reed and Carroll establish that yellow fever is caused by a virus

Physics

Richardson formulates a law to explain the emission of electrons from hot surfaces

Technology

Marconi makes first transatlantic radio transmission

1902

Biology

Landsteiner announces his discovery of the ABO blood-group system

Bayliss and Starling discover the role of the hormone secretin in digestion

Medicine

Richet coins the term anaphylaxis to describe the reaction whereby a second injection of an antigen proves fatal

Physics

Heaviside (and Kennelly) propose the existence of the Kennelly–Heaviside layer in the upper atmosphere

1903

Astronomy

Exploration of Cosmic Space by means of Reaction Devices (Tsiolkovsky)

Chemistry

Zsigmondy and Siedentopf invent the ultramicroscope

Birkeland and Eyde develop their process of nitrogen fixation

Physics

Rutherford and Soddy publish account of radioactive series involving transmutation of elements

Technology

Wilbur Wright pilots the first powered flight on December 14; Orville Wright pilots the second flight on December 17

1904

Astronomy

Moulton and Chamberlin formulate planetismal theory

Hartmann finds first evidence of interstellar gas

Solar observatory set up on Mount Wilson at the south end of the Sierra Madre range by G. E. Hale

Chemistry

Ramsay and Whytlaw-Gray codiscover niton (now known as radon)

Medicine

Aschoff describes inflammatory nodules in heart muscle (Aschoff's bodies)

Physics

Lorentz and Fitzgerald independently propose Lorentz–Fitzgerald contraction

Lorentz publishes transformations for space and time coordinates between frames of reference (Lorentz transformations)

J. A. Fleming invents thermionic vacuum tube

Barkla observes the polarization of x-rays

1905

Biology

Optima and Limiting Factors (Blackman)

Elements of Heredity (Johannsen)

J. S. Haldane and J. G. Priestley demonstrate the role of carbon dioxide in the regulation of breathing

Johannsen introduces the terms genotype and phenotype

(to 1909) Lucas formulates all-or-none law of nervous stimulation

(to 1915) Willstätter works out formulae of chlorophylls a and b

Chemistry

Goldschmidt introduces his method for the reduction of metallic oxides to metals – the Thermit process

Earth Science

On the Influence of the Earth's Rotation on Ocean Currents (Ekman)

Medicine

Schaudinn and Hoffmann isolate the spirochete that causes syphilis

Physics

Boltwood demonstrates that lead is final product of uranium decay

Rutherford and Soddy publish theory of nuclear transmutation

Einstein publishes papers on Brownian motion, the photoelectric effect, and special relativity; relates mass and energy ($E = mc^2$)

1906

Biology

The Integrative Action of the Nervous System (Sherrington)

(to 1907) Hopkins shows that a diet of proteins, carbohydrates, fats, and salts will not support growth in mice and postulates other essential accessory substances (later to be called vitamins) in the normal diet

Chemistry

Tsvet coins the term chromatograph for the analytic procedure he developed to separate plant pigments

Earth Science

Oldham provides evidence that the Earth has a central core

Medicine

Wasserman develops the Wasserman test to diagnose syphilis

Physics

Nernst formulates the Nernst heat theorem (third law of thermodynamics)

Lyman series identified in hydrogen spectrum

Technology

First music and speech broadcast in America (transmitted on Christmas Eve by Fessenden)

1907

Biology

Hopkins and Fletcher demonstrate that lactic acid accumulates in working muscle

Harrison develops the technique of tissue culture

Chemistry

Urbain discovers lutetium

(to 1909) Haber demonstrates his process for synthesizing ammonia from nitrogen and hydrogen

Medicine

Alois Alzheimer diagnoses Alzheimer's disease -

Physics

Minkowski puts forward concept of 4-dimensional space–time

Technology

De Forest patents the Audion tube

1908

Astronomy

Hale finds first extraterrestrial magnetic field in sunspots

Henrietta Leavitt shows that cepheid variables can be used to estimate stellar distances

Biology

Inborn Errors of Metabolism (Garrod) – introduces the idea of genetic diseases

Hardy and Weinberg discover Hardy–Weinberg law

Medicine

Landsteiner manages to transmit polio from humans to monkeys

Physics

Kamerlingh-Onnes succeeds in liquefying helium

Perrin confirms experimentally Einstein's predictions concerning Brownian motion

Technology

Wilbur Wright first demonstrates powered flight publicly at Le Mans in August; Orville Wright gives a demonstration a few days later at Fort Meyer, Virginia

1909

Biology

Ricketts describes the microorganism causing Rocky Mountain spotted fever – an organism intermediate between a bacterium and a virus

Correns obtains the first evidence for cytoplasmic inheritance

Johannsen introduces the term genes to describe Mendel's factors of inheritance

Chemistry

Levene shows that the carbohydrate in yeast nucleic acid is the pentose sugar ribose

Bakelite is invented by Baekeland

Earth Science

Mohorovičić discovers discontinuity between Earth's mantle and crust (Mohorovičić discontinuity)

Charles Dolittle Walcott discovers the Burgess Shale fossils

Medicine

Nicolle discovers that typhus is carried by the louse

Physics

Millikan starts series of experiments to determine the charge on the electron

1910

Geology

The California Earthquake of April 19, 1906 (Harry Fielding Reid) – formulates the elastic rebound theory

Mathematics

(to 1913) *Principia Mathematica* (B. Russell and Whitehead)

Medicine

Ehrlich finds a chemical – Salvarsan – effective in treating syphilis

Psychology

Formation of the International Psycho-Analytical Association

Technology

Claude introduces neon lighting

1911

Biology

Krogh shows that movement of oxygen from the lungs is by simple diffusion (no active secretion is involved)

T. H. Morgan and colleagues produce the first chromosome maps

Medicine

Rous shows that cancer in chickens can be transmitted by a virus

Physics

C. T. R. Wilson invents cloud chamber

Rutherford proposes nuclear model of the atom

Kamerlingh-Onnes discovers superconductivity

(to 1912) V. F. Hess discovers cosmic rays

Einstein predicts gravitational field should deflect light

General

The Kaiser Wilhelm Gesselschaft founded in the Dahlem suburb of Berlin under the directorship of the historian Adolf von Harnack – the forerunner of the Max Planck Institute

1912

Anthropology

A. S. Woodward and Dawson find Piltdown man

Astronomy

Slipher measures velocity of Andromeda

Leavitt discovers period–luminosity relation of Cepheid variables

Biology

Funk suggests that certain diseases are caused by deficiencies of certain ingredients (vitamins) from the diet

Physics

Von Laue discovers x-ray diffraction by crystals

W. L. Bragg formulates *Bragg's law* for x-ray diffraction

1913

Astronomy

H. N. Russell publishes Hertzsprung–Russell diagram

Biology

Michaelis and Menten propose the Michaelis–Menten equation to describe the variation in rate found when an enzyme acts on a substrate

Sturtevant publishes a linkage map constructed from data on recombinant frequencies in *Drosophila*

Earth Science

Gutenberg identifies the Earth's core as being liquid from seismological evidence

A. Holmes proposes the first quantitative geological time scale

Physics

Soddy proposes existence of isotopes

Stark discovers splitting of spectral lines in strong electric field (Stark effect)

On the Constitution of Atoms and Molecules (N. Bohr) – introduces his quantum theory of the atom and atomic spectra

Moseley demonstrates characteristic x-ray wavelengths of elements depend on squares of atomic number plus a constant (Moseley's law)

Fajans proposes laws governing products of radioactive decay (independently of Soddy)

1914

Astronomy

Nicholson discovers Sinope (satellite of Jupiter)

W. S. Adams investigates spectra of stars; leading to stellar parallax method of finding distances

Biology

Ewins and Dale isolate acetylcholine from ergot

Kendall isolates the active ingredient of the thyroid gland

Medicine

Respiratory Function of the Blood (Barcroft)

Physics

Frank and G. Hertz demonstrate quantized nature of energy transfer

1915

Astronomy

Shapley proposes disk-shaped structure for Galaxy

W. S. Adams identifies first white dwarf (Sirius B)

Einstein and Grossmann explain advance in the perihelion of Mercury

Biology

D'Herelle and Twort independently discover the bacteriophage

Chemistry

Debye gives theory of electron diffraction by gases

Earth Science

Die Enstehung der Kontinente und Ozeane (Wegener) – postulates original supercontinent of Pangaea and idea of continental drift

Mathematics

Fisher describes a solution for the exact distribution of the correlation coefficient in statistics

Physics

W. H. Bragg constructs first x-ray spectrometer

1916

Astronomy

E. E. Barnard discovers Barnard's star

Schwarzschild introduces Schwarzschild radius

Biology

The Involuntary Nervous System (Gaskell)

Physics

Sommerfeld proposes elliptical orbits for electrons in atoms

N. Bohr formulates correspondence principle

Einstein publishes general theory of relativity

1917

Astronomy

De Sitter proposes model of universe (de Sitter universe)

The 100-inch reflector first used at the Mount Wilson Observatory

Chemistry

Meitner and Hahn discover protactinium

Physics

Chapman predicts phenomenon of thermal diffusion of gases

1918

Astronomy

100-inch Hooker telescope in operation at Mount Wilson (largest until 1948)

(to 1924) *Henry Draper Catalogue* (E. C. Pickering and A. Cannon) – records spectra of stars

Biology

The Correlation between Relatives on the Supposition of Mendelian Inheritance (Fisher) – demonstrates that continuous variations are inherited in Mendelian fashion

Meyerhof investigates cellular metabolism – leads to discovery of Embden–Meyerhof pathway

1919

Astronomy

Eddington reports results of observations during solar eclipse, verifying bending of light passing close to Sun, as predicted by general theory of relativity

Physics

Aston produces his first mass spectrograph

Barkhausen discovers that magnetization tends to occur in discrete steps

Rutherford identifies first artificial transmutation of a nucleus

1920

Astronomy

Baade discovers the asteroid Hidalgo

Saha publishes the equation for degree of ionization of atoms in stars

Mathematics

Thoralf Albert Skolem contributes to the Lowenheim–Skolem theorem and constructs the Skolem paradox inset theory

Medicine

Goldberger finds a cure for pellagra

Physics

O. Stern confirms experimentally the phenomenon of space quantization

General

The Throop Polytechnic Institute in Pasadena, California is renamed the California Institute of Technology

c. 1920

Biology

(to *c.* 1925) Keilin discovers cytochrome

1921

Biology

Banting and Best isolate insulin and show its effectiveness in treating diabetes

Loewi discovers that chemicals are released from nerve endings when the nerve is stimulated

Chemistry

Midgley discovers tetraethyl lead as an antiknock additive for fuel

Earth Science

On the Dynamics of the Circular Vortex with Applications to the Atmospheric Vortex and Wave Motion (V. Bjerknes)

Physics

Hahn defines nuclear isomerism

Kaluza supplements Einstein's 4-dimensional space– time model with a fifth dimension

1922

Biology

A. Fleming publishes his discovery of lysozyme

Hopkins isolates glutathione

Chemistry

Kraus develops processes for the commercial production of tetraethyl lead

Heyrovský describes polarography

Earth Science

Weather Prediction by Numerical Process (Richardson) – the first attempt to apply mathematical techniques to weather prediction

Physics

Friedmann publishes his paper on the expanding universe

Technology

Sabine publishes his papers on architectural acoustics

1923

Astronomy

Wolf devises Wolf diagram for dark nebulae

Biology

Conant shows that oxyhemoglobin contains ferrous iron

Euler-Chelpin works out the structure of the yeast coenzyme

Heidelberger and Avery show that certain polysaccharides in the capsules of pneumococci are responsible for specific antigenic properties

Hevesy makes first application of a radioactive tracer – ^{212}Pb – to a biological system

Whipple reports that liver in the diet increases hemoglobin production

Warburg designs instrument (Warburg manometer) to measure uptake of oxygen by human tissue

Chemistry

Lowry and Brønsted independently formulate a theory of acids and bases (the Lowry–Brønsted theory)

Valence and the Structure of Atoms and Molecules (G. N. Lewis) – proposes octet theory of valence

Hevesy and Coster discover hafnium

Debye and Huckel publish their theory of electrolytes

Physics

Zworykin constructs the first iconoscope

Compton discovers scattering effect of radiation by electrons (Compton effect)

1924

Archeology

Dart describes the Taung skull

Astronomy

Eddington introduces mass–luminosity relationship for stars

Biology

Berger makes the first human encephalogram

Chemistry

Svedberg introduces the ultracentrifuge as a technique for investigating the molecular weights of very large molecules

Earth Science

The Earth: Its Origin, History, and Physical Constitution (Jeffreys)

Mathematics

Banach and Tarski prove the Banach–Tarski paradox

Physics

Pauli proposes his exclusion principle

De Broglie proposes that particles can behave as waves

Appleton establishes experimentally the presence of the Heaviside-Kennelly layer

1925

Astronomy

The Draper Extension first published by Harvard College Observatory, Massachusetts

Biology

Adrian finds that nerve messages are relayed by changes in the frequency of the discharge

Chemistry

Nieuwland polymerizes acetylene to give divinylacetylene

Physics

Giauque introduces the method of adiabatic demagnetization for low temperatures

Goudsmit and Uhlenbeck propose electron spin

Tuve and Breit use pulse-ranging to determine the height of the ionosphere

Heisenberg formulates matrix mechanics

Born and Jordan develop matrix mechanics

Auger discovers that an excited atom can emit an electron in reverting to a lower energy state (Auger effect)

(to 1926) Schrödinger develops wave mechanics

c. 1925

Biology

Hecht formulates photochemical theory of visual adaptation

1926

Astronomy

The Internal Constitution of the Stars (Eddington)

Hubble publishes Hubble's classification of galaxies

Lindblad proposes rotation of Galaxy

Biology

Introduction to Experimental Biology (de Beer) – disproves germ-layer theory

Windaus discovers that ergosterol is a precursor of vitamin D

Sumner achieves the first isolation of a pure enzyme (urease) and shows it to be a protein

J. J. Abel announces the crystallization of insulin

H. J. Muller discovers that x-rays can induce mutations

Chemistry

I. Noddack, W. Noddack, and O. Berg discover rhenium

Ingold introduces the concept of mesomerism

Medicine

Minot and Murphy discover a cure for pernicious anemia

Physics

Oskar Klein revises Kaluza's theory of a fifth dimension by formulating the Kaluza–Klein theory

Technology

Goddard launches first successful liquid-fuel rocket flight

Baird demonstrates his apparatus for transmitting images

1927

Astronomy

Lemaître provides cosmological model of expanding universe

Oort confirms galactic rotation

Biology

Landsteiner discovers the MN and the P blood-group systems

Chemistry

Electronic Theory of Valency (Sidgwick)

Medicine

Stokes manages to transmit yellow fever to the rhesus monkey

Physics

Wigner introduces parity as a conserved property of nuclear reactions

G. Thomson and (independently) Davisson and Germer demonstrate wave property (diffraction) of electrons

N. Bohr formulates complementarity principle

Heisenberg formulates his uncertainty principle

(to 1932) Fock and Hartree show how

Schrödinger's wave equation can be applied to atoms with more than one electron

Psychology

Practice and Theory of Individual Psychology (Adler)

1928

Astronomy

Bowen explains forbidden emission lines in spectra of nebulae

Biology

Riddle isolates prolactin

Griffith discovers bacterial transformation in pneumococci

Medicine

A. Fleming discovers penicillin

Physics

Geiger–Müller counter invented

Dirac introduces relativity into the Schrödinger wave equations to account for electron spin

Raman discovers Raman scattering effect

Ruska produces the first electron microscope

1929

Astronomy

Struve shows interstellar matter exists throughout Galaxy

Hubble announces his law that the recessional velocity of galaxies is proportional to their distance (Hubble's law)

Biology

Butenandt isolates the first pure sex hormone, estrone

Edward Adelbert Doisy isolates the hormone oestrone and soon afterward, oestradiol

(to 1931) Barbara McClintock establishes linkage groups in maize

Chemistry

Paneth demonstrates the existence of the methyl radical

Levene identifies the carbohydrate in thymus nucleic acid as deoxyribose

The Constitution of the Sugars (Haworth) – introduces the idea that sugar molecules can exist in ring form

H. Fischer synthesizes hemin

Eyring and Polyani calculate potential-energy surface for chemical reaction –

Eyring later develops absolute-rate theory of reaction rates

Earth Science

A. Holmes proposes his convection-current theory to explain continental drift

On the Direction of Magnetization of Basalt (Matuyama) – discovery of remnant magnetization

Medicine

Forssman introduces the technique of cardiac catheterization

Physics

Bothe uses coincidence method to show cosmic rays are particles

(to 1933) Rabi invents the atomic- and molecular-beam magnetic-resonance method

1930

Aeronautics

B. N. Wallis invents the geodetic construction

Astronomy

Tombaugh discovers Pluto

Trumpler discovers interstellar absorption

Lyot invents the coronagraph

Biology

Karrer determines the structure of carotene

Physics

Lawrence begins to construct cyclic particle accelerator (cyclotron)

Pauli suggests the existence of the neutrino

Dirac proposes negative energy states for the electron, which led subsequently to the appreciation of antimatter

Néel proposes the existence of antiferromagnetism

1931

Biology

Goodpasture introduces the method of culturing viruses in fertile eggs

Karrer determines the structure of, and synthesizes, vitamin A

C. Stern provides experimental evidence for crossing-over between homologous chromosomes

Chemistry

Carothers produces the first synthetic rubber (neoprene)

Urey discovers heavy water (deuterium oxide)

Mathematics

Gödel proves incompleteness of arithmetic

Physics

Van de Graaf builds his high-voltage electrostatic generator

1932

Astronomy

Jansky publishes his discovery of radio interference from the stars, so founding the new field of radio astronomy

Biology

Haldane makes the first estimate of mutation rates in humans

Krebs and Henselheit introduce the urea cycle

King and Szent-Györgi announce their (independent) isolations of vitamin C

Chemistry

Pauling introduces the idea of resonance hybrids

Bergmann discovers the carbobenzoxy method of peptide synthesis

Physics

Chadwick discovers the neutron

Anderson discovers the positron

Cockcroft and Walton achieve first artificial nuclear transformation

1933

Biology

King determines the formula of vitamin C

The first synthesis of a vitamin, vitamin C, by Haworth and Hirst

Brachet demonstrates that both DNA and RNA occur in animal and in plant cells

Bernal obtains the first x-ray photograph of a single-crystal protein

Mathematics

The Foundations of the Theory of Probability (Kolmogorov)

Physics

Anderson discovers the muon

Occhialini and Blackett obtain cloud-chamber tracks of the positron

Fermi proposes weak interaction as one of fundamental interactions in physics

Walther Meissner and R. Oschenfeld discover the Meissner effect, now used as a routine test for superconductivity

General

Institute for Advanced Study opens in Princeton, New Jersey

1934

Biology

R. R. Williams works out the formula of vitamin B_1

Ružička is the first to synthesize a sex hormone, androsterone

(to 1935) Theorell gives the first detailed account of enzyme action

Chemistry

Oliphant and Harteck produce the hydrogen isotope tritium

Earth Science

(to 1939) *On Seismic Waves* (Gutenberg and Richter)

Physics

Casimir and Gorter advance a two-fluid model of superconductivity

Cherenkov discovers radiation from fast particles (Cherenkov radiation)

Fermi discovers that slow neutrons more readily interact with nuclei

Noddack anticipates Frisch in suggesting the hypothesis of nuclear fission

I. and P. Joliot-Curie discover artificial radioactivity

Goldhaber and Chadwick discover the nuclear photoelectric effect

1935

Biology

Dam discovers vitamin K

Stanley crystallizes the tobacco mosaic virus and demonstrates the retention of infectivity after crystallization

Von Euler isolates the first of the prostaglandins

Chemistry

Carothers produces nylon

Earth Science

Seismological Tables (Jeffreys and Bullen)

Richter develops scale for earthquake magnitudes (Richter scale)

Mathematics

The Concept of Truth in Formalized Languages (Tarski)

Medicine

Egas Moniz introduces the operation of prefrontal leukotomy

Domagk reports on the effectiveness of prontosil against streptococcal infection

Physics

Yukawa predicts the existence of the pion

Can Quantum Mechanical Description of Physical Reality be Considered Complete? (Albert Einstein, Boris Podolsky, and Nathan Rosen)

Technology

The Detection of Aircraft by Radio Methods (Watson-Watt)

1936

Biology

Kuhn synthesizes vitamin B_6

Rose discovers the first essential amino acid – threonine

Experimentelle Beiträge zu einer Theorie der Entwicklung (Spemann)

Dale demonstrates that acetylcholine is released at motor-nerve endings of voluntary muscle

Computers

Zuse invents the computer "out of laziness"

Earth Science

Daly suggests existence of turbidity currents in oceans

Physics

Wigner and Breit work out the Breit–Wigner formula

Mueller invents the field-emission microscope

The Structure of Metals and Alloys (Hume Rothery)

1937

Biology

Gorer discovers the histocompatibility antigens and establishes their control at the genetic level

Williams synthesizes vitamin B_1

Electrical Signs of Nervous Activity (Erlander and Gasser)

Bawden and Pirie demonstrate that tobacco mosaic virus contains RNA

Blakeslee discovers that colchicine induces multiple sets of chromosomes in plants

Krebs discovers the tricarboxylic acid cycle (Krebs cycle)

Genetics and the Origin of Species (Dobzhansky)

Sonneborn discovers sexuality in the protozoa

Chemistry

Segrè discovers technetium

Computers

George Robert Stibitz builds his first calculator

Earth Science

Our Wandering Continents (Du Toit) – suggests separation of Pangaea into Laurasia and Gondwanaland

Mathematics

On Computable Numbers (Alan Turing)

Medicine

Bovet develops the antihistamine drug 933F

Theiler and Smith announce the development of a vaccine against yellow fever

Elvehjem shows active ingredient in pellagra-preventive factor is nicotinic acid

Physics

Frank and Tamm explain Cherenkov radiation

Kapitza discovers the superfluidity of helium

Technology

Chester Floyd Carlson and Otto Kornei make the first electrostatic (xerographic) copier

1938

Astronomy

Nicholson discovers Lysithea and Carme (satellites of Jupiter)

Hahn discovers nuclear fission (interpreted by Meitner and Frisch)

Physics

Alvarez describes K-capture

Technology

Ladislao and Georg Biró patent the ballpoint pen

1939

Astronomy

Introduction to the Study of Stellar Structure (Chandrasekhar) – introduces idea of Chandrasekhar limit

Biology

Dam and Karrer isolate vitamin K

Doisy synthesizes and characterizes vitamin K

Chemistry

The Nature of the Chemical Bond (Pauling)

Perey discovers francium

Earth Science

Bergeron–Findeisen theory of precipitation

Medicine

Ewin's research team develops the drug sulfapyridine

Dubos discovers the antibiotic tyrothricin

Florey and Chain extract penicillin

Physics

Energy Production in Stars (Bethe)

Meitner and O. Frisch interpret Hahn's experiments as evidence of nuclear fission

Meitner announces the discovery of light nuclei (fission products) following neutron bombardment of uranium nuclei

Luis Walter Alvarez and Felix Bloch make the first measurement of the magnetic moment of the neutron

Alvarez demonstrates that tritium is radioactive

Boot and Randall develop the cavity magnetron

Technology

The first jet flight is powered by an engine designed by von Ohain

1940

Astronomy

Reber publishes first radio map of sky

Biology

Landsteiner announces his discovery of the rhesus factor

Chemistry

McMillan and Abelson discover the first transuranic element – neptunium

Patent taken out on the insecticide DDT (P. H. Müller)

Kamen and Ruben discover the radioisotope carbon–14

Earth Science

Rossby discovers long sinusoidal atmospheric waves of large amplitude (Rossby waves)

Physics

Hillier builds the first successful American high-resolution electron microscope

(to 1950) Development of modern theory

of quantum electrodynamics by Feynman, Schwinger, and Tomonaga (independently)

1941

Aeronautics

The jet engine, designed by Whittle and fitted to a Gloster E28/39 aircraft, makes its first flight (May 15)

Astronomy

Edlen shows "coronium" to be highly ionized heavy atoms

Chemistry

Martin and Synge develop partition chromatography

Medicine

Cournand and Ranges develop cardiac catheterization

Huggins pioneers the use of female sex hormones in treating cancer of the prostate gland

Physics

(to 1943) Tomonaga develops a quantum field theory consistent with the theory of special relativity

1942

Biology

Brachet suggests RNA granules might be the agents of protein synthesis

(to 1953) K. E. Bloch and others determine biosynthesis of cholesterol

Computers

John Vincent Atanasoff and Clifford Berry complete the Atanasoff–Berry Computer (ABC)

Earth Science

Belousov suggests that Earth movements caused by density of crust

Physics

First self-supporting nuclear-fission chain reaction (Stagg Field, Chicago)

Alfvén postulates hydromagnetic waves (Alfvén waves) in plasmas

1943

Astronomy

MKK system of stellar classification introduced (by W. W. Morgan, Keenan, and Kellman)

Seyfert discovers Seyfert galaxies

Baade introduces Populations I and II classification of stars

Biology

Luria and Delbrück demonstrate spontaneous mutation in bacteria

B. Chance provides experimental evidence for the formation of an enzyme–substrate complex, as proposed by Michaelis

Waksman isolates streptomycin from the mold *Streptomyces griseus*

Chemistry

Longuett-Higgins suggests that borane contains hydrogen bridges

Computers

Howard Hathaway Aiken completes the Harvard Mark I or ASCC (Automatic Sequence – Controlled Calculator)

Technology

Luis Walter Alvarez guides a distant plane to land using radar

1944

Biology

An artificially produced plant species *Ehrharta erecta* is established in a natural environment

MacLeod, Avery, and McCarty provide evidence that DNA is responsible for bacterial transformation

Wyckoff and R. C. Williams develop the metal-shadowing technique to give three-dimensional photographs with the electron microscope

What is Life? (Schrödinger)

Earth Science

Principles of Physical Geography (A. Holmes)

Physics

Veksler invents synchrocyclotron

1945

Biology

Beadle and Tatum formulate the one gene–one enzyme hypothesis

Hershey demonstrates (independently of Luria) spontaneous mutations in bacteriophages

Computers

Mauchly and Eckert complete ENIAC (Electronic Numerator Integrator and Calculator)

Physics

Atomic bomb first tested (July 16)

General

Studies in the Logic of Confirmation (Carl Gustav Hempel) – challenges the foundations of inductive logic

1946

Astronomy

Tousey photographs the solar spectrum from above the ozone layer

Biology

Delbrück and Hershey demonstrate genetic recombination in viruses

Von Euler isolates noradrenaline (norepinephrine)

Tatum and Lederberg demonstrate occurrence of sexual reproduction in bacteria

Cohen introduces radioactive labeling of microorganisms

Earth Science

Schaefer seeds clouds and produces the first artificial rainfall

Physics

Bloch and Purcell independently introduce the technique of nuclear magnetic resonance

General

The Kaiser Wilhelm Gesselschaft in Berlin is renamed the Max Planck Institute

1947

Astronomy

Bok discovers Bok globules

Ambartsumian introduces idea of stellar association

Biology

Lipmann discovers coenzyme A

Todd synthesizes ADP and ATP

Chemistry

Libby develops the radiocarbon dating technique

Physics

Kusch measures the magnetic moment of the electron and finds a discrepancy between the experimental and theoretical values

Brattain, Bardeen, and Shockley invent the point-contact transistor

Lamb announces the *Lamb shift*

Occhialini and Powell observe tracks of the pion

1948

Anthropology

Sexual Behavior in the Human Male (Kinsey)

Astronomy

Burnright detects solar x-rays

H. D. and H. W. Babcock develop magnetograph and detect solar and stellar magnetic fields

Alpher, Bethe, and Gamow publish theory on origin of elements

Alpher and Herman first predict cosmic background radiation from big bang

The Steady-State Theory of the Expanding Universe (Gold and Bondi)

Kniper discovers Miranda (satellite of Uranus)

200-inch Hale telescope in operation at Mount Palomar (largest until 1977)

Biology

Folkers isolates vitamin B_{12}

The Functional Organization of the Diencephalon (W. H. Hess)

Medicine

Weller and Neva succeed in growing the rubella virus in tissue culture

Duggar discovers chlortetracycline (Aureomycin), the first tetracycline antibiotic

Hench introduces cortisone to treat rheumatoid arthritis

Physics

Shockley develops the junction transistor

Gabor invents the technique of holography

Feynman's paper *Space–Time Approach to Non-Relativistic Quantum Mechanics*, in which he introduces path integrals, is turned down by *Physical Review*

General

Studies in the Logic of Explanation (Hempel and Openheim) – proposes the Hypothetico-Deductive method

1949

Astronomy

Kniper discovers Nereid (satellite of Neptune)

Baade discovers asteroid Icarus

Biology

Enders, Weller, and Robbins cultivate polio virus *in vitro* on human embryonic tissue

Burnet postulates that immunological tolerance has not yet developed in the embryo stage

Murray Llewellyn Barr with Ewart Bertram discover Barr bodies in female somatic cells

Chemistry

G. Porter and Norrish begin developing methods of flash photolysis

Computers

Wilkes builds EDSAC, the first working computer with a stored program

Mathematics

A Mathematical Theory of Communication (Shannon and Weaver)

Medicine

Burnet discovers the phenomenon of acquired immunologic tolerance

Physics

Shull demonstrates antiferromagnetism using neutron diffraction

Space–Time Approach to Quantum Electrodynamics (Richard Feynman) – introduces use of Feynman diagrams

1950

Astronomy

The Nature of the Universe (Hoyle)

Oort proposes comets originate from reservoir far out in solar system (Oort's cloud)

Whipple proposes icy-nucleus theory of comets

R. H. Brown plots the first radio map of an external galaxy

Biology

Pontecorvo and Roper discover the parasexual cycle in fungi

Chargaff announces base ratios of DNA, important in the construction of Watson–Crick model of DNA

(to 1952) Harris shows that release of pituitary hormones is controlled by the hypothalamus

Computers

Computing Machinery and Intelligence (Alan Turing)

Physics

The betatron at the University of Illinois is completed

Rainwater suggests his modification to the shell model of nuclear structure

(to 1953) Mottelson and A. Bohr advance a theory of nuclear structure

Sakharov and Tamm describe a process whereby a deuterium plasma could be confined in a magnetic bottle so as to extract energy produced by nuclear fusion – the tokamak

1951

Astronomy

Brouwer, Clemence, and Eckert publish table for accurate orbits of outer planets

Purcell and Ewen detect 21-centimeter hydrogen emission line (predicted 1944, van de Hulst)

Nicholson discovers Ananke (satellite of Jupiter)

Biology

The Study of Instinct (Tinbergen)

Chromosome Organization and Genetic Expression (McClintock) – description of transposition of genes

Chemistry

Pauling suggests protein molecules are arranged in helices

Physics

The first breeder reactor is built following Zinn's design

1952

Astronomy

Merrill detects technetium in S-type stars

Biology

Hershey and Chase prove that DNA is the genetic material of bacteriophages

Wilkins and Franklin obtain evidence for the double helical structure of DNA

Lederberg and Zinder discover bacterial transduction

Cohen and Levi-Montalcini determine the nature of a nerve-growth factor from mouse tumor cells

Chemistry

E. O. Fischer confirms sandwich structure for ferrocene by x-ray crystallography

Computers

EDVA (Electronic Digital Variable Computer) is completed

Earth Science

Heezen provides evidence of turbidity currents in oceans

Medicine

Pathology of the Cell (Cameron)

Physics

Glaser produces the first bubble chamber

Bohr and Mottelson propose their collective model of nuclear structure

CERN (Conseil Européen pour la Recherche Nucléaire) set up by eleven European governments in Geneva under its first director, Felix Bloch

1953

Anthropology

Sexual Behavior in the Human Female (Kinsey)

Biology

H. E. Huxley and Hanson propose the sliding-filament theory of muscle contraction

Medawar shows that adult mammals injected with foreign tissues at the embryonic stage or at birth, will later accept grafts from the original tissue donor

Watson and Crick construct a three-dimensional model of the DNA molecule

Kettlewell demonstrates industrial melanism in moths

Chemistry

Ziegler introduces the Ziegler catalysts for polymerization of ethane

Karl and Hauptman publish *The Phases and Magnitudes of the Structure Factors*, in which they show how phase structures could be inferred directly from diffraction patterns

Physics

Lax detects cyclotron resonance in germanium

Gell-Mann introduces the concept of strangeness

Townes makes working model of maser

1954

Biology

Du Vigneaud synthesizes the first protein – oxytocin

Chemistry

Natta uses improved Ziegler catalysts to produce stereospecific polymers

Eigen introduces relaxation techniques to study extremely fast chemical reactions

Earth Science

Seismicity of the Earth (Richter and Gutenberg)

Medicine

First clinical trials of oral contraceptives are conducted

Joseph Edward Murray carries out the first kidney transplant into the pelvis of the recipient

Physics

Construction of the 25 GeV Synchrotron begins at CERN in Geneva

1955

Astronomy

U.S. navy begins Vanguard project to launch U.S. satellite

Biology

Ochoa discovers the enzyme polynucleotide phosphorylase, later used to synthesize artificial RNA

The complete amino-acid sequence of a protein (insulin) is established by Sanger

Chemistry

Thermodynamics of Irreversible Processes (Prigogine)

Medicine

Jerne proposes the clonal selection theory of antibody selection to account for white blood cells being able to produce a large range of antibodies

Physics

Chamberlain, Segrè, Weigand, and Ypsilantis discover the antiproton

Basov and Prokhorov develop the maser

Bridgman transforms graphite into synthetic diamond using extremely high–pressures

Dehmelt begins work on the Penning trap, to isolate a single electron

1956

Astronomy

Oort and Walraven show that light from the Crab nebula is synchrotron radiation

Sir Richard van der Riet declares that space travel is "utter bilge"

Biology

Kornberg discovers DNA polymerase

Li determines the sequence of amino acids in adrenocorticotropic hormone

Berg identifies the molecule later known as transfer RNA

Hodgkin establishes the structure of vitamin B_{12}

Earth Science

Ewing plots Mid-Atlantic Ridge

Physics

Lee and Yang argue that parity is not conserved in weak interactions

Reines and Cowan confirm the existence of the neutrino

Wu experimentally confirms that parity is not conserved in beta disintegration

Cooper shows that, at low temperatures, electrons in a conductor can act as bound pairs (Cooper pairs)

1957

Astronomy

Hoyle, Fowler, and E. M. and G. Burbidge publish theory of formation of elements in stars

250-foot radio telescope in use at Jodrell Bank

Launch (Oct. 4) of Soviet satellite Sputnik 1 – first artificial satellite

Launch of Soviet satellite Sputnik 2 with dog Laika – proves living organisms can survive in space

Biology

The Physiology of Nerve Cells (Eccles)

Sutherland discovers cyclic AMP

Isaacs and Lindenmann report discovery of interferon

Kendrew determines the first three-dimensional model of a protein – myoglobin

Leloir announces his discovery of the mechanism whereby glycogen is synthesized in the body

The Path of Carbon in Photosynthesis (Calvin)

Antibody Production Using the Concept of Clonal Selection (Burnett)

Computers

McCarthy sets up the Artificial Intelligence Laboratory at the Massachusetts Institute of Technology

Physics

Bardeen, Cooper, and Schrieffer formulate their theory of superconductivity

Mössbauer discovers recoilless nuclear resonance absorption (Mössbauer effect)

1958

Astronomy

Launch of Explorer 1, which discovers Van Allen belts – first in major series of U.S. research satellites

Launch of Pioneer 1 – start of series of U.S. probes to study Moon and solar system

Ephemeris time adopted by astronomical scientists

The Royal Greenwich Observatory moved to Herstmonceux Castle in Sussex

Biology

Evolution of Genetic Systems (Darlington)

Meselson and Stahl demonstrate the semiconservative nature of DNA replication

Dausset discovers the human histocompatibility system

Medicine

Burkitt publishes his first account of Burkitt's lymphoma

Physics

Esaki discovers tunneling effect in semiconductor junctions

Technology

Kilby makes the first integrated circuit using silicon

1959

Astronomy

Third Cambridge Catalogue (3C) – catalog of known radio sources

Launch of Lunar 1 – first in series of Soviet lunar space probes

Launch of Discoverer 1 – first in series of U.S. unmanned probes in orbit over poles; later Discoverer probes used for military surveillance

Biology

Dulbecco introduces the idea of cell transformation

Moore and Stein establish the amino-acid sequence of the enzyme ribonuclease

Medicine

Sabin announces successful results from testing live attenuated polio vaccine

Kouwenhoven introduces closed-chest cardiac massage

Physics

Luis Walter Alvarez builds a 72″ bubble chamber

Lederman, Lee, Schwartz, and Steinberger carry out the two-neutrino experiment

1960

Anthropology

Louis Leakey discovers the skull of *Homo erectus* at Olduvai

Astronomy

Sandage and Matthews discover quasars

Launch of Tiros 1 – first in series of U.S. weather satellites

Biology

R. B. Woodward synthesizes chlorophyll

Jacob and Monod propose the existence of the operon

Physics

Giaever investigates electron tunneling in superconducting junctions

Maiman designs the laser

Technology

Echo I, simple radio reflector balloon, launched

1961

Astronomy

Launch of Venera 1 (also called Venus 1) – first in series of Soviet Venus space probes (first mission failed)

Launch of Vostok 1 – first in series of Soviet manned space flights putting first man in space (Yuri Gagarin, Apr. 12)

Launch (May 5) of U.S. Mercury-Redstone 3 mission – first American in space (Alan B. Shepard in suborbital flight)

Launch of Ranger 1 – first in series of U.S. probes to investigate Moon (detailed photographs by Ranger 7, 1964)

Biology

Brenner and Crick show that the genetic code consists of a continuous string of nonoverlapping base triplets

Good and J. Miller independently discover the role of the thymus in the development of immunity

Nirenberg makes the first step in breaking the genetic code by finding that UUU codes for phenylalanine

Physics

Brans and Dicke propose Brans–Dicke theory of gravitation

Ne'eman and Gell-Mann independently develop a mathematical representation for the classification of elementary particles

1962

Astronomy

Rossi detects cosmic x-ray source in Scorpio (Sco X–1)

Launch (Feb. 20) of U.S. Mercury–Atlas 6

mission – first American in orbit (John H. Glenn)

Launch of OSO1 (Orbiting Solar Observatory) – first in series of U.S. probes for studies of Sun

Launch of Ariel 1 – first in series of U.S.-launched British satellites for studies of ionosphere and x-ray sources

Launch of Mariner 1 and Mariner 2 – first in series of U.S. planetary space probes: Mariner 2 flies past Venus

Launch of Mars 1 – first in series of Soviet probes to study Mars

Chemistry

Bartlett demonstrates that not all noble gases are inert by forming the compound xenon fluoroplatinate

Earth Science

History of Ocean Basins (H. H. Hess) – introduction of sea-floor spreading hypothesis

Physics

Josephson predicts effects occurring in superconducting junctions (Josephson effects)

General

The Structure of Scientific Revolutions (Kuhn)

1963

Astronomy

Schmidt investigates red shifts of quasars

Launch of Soviet spacecraft Vostok 6 – first woman in space (Valentina Tereshkova, June 16)

Biology

Blumberg discovers the Australian antigen

On Aggression (Lorenz)

Medicine

Gajdusek describes the first slow-virus infection to be identified in humans

Physics

(to 1964) Cormack publishes papers on the mathematical basis of x-ray tomography

1964

Astronomy

Dicke and Peebles predict cosmic background radiation and start searching for it

Penzias and Wilson discover cosmic microwave background radiation

Launch of unmanned test flight Gemini 1

– first in a U.S. series of manned space missions

Ranger 7 takes first detailed photographs of Moon's surface

Launch of U.S. planetary probe Mariner 4 to investigate Mars (1965)

Biology

Merrifield synthesizes bradykinin

Conduction of the Nervous Impulse (A. L. Hodgkin)

Genetical Theory of Social Behaviour (W. D. Hamilton) – beginning of sociobiology

Medicine

Clarke announces injection of Rh-negative mothers with Rh-antibodies prevents subsequent Rhesus babies

Physics

The Eightfold Way (Gell-Mann and Ne'eman)

Cronin, Fitch, Christenson, and Turley find that charge-conjugation-parity (CP) conservation is violated in the decay of neutral kaons

On the Einstein–Podolsky–Rosen Paradox (Bell) – includes Bell's theorem on quantum mechanics

Higgs first postulates the Higgs field and the Higgs boson

1965

Astronomy

Nucleosynthesis in Massive Stars and Supernovae (Hoyle and Fowler)

Friedman first accurately locates nonsolar x-ray source in Crab nebula (Tau X–1)

Mariner 4 flies past Mars and relays photographs of surface

Biology

Holley announces the nucleotide sequence of alanine tRNA

R. B. Woodward and Eschenmoser synthesize vitamin B_{12}

Earth Science

Launch of U.S. probe Explorer 29; Geodetic Earth-Orbiting Satellite (GEOS), used for geodetic measurements

Physics

Weber completes building his detector for gravitational waves

Technology

Launch of Intelsat 1 (called Early Bird) – International Communications Satellite stationed over Atlantic

1966

Astronomy

Launch of Soviet Moon probe Luna 9 – first probe to make soft landing on Moon and return photographs

Launch of Apollo 1 – the first in a series of U.S. manned space probes in program to land men on the Moon (Apollo 11, 1969)

Launch of Soviet Moon probe Luna 10 – first probe to go into lunar orbit

Launch of OAO1 (Orbiting Astronomical Observatory) – first in series of U.S. probes containing telescopes, spectrometers, and detectors for ultraviolet and x-ray studies of universe

Launch of Surveyor 1 – first in series of U.S. Moon probes to make soft landing and relay photographs and data on Moon's surface

Launch of Lunar Orbiter 1 – first in series of U.S. Moon probes to photograph lunar surface

Biology

Gilbert and Muller-Hill isolate the lac repressor

1967

Astronomy

Bell and Hewish discover first pulsar

Launch of Soyuz 1 – first in major series of Soviet manned spacecraft (Vladimir Komarov killed during reentry on first mission)

Chemistry

Pederson publishes work on crown ethers

Earth Science

A Revolution in Earth Science (J. T. Wilson)

Medicine

The first heart transplant performed on a human patient (by C. N. Barnard)

Physics

Friedman, Kendall, and Taylor demonstrate that the proton has an inner structure

A Model of Leptons (Weinberg) – introduces electroweak theory

1968

Astronomy

Discovery of first mascons on Moon's surface – local areas of increased gravity discovered by tracking spacecraft Lunar Orbiter 5

Physics

Salam and Weinberg independently formulate gauge theory to give unified description of weak and electromagnetic interactions – predict existence of neutral currents

Charpak describes his drift chamber

Feynman introduces the idea of "partons"

Sakharov publishes *Progress, Peaceful Coexistence and Intellectual Freedom*, arguing for a global reduction in nuclear weapons

1969

Astronomy

Armstrong and Aldrin make first manned lunar landing (Apollo 11, July 20 in Sea of Tranquillity) – bring back samples of lunar material

Van de Kamp detects planet orbiting Barnard's star

Mount Wilson and Palomar Observatories renamed the Hale Observatories

Biology

Edelman announces the amino-acid sequence of immunoglobulin G

Guillemin and Schally independently determine structure of thyrotropin-releasing factor

1970

Astronomy

Launch of Soviet Moon probe Luna 16 – first successful automatic return of lunar sample

Launch of Explorer 42 (called Uhuru) – U.S. probe for research on cosmic x-rays

Biology

Baltimore and Temin independently discover the enzyme reverse transcriptase

Khorana announces the synthesis of the first artificial gene

H. O. Smith identifies the first restriction enzyme (Hind II)

Neher and Sakmann develop the patch-clamp technique for studying ion channels in cell membrane

Duesberg discovers oncogenes

Physics

Glashow extends the Weinberg–Salam theory by introducing the property of charm

Yoichipo Nambu introduces string theory

1971

Astronomy

Launch of Salyut 1 – first in a series of Soviet space stations for scientific research and military surveillance

Launch of Mariner 9 – goes into orbit around Mars and relays data and photographs of surface

1972

Anthropology

Richard Erskine discovers *Homo Habilis*

Astronomy

Launch of U.S. planetary probe Pioneer 10 to investigate Jupiter (1973)

Biology

Nathans determines the order of the 11 cleavage fragments of the SV40 virus

Gould and Eldredge propose the punctuated equilibrium hypothesis, that views evolution as episodic rather than continuous

Medicine

Gallo and his team identify interleukin-2 – a factor that stimulates growth in human T-cells

Technology

Land launches the first polaroid camera

1973

Astronomy

Launch of U.S. planetary probe Pioneer 11 to investigate asteroid belt, Jupiter (1974), and Saturn (1979)

Launch of Skylab 1 – first in series of U.S. space stations for scientific research

Launch of Skylab 3 – observations made on solar flares

Pioneer 10 flies past Jupiter – relays photographs of planet and satellites

Launch of U.S. planetary probe Mariner 10 – to investigate Venus and Mercury (1974)

Large Scale Structure of Space and Time (Hawking and Ellis)

Biology

Snyder and Pert find receptor sites for opiates in the limbic system of the brain

Boyer and Helling construct functional DNA by joining together DNA from two different sources

Medicine

CAT body scanners introduced

Physics

Dehmelt isolates and traps a single electron

1974

Anthropology

Johanson discovers the oldest-known human fossil Australopithecus afarensis (known as "Lucy")

Astronomy

Mariner 10 flies past Venus and Mercury and relays photographs of surface

Pioneer 11 flies past Jupiter

Hawking proposes that black holes can emit particles

Biology

The Berg letter warns of the dangers of uncontrolled experiments on DNA recombinants

Chemistry

Rowland and Molina point out that CFCs in the stratosphere attack ozone

Physics

Richter and Ting independently discover the J/psi particle

Perl identifies a heavy lepton

Penrose shows that a nonperiodic tiling can have an almost fivefold symmetry

The Physics of Liquid Crystals (de Gennes)

1975

Anthropology

Richard Leakey discovers *Homo erectus*

Astronomy

Launch of Venera 9 and Venera 10 – Soviet probes that land and relay data and photographs of surface of Venus

Apollo–Soyuz Test Project – joint U.S. and Soviet space project with docking of two spacecraft in orbit

Biology

Milstein produces monoclonal antibodies

Kosterlitz and Hughes discover endogenous opiates (enkephalins) in brain tissue

1976

Chemistry

The National Academy of Sciences publish a report supporting the work of Rowland and Molina on the effect of CFCs on the ozone layer

Mathematics

Haker and Appel announce the solution of the four-color map problem

Medicine

Varmus, Bishop, Stehelin, and Vogt show that viral oncogenes are derived from the genes of the host, incorporated into the genehi material of the virus in a modified form

Physics

The 450 GeV Super Proton Synchrotron is installed at CERN

1977

Astronomy

Soviet 6-meter reflector in operation at Zelenchukskaya

Launch of Voyager 1 and Voyager 2 (originally Mariner 11 and Mariner 12) – U.S. planetary probes to study Jupiter (1979) and Saturn (1980/81)

Biology

The first complete nucleotide sequence of the genetic material of an organism, the bacteriophage OX174, is published

Physics

Lederman and co-workers discover the bottom quark

Fairbank announces the first experimental evidence for an isolated quark

1978

Medicine

Edwards and Steptoe achieve successful transplantation of human ova fertilized *in vitro*

1979

Astronomy

Voyager 1 and Voyager 2 fly by Jupiter – study and photograph atmosphere and surfaces of main satellites

Pioneer 11 flies past Saturn

1980

Anthropology

Pilbeam discovers a partial skull of a hominid fossil, *Sivapithecus*

Astronomy

Voyager 2 flies past Saturn – relays pictures of rings

Physics

Alan Guth proposes his inflationary universe model

Fred Hoyle suggests that cosmic dust contains bacterial cells

Geology

Luis Alvarez publishes his impact theory of the extinction of dinosaurs

Physics

von Klitzing discovers the quantum Hall effect

1981

Astronomy

Successful launch and recovery of space shuttle – first reusable spacecraft

Biology

K. E. Davies and J. M. Murray discover a restriction fragment length polymorphism (RFLP) on the X chromosome linked with Duchenne muscular dystrophy

Bining and Roher use their scanning-tunneling microscope (STM) to resolve surface details of crystals

1982

Astronomy

Venera 13 and 14 land on Venus and relay color pictures of surface

John Huchra and colleagues put forward evidence for *The Great Attractor* lying beyond the Hydra–Centaurus supercluster

Biology

Hartmut Michael crystallizes the membrane proteins of the bacterium *Rhodopseudomonas viridis*

Thomas Cech concludes that RNA is self-splicing and proposes the term "ribozyme"

Chemistry

Huffman and Kratschmer find spectral evidence for what is later recognized to be a new form of carbon (fullerene)

Mathematics

Mandelbrot introduces the term "fractal"

Medicine

Robert Gallo discovers the viruses HTLV-1 and HTLV-2

Discovery of cancer-causing genes (oncogenes)

1983

Astronomy

First American woman in space (Sally Ride on space-shuttle flight)

Biology

Mullis invents his technique for producing copies of DNA – the polymerase chain reaction

Medicine

Wexler and Gusella discover the position of the gene responsible for Huntington's disease

Montagnier becomes convinced that LAV (lymphadenopathy associated virus) is the cause of AIDS

Gallo isolates the virus HTLV-3

Physics

Rubbia and Charpak show evidence for the W particle at CERN

1984

Astronomy

The 98-inch Isaac Newton telescope is moved from the Royal Greenwich Observatory at Herstmonceux Castle, Sussex, to a new site at La Palma in the Canary Islands

Biology

Jeffreys discovers the technique of genetic fingerprinting

Chemistry

Dany Schectman and colleagues find crystals with a fivefold symmetry (quasicrystals)

Physics

Sagan and colleagues publish the controversial *Nuclear Winter: Global Consequences of Multiple Nuclear Explosions*

1985

Chemistry

Smalley, Kroto, and others discover a new form of carbon C_{60} and propose the name "buckminsterfullerene"

Joe Farman publishes his results on the connection between ozone depletion and atmospheric CFCs

Biology

Leroy Hood and Lloyd Smith develop the automatic sequencer for determining the sequence of DNA base pairs – a useful tool for mapping the human genome

Medicine

Gallo patents a test for HIV

Montagnier isolates the virus HIV-2

1986

Astronomy

The space shuttle Challenger blows up shortly after launch on Jan 28 with the death of six astronauts and an observer

Voyager 2 passes close to Uranus – 10 more satellites discovered

Mir (meaning "Peace") launched by the Soviet Union – the first permanently manned space station

Biology

DeLisi organizes a meeting in Santa Fe, New Mexico, to initiate the setting up of the Human Genome Project

Medicine

The International Committee on the Taxonomy of Viruses officially names the AIDS virus as HIV (human immunodeficiency virus)

Gallo and Montagnier agree to share the patent for the AIDS test

Physics

Bednorz and Muller discover a new type of semiconductor with a high critical temperature (35K)

1987

Physics

Paul Ching-Wu Chu makes a stable mixed yttrium–barium–copper oxide with the high critical temperature of 93K

Superstring Theory (John Henry Schwarz, Michael Green, and Ed Witten)

John Stuart Bell publishes *Speakable and Unspeakable in Quantum Mechanics*, giving his own views on "Bell's paradox"

1988

Biology

R. White announces that preliminary maps have been completed for most of the human chromosome

Physics

Fleischmann and Pons claim to have discovered an electrolytic method of achieving cold nuclear fusion – other research groups fail to reproduce the effects

1989

Astronomy

Huchra and Geller find the cluster of galaxies "The Great Wall"

Voyager 2 passed Neptune – discovers a "Great Dark Spot" and 4 complete rings

Biology

Lap-Chee Tsui, Jack Riordan, and Francis Collins announce the location of the cystic fibrosis gene

Earth Science

Global Warming (Schneider) – discussing the greenhouse effect

Physics

The Large Electron–Positron Collider is installed at CERN, Geneva

Richard Muller publishes *Nemesis*, claiming that the Sun has a companion star

1990

Astronomy

The Hubble Space Telescope is launched – a fault in the primary mirror means that it has a lower angular resolution than expected

The Cosmic Background Explorer starts mapping the sky

An 18th moon of Saturn is discovered (from Voyager 2 results)

Medicine

Start of The Human Genome Project with the selection of six institutions to do the work

1991

Astronomy

First British woman in space (Helen Sharman on a Russian Mir mission)

Chemistry

Doped fullerenes discovered to have superconductivity

1993

Astronomy

Results from COBE show ripples in the cosmic background radiation (supporting the inflationary theory of the universe)

NASA send space shuttle mission to repair Hubble Space Telescope

Carolyn and Eugene Shoemaker and David Levy discover a new comet Shoemaker–Levy 9

Mathematics

Wiles claims to have proved Fermat's last theorem

1994

Astronomy

Comet Shoemaker–Levy crashes into the atmosphere of Jupiter

Mathematics

A gap in Wiles's proof of Fermat's last theorem is discovered. Wiles produces a revised version of the proof

Physics

Workers at Fermilab, Chicago, tentatively claim discovery of the top quark

1995

Astronomy

Alan Hale and Thomas Bopp discover a new comet. Hale–Bopp is expected to make its closest approach to the Sun in early 1997

The U.S. space shuttle *Endeavor* docks with the Russian station *Mir*

The Galileo unmanned spacecraft launches a probe into the atmosphere of Jupiter

Mathematics

Wiles's proof of Fermat's last theorem is finally established

Medicine

Teams in Toronto and in Seattle, Washington, and Boston identify two genes responsible for early-onset forms of Alzheimer's disease

Clinical trials are conducted on a new class of anti-HIV drugs, protease inhibitors, designed to attack the virus at different stages in its life cycle

Physics

The discovery of the top quark at Fermilab is confirmed

Researchers in Colorado and at Rice University, Texas, obtain temperatures of less than 200 billionths of a degree above absolute zero. They observe Bose–Einstein condensation, in which thousands of atoms combine to behave as a single quantum entity

1996

Astronomy

Scientists at NASA detect fossil microbes in a meteorite found in Antarctica and originating on Mars, leading to renewed debate about life on Mars

Medicine

A link is established between BSE (bovine spongiform encephalopathy) in cattle and a form of Creutzfeldt-Jacob disease in humans. The agent is thought to be a prion, a type of protein transmitted in infected beef

INDEX

Boss, Lewis **2**: 16
Botanists: **1**: 32, 114, 136, 160, 199, 201; **2**: 15, 63, 94, 96, 100, 128, 149, 150; **4**: 41, 46, 53, 124, 157, 191; **5**: 75, 85, 86, 93, 121, 133, 139, 154, 166; **6**: 22, 120, 135; **7**: 40, 87, 133, 141; **8**: 37, 89, 200, 212, 220; **9**: 19, 20, 38, 50, 138, 162, 180, 208; **10**: 1, 33, 79, 140
Bothe, Walther Wilhelm Georg Franz **2**: 17
Boucher de Crevecoeur de Perthes, Jacques **2**: 18
Bouguer, Pierre **2**: 19
Boulton, Matthew **2**: 20
Bourbaki, Nicolas **2**: 20
Boussingault, Jean Baptiste **2**: 21
Boveri, Theodor Heinrich **2**: 22
Bovet, Daniel **2**: 23
Bowen, Edmund John **2**: 24
Bowen, Ira Sprague **2**: 25
Bowman, Sir William **2**: 26
Boyd, William Clouser **2**: 27
Boyer, Herbert Wayne **2**: 27
Boyle, Robert **2**: 28
Boys, Sir Charles Vernon **2**: 30
Brachet, Jean **2**: 31
Braconnot, Henri **2**: 32
Bradley, James **2**: 32
Bragg, Sir William Henry **2**: 33
Bragg, Sir William Lawrence **2**: 34
Brahe, Tycho **2**: 35
Brahmagupta **2**: 37
Braid, James **2**: 38
Brain: **4**: 10; **5**: 42, 65, 205; **9**: 96; **10**: 32
Bramah, Joseph **2**: 39
Brambell, Francis **2**: 39
Brand, Hennig **2**: 40
Brandt, Georg **2**: 40
Brans, Carl Henry **2**: 41
Brattain, Walter Houser **2**: 42
Braun, Karl Ferdinand **2**: 43
Bredt, Konrad Julius **2**: 44
Breit, Gregory **2**: 44
Brenner, Sydney **2**: 45
Bretonneau, Pierre Fidèle **2**: 47
Brewster, Sir David **2**: 48
Bricklin, Daniel **2**: 49
Bridgman, Percy Williams **2**: 50
Briggs, Henry **2**: 51
Bright, Richard **2**: 51
British aeronautical engineer: **10**: 119
British agricultural scientists: **6**: 72; **8**: 196; **10**: 2
British anatomists: **5**: 117, 185; **6**: 95; **7**: 205; **10**: 121
British anthropologists: **4**: 72; **6**: 77, 78, 95; **7**: 179; **8**: 46
British archeologist: **6**: 77
British architect: **9**: 172
British astronomers: **1**: 8, 19, 105, 155, 202; **2**: 32, 64, 79, 80, 152; **3**: 22, 31, 45, 111, 117; **4**: 22, 144, 198; **5**: 2, 18, 29, 30, 31, 45, 95, 108, 146, 148; **6**: 67, 148, 170; **7**: 6, 12, 76; **8**: 61, 67, 90, 206; **9**: 87, 97, 109,

183; **10**: 7, 168
British bacteriologists: **2**: 66; **4**: 3; **6**: 100; **10**: 8
British biochemists: **1**: 196; **2**: 129; **4**: 207; **5**: 54, 89, 193; **6**: 25; **7**: 85, 142, 143; **8**: 32, 34, 50, 77; **9**: 7, 204
British biologists: **1**: 73; **2**: 45, 203; **4**: 164, 201, 209; **5**: 124, 126, 127, 138, 183; **6**: 176; **7**: 21, 78, 211; **8**: 13, 39, 157, 197; **9**: 186, 190; **10**: 135
British botanists: **1**: 114, 136, 160, 199; **2**: 63, 189; **4**: 124; **5**: 85, 86, 121; **6**: 120; **8**: 200, 220; **9**: 38, 50, 162; **10**: 79, 140
British chemical engineers: **1**: 21, 149, 185; **2**: 134, 208; **3**: 34; **4**: 75, 112; **7**: 91; **9**: 107; **10**: 96
British chemists: **1**: 4, 24, 49, 69, 74, 120, 131, 144, 196; **2**: 24, 28, 196, 197, 207, 209; **3**: 5, 9, 13, 29, 65, 87, 145, 173, 183, 187; **4**: 1, 30, 147, 206, 209, 219; **5**: 5, 21, 53, 56, 60, 69, 88, 134, 137, 160, 184, 202, 209; **6**: 29, 64, 106, 136, 158; **7**: 3, 4, 38, 46, 75, 143, 152, 162, 174, 183, 218; **8**: 1, 27, 28, 39, 58, 66, 71, 75, 86, 95, 109, 151, 159, 160, 170, 200; **9**: 64, 94, 100, 147, 157, 168, 176, 185, 187, 196, 197, 203, 215; **10**: 6, 14, 65, 137, 139, 161, 186
British computer scientists: **2**: 90; **9**: 138; **10**: 133
British crystallographers: **1**: 168; **6**: 159
British earth scientists: **1**: 139; **2**: 75, 139, 177, 205; **3**: 22, 44, 216; **4**: 54, 93, 195; **5**: 80, 122, 148; **6**: 47, 64, 120, 169, 184, 211; **7**: 8, 70, 77, 125, 127, 163, 190; **8**: 81, 85, 93, 120, 191, 210; **9**: 41, 84, 85, 97, 102; **10**: 39, 113, 118, 166
British ecologist: **3**: 143
British Egyptologist: **10**: 187
British electrical engineers: **4**: 4; **5**: 7
British embryologists: **5**: 55; **10**: 59, 162
British endocrinologist: **4**: 213
British engineers: **1**: 180; **2**: 20, 39, 67; **5**: 93; **7**: 12, 23, 138, 151, 220; **8**: 113; **9**: 10, 69, 126, 172, 183; **10**: 120
British entomologists: **5**: 183; **10**: 127
British ethologists: **3**: 32; **9**: 198
British explorers: **1**: 133; **2**: 178; **4**: 54, 72; **5**: 85
British geneticists: **1**: 135, 186; **3**: 16, 213; **4**: 14, 186; **5**: 147, 199; **7**: 7; **8**: 70; **10**: 59
British herbalist: **4**: 101
British horticulturist: **1**: 186
British immunologists: **4**: 145; **7**: 31
British inventors: **1**: 68, 106, 151, 180; **2**: 39, 111, 124, 191; **4**: 211; **7**: 12, 51, 218; **9**: 10, 126,

153; **10**: 2, 82
British mathematicians: **1**: 90, 128, 179; **2**: 7, 123, 139, 175, 196; **3**: 74, 117, 213; **4**: 159, 208; **5**: 67, 146; **6**: 47, 145, 169, 198; **7**: 76, 101; **8**: 22, 93, 195; **9**: 41, 75, 135, 155, 166; **10**: 3, 113, 116, 117, 131
British metallurgists: **2**: 191, 193; **3**: 15, 60; **4**: 179; **5**: 60, 115
British meteorologists: **3**: 13, 216; **6**: 48; **8**: 143; **9**: 56, 72
British mineralogist: **4**: 160
British naturalists: **1**: 133; **2**: 72; **3**: 18; **4**: 13; **7**: 142; **10**: 66, 114
British ornithologists: **6**: 40; **7**: 153
British paleontologists: **7**: 205, 219; **10**: 77, 164
British pathologists: **3**: 153; **5**: 70, 138
British pharmacologists: **6**: 18; **10**: 25
British philosophers: **1**: 97; **2**: 121; **5**: 114; **7**: 208; **8**: 66, 73, 195; **9**: 108; **10**: 110, 116
British physicians: **1**: 12, 30, 105, 144, 152, 196, 202; **2**: 26, 38, 51, 54, 72, 73, 82, 158; **3**: 21, 141, 197; **4**: 77, 196; **5**: 21, 87, 117, 118, 141, 150; **6**: 118, 131, 143, 195, 201, 210; **7**: 219; **8**: 162, 172; **9**: 74, 90; **10**: 79, 121, 153, 170, 187
British physicists: **1**: 50, 59, 73, 74, 87, 122, 125, 134, 153, 159, 197; **2**: 8, 28, 30, 33, 34, 48, 100, 110, 128, 164, 179, 193, 196, 207; **3**: 9, 56, 65, 74, 87, 171, 183; **4**: 4, 33, 49, 57, 118, 166, 198; **5**: 2, 7, 48, 146, 162, 163, 189, 198; **6**: 37, 127, 134, 144, 149, 156, 177, 209; **7**: 17, 51, 109, 111, 163; **8**: 17, 21, 22, 49, 79, 80, 112, 113, 116, 119, 144, 158, 177, 189; **9**: 31, 71, 130, 135, 144, 167, 192, 193; **10**: 9, 76, 79, 80, 108, 117, 136, 145, 160, 161, 187
British physiologists: **1**: 15, 137; **3**: 6; **4**: 17, 78, 187; **5**: 54, 68, 123, 181; **6**: 58, 177, 197; **7**: 36, 211; **8**: 95, 193; **9**: 55, 59, 118
British psychologist: **2**: 86
British zoologists: **1**: 110; **2**: 39; **3**: 35; **4**: 24, 139, 143; **6**: 61, 212; **7**: 127; **8**: 79; **9**: 198; **10**: 180, 199
Broca, Pierre Paul **2**: 52
Brockhouse, Bertram **2**: 53
Brodie, Sir Benjamin **2**: 54
Brodie, Bernard Beryl **2**: 55
Brongniart, Alexandre **2**: 55
Bronk, Detlev Wulf **2**: 56
Brønsted, Johannes **2**: 57
Broom, Robert **2**: 58
Brouncker, William Viscount **2**: 59
Brouwer, Dirk **2**: 59
Brouwer, Luitzen **2**: 60
Brown, Herbert Charles **2**: 61

Chinese pharmacologist: **6:** 121
Chittenden, Russell Henry **2:** 150
Chladni, Ernst Florens **2:** 151
Chlorophyll: 3: 212; **8:** 19, 212; **10:** 142, 167
Cholera: 6: 4; **9:** 90
Cholesterol: 1: 204; **2:** 62, 87, 190; **4:** 134; **8:** 204; **10:** 150, 167
Chou Kung 2: 152
Christie, Sir William Henry Mahoney **2:** 152
Chromatography: 10: 1
Chromosomes: 4: 6; **7:** 103; **9:** 127, 145
Chu, Paul Ching-Wu **2:** 153
Chu Shih-Chieh 2: 154
Civil Engineer: 3: 140
Clairaut, Alexis Claude **2:** 155
Claisen, Ludwig **2:** 156
Clark, Alvan Graham **2:** 157
Clarke, Sir Cyril Astley **2:** 158
Claude, Albert **2:** 159
Claude, Georges **2:** 160
Clausius, Rudolf **2:** 161
Clemence, Gerald Maurice **2:** 162
Cleve, Per Teodor **2:** 163
Climate: 3: 14; **6:** 48
Cloud chamber: 1: 198; **10:** 145
Cloud formation: 1: 164
Coblentz, William Weber **2:** 164
Cockcroft, Sir John **2:** 164
Cocker, Edward **2:** 165
Coenzymes: 3: 168; **4:** 207; **9:** 181, 205; **10:** 74
Cohen, Paul Joseph **2:** 166
Cohen, Seymour Stanley **2:** 166
Cohen, Stanley **2:** 167
Cohn, Ferdinand Julius **2:** 168
Cohnheim, Julius **2:** 169
Colloids: 4: 153; **10:** 198
Colombo, Matteo Realdo **2:** 170
Comets: 7: 195; **10:** 112
Compton, Arthur Holly **2:** 171
Computer Scientists: 1: 18, 41, 76, 96; **2:** 49, 90; **3:** 116, 190; **4:** 15; **5:** 71, 76, 90, 153, 176, 204; **6:** 2, 106; **7:** 10, 24, 81, 151, 192; **9:** 12, 131, 138; **10:** 133, 151, 200
Comte, Auguste Isidore **2:** 172
Conant, James Bryant **2:** 174
Conon of Samos 2: 174
Continental drift: 1: 198; **2:** 76; **3:** 109; **5:** 80, 148; **8:** 191; **10:** 88
Contraceptive pill: 8: 48; **9:** 100
Conway, John Horton **2:** 175
Conybeare, William **2:** 177
Cook, James **2:** 178
Cooke, Sir William **2:** 179
Cooper, Leon Neil **2:** 180
Cope, Edward Drinker **2:** 181
Copernicus, Nicolaus **2:** 182
Corey, Elias James **2:** 184
Cori, Carl Ferdinand **2:** 185
Cori, Gerty Theresa **2:** 186
Coriolis, Gustave-Gaspard **2:** 187
Cormack, Allan Macleod **2:** 188
Corner, Edred **2:** 189
Cornforth, Sir John **2:** 190
Correns, Karl Erich **2:** 190

Cort, Henry **2:** 191
Corvisart, Jean-Nicolas **2:** 192
Cosmic background radiation: 3: 69; **8:** 25
Cosmic rays: 1: 198; **2:** 17, 171; **5:** 41; **7:** 73; **8:** 80
Cosmologists: 2: 4; **3:** 3; **4:** 173; **5:** 2, 99; **6:** 102
Coster, Dirk **2:** 193
Cottrell, Sir Alan **2:** 193
Coulomb, Charles Augustin de **2:** 194
Coulson, Charles Alfred **2:** 196
Couper, Archibald Scott **2:** 197
Cournand, André **2:** 198
Courtois, Bernard **2:** 199
Cousteau, Jacques Yves **2:** 200
Crafts, James Mason **2:** 201
Craig, Lyman Creighton **2:** 201
Cram, Donald James **2:** 202
Crick, Francis **2:** 203
Croatian earth scientist: **7:** 88
Croatian mathematician: **7:** 68
Croll, James **2:** 205
Cronin, James Watson **2:** 206
Cronstedt, Axel Frederic **2:** 207
Crookes, Sir William **2:** 207
Cross, Charles Frederick **2:** 208
Crum Brown, Alexander **2:** 209
Crutzen, Paul **2:** 210
Crystallographers: 1: 168; **5:** 178; **6:** 159; **10:** 179
Crystallography: 9: 125
Cuban physician: **3:** 206
Cugnot, Nicolas-Joseph **2:** 211
Culpeper, Nicholas **2:** 211
Curie, Marie Skłodowska **2:** 212
Curie, Pierre **2:** 215
Curtis, Heber Doust **2:** 217
Curtius, Theodor **2:** 218
Cushing, Harvey **2:** 218
Cuvier, Baron Georges **2:** 219
Cybernetics: 10: 125
Cytologists: 1: 159; **2:** 114; **3:** 103; **4:** 6, 136; **7:** 56
Czech chemist: **5:** 47
Czech physiologist: **8:** 100

d'Abano, Pietro **3:** 1
Daguerre, Louis-Jacques-Mandé **3:** 2
d'Ailly, Pierre **3:** 3
Daimler, Gottlieb Wilhelm **3:** 4
Dainton, Frederick Sydney **3:** 5
Dale, Sir Henry Hallett **3:** 6
d'Alembert, Jean Le Rond **3:** 7
Dalén, Nils Gustaf **3:** 8
Dalton, John **3:** 9
Dam, Carl Peter Henrik **3:** 11
Dana, James Dwight **3:** 12
Daniell, John Frederic **3:** 13
Daniels, Farrington **3:** 14
Danish anatomist: **9:** 125
Danish archeologists: **9:** 188; **10:** 169
Danish astronomers: **2:** 35; **3:** 94; **5:** 36; **8:** 167; **9:** 141
Danish bacteriologist: **4:** 154
Danish biochemist: **3:** 11
Danish biologist: **9:** 22
Danish botanist: **5:** 154
Danish chemists: **1:** 195; **2:** 57; **5:** 216; **9:** 103, 189

Danish earth scientists: **6:** 96; **7:** 173; **9:** 125
Danish geneticist: **5:** 154
Danish immunologist: **5:** 152
Danish mathematicians: **1:** 129; **7:** 173
Danish meteorologist: **3:** 14
Danish physicians: **3:** 203, 207
Danish physicists: **1:** 215, 216; **7:** 112, 120, 184
Danish physiologist: **6:** 27
Danish zoologist: **9:** 122
Dansgaard, Willi **3:** 14
Darby, Abraham **3:** 15
Dark matter: **8:** 187
Darlington, Cyril Dean **3:** 16
Dart, Raymond Arthur **3:** 17
Darwin, Charles Robert **3:** 18
Darwin, Erasmus **3:** 21
Darwin, Sir George **3:** 22
Daubrée, Gabriel Auguste **3:** 23
Dausset, Jean **3:** 24
Davaine, Casimir Joseph **3:** 25
Davenport, Charles **3:** 26
Davis, Raymond **3:** 26
Davis, William Morris **3:** 27
Davisson, Clinton Joseph **3:** 28
Davy, Sir Humphry **3:** 29
Dawes, William Rutter **3:** 31
Dawkins, Richard **3:** 32
Day, David Talbot **3:** 33
Deacon, Henry **3:** 34
de Bary, Heinrich Anton **3:** 34
De Beer, Sir Gavin **3:** 35
Debierne, André Louis **3:** 36
de Broglie, Prince Louis Victor Pierre Raymond **3:** 37
Debye, Peter **3:** 38
Dedekind, (Julius Wilhelm) Richard **3:** 39
de Duve, Christian René **3:** 40
Deficiency diseases: **3:** 130; **4:** 56, 130; **6:** 131
De Forest, Lee **3:** 41
De Geer, Charles **3:** 42
Dehmelt, Hans Georg **3:** 43
De la Beche, Sir Henry **3:** 44
Delambre, Jean Baptiste **3:** 45
De la Rue, Warren **3:** 45
Delbrück, Max **3:** 46
D'Elhuyar, Don Fausto **3:** 48
DeLisi, Charles **3:** 49
Del Rio, Andrès Manuel **3:** 50
De Luc, Jean André **3:** 50
Demarçay, Eugene Anatole **3:** 52
Demerec, Milislav **3:** 52
Democritus of Abdera 3: 53
De Moivre, Abraham **3:** 54
Dempster, Arthur Jeffrey **3:** 55
Dendrochronologist: **3:** 90
Dentists: **7:** 107; **10:** 98
Derham, William **3:** 56
Desaguliers, John **3:** 57
Desargues, Girard **3:** 57
Descartes, René du Perron **3:** 58
Desch, Cyril Henry **3:** 60
de Sitter, Willem **3:** 61
Desmarest, Nicolas **3:** 61
Désormes, Charles Bernard **3:** 62
Deville, Henri **3:** 63
de Vries, Hugo **3:** 64
Dewar, Sir James **3:** 65

Epicurus **3**: 152
Epstein, Sir Michael **3**: 153
Erasistratus of Chios **3**: 154
Eratosthenes of Cyrene **3**: 155
Ercker, Lazarus **3**: 155
Erdös, Paul **3**: 156
Erlanger, Joseph **3**: 157
Erlenmeyer, Richard **3**: 158
Ernst, Richard Robert **3**: 158
Esaki, Leo **3**: 160
Eschenmoser, Albert **3**: 161
Eskola, Pentti Elias **3**: 161
Espy, James Pollard **3**: 162
Estonian biologist: **1**: 101
Estonian physicist: **9**: 21
Estrogen: **1**: 31; **2**: 87
Ethnographers: **4**: 50; **8**: 116
Ethologists: **3**: 32; **4**: 47; **6**: 165; **9**: 198
Euclid **3**: 163
Eudoxus of Cnidus **3**: 165
Euler, Leonhard **3**: 166
Euler-Chelpin, Hans Karl August Simon von **3**: 168
Eustachio, Bartolommeo **3**: 169
Evans, Robley Dunglison **3**: 170
Everett iii, Hugh **3**: 170
Evolution: **1**: 86; **3**: 18; **6**: 47; **10**: 66
Ewing, Sir James Alfred **3**: 171
Ewing, William Maurice **3**: 172
Ewins, Arthur James **3**: 173
Expanding universe: **5**: 100
Explorers: **1**: 133; **2**: 89, 178; **4**: 54, 72; **5**: 85, 112; **6**: 41; **7**: 136, 173, 174; **8**: 102
Eyde, Samuel **3**: 174
Eyring, Henry **3**: 175

Fabre, Jean Henri **3**: 177
Fabricius, David **3**: 178
Fabricius ab Aquapendente, Hieronymus **3**: 178
Fahrenheit, (Gabriel) Daniel **3**: 179
Fairbank, William **3**: 180
Fajans, Kasimir **3**: 181
Fallopius, Gabriel **3**: 182
Faraday, Michael **3**: 183
Farman, Joe **3**: 187
Fechner, Gustav Theodor **3**: 188
Fehling, Hermann Christian von **3**: 189
Feigenbaum, Edward Albert **3**: 190
Fermat, Pierre de **3**: 191
Fermentation: **2**: 71, 91; **4**: 208; **8**: 4; **9**: 32
Fermi, Enrico **3**: 192
Fernel, Jean François **3**: 195
Ferrel, William **3**: 196
Ferrier, Sir David **3**: 197
Fessenden, Reginald **3**: 198
Feyerabend, Paul Karl **3**: 199
Feynman, Richard **3**: 200
Fibiger, Johannes **3**: 203
Fibonacci, Leonardo **3**: 204
Finch, George Ingle **3**: 205
Finlay, Carlos Juan **3**: 206
Finnish cartographer: **7**: 173
Finnish chemists: **4**: 59; **10**: 42
Finnish earth scientists: **3**: 161; **7**: 173

Finnish explorer: **7**: 173
Finnish physiologist: **4**: 155
Finsen, Niels Ryberg **3**: 207
Fischer, Edmond H. **3**: 208
Fischer, Emil Hermann **3**: 209
Fischer, Ernst Otto **3**: 210
Fischer, Hans **3**: 211
Fischer, Otto Philipp **3**: 212
Fisher, Sir Ronald **3**: 213
Fitch, Val Logsdon **3**: 214
Fittig, Rudolph **3**: 215
Fitzgerald, George Francis **3**: 215
Fitzroy, Robert **3**: 216
Fizeau, Armand **3**: 217
Flammarion, Nicolas **3**: 218
Flamsteed, John **3**: 219
Fleischmann, Martin **4**: 1
Fleming, Sir Alexander **4**: 3
Fleming, Sir John Ambrose **4**: 4
Fleming, Williamina **4**: 5
Flemish astronomer: **8**: 103
Flemish cartographer: **7**: 200
Flemish chemist: **5**: 14
Flemish engineer: **9**: 129
Flemish mathematicians: **8**: 103; **9**: 129
Flemish physician: **5**: 14
Flemish sociologist: **8**: 103
Flemming, Walther **4**: 6
Flerov, Georgii Nikolaevich **4**: 7
Florey, Howard Walter **4**: 8
Flory, Paul John **4**: 9
Flourens, Jean Pierre Marie **4**: 10
Floyer, Sir John **4**: 11
Fock, Vladimir **4**: 12
Folkers, Karl August **4**: 12
Forbes, Edward **4**: 13
Ford, Edmund Brisco **4**: 14
Forrester, Jay **4**: 15
Forssmann, Werner **4**: 16
Fossils: **1**: 51; **3**: 97; **7**: 70; **9**: 125
Foster, Sir Michael **4**: 17
Foucault, Jean Bernard **4**: 18
Fourcroy, Antoine François de **4**: 19
Fourier, Baron (Jean Baptiste) Joseph **4**: 20
Fourneau, Ernest **4**: 21
Fourneyron, Benoît **4**: 21
Fowler, Alfred **4**: 22
Fowler, William Alfred **4**: 23
Fox, Harold Munro **4**: 24
Fox, Sidney Walter **4**: 25
Fracastoro, Girolamo **4**: 26
Fractals: **6**: 207
Fraenkel-Conrat, Heinz L. **4**: 27
Francis, Thomas Jr. **4**: 28
Franck, James **4**: 29
Frank, Ilya Mikhailovich **4**: 30
Frankland, Sir Edward **4**: 30
Franklin, Benjamin **4**: 31
Franklin, Rosalind **4**: 33
Frasch, Herman **4**: 34
Fraunhofer, Josef von **4**: 35
Fredholm, Erik Ivar **4**: 36
Frege, Gottlob **4**: 36
French agricultural scientists: **2**: 21; **3**: 101
French anatomists: **2**: 219; **4**: 10; **8**: 14, 30
French anthropologist: **2**: 52

French archeologist: **2**: 18
French architect: **8**: 30
French astronomers: **2**: 9, 115; **3**: 45, 82, 218; **5**: 145; **6**: 39, 45, 62, 111, 187; **7**: 13, 55; **8**: 42, 69, 145
French bacteriologist: **7**: 164
French balloonists: **7**: 99
French biochemists: **2**: 32; **7**: 95
French biologists: **2**: 219; **3**: 103; **4**: 100; **5**: 142; **6**: 46, 183; **8**: 3, 180, 213
French botanists: **5**: 166; **7**: 141
French chemists: **1**: 109, 175, 176; **2**: 92, 122, 141, 143, 145, 149, 160, 199, 212; **3**: 36, 52, 62, 63, 100, 105; **4**: 19, 42, 86, 102, 165, 176; **5**: 26; **6**: 68, 70, 71, 83, 86, 88, 97, 103, 199; **7**: 89; **8**: 3, 11, 18, 19, 26, 94, 115, 126, 178, 208, 213; **9**: 179; **10**: 14, 32, 101, 178
French cosmologist: **3**: 3
French cytologists: **3**: 103; **7**: 56
French earth scientists: **1**: 140; **2**: 55, 200; **3**: 23, 61; **4**: 168
French engineers: **2**: 140, 211; **3**: 57; **4**: 21; **6**: 87; **8**: 30
French entomologists: **3**: 177; **8**: 121
French explorer: **6**: 41
French geographers: **2**: 68; **3**: 3; **6**: 41; **10**: 37
French histologist: **8**: 114
French horticulturist: **7**: 141
French immunologist: **3**: 24
French inventors: **1**: 58; **3**: 2; **4**: 21; **6**: 87; **7**: 165, 212
French mathematicians: **1**: 13, 43; **2**: 9, 19, 109, 117; **3**: 7, 45, 54, 57, 58, 191; **4**: 20, 71, 103, 178; **5**: 24, 160; **6**: 43, 62, 84, 119, 137; **7**: 13, 49, 94; **8**: 2, 62, 64, 67, 161; **9**: 47; **10**: 35, 37, 89
French metallurgist: **8**: 121
French military scientist: **6**: 206
French mineralogists: **1**: 147; **5**: 1
French paleontologists: **2**: 55; **6**: 66
French pathologists: **1**: 185; **6**: 69; **7**: 98
French pharmacologists: **2**: 122; **4**: 21
French philosophers: **2**: 81, 172; **3**: 7, 58, 102; **4**: 80; **7**: 49; **8**: 2, 62
French physicians: **2**: 47, 52, 65, 108, 142, 192; **3**: 24, 25, 195; **4**: 10; **6**: 42, 69, 85, 168, 199; **7**: 217; **8**: 35, 48; **10**: 38
French physicists: **1**: 38, 43, 60, 80, 94, 143, 189; **2**: 19, 91, 92, 106, 115, 145, 146, 155, 187, 194, 215; **3**: 2, 102, 105, 191, 217; **4**: 18, 37, 80, 86, 99; **5**: 157, 158, 181; **6**: 43, 57, 62, 140, 142, 206, 220; **7**: 13, 144, 172, 212; **8**: 2, 19, 31, 35, 54, 64, 121, 126
French physiologists: **1**: 170, 174; **2**: 65; **3**: 109; **6**: 200, 216; **8**: 146

Goddard, Robert 4: 121
Gödel, Kurt 4: 122
Godwin, Sir Harry 4: 124
Goeppert-Mayer, Maria 4: 125
Goethe, Johann Wolfgang von 4: 126
Gold, Thomas 4: 128
Goldberger, Joseph 4: 130
Goldhaber, Maurice 4: 131
Goldschmidt, Johann Wilhelm 4: 132
Goldschmidt, Victor 4: 132
Goldstein, Eugen 4: 133
Goldstein, Joseph 4: 134
Golgi, Camillo 4: 136
Gomberg, Moses 4: 137
Good, Robert Alan 4: 138
Goodall, Jane 4: 139
Goodman, Henry Nelson 4: 141
Goodpasture, Ernest 4: 142
Goodrich, Edwin Stephen 4: 143
Goodricke, John 4: 144
Gordan, Paul Albert 4: 144
Gorer, Peter Alfred 4: 145
Gorgas, William 4: 146
Gossage, William 4: 147
Goudsmit, Samuel 4: 148
Gould, Benjamin 4: 149
Gould, Stephen Jay 4: 150
Graaf, Regnier de 4: 151
Graebe, Karl 4: 152
Graham, Thomas 4: 152
Gram, Hans Christian 4: 154
Granit, Ragnar Arthur 4: 155
Grassi, Giovanni Battista 4: 156
Gray, Asa 4: 157
Gray, Harry Barkus 4: 158
Gray, Stephen 4: 159
Greek anatomists: 3: 154; 5: 25
Greek astronomers: 1: 65; 2: 93, 174; 3: 155, 165; 5: 23, 57; 7: 57; 8: 78, 102; 9: 177
Greek botanist: 9: 180
Greek earth scientists: 1: 56; 9: 177
Greek explorer: 8: 102
Greek-French astronomer: 1: 55
Greek geographers: 3: 67; 5: 7, 57; 9: 137
Greek inventor: 5: 25
Greek mathematicians: 1: 56, 62; 2: 174; 3: 73, 163, 165; 5: 25, 131; 7: 214; 8: 101
Greek philosophers: 1: 24, 45, 46, 65; 3: 53, 67, 146, 152; 5: 23; 6: 108; 7: 219; 8: 40, 55, 78, 91, 101; 9: 93, 140, 177, 180; 10: 181, 192
Greek physicians: 1: 24; 3: 73, 154; 4: 62; 5: 25, 58; 8: 82
Greek scientists: 1: 65; 8: 41
Green, George 4: 159
Greenhouse effect: 8: 134
Greenstein, Jesse Leonard 4: 160
Gregor, William 4: 160
Gregory, James 4: 161
Griess, Johann Peter 4: 162
Griffin, Donald Redfield 4: 163
Griffith, Fred 4: 164
Grignard, François 4: 165
Grimaldi, Francesco 4: 166
Group theory: 1: 6; 4: 72; 5: 161
Grove, Sir William 4: 166

Guericke, Otto von 4: 167
Guettard, Jean Etienne 4: 168
Guillaume, Charles 4: 169
Guillemin, Roger 4: 170
Guldberg, Cato 4: 171
Gullstrand, Allvar 4: 172
Gutenberg, Beno 4: 172
Guth, Alan Harvey 4: 173
Guthrie, Samuel 4: 174
Guyot, Arnold Henry 4: 175
Guyton de Morveau, Baron Louis Bernard 4: 176

Haber, Fritz 4: 177
Hadamard, Jacques 4: 178
Hadfield, Sir Robert 4: 179
Hadley, George 4: 180
Hadley, John 4: 180
Haeckel, Ernst Heinrich 4: 181
Hahn, Otto 4: 183
Haken, Wolfgang 4: 185
Haldane, John Burdon Sanderson 4: 186
Haldane, John Scott 4: 187
Hale, George Ellery 4: 189
Hales, Stephen 4: 191
Hall, Asaph 4: 192
Hall, Charles Martin 4: 193
Hall, Edwin Herbert 4: 194
Hall, James 4: 195
Hall, Sir James 4: 195
Hall, Marshall 4: 196
Haller, Albrecht von 4: 197
Halley, Edmond 4: 198
Halsted, William Stewart 4: 200
Hamilton, William 4: 201
Hamilton, Sir William Rowan 4: 202
Hämmerling, Joachim 4: 203
Hammond, George Simms 4: 204
Hansen, Gerhard Henrik 4: 205
Hantzsch, Arthur Rudolf 4: 206
Harcourt, Sir William 4: 206
Harden, Sir Arthur 4: 207
Hardy, Godfrey Harold 4: 208
Hardy, Sir William Bate 4: 209
Hare, Robert 4: 210
Hargreaves, James 4: 211
Hariot, Thomas 4: 211
Harkins, William Draper 4: 212
Harris, Geoffrey Wingfield 4: 213
Harrison, Ross Granville 4: 214
Hartline, Haldan Keffer 4: 215
Hartmann, Johannes 4: 215
Harvey, William 4: 216
Hassell, Odd 4: 218
Hatchett, Charles 4: 219
Hauksbee, Francis 4: 219
Hauptman, Herb Aaron 4: 220
Haüy, René Just 5: 1
Hawking, Stephen William 5: 2
Haworth, Sir (Walter) Norman 5: 5
Hays, James Douglas 5: 6
Heat: 1: 197; 5: 163; 8: 190
Heaviside, Oliver 5: 7
Hecataeus of Miletus 5: 7
Hecht, Selig 5: 8
Heezen, Bruce Charles 5: 8
Heidelberger, Michael 5: 9
Heisenberg, Werner Karl 5: 10
Helmholtz, Hermann Ludwig

von 5: 13
Helmont, Jan Baptista van 5: 14
Hemoglobin: 2: 174; 5: 135; 8: 33; 10: 113
Hempel, Carl Gustav 5: 15
Hench, Philip Showalter 5: 17
Henderson, Thomas 5: 18
Henle, Friedrich 5: 19
Henry, Joseph 5: 20
Henry, William 5: 21
Hensen, Viktor 5: 22
Heracleides of Pontus 5: 23
Heraclitus of Ephesus 5: 23
Herbalist: 4: 101
Hermite, Charles 5: 24
Hero of Alexandria 5: 25
Herophilus of Chalcedon 5: 25
Héroult, Paul 5: 26
Herring, William Conyers 5: 27
Herschbach, Dudley 5: 28
Herschel, Caroline 5: 29
Herschel, Sir (Frederick) William 5: 30
Herschel, Sir John Frederick William 5: 31
Hershey, Alfred Day 5: 32
Hertz, Gustav 5: 33
Hertz, Heinrich Rudolf 5: 34
Hertzsprung, Ejnar 5: 36
Herzberg, Gerhard 5: 38
Hess, Germain Henri 5: 39
Hess, Harry Hammond 5: 39
Hess, Victor Francis 5: 40
Hess, Walter Rudolf 5: 42
Hevelius, Johannes 5: 43
Hevesy, George Charles von 5: 44
Hewish, Antony 5: 45
Heymans, Corneille 5: 46
Heyrovský, Jaroslav 5: 47
Higgins, William 5: 48
Higgs, Peter Ware 5: 48
Hilbert, David 5: 49
Hildebrand, Joel Henry 5: 52
Hilditch, Thomas Percy 5: 53
Hill, Archibald Vivian 5: 54
Hill, James Peter 5: 55
Hillier, James 5: 55
Hinshelwood, Sir Cyril 5: 56
Hipparchus 5: 57
Hippocrates of Cos 5: 58
Hirsch, Sir Peter Bernhard 5: 60
Hirst, Sir Edmund 5: 60
His, Wilhelm 5: 61
Hisinger, Wilhelm 5: 62
Histologists: 4: 136; 6: 11, 204; 8: 108, 114; 9: 106
Hitchings, George Herbert 5: 63
Hittorf, Johann Wilhelm 5: 64
Hitzig, Eduard 5: 65
HIV: 4: 70; 7: 98
Hjelm, Peter Jacob 5: 66
Hoagland, Mahlon Bush 5: 66
Hodge, Sir William 5: 67
Hodgkin, Sir Alan Lloyd 5: 68
Hodgkin, Dorothy 5: 69
Hodgkin, Thomas 5: 70
Hoff, Marcian Edward 5: 71
Hoffmann, Friedrich 5: 72
Hoffmann, Roald 5: 73
Hofmann, Johann Wilhelm 5: 74
Hofmeister, Wilhelm 5: 75
Hofstadter, Douglas 5: 76

Just, Ernest Everett 5: 167

Kaluza, Theodor 5: 168
Kamen, Martin David 5: 169
Kamerlingh-Onnes, Heike 5: 170
Kamin, Leon 5: 171
Kammerer, Paul 5: 172
Kane, Sir Robert John 5: 173
Kant, Immanuel 5: 174
Kapitza, Pyotr 5: 175
Kapoor, Mitchell David 5: 176
Kapteyn, Jacobus Cornelius 5: 177
Karle, Isabella Helen 5: 178
Karle, Jerome 5: 179
Karrer, Paul 5: 180
Kastler, Alfred 5: 181
Katz, Bernard 5: 181
Keeler, James Edward 5: 182
Keenan, Philip Childs 5: 183
Keilin, David 5: 183
Keir, James 5: 184
Keith, Sir Arthur 5: 185
Kekulé von Stradonitz, Friedrich August 5: 186
Kellner, Karl 5: 189
Kelvin, William Thomson, Baron 5: 189
Kemeny, John George 5: 191
Kendall, Edward Calvin 5: 192
Kendall, Henry Way 5: 193
Kendrew, Sir John 5: 193
Kennelly, Arthur Edwin 5: 194
Kenyan anthropologist: 6: 79
Kepler, Johannes 5: 195
Kerr, John 5: 198
Kerst, Donald William 5: 198
Kettlewell, Henry 5: 199
Kety, Seymour Solomon 5: 200
Khorana, Har Gobind 5: 201
Kidd, John 5: 202
Kiddinu 5: 202
Kilby, Jack St. Clair 5: 203
Kildall, Gary 5: 204
Kimura, Doreen 5: 205
Kimura, Hisashi 5: 206
Kimura, Motoo 5: 207
Kinetic theory: 2: 2, 161; 5: 163; 7: 18; 10: 76
King, Charles Glen 5: 207
Kinsey, Alfred Charles 5: 208
Kipping, Frederic Stanley 5: 209
Kirchhoff, Gustav Robert 5: 210
Kirkwood, Daniel 5: 211
Kirwan, Richard 5: 212
Kistiakowsky, George Bogdan 5: 213
Kitasato, Baron Shibasaburo 5: 214
Kittel, Charles 5: 215
Kjeldahl, Johan Gustav Christoffer Thorsager 5: 216
Klaproth, Martin 5: 217
Klein, (Christian) Felix 5: 218
Klingenstierna, Samuel 5: 219
Klitzing, Klaus von 5: 220
Klug, Sir Aaron 6: 1
Knuth, Donald Ervin 6: 2
Koch, (Heinrich Hermann) Robert 6: 3
Kocher, Emil Theodor 6: 5
Köhler, Georges J. F. 6: 6
Kohlrausch, Friedrich 6: 7

Kohn, Walter 6: 8
Ko Hung 6: 9
Kolbe, Adolph 6: 10
Koller, Carl 6: 10
Kölliker, Rudolph Albert von 6: 11
Kolmogorov, Andrei 6: 12
Kopp, Hermann Franz Moritz 6: 13
Köppen, Wladimir Peter 6: 14
Kornberg, Arthur 6: 15
Korolev, Sergei Pavlovich 6: 16
Kossel, Albrecht 6: 17
Kosterlitz, Hans Walter 6: 18
Kouwenhoven, William 6: 19
Kovalevski, Aleksandr Onufrievich 6: 19
Kovalevsky, Sonya 6: 20
Kozyrev, Nikolay 6: 21
Kraft, Robert Paul 6: 22
Kramer, Paul Jackson 6: 22
Kratzer, Nicolas 6: 23
Kraus, Charles August 6: 24
Krebs, Edwin Gerhard 6: 24
Krebs, Sir Hans Adolf 6: 25
Krogh, Schack August Steenberg 6: 27
Kronecker, Leopold 6: 28
Kroto, Harold Walter 6: 29
Kuffler, Stephen William 6: 30
Kuhn, Richard 6: 31
Kuhn, Thomas Samuel 6: 32
Kühne, Wilhelm Friedrich 6: 33
Kuiper, Gerard Peter 6: 34
Kundt, August 6: 35
Kurchatov, Igor Vasilievich 6: 36
Kurti, Nicholas 6: 37
Kusch, Polykarp 6: 37

Lacaille, Nicolas Louis de 6: 39
Lack, David Lambert 6: 40
La Condamine, Charles Marie de 6: 41
Laënnec, René Théophile Hyacinthe 6: 42
Lagrange, Comte Joseph Louis 6: 43
Lakatos, Imre 6: 44
Lalande, Joseph de 6: 45
Lamarck, Jean Baptiste, Chevalier de 6: 46
Lamarckism: 2: 181; 5: 172; 6: 47; 10: 58
Lamb, Sir Horace 6: 47
Lamb, Hubert Horace 6: 48
Lamb, Willis Eugene, Jr. 6: 49
Lambert, Johann Heinrich 6: 50
Lamont, Johann von 6: 51
Lancisi, Giovanni Maria 6: 52
Land, Edwin Herbert 6: 52
Landau, Lev Davidovich 6: 53
Landolt, Hans Heinrich 6: 54
Landsteiner, Karl 6: 55
Langevin, Paul 6: 57
Langley, John Newport 6: 58
Langley, Samuel Pierpont 6: 59
Langmuir, Irving 6: 60
Lankester, Sir Edwin Ray 6: 61
Laplace, Marquis Pierre Simon de 6: 62
Lapworth, Arthur 6: 64
Lapworth, Charles 6: 64
Larmor, Sir Joseph 6: 65

Lartet, Edouard Armand Isidore Hippolyte 6: 66
Laser: 6: 202
Lassell, William 6: 67
Laurent, Auguste 6: 68
Laveran, Charles 6: 69
Lavoisier, Antoine Laurent 6: 70
Lavoisier, Marie Anne Pierrette 6: 71
Lawes, Sir John Bennet 6: 72
Lawless, Theodore 6: 73
Lawrence, Ernest Orlando 6: 74
Lax, Benjamin 6: 75
Lazear, Jesse Williams 6: 76
Leakey, Louis 6: 77
Leakey, Mary 6: 78
Leakey, Richard Erskine 6: 79
Leavitt, Henrietta Swan 6: 80
Lebedev, Pyotr 6: 82
Le Bel, Joseph Achille 6: 83
Lebesgue, Henri Léon 6: 84
Leblanc, Nicolas 6: 85
Le Chatelier, Henri Louis 6: 86
Leclanché, Georges 6: 87
Lecoq de Boisbaudran, Paul-Emile 6: 88
Lederberg, Joshua 6: 88
Lederman, Leon Max 6: 90
Lee, Tsung-Dao 6: 91
Lee, Yuan Tseh 6: 92
Leeuwenhoek, Anton van 6: 93
Leffall, LaSalle 6: 95
Le Gros Clark, Sir Wilfrid Edward 6: 95
Lehmann, Inge 6: 96
Lehn, Jean Marie Pierre 6: 97
Leibniz, Gottfried Wilhelm 6: 98
Leishman, Sir William 6: 100
Leloir, Luis Frederico 6: 101
Lemaître, Abbé Georges Edouard 6: 102
Lémery, Nicolas 6: 103
Lenard, Philipp Eduard Anton 6: 104
Lenat, Douglas 6: 106
Lennard-Jones, Sir John 6: 106
Lenoir, Jean Joseph Etienne 6: 107
Lenz, Heinrich 6: 108
Lepidopterist: 5: 199
Leucippus 6: 108
Leuckart, Karl 6: 109
Levene, Phoebus Aaron Theodor 6: 110
Le Verrier, Urbain Jean Joseph 6: 111
Levi-Montalcini, Rita 6: 112
Levinstein, Ivan 6: 114
Lewis, Edward B. 6: 115
Lewis, Gilbert Newton 6: 116
Lewis, Julian Herman 6: 117
Lewis, Timothy Richard 6: 118
L'Hôpital, Marquis Guillaume François Antoine de 6: 119
Lhwyd, Edward 6: 120
Li, Choh Hao 6: 120
Li, Shih-Chen 6: 121
Libavius, Andreas 6: 122
Libby, Willard Frank 6: 123
Lie, (Marius) Sophus 6: 124
Liebig, Justus von 6: 124
Lighthill, Sir Michael 6: 127
Lilienthal, Otto 6: 128

Shizuki, Tadao 9: 61
Shockley, William Bradford 9: 62
Shull, Clifford Glenwood 9: 63
Sidgwick, Nevil Vincent 9: 64
Siebold, Karl Theodor Ernst von 9: 65
Siegbahn, Kai Manne Börje 9: 66
Siegbahn, Karl Manne Georg 9: 67
Siemens, Ernst Werner von 9: 68
Siemens, Sir William 9: 69
Sierpiński, Waclaw 9: 70
Silliman, Benjamin 9: 70
Simon, Sir Francis Eugen 9: 71
Simpson, Sir George Clark 9: 72
Simpson, George Gaylord 9: 73
Simpson, Sir James Young 9: 74
Simpson, Thomas 9: 75
Škoda, Josef 9: 75
Skolem, Thoralf Albert 9: 76
Skraup, Zdenko Hans 9: 77
Slipher, Vesto Melvin 9: 77
Smalley, Richard Errett 9: 79
Smallpox: 5: 150
Smellie, William 9: 79
Smith, Hamilton Othanel 9: 80
Smith, Henry John 9: 81
Smith, Michael 9: 82
Smith, Theobald 9: 83
Smith, William 9: 84
Smithson, James 9: 85
Smoot, George Fitzgerald III 9: 86
Smyth, Charles Piazzi 9: 87
Snell, George Davis 9: 88
Snell, Willebrord van Roijen 9: 89
Snow, John 9: 90
Snyder, Solomon Halbert 9: 90
Sobrero, Ascanio 9: 92
Sociologists: 7: 50; 8: 103
Socrates 9: 93
Soddy, Frederick 9: 94
Software Designer: 4: 82
Sokoloff, Louis 9: 95
Solar system: 1: 27
Solvay, Ernest 9: 96
Somerville, Mary 9: 97
Sommerfeld, Arnold Johannes Wilhelm 9: 99
Sondheimer, Franz 9: 100
Sonneborn, Tracy Morton 9: 101
Sorby, Henry Clifton 9: 102
Sørensen, Søren Peter Lauritz 9: 103
Sosigenes 9: 103
South African anatomist: 2: 58
South African biologist: 6: 1
South African earth scientist: 3: 108
South African paleontologist: 2: 58
South African physician: 1: 123
South African physicist: 2: 188
Spallanzani, Lazzaro 9: 104
Spanish alchemists: 1: 69; 4: 88
Spanish-American biologist: 1: 86
Spanish chemist: 3: 48
Spanish histologist: 8: 108
Spanish mineralogists: 3: 48, 50
Spanish-Muslim philosopher: 1: 81

Spanish-Muslim physician: 1: 81
Spanish physician: 9: 49
Spectroscopy: 5: 38; 7: 111
Spectrum: 2: 77; 4: 35; 5: 210; 7: 158
Spedding, Frank Harold 9: 105
Speed of light: 1: 60; 3: 133, 217; 4: 18; 7: 64; 8: 167
Spemann, Hans 9: 106
Spence, Peter 9: 107
Spencer, Herbert 9: 108
Spencer Jones, Sir Harold 9: 109
Sperry, Elmer Ambrose 9: 110
Sperry, Roger Wolcott 9: 111
Spiegelman, Sol 9: 112
Spitzer, Lyman Jr. 9: 113
Spontaneous generation: 9: 104; 10: 17
Spörer, Gustav Friedrich Wilhelm 9: 114
Stahl, Franklin William 9: 114
Stahl, Georg Ernst 9: 115
Stanley, Wendell Meredith 9: 116
Stark, Johannes 9: 117
Starling, Ernest Henry 9: 118
Stas, Jean Servais 9: 119
Staudinger, Hermann 9: 120
Steady-state theory: 2: 5; 4: 129; 5: 95
Steam engine: 2: 211; 3: 57; 5: 25; 7: 151, 212; 8: 113; 10: 82
Stebbins, George Ledyard 9: 121
Steel: 1: 181; 4: 112, 179; 9: 185
Steenstrup, Johann Japetus Smith 9: 122
Stefan, Josef 9: 123
Stein, William Howard 9: 123
Steinberger, Jack 9: 124
Steno, Nicolaus 9: 125
Stephenson, George 9: 126
Stereochemistry: 8: 84; 10: 28
Stern, Curt 9: 127
Stern, Otto 9: 128
Steroids: 5: 192; 8: 129; 10: 150
Stevin, Simon 9: 129
Stewart, Balfour 9: 130
Stibitz, George Robert 9: 131
Stirling, Robert 9: 132
Stock, Alfred 9: 133
Stokes, Adrian 9: 134
Stokes, Sir George Gabriel 9: 135
Stoney, George 9: 136
Strabo 9: 137
Strachey, Christopher 9: 138
Strasburger, Eduard Adolf 9: 138
Strassmann, Fritz 9: 139
Strato of Lampsacus 9: 140
String theory: 7: 136; 9: 34
Strohmeyer, Friedrich 9: 140
Strömgren, Bengt Georg Daniel 9: 141
Struve, Friedrich Georg Wilhelm von 9: 142
Struve, Otto 9: 143
Sturgeon, William 9: 144
Sturtevant, Alfred Henry 9: 145
Suess, Eduard 9: 146
Sugden, Samuel 9: 147
Sugita, Genpaku 9: 148
Sumner, James Batcheller 9: 148

Sunspots: 4: 190; 7: 13; 9: 16
Superconductivity: 1: 48, 119, 212; 2: 113, 180; 5: 170; 6: 54; 9: 26
Superfluid: 1: 49, 212
Superstring theory: 9: 34; 10: 154
Surgery: 1: 187; 3: 125; 7: 217; 8: 35
Su Sung 9: 149
Sutherland, Earl 9: 150
Svedberg, Theodor 9: 151
Swammerdam, Jan 9: 152
Swan, Sir Joseph Wilson 9: 153
Swedish anatomist: 8: 134
Swedish astronomers: 1: 54; 2: 126; 6: 132, 181
Swedish biochemists: 1: 167; 3: 168; 9: 3, 181
Swedish botanists: 4: 46; 6: 135
Swedish chemists: 1: 70, 165, 177; 2: 40, 163, 207; 3: 139; 4: 60; 5: 44, 66; 7: 108, 166, 168; 9: 15, 43, 151, 201
Swedish cytologist: 2: 114
Swedish earth scientists: 3: 140; 4: 90
Swedish engineers: 3: 8; 7: 168
Swedish entomologist: 3: 42
Swedish inventor: 7: 168
Swedish mathematicians: 4: 36; 5: 219
Swedish metallurgist: 5: 66
Swedish meteorologist: 1: 164
Swedish mineralogists: 2: 207; 4: 60; 5: 62
Swedish naturalist: 8: 188
Swedish physician: 4: 172
Swedish physicists: 1: 27, 54; 3: 123; 5: 219; 7: 34; 8: 205; 9: 66, 67; 10: 129
Swedish physiologists: 10: 50, 126
Swiss-American biologist: 1: 16
Swiss anatomist: 5: 61
Swiss astronomer: 10: 158
Swiss bacteriologist: 10: 185
Swiss biochemists: 7: 67; 8: 129
Swiss biologist: 1: 61
Swiss botanists: 2: 96; 4: 41; 7: 133
Swiss chemists: 3: 158, 161; 5: 120, 180; 6: 219; 7: 120; 8: 45, 84, 204
Swiss earth scientists: 2: 147; 3: 50; 9: 9
Swiss embryologist: 6: 11
Swiss histologist: 6: 11
Swiss mathematicians: 1: 111, 171, 172, 173; 3: 166
Swiss meteorologist: 3: 50
Swiss naturalists: 2: 6; 4: 105
Swiss physicians: 4: 105; 6: 5
Swiss physicists: 4: 169; 7: 115; 8: 7, 42, 45, 85, 164; 9: 9
Swiss physiologists: 4: 197; 5: 42, 61
Swiss psychiatrist: 5: 165
Swiss psychologist: 5: 165
Swiss zoologist: 9: 215
Sydenham, Thomas 9: 154
Sylvester, James Joseph 9: 155
Sylvius, Franciscus 9: 156
Synge, Richard Laurence Millington 9: 157

Walker, Sir James **10**: 65
Wallace, Alfred Russel **10**: 66
Wallach, Otto **10**: 69
Wallis, John **10**: 70
Walton, Ernest **10**: 71
Wankel, Felix **10**: 72
Warburg, Otto Heinrich **10**: 73
Ward, Joshua **10**: 75
Wassermann, August von **10**: 76
Waterston, John James **10**: 76
Watson, David Meredith Seares **10**: 77
Watson, James Dewey **10**: 78
Watson, Sir William **10**: 79
Watson-Watt, Sir Robert **10**: 80
Watt, James **10**: 82
Weather forecasting: 1: 1; **2**: 145; **8**: 143
Weber, Ernst Heinrich **10**: 83
Weber, Joseph **10**: 84
Weber, Wilhelm Eduard **10**: 85
Wegener, Alfred Lothar **10**: 86
Weierstrass, Karl Wilhelm Theodor **10**: 88
Weil, André **10**: 89
Weinberg, Steven **10**: 90
Weismann, August Friedrich Leopold **10**: 92
Weizmann, Chaim Azriel **10**: 93
Weizsäcker, Baron Carl Friedrich von **10**: 94
Welch, William Henry **10**: 95
Weldon, Walter **10**: 96
Weller, Thomas Huckle **10**: 97
Wells, Horace **10**: 98
Wendelin, Gottfried **10**: 99
Wenzel, Carl Friedrich **10**: 99
Werner, Abraham Gottlob **10**: 100
Werner, Alfred **10**: 101
Wernicke, Carl **10**: 102
West, Harold Dadford **10**: 103
Westinghouse, George **10**: 104
Wexler, Nancy **10**: 105
Weyl, Hermann **10**: 106
Wharton, Thomas **10**: 107
Wheatstone, Sir Charles **10**: 108
Wheeler, John Archibald **10**: 109
Whewell, William **10**: 110
Whipple, Fred Lawrence **10**: 111
Whipple, George Hoyt **10**: 112
Whiston, William **10**: 113
White, Gilbert **10**: 114
White, Ray **10**: 114
Whitehead, Alfred North **10**: 116
Whittaker, Sir Edmund **10**: 117
Whittington, Harry Blackmore **10**: 118
Whittle, Sir Frank **10**: 119
Whitworth, Sir Joseph **10**: 120
Whytt, Robert **10**: 121
Wieland, Heinrich Otto **10**: 122
Wien, Wilhelm Carl Werner Otto Fritz Franz **10**: 123
Wiener, Norbert **10**: 124
Wieschaus, Eric **10**: 125

Wiesel, Torsten Nils **10**: 126
Wigglesworth, Sir Vincent Brian **10**: 127
Wigner, Eugene Paul **10**: 128
Wilcke, Johan Carl **10**: 129
Wild, John Paul **10**: 130
Wildt, Rupert **10**: 131
Wiles, Andrew John **10**: 131
Wilkes, Maurice Vincent **10**: 133
Wilkins, John **10**: 134
Wilkins, Maurice Hugh Frederick **10**: 135
Wilkins, Robert Wallace **10**: 136
Wilkinson, Sir Denys Haigh **10**: 136
Wilkinson, Sir Geoffrey **10**: 137
Williams, Robert R. **10**: 138
Williams, Robley Cook **10**: 138
Williamson, Alexander William **10**: 139
Williamson, William Crawford **10**: 140
Willis, Thomas **10**: 141
Willstätter, Richard **10**: 142
Wilson, Alexander **10**: 143
Wilson, Allan Charles **10**: 143
Wilson, Charles Thomson Rees **10**: 145
Wilson, Edward Osborne **10**: 146
Wilson, John Tuzo **10**: 147
Wilson, Kenneth G. **10**: 148
Wilson, Robert Woodrow **10**: 149
Windaus, Adolf Otto Reinhold **10**: 150
Winkler, Clemens Alexander **10**: 151
Winograd, Terry Allen **10**: 151
Wislicenus, Johannes **10**: 152
Withering, William **10**: 153
Witten, Ed(ward) **10**: 154
Wittig, Georg **10**: 155
Wöhler, Friedrich **10**: 156
Wolf, Johann Rudolf **10**: 158
Wolf, Maximilian Franz Joseph Cornelius **10**: 159
Wolff, Kaspar Friedrich **10**: 160
Wolfram, Stephen **10**: 160
Wollaston, William Hyde **10**: 161
Wolpert, Lewis **10**: 162
Women Scientists: 1: 155; **2**: 79, 90, 98, 121, 147, 186, 212; **4**: 5, 33, 95, 103, 125, 139; **5**: 29, 69, 90, 130, 131, 158, 178, 205; **6**: 20, 71, 78, 80, 96, 112, 159, 212, 218; **7**: 15, 25, 34, 84, 142, 170, 178; **8**: 26, 186; **9**: 97; **10**: 105, 174, 175, 182
Wood, Robert Williams **10**: 163
Woodward, Sir Arthur Smith **10**: 164
Woodward, John **10**: 166
Woodward, Robert Burns **10**: 167

Woolley, Sir Richard van der Riet **10**: 168
Worsaae, Jens Jacob Asmussen **10**: 169
Wright, Sir Almroth Edward **10**: 170
Wright, Sewall **10**: 171
Wright, Wilbur **10**: 172
Wright, Orville **10**: 172
Wrinch, Dorothy **10**: 174
Wróblewski, Zygmunt Florenty von **10**: 175
Wu, Chien-Shiung **10**: 175
Wu, Hsien **10**: 176
Wunderlich, Carl Reinhold August **10**: 177
Wurtz, Charles Adolphe **10**: 178
Wyckoff, Ralph Walter Graystone **10**: 179
Wynne-Edwards, Vero Copner **10**: 180

Xenophanes of Colophon **10**: 181
X-ray crystallography: 1: 73, 169; **4**: 33; **5**: 194; **8**: 32; **10**: 135
X-ray diffraction: 2: 34, 34; **3**: 39; **10**: 53
X-rays: 1: 122; **7**: 117; **8**: 168
X-ray spectrum: 2: 34; **7**: 109; **9**: 66
X-ray tomography: 2: 188; **5**: 94;

Yalow, Rosalyn Sussman **10**: 182
Yang, Chen Ning **10**: 183
Yanofsky, Charles **10**: 184
Yersin, Alexandre Emile John **10**: 185
Yoshimasu, Todu **10**: 185
Young, James **10**: 186
Young, Thomas **10**: 187
Yukawa, Hideki **10**: 189

Zeeman, Pieter **10**: 191
Zeno of Eelea **10**: 192
Zernike, Frits **10**: 193
Ziegler, Karl **10**: 194
Zinder, Norton David **10**: 195
Zinn, Walter Henry **10**: 196
Zoologists: 1: 110; **2**: 22, 39; **3**: 12, 24, 35; **4**: 24, 47, 139, 143, 156, 163; **5**: 130, 172, 208; **6**: 19, 61, 109, 212; **7**: 23, 56, 127; **8**: 79; **9**: 13, 30, 65, 106, 122, 198, 215; **10**: 180, 199,
Zozimus of Panopolis **10**: 197
Zsigmondy, Richard Adolf **10**: 197
Zuckerandl, Emile **10**: 198
Zuckerman, Solly, Baron Zuckerman **10**: 199
Zuse, Konrad **10**: 200
Zwicky, Fritz **10**: 201
Zworykin, Vladimir Kosma **10**: 202